Fugitive Father

by
Robert C. Mowry

Chapter 1

With a shrill squeal from its locked tires, the black limo rocked to a stop. Clayton Kingston then exited the curbside, rear door before the driver could get around to open it for him. Doing a quick scene assessment before moving from the car, Kingston's eyes locked on the group photographing the body.

One man, who stood several feet away from the others, turned and looked his way. Appearing to recognize Secretary Kingston, the man reached up and straightened his tie, then he hurried toward the car. Secretary Kingston stood motionless with his hand still on the limo door as he peered at the approaching man.

In seconds this man reached the limo, swallowed hard, stared into Kingston's eyes, then he spoke. "Secretary Kingston, this is an honor, sir. I'm Agent Winger, FBI Airport Security, DC Unit Commander, sir."

Kingston nodded, then looked back at the body stretched out on the floor of the airport parking garage.

"I'm surprised to see you here, sir. We have this under control," agent Winger said while he reached up with his left hand and again straightened his tie. "No need to involve Homeland Security, I mean I know how busy you are and…"

"The President's idea. He even considered coming himself. Lay it out for me."

"Sure, well—" agent Winger cleared his throat. "Someone, or something, must have distracted this guy while the perp slipped up behind him and at point blank put a slug in our guy's brain. Looks like a robbery. That metal attaché case is cuffed to our stiff's wrist. You can see where someone tore away at the flesh on his hand trying to yank it off. Something must have scared the killer off before he could break, or cut off, the cuff— or the guy's hand."

Agent Winger paused for a second, then continued. "My guys are just finishing up the prints and pictures now. Ah… Can we move the body, sir?"

"Aba Saad," Kingston said.

"Really? This stiff's a wanted terrorist?"

"Aswad Hamal's faithful Lieutenant. What's he carrying? Computer? Any notes or planner?"

"Yeah, all of that," Agent Winger said. "Looks like all the writing is in code. Of course that's all been secured. We'll check out that computer—"

"No! Secure it and get it to the Decoding and Deciphering unit at Los Alamos."

"Los Alamos? Sure, I'll have it forwarded to DAD with an agent first thing in the morning," Agent Winger said.

"Two men—no, make it three. Arrange for a couple of air marshals on the flight too," Secretary Kingston said. He stepped back and leaned against the limo. He stared over at the body once more.

"Surveillance in New York spotted Saad getting off a private jet, but lost him," Secretary Kingston said. "This was no ordinary robbery attempt, Winger. We need to find out who Saad was here to meet. Most of all, we need to find out what he was carrying. He must have been passing on some mighty important stuff to be doing it himself. Maybe he was turning sides or something. God help us if we have some sort of turf war among terrorists breaking out."

Secretary Kingston paused for a moment, and then spoke as he slid back into the safety of his limo. "Bombs, Winger. Saad was a bomb man. This has something to do with killing a bunch of us."

★★★

Four days later, high on a mesa in northern New Mexico, dawn's hazy gray gave way to a blanket of cloudless, blue sky as the high-desert's morning sun inched its way over the mountainous horizon. Piercing rays suddenly penetrated through the narrow slits in the lab's easterly facing window blinds, cutting directly across Dr. Alex Vincent's bleary eyes. Looking up from his computer, Alex blinked, then turned his head off to the right and looked at the clock: five minutes until six. The silence of the room was broken only by the faint whir of the tiny computer cooling fans and the even fainter hum of the fluorescent lights.

Smelling the aroma of the coffee one of his assistants, Carla Hunter, had made moments ago, Alex picked up his cup and walked to the coffee maker. Those footsteps, though barely audible on the tightly woven, thick-pile carpet, seemed to fracture a sacred stillness.

Alex filled his cup with the steamy brew, and then turned to observe his two assistants. Carla sat with both elbows on her desk, her head resting on her hands, her eyes closed. Kurt Stein, on the other hand, sat staring intently at his computer screen while rhythmically, yet silently, tapping a pencil against his chin.

Alex raised his cup and let the hot coffee touch his lips. He instantly backed it away. He looked at the clock again: three minutes before six.

He walked back to his desk, set his cup on a leather coaster, and then eased into his plush, calf-skin and chrome chair. He scrolled the open file on his screen to its beginning. It was a copy of everything on Aba Saad's computer, plus a scanning of all his papers and planner pages found in his briefcase and pockets.

For the last three days, Alex had spent nearly every waking moment studying the almost 1,000 pages the fallen terrorist had been carrying. All of it defied their computer models. Then there were the maps. Mixed in with the pages of code were dozens of pages of maps showing in great detail fifteen of the nation's top airports, including their parking areas, entry ways and exits, and the adjacent streets and neighborhoods.

Alex had a thing about maps, not a good thing. The summer after his junior year at MIT he'd worked on a highway survey corps and did both the outside, physical, rough survey work as well as then drawing the corresponding maps. Working outside with bugs, snakes, and foul weather wasn't to his liking. Sitting in a poorly lit, overly cluttered office at an antiquated drafting table wasn't much better. He much preferred his well-furnished, well-organized, office here at the lab with its colorful artwork and other high end furnishings.

Alex looked at the clock: one-minute before six. He again tried to sip his coffee—still too hot. He got up and went to the water cooler, filled a paper cup, then returned to his desk. He took a sip of the cool water, and softly cleared his throat.

"This is it, guys. Any comments?" he asked.

Carla raised her head, looked at Alex, and then shook it slowly in the negative. Kurt pushed himself back in his chair, slammed his pencil down on his desk and threw up his hands.

"This is impossible. Utterly impossible. You know I've worked on this kind of stuff for nearly ten years now, but this beats all I've ever seen. Some of this seems to refer to hardware, bombs probably. Other parts, like these lists here, must be locations, times, people, and who knows what else. Without some direction, a beginning point at least, we're racing down an endless spiral."

"You can tell that to the President then. I'll let you handle this call," Alex said.

"Whoa now Alex. Keep me out of it. You're the—"

Bzzzzz. The phone rang. Alex stared at it. It was the direct line, the secure one. Bzzzzz. On the second buzz, he picked it up.

"Good morning. This is Doctor Alex Vincent."

"Good morning Doctor Vincent. Clayton Kingston here. Some of my Homeland Security staff and I are in the Oval Office with President Daugherty. We're on a speaker system. Your staff with you?"

"Yes, Mr. Secretary." Alex glanced at the sound-proof security door one more time as he flipped on the speaker switch, then he cradled the receiver.

"I know it's early out in Los Alamos," Secretary Kingston said. "I appreciate all of you being there. You've had three days to analyze Aba Saad's documents. Any success?"

Alex swallowed hard, trying to moisten his parched mouth. He rapidly looked at Kurt, then Carla. Both stared blankly back at him.

"We need time, sir," Alex said, leaning slightly toward the phone. "This is a monumental challenge."

"Then you're saying, Doctor, that you don't think you'll have this for us in the next few days? Well, the FBI, along with every other allied intelligence agency, is looking at every possible angle as to what Abba Saad was up to. Not knowing what is going on isn't our style. When middle-eastern, terrorist leaders start turning up dead in DC airport parking garages, we've got problems. We didn't know Saad was coming here, but someone did. To know what to prepare against, we've got to know his business here and who took him out.

"If any of this leaks out to the public…" Secretary Kingston paused, and then cleared his throat. There was a long moment of silence. "Well, do whatever you have to, but we need to know what's in that computer. It's key to all else we need to know. I'm sure I'm being redundant. We're all wound pretty tightly around here these days. You get the picture. I'm sure."

"This has our full attention, sir. Codes are tricky. Sometimes things just fall into place. Surely, one of us will find the key soon," Alex said, and then he wiped the perspiration from his forehead with a tissue.

"This seems to have something to do with our airports," Secretary Kingston said. "I'm sure you realize that without my saying anything. We'll forward any new information we turn up on this end. Any questions?"

Alex again looked at Carla and Kurt. Carla shrugged her shoulders and shook her head slightly. Kurt just stared down at his desk, and then softly mumbled, "No, not at this time."

"Nothing more now," Alex said. "Anything comes up that we think you can add to, I'll call you."

"Doctor Vincent, this is President Daugherty. My office is open to you anytime for whatever help we can be. I understand this is a heavy load we're laying on you. I'm aware you've accomplished much in your distinguished career of service to our country. I truly believe you're the best person in the entirety of this great nation to pull this off. I'm asking for a commitment like never before. This will take a sacrifice not only from you and each of your people, but from your families as well. I challenge you to be up to the task."

No! Tell him you can't do this now. Tell him…

"I ah, we're up to it, Mr. President. We at Decoding and Deciphering at Los Alamos National Laboratories will come through for you, sir. We're honored to have been chosen for this challenge. We'll not let our country down."

"I believe you, Doctor Vincent. May God help you," President Daugherty said. "I'll turn you back to Secretary Kingston now."

"Thank you, Mr. President," Alex said. *Could have done without that God thing.*

"Dr. Vincent, I'll be out to see you shortly," Secretary Kingston said. "Keep my office posted on your progress. If you have nothing else, we'll end for now."

"Nothing now, sir," Alex said. "Good bye then."

The phone went dead. Alex flipped off the speaker switch, then slid back in his chair. Silence again dominated the room. After a moment, Alex got up, picked up his cup, and walked over to a window and pulled open the blinds. Succumbing to one of his frequent habits, Alex stared out into the rugged canyon's rocky precipice that lay only a few yards from the edge of the building. Slowly, he sipped his still-hot coffee.

Kurt spun around in his chair to face Carla. "Look, logic tells us the only way we can come up with a quick fix is to first figure out the subject of each section here. There's this stuff in Arabic letters, then that section in French and, well, breaking it into sections is elementary. We can work out the details after that. I know Homeland Security thinks this is all about some new super bomb or some other high-tech gizmo, but I'm still skeptical. These guys just aren't that sophisticated. They usually strap on some dynamite and blow themselves, and everything around them, to pieces."

"Oh please, Kurt, cut with the lecture," Carla said. "Remember, there are reports all over the world claiming Aswad Hamal has half-a-dozen agents with some new, high-tech bomb ready to deploy on us. There might even be sleepers here already. You remember the briefing about that guy Israeli Intel picked up last month? He claims something big, some new bio thing, is going to happen here around the next remembrance of the nine-eleven, twin tower disaster. If that's so, we have maybe ten weeks. That's all we have before they spread some new body- destroying bug, and Lord knows what else, across our country. The key to all of that is probably right here. Right here in our hands—we just need to break it. That's what we do here, break codes, right?"

"Rumors of this will leak out," Kurt said. "Washington will deny anything's going on, but you know the rumors are going to fly across the airwaves faster than Spiderman across town. I don't see how we can do this, even if we work 24/7. Still, I— what do you suggest, Alex? Alex?"

"I, well…"

"Get a grip, Alex. You're the department head here, but you can't even get your mind together enough to join the conversation," Kurt said, snapping his pencil in two, and then slamming the pieces in a wastebasket. "If anyone at this lab, maybe anyone in the entire country, can pull this off it's you. However, lately there's been nothing but empty air in that head of yours."

"Easy, Kurt," Carla cut in, "let's not get personal."

"Not get personal! We're faced with maybe the end of the world as we know it, and you don't want to get personal? This is on our shoulders, us, the three of us right here. We're the ones given this charge by the President himself. Got that? If we fail—"

"Let's start over," Carla said, quickly rising and stepping toward the coffee pot while she continued to talk. "We know our goal, mandate really. We know generally what we're facing. We just need to start randomly running samples against all models and code history, and surely we'll get a break. How does that sound to you, Alex?"

"Yeah, sure, that's what I'm thinking," Alex said. "Sure, let's start breaking out samples." Alex walked back to his desk, took a yellow legal pad from his side drawer, pulled a custom made, ebony and gold pen from his shirt pocket, then he looked at Kurt, then Carla as she sat down with her coffee.

Stay focused. Tucker's gotten through every other crisis he's faced. He'll make it through whatever's bugging him now. Work comes first—it always has.

Nearly eight hours later, just before two o'clock in the afternoon, they finally broke for lunch.

"Be back in an hour, probably less," Kurt said, as he quickly exited the room. Alex went to the coffee pot, poured the last of the morning's coffee into his cup, and then walked over to the window and stared out into the canyon.

"Bill and the boys are meeting me over at Pepper's Cantina," Carla said, hanging up the phone. "Come join us, Alex. You can't just stay here and live on coffee. You're already so thin—you're losing weight again, I know you are. Come—please."

"Some other day, really I will. Thanks anyway. I promised Tucker I'd call and…" he looked away, avoiding eye contact with Carla.

"Look, I know I'm butting in, but whatever it is that's got you so preoccupied… Well, if I can help, you know, just talking sometimes really helps," Carla said, staring at her co-worker and boss of five years. "You've been through a lot. I can imagine how hard it must have been when Evelina left. Tucker—well, if this has something to do with Tucker, remember, I have two boys myself."

Alex nodded. "Thanks, but I'm alright, really I am. I'll ah— I'll go and get a salad at the cafeteria. Go on now. Don't keep Bill waiting."

The next morning Alex Vincent jerked and dropped his pen at the unexpected ringing of his cell phone. He looked away from the sample of code he'd been studying. "Hello," he answered after nearly dropping the phone to the floor when he tried to open it with one hand.

"Dad? Where are you? Mom's out in her car. She brought me up here when you didn't come get me. Mom figured you was hangin' out in the garage or somethin' and just forgot to come. She wants to go. When you gonna be here?"

"Tucker! I, well, yeah," Alex looked at the clock. It was after ten in the morning. *This must be Saturday.* "I'll be right home. Guess I wasn't watching the clock."

"Hurry Dad. Mom's in like one of her moods. I'll tell her to go on back home. You're comin' now, right Dad? I sorta don't wanna be here alone for long. Not that I'm 'fraid a bein' alone. I just want you here."

"Yeah, sure Son. I'm on my way out the door now. See you in ten minutes, or less. Tell your mother to go on. Just lock the door until I get there."

Alex slid his phone into its leather case on his belt while walking past the security guard.

"Ya'll been puttin' in some mighty long hours, Doc Vincent. Hear you're a workin' on something real special this time. Makes me proud just to be a wee bit part of whatever that is. Nothin' gets in or out past old Lester, ya know," the silver haired, bi- spectacled guard said when Alex walked by.

"I'll bet nothing does get past you, Lester. Got to go see my boy. Maybe I'll be back before you leave. Might work all night again. Kurt's down the hall. Carla hasn't come in yet today. No one else is here that I know of. Keep the bad guys out," Alex said while walking toward the door.

"Ain't no bad guys around here, Doc Vincent, just good folks, like you and me."

★★★

"Hey Dad. Eight minutes and fifty-four seconds. Right on! Told Mom you'd beat ten minutes. She's gonna call in 'bout fifteen minutes, and she said you'd not be home yet. Hey Dad, when she calls—I mean I know you don't want to talk to her— but could you maybe say something to me loud enough so's she can hear ya? That's so's she'll know for sure you're really here?"

"Yeah, I've been trying to be better about all that. It's just that right now we're—" Alex cut himself off. "Well, I guess I have a lot of fathering to catch up on. It seems there is always something going on with my work. Better days are coming. I promise."

7

"Yeah, sure Dad. Hey, can we go to the ballpark? Saw a bunch of guys, big guys, playing there when Mom and me drove by. Can we go watch 'em, Dad? Can we?"

"Yeah, let me change clothes. After your mother calls, we'll go."

★★★

Three hours later, while father and son munched on cheeseburgers and fries, Tucker started asking questions. "Can I stay the night, Dad? Mom won't care, 'cause I asked her. She said just call. Can I Dad? You know, just me and you, Dad."

"Well... tell you what, in a month or so, when I get this new project done, you and I will take a trip somewhere. How's that sound?"

"Wow! Just you and me? When, Dad? When can we go?" "Soon, couple of weeks, maybe. Until then—"

"You saying I can't stay tonight? Ah, Dad, I really wanna. I ain't slept much at home and—"

Alex looked at his watch. He needed to work tonight. But then, he'd worked nearly all night for the last four. Suddenly, his cell phone rang.

"Alex? Where are you? I turned around and you were gone. That was hours ago. Carla came in and said she saw your car at the baseball fields. What are you doing? You forget the country turns into a cemetery in a few weeks? Come on man, get back in here."

"Easy, Kurt. I've got Tucker and he wants to spend the night and—"

"You crazy? Look, I think we're on to something here. I ran one sample by that old alpha run and got some hits. Come on, get your priorities straight."

"But—yeah. OK. I'll be in. See ya."

Tucker was silent. Alex saw him drag the back of his forearm across his cheek as he turned away.

"Tell you what, big guy, since you're all of twelve years old now, how 'bout I dig out my old sleeping bag, and you come down to the lab with me. You can sack out there, in the reception area, you know, out by the guard station. I'll be working right down the hall. I'll come out often and check on you."

"For sure Dad? Me and you down at the lab all night?"

"Yeah. I can make that work. Is it a deal?"

"Super deal! Wait'll I tell the guys back home 'bout this. Wow, me spending the night at the big ol' Los Alamos Lab with my dad. Bet you're workin' on something as big as that bomb thing was back when grandpa was alive."

Was this? Alex wondered. Could this be as important as the Manhattan Project had been? Failure might be a whole lot more devastating to the people who lived in the United States. Alex was sure they wouldn't fail though. He'd never failed on a project yet—not one at the lab anyway.

The sun was starting to lower into the west when Alex drove into the parking lot. He and Tucker walked toward the Area 622 building, the one that housed the DAD unit. Lester would be gone, but that wouldn't matter. Whoever was on duty would let Tucker stay with them. Alex looked over at his son and matched his son's smile with his own.

Keep smiling. Pretend everything's alright anyway.

"Breakfast?" Alex asked Tucker the next morning when they left the lab.

"Pancakes," came the reply. Tucker had slept well while his father worked all night. From that, Alex was now bleary-eyed and his head throbbed. Actually, he'd had little sleep for days, never more than three or four hours a night. Lately, he'd come to work unshaven, something he'd never done in all his time here. At times he wondered what pushed him the hardest: the urgency of this project or Kurt? There was no question this young man was a brilliant code-man. He was ambitious, with lots of drive to move up the ladder. The only thing in his way was Dr. Alex Vincent. With his fifteen years there, his impeccable record and wall full of commendations and awards, Alex Vincent was well entrenched as head of DAD.

"We goin' to our old home now?" Tucker asked when his dad drove the car out of the restaurant parking lot and headed down the street.

"Yeah. I couldn't drive you back to Santa Fe as tired as I am now. I need some sleep first. I guess your mother could come get you."

"No way! I want you to take me home. Mom brought me up here."

"All right. Just later then."

Hours later, when they reached the streets of Santa Fe and slowed down, Alex pushed the button and closed his car's sunroof, keeping out the intense afternoon heat. He turned the silver BMW up the street toward where his ex-wife now lived. Tucker had said very little the entire trip from Los Alamos. He'd sat looking at the dashboard, his hands tapping lightly on whatever they were near. When they approached a park, Tucker suddenly spoke up.

"Over there, Dad." Tucker pointed to the parking area for the park. "Can we stop there for a minute? Got something to ask you."

Without saying anything, Alex turned into the parking lot and parked under a cottonwood tree. He lowered the windows, and then turned off the ignition.

"So, what is it you want to ask?"

"Oh—well," Tucker hesitated. "Guess I was just thinking. Dad, well like I said I was just thinking that maybe I could like come live with you. I'd be no problem, no problem at all."

"Whoa! What's brought this on?" Alex was surprised—yet not entirely. For weeks now Tucker had been acting strange. He'd tossed out several trial balloons over the last few visits, commenting about what it would be like living with his dad.

"Oh—things. Just things, Dad."

Alex studied his son as Tucker stared out the windshield toward some children playing soccer. He sat only inches away, yet his mind seemed to be miles away.

Tucker's thick, sandy hair was cut in a fashionable style. His clothes were new and neat. Alex was glad to see that at least some of the money he sent Evelina each month was going to care for Tucker. It suddenly crossed his mind that Tucker looked very much like he did at that age. He remembered a picture of him at about the same age that his grandmother kept hanging on her parlor wall. Those were carefree years, those childhood ones growing up in Iowa.

Alex knew things weren't so carefree for Tucker. Alex reminisced back to the good times he had had with his extended family—from grandparents to cousins—at so many family outings. Tucker had none of that. Tucker had, well, he had his mother. Guilt cut through Alex as he thought of how little of himself he'd given his son. Why? That was what tormented him now. How could he change this now?

"What would your mother say about this?" Alex asked, getting back to the question at hand. "You talk to her about this?"

Tucker said nothing.

"You mad at your mother?"

"Ain't just mad, Dad."

"What then?"

"Awful scared."

"Scared?"

"Yeah."

Alex waited for Tucker to go on. He didn't know what this was all about, but somehow he knew it wasn't going to be good for him.

"When Melissa came to us," Tucker finally said slowly, "well, I don't know much about all that, but mom said you weren't her father. I don't know who—I guess all kids gotta have a father. Well, mom didn't care much about her. When little Melissa went missing…"

Alex tried to figure where Tucker was going with his thoughts. Yes, his ex-wife had given birth to a little girl about a year ago, long after their divorce. Then, about six months back the baby turned up missing. He'd never talked with Tucker about this. Now seemed like the best time to get his son's thoughts out into the open.

"It must have been hard, having your little sister disappear like that. I'll bet you miss her greatly."

"Yeah. Sure do. Me and her was just becoming like—like somethin'. Anyway, I miss her a bunch. It scares me, Dad."

"What's that, Son?"

"Ahh—I know I shouldn't a done it, but mom, she's been funny lately and, well—"

Alex let his son get his thoughts together and start again.

"See, I kinda listened in when mom was on the phone. Don't know who she was talking to, but that's why I'm scared, Dad. I heard mom talkin'. She had something to do with little Melissa. Heard her say—"

When Tucker paused again, Alex continued to sit in silence.

"Heard Mom tellin' someone that she was right there when they," again Tucker paused. "When they stuck like a big ol' dagger thing right down into little Melissa's heart."

Chapter 2

Attempts by Alex to get some sleep before returning to the lab were futile. He lay on his bed, staring at the ceiling. His mind raced with thoughts of how all through his life other people, other things, some project or some problem had tugged him, one way or another. Sometimes it had been more than one thing and in more than one direction at the same time. This was one of those times—and the timing couldn't be worse.

After getting his Doctorate, he'd gone back home to Iowa to visit friends and family before starting his position with Los Alamos National Laboratory. It was then that Evelina suggested, rather forcefully he now remembered, that they get married. She had already applied for a kindergarten teaching position in Los Alamos and planned to move there to be with him.

Guess with me not being much with women, that really stroked my ego.

Zzzzzing, zzzzzing, Alex's phone rang again—for the fifth time. Kurt had left four messages; each one harsher than the last, but this time it was Carla.

"Alex, if you're sick or something, please let us know. We've come up with something, but need your input before we go any further. Please, at least call us."

When the recorder beeped its end of message signal, Alex closed his eyes. He thought about getting up—yet not a muscle moved.

★★★

Tucker stared listlessly across the room at his computer. He'd opened up his favorite game to the screen over an hour ago, but had yet to make the opening move. From his perch on the sofa, Tucker was then drawn to the calls from little Kreg Browning to his mother. Kreg was a normal two-year-old. Sally Browning had been Evelina Vincent's housekeeper and Tucker's baby sitter ever since Tucker and his mother had left Alex and moved to Santa Fe. That was a few months after Kreg was born.

Tucker liked Sally, little Kreg too. When she first came to their home, Sally would take spells when she would sit in a chair and just cry. Tucker soon learned that her husband, Buck, who of course was little Kreg's father, had then recently been killed somewhere far away. Sally said he'd been killed by a suicide- bomber, whatever that was.

Sally seemed some better now; at least she didn't cry as much. Tucker felt sad for little Kreg, his not having a father. With his own father working at the lab and all, Tucker and his father spent a minimal amount of time together, but at least he had one.

Bzzzzzzzz. Urrrrrrrrr. Mmmmmm." Kreg pushed his favorite toy, a large plastic truck, across the floor towards Tucker. "Tata, play with me," he said to Tucker.

"Push me the truck," Tucker said, and then he slid off the couch and got down on the floor and pushed the truck back to Kreg. From the corner of his eye, Tucker saw Sally Browning watching them play. After a few moments, she came over and sat on a chair beside them.

"Thank you for being so good to Kreg, Tucker."

"Oh, we have fun, I guess," Tucker said. "Sometimes I— well, I pretend he's little Melissa. I think sorta like it's me and Melissa playing. That's not bad, is it?"

"Bad? No, that's not bad. That must have been hard on you, losing your baby sister like you did. Sure was hard on me losing Buck. If anything like that ever happened to my little Kreg, why, I'd just lose my mind. I'd go stark crazy, so I would."

Tucker thought about that.

Do people really lose their minds? Is that what's happened to Mom?

Soon Kreg fell asleep on a soft rug, and Sally picked him up and put him up on the sofa.

"Sally," Tucker said when she again sat on a chair near him. "You know much about Mom's church thing? You know, that Saints thing."

"Oh, that. I don't know about calling that a church—maybe they do. She's never talked to me about it at all. It seems to be for people who are well off and well educated. I'm just..." Sally didn't finish her thought. After a few seconds, she continued.

"One day when I dusted the bookshelf, up on the top shelf, I found a little pamphlet about the Saints of Seven. I don't think anyone outside the group is to see it."

"Pamphlet?"

"Yeah, that's a small book-like thing, just a few pages really." "Oh. Can I see it?" Tucker asked.

"I don't know. I don't think it would be good for you. In fact, I put it back myself after about the second page," Sally said. "You'd better ask your mother."

"Yeah, all right. I just wanna know sorta what that's about. I think that's what changed Mom a bunch. Dad didn't see it, him being so busy and all, but I saw it. Mom ain't been the old Mom since she got into all of that stuff. What do people need a church thing for anyway?"

"I used to go to church," Sally said quietly. "It's been a long time now though. Guess I'm still too mad at God."

★★★

Late that afternoon, Alex Vincent showed up at the lab. The moment he walked through the door Kurt jumped on him.

"Where have you been? Another hour and I'd have called the police. We've lost nearly a whole day. If I could—"

"Kurt!" Carla cut in. "Give him a chance."

"Sorry, guys. I got your messages Kurt, yours too Carla. I just couldn't do anything."

"Look, Alex, if you're sick, for heaven's sake go check into the hospital," Kurt said. "Do whatever you must to get up to speed. Look at the calendar. Look at—"

"Alright, alright," Alex said, and then he walked over to his favorite window as he did so often when under pressure. He looked down into the peace of the forested canyon.

"I'll tell you. I'll tell you what's gotten a grip on my mind, but you've got to swear to secrecy. This has to be between the three of us. No one above us or no one outside the lab, just us, all right?"

"Of course, Alex," Carla said. Kurt just stared at his boss.

"Kurt," Carla said, "you want things out in the open. Alex is giving us a chance. Don't be like this."

"This is a time to put all personal things on hold. I don't care what they are," Kurt said. "I don't care if you're dying of cancer, or it's your kid. I don't want to talk about it. That means we then come to some resolution. I don't want a resolution. I only want to see the same level of commitment from my supervisor that I have when the security of the nation calls for it."

"Personal lives can't always be put on hold, Kurt," Carla said.

"I've done it."

"No offense, Kurt, but you don't have much of a personal life," Carla said. "What is there besides your career? You've no children, no wife or even a girlfriend. Your health is good, and you don't have so much as a cat. Come on, you don't know what others face. We can't go on like this."

"All right," Kurt said. "Out with it. Then let's get back to work. Time is running out. So what's the big deal?"

"It's Tucker," Alex said. "He's been acting quite strange for weeks— months really. I didn't know what was on his mind. Then the other night when I took him home, well, he finally talked to me. He's scared silly. He wants to come live with me. He—" Alex swallowed hard. Carla quickly grabbed Alex's coffee cup, went to the sink and dumped its cold, stale coffee, then refilled it with fresh and brought it to him. He slipped his index finger through the handle, then aimlessly twisted the cup back and forth. After a few seconds, Alex started talking again.

"He's overheard—oh, thanks for the coffee—he overheard his mother talk of being part of the disappearance of, and then the, and the—" he paused again and cleared his throat for a second. "He heard her talk of being part of the ritualistic killing of her little girl."

"No!" Carla gasped.

"You believe him?" Kurt asked. "He's eight years old and you believe him?"

"He's twelve, and wouldn't make something such as this up. Evelina is involved in something weird. The Saints of Seven they call it."

"I've heard of that," Carla said. "Yes, down in Santa Fe it's said there's a group of otherwise respectable people involved in that. Rumors are, some city officials, even top police are involved. I hear they're part old time Indian worship mixed in with the worship of ancient Greek gods. Human sacrifice might well work its way in with that. Oh, surely not. Come to think of it though, you don't hear anything about the disappearance of Evelina's little girl."

"Can't this wait, Alex? Just a few weeks? I know he's your kid, but we've got the responsibility of saving the nation. Think of what that will do for your career? Think of all the things you'll be able to do for Tucker then. Think of how proud he'll be of you when you're a hero."

"Is that what's sparked your fire so much?" Carla asked. "Is it, Kurt? Are we working here to save lives or to become heroes?"

"Both. You won't turn it down, neither one of you. Don't be so self-righteous. We've got to do this, and yes, you bet I want the glory for doing it once we're done."

"You're so wrong, Kurt. Becoming famous would mess up my life. All I want is to be a mom and wife who has a chance to use the gifts and training I have to do good things. I'd be just as happy doing medical research. You don't get it, do you Kurt?"

"We're getting way off track," Alex said. "No one's motives are important now. We need to accomplish our project and do it quickly. Here's what we're going to do. You know that for the last several years now I've been working on that new program, Code Dog as I've tagged it. It takes the five legs of code theories I developed ten years ago and combines them into a new zone of artificial intelligence. It's taken me until now to get the program to where it will work through all five legs and not bog down and draw false conclusions. I believe it only needs my tweaking on a few things before trying it on raw data. I figured it would take another six months in my spare time. You know how little of that we've had these last few years. I'm going to get on Code Dog full-time while you two keep working at the conventional avenues. Maybe in a very short time—one way or the other— we'll have this beat."

"What about Tucker? What are you going to do, Alex?" Carla asked.

"I don't know. I can't just take Tucker. There are the courts and all that."

"Yeah… maybe you need some legal help," Carla said. "I think I know just the man— Wade Hawkins. He's an attorney down in Santa Fe who spends much of his time on desperate family situations. He lost his wife and son years ago. They were murdered, and he seems to have a calling to help families in trouble."

"A calling? How do you know this guy?" Alex asked.

"He spoke at a woman's group at my church a year or so ago. Bill knows him too."

"Figures. Is he going to tell me what *God* is telling me to do? Look, I know you believe all that stuff, how I don't know, but I'm a realist. I've got too much science, provable facts, in my head and—"

"Alex, I've got just as much education as you do. If you'd only take a look at some of the new, truly scientific evidence out there—"

"Whoa!" Kurt cut in. "This is getting way off track again. Fine, Alex, go see that attorney. Maybe if he gets involved, that will keep your kid safe until we get through this. He might get him into foster care or something."

"Foster care! I'll never— look; I've rarely been there for Tucker. Even during the divorce I never once talked to him about it or any of his feelings. Call me a late bloomer, or whatever, but I'm just realizing I'm his father. I've never been that and now he needs me more than ever and terrorist code or no code I'm going to do whatever I can."

"Then resign," Kurt said.

"Kurt!" Carla shot back at him. "There's no one else to spearhead this. No one else can complete Code Dog. Besides, the lab wouldn't accept any resignation at this point."

"They won't accept the level of commitment, or rather non-commitment, we've been getting either," Kurt said. "Alex goes down, we all go down. If he doesn't carry his load, we fail. Then we all might as well go to teaching school or driving a bus. You all remember what a mess we were left in when Miles Groman up and took off in the middle of a major project. For what he did, I hope that wherever he fled to, they figured out what a cutthroat he was and took his head off."

"The Feds put Miles under immense pressure, so they did. They accused him of some horrendous things. I don't know what evidence they had, but I still don't believe Miles was a spy or whatever else they claimed," Alex said. "I'll do better. I really will. I'll call this attorney Hawkins in the morning. Let's pull back together and get the needed fix. Really now, we all know that no backward thinking ideologues from some cave or tent out in that sand can get up on us."

The sun was behind the western mountains when Wade Hawkins walked his horse into its stall. He put the blanket and saddle on the rail, and then hung up the rest of the tack.

"There now, Kicks," he said, scooping the horse some mixed grain, throwing on a handful of dried molasses. He rubbed the large palomino animal down with a handful of straw, then he used a curry comb to finish up.

"Sure is a pretty one tonight," Wade said half to himself and half to his horse as he gazed at the sunset. He looked over towards his house and saw his mother sitting on a banco under the latilla-covered patio off the kitchen. From the large stone grill, Wade noticed a skiff of smoke rising and his nose detected the aroma of sizzling steak.

"You see that sky?" Wade's mother, Nita, asked when he approached. "With a sky like that, there's little chance of rain tomorrow. Lord knows we need it. It'll come. It'll come when it's our turn. Come now, Son. Got the table here all set. Wash up and dish yourself up some of those fresh greens while these steaks finish grilling."

When his father died twelve years ago, Wade took over the law office, all but the bookkeeping and other paper work. Nita Hawkins still sent out the bills and collected the money using only the old Royal typewriter that for over forty years had rested on her worn and stained, roll-top desk.

"Thank you Mom," Wade said after dinner. "I'm going to read a little of that new book you got me, then turn in early. I've got court tomorrow. Got to go in early and get ready."

"You wear that new jacket I bought you, Son. That's real suede on the shoulders and elbows, not some fake, make-believe polyester. Some cow gave it's all for that, so you wear it and do the same."

★★★

The next morning, Wade's phone rang soon after he arrived at his office. He looked at his watch—not yet seven. Needing to prepare for court, he ignored the ringing. Every few minutes it rang again, but he never picked it up. When Nita came in shortly after eight, she answered it, put the caller on hold and walked back to Wade's office.

"I think you need to take this call, Son. It's a Dr. Alex Vincent from Los Alamos. He works with that Carla Hunter woman, Bill Hunter's wife, you know? It's Vincent's ex-wife whose baby turned up missing a few months back. You remember that? Well, he sounds very desperate, scared even. Poor man sounds as if he really needs some help."

Wade nodded, and then picked up his phone. "This is Wade Hawkins. How can I help you?"

"I'm—well, she told you, I'm sure, who I am. I—I need your help. It's my son. He—please, I've got to talk to you."

Chapter 3

With caution and near silence, Tucker quietly carried the kitchen chair over to the bookcase. His mother had entered her bedroom and closed the door nearly an hour ago. It had taken Tucker that long to get up the courage to try and find that pamphlet Sally Browning had told him about. Sally wouldn't get it for him, and she was always there when his mother wasn't, so he had to get it when his mother was home, but occupied in her room. Since that was most of the time, it wasn't time he needed; it was getting up the nerve to look at something he didn't think his mother would want him to see. Maybe he wouldn't really want to see it either once he got his hands on it.

He got up on the chair, then reached up on the top shelf. No books were on that shelf, only some figurines and antique Indian bowls. Tucker pushed himself up on his toes as he reached around for the pamphlet. He had to move the chair three times before his fingers felt what he searched for. He stood there on that chair, up on his toes, as he contemplated what he was doing. Then he slid the pamphlet to the edge of the shelf and quickly took it down. He started to step off the chair. At the same time, he tried to stuff the pamphlet in his shirt. Distracted, he fell off the chair, knocking it over as he hit the floor. As the chair flipped over, it knocked a ceramic lamp off an end table by the sofa. Tucker hit his head on the edge of the table. The lamp shattered into dozens of pieces as it hit the hard, tile floor.

Bouncing to his feet, he grabbed hold of the chair and, as quickly as he could, took it back to the kitchen. He was barely back to the sofa when his mother burst out through her bedroom door.

"What are you doing? Look what you did! You know my mother gave me that lamp." Evelina stooped to pick up some of the larger pieces.

Tucker couldn't look. His eyes were glued to the corner of the pamphlet sticking out by the sofa leg. It had slid out of his shirt in the fall. He slowly swung his foot around to push the booklet completely under the sofa skirting.

"Well, get me a trash bag to put these pieces in. No, I'll get that. You go get the vacuum cleaner. Where does Sally keep that anyway?"

With one last little push with his foot to hide the pamphlet better, Tucker breathed easier.

"Sorry, Mom. I must have tripped on the cord or something. I'll clean it up. You go on. I can do it. Sally can finish up tomorrow if I don't get it all."

"Be more careful from now on. You interrupted something very important. Clean that up then go to bed. I'll see you tomorrow." With that Evelina stormed back into her room and slammed the door.

Tucker picked up the larger broken lamp pieces but left the vacuuming for Sally. He then reached down, retrieved the pamphlet and slipped it back inside his shirt. Slowly, even fearfully, he headed for his room.

When Tucker started reading the pamphlet he got about as far into it as Sally said she did. He closed it and slid it under his pillow. Sally was right. He really didn't want to know what the Saints of Seven was all about.

Why? Why was his mother involved in something such as this? Tomorrow he'd have to get this back up on the bookcase— without doing any more damage.

★★★

Wade Hawkins got out of court and back to his office shortly before three, the time he'd told Alex Vincent to meet him. He hung his hat over the inverted-horseshoe rack, then he dropped wearily into his old leather chair—purchased over forty years ago by his father— and leaned his head back. In a few seconds Nita buzzed him and let him know that Dr. Alex Vincent was there.

"Send him in. I'll do this court follow-up later."

Wade stood and walked to his office doorway and watched the other man walk down the hallway toward him. He reached out his hand when Alex Vincent neared him.

"I'm Wade Hawkins. Pleased to meet you."

"Alex Vincent. Thank you for meeting with me," Alex said when he shook Wade's hand. "Carla, that's Carla Hunter, I work with her, she, well, she suggested I meet with you."

"Please, come in and take a seat. Would you like coffee or cold water?" Wade asked.

"No. No thank you. I just finished a bottle of water driving over here."

"How can I help you?" Wade asked as he sat back into his chair. He then slid open a side drawer and took out a legal pad and prepared to make notes.

"Well—I—where do I begin? I guess with what I need you to do. I need to get custody of my son, immediately."

Wade looked at Alex Vincent and waited for him to continue. When nothing more came, Wade quizzed Alex.

"So, how old is your son?"

"Tucker is twelve."

"Tucker, you said. That's a great name for a boy. Twelve's a good age too. Does he like football?"

"I—I don't know. He does like baseball, but I guess there's a whole lot I don't know. You see, I supervise the Decoding and Deciphering unit up at the lab and—well, I've never been much of a father. Wasn't much of a husband either it seems. My wife left about two years back."

"So, why do you feel the need for custody now?" Wade asked.

"Tucker's in danger. See, his little sister—my ex-wife had a little girl about a year ago—his little sister went missing about six months back and—" Alex suddenly got a serious look on his face. He leaned forward in his chair, and stared deep into Wade's eyes.

"What I tell you is confidential, right? I mean, you won't tell anyone, will you?"

"I'm bound to confidentiality by law. You can tell me anything. Those associated with me are bound also."

"I thought so, just needed to make sure," Alex said, as he slid back part way in his chair. "Well, Evelina, that's my ex-wife, she had this little girl, as I said before, and then six months ago the baby turned up missing. Well, Evelina is involved in a very strange group, the Saints of Seven. You ever hear of them?"

The Saints of Seven!

At that Wade leaned forward in his seat. Yes, he knew a lot about the Saints of Seven. Several years back he'd fought hard to help get a young woman out of that group. A group that on the outside appeared to be sophisticated and intellectual but, according to what Wade had learned, were actually very power hungry and worshipped ancient gods and powers. He also remembered hearing the news about the little Vincent baby turning up missing back when it happened, but couldn't remember hearing anything on that case for months now. If Evelina Vincent was in the Saints of Seven…

"I'm familiar with them. Go on," Wade said.

"Well, I've been trying to pay more attention to Tucker. I know he's very stressed, and I guess I'm feeling quite guilty for the lack of time and, well, just any of myself, I've given him all these years. At the same time, I'm involved in the most intense project at the lab in all my years on the job. I should be spending twenty hours every day there until we accomplish our mandate. It's a national security thing—big really. I'm letting down my team, maybe the entire country, by getting involved with Tucker at this time."

Alex got a distant look on his face while he sat in silence for a moment, then he proceeded. "But last Sunday night when Tucker told me he'd overheard his mother on the phone admitting that she was involved in the disappearance and killing of her own daughter, that's when I knew I had to do something for Tucker. I must get him out of that house."

The killing of her own daughter! This echoed around in Wade's head. He eyed the man across the desk from him, then pushed back in his chair and looked away from Alex Vincent to be less intimidating, hoping Alex would relax a little.

"You believe that?" Wade asked.

"Yeah—oh, I never would have years ago—but the way Evelina's acted these last few years—Tucker wouldn't lie. He's truly scared."

"Does Evelina have a career or job?" Wade asked.

"Yes," Alex Vincent said. "She's a kindergarten teacher over at Taos Street Elementary here in Santa Fe."

"She ever had any trouble with the law?" Wade asked.

"No."

"She ever accused of not taking care of Tucker?"

"No."

"You be the judge," Wade said. "Play this out with me. On one side is an apparently upstanding kindergarten teacher with no public negative record and on the other side is a man who works twenty hours a day and has forever neglected his son. Who do you give a twelve-year-old child to?"

"But she killed her own daughter!"

"On the word of a twelve-year-old boy who wants to go and live with his father. Look, I'm not saying all you said is wrong— actually I find you quite believable—I'm just telling you what will happen in a court. I've been there too many times. Unless the mother is a real dog, she gets the kids. Your ex-wife may be that real dog, but we have no proof that would be admissible in court. How do we go about proving that what Tucker said is true?"

"I—I don't know," Alex said.

"That's what we'd have to do, you know," Wade said.

"What about that cult?"

"The Saints of Seven may be a baby-killing, blood-sucking group on the inside, but on the outside, it plays the upstanding role, and it has some of the city's best known and most respected citizens among its ranks. I know," Wade said. "I beat them once in court, but it wasn't easy. I got them barred from harassing a young woman after she was taken out of that mess and got her head cleared. In all of that, nothing about human sacrifice came out—though that was before this missing child. It wouldn't surprise me though if they've slipped to this depth. I know there were some weird things going on in that group."

Alex slumped back into his chair as if someone pulled a plug and drained all the hope out of him. Wade looked at him, but Alex just stared at the floor.

After a moment of silence, Alex looked up at Wade, then nodded his head. "I was afraid of this. If something happens to Tucker…"

"Tomorrow, call me about this time tomorrow. I'll do some digging around. Just one more day. Call me then."

"Sure will, Mr. Hawkins. I surely will."

★★★

Late the next morning, Wade walked up to a small building on a side-street behind the main Santa Fe Police Station. Once inside the police forensic lab, he was warmly greeted.

"Hey Wade! Haven't seen you for ages. What have you been working on?"

"Most of it's been pretty dull, Carlos. How about you?"

"Anything but dull. Weird stuff going on around here, man. Weird stuff."

"The Saints of Seven involved in any of it?" Wade asked.

"You shouldn't ask things like that," Carlos said. "You know I can't tell you who or what. You bumped into that group. You should know all about them."

"Any human sacrifice? Any baby killing or the like?"

At that Carlos looked around to make sure no one had heard what Wade had asked. "Man, don't talk about that. You know I couldn't say anything about the likes of that. You know how things are, but as I said, there's some awful strange and sickening stuff going on."

"That little Vincent girl, she part of it?" Wade asked.

"Come on, Wade," Carlos said, again looking around.

"Who's heading up that missing child case?"

"Detective Luke Lane, but old Max Pace has this one shut up like glue," Carlos said. "That much I can tell you."

"Thanks, Carlos. I owe you lunch. Maybe next week?"

"That's a deal, but no shop talk, all right Wade?"

"Yeah, sure."

Wade next walked up the street to the main police office where the detectives worked. Wade stopped and looked around before going inside. He hated cases that involved the police. He rarely was around any of the detectives, especially those in homicide. Opening the old, hand-carved, cedar door, Wade went inside and asked to see Luke Lane. The secretary called Lane, who then had Wade sent back to his desk. Wade eyed up Luke Lane as he walked toward Lane's desk. He'd seen this young detective around, but never had any dealings with him and hadn't ever tried to get a line on what made the young cop tick. Wade now quickly observed that Luke Lane most likely was very image conscious. He wore what appeared to be an expensive Italian suit and had a haircut that looked like Hollywood.

"Luke Lane," the young man said when he rose to shake Wade's hand.

"Wade Hawkins. I'm an attorney here."

"Yeah, I've seen you around. What do you want?"

"I'm working on a project for Dr. Alex Vincent, the code department head up in Los Alamos. The disappearance of his ex-wife's little girl might have some bearing. What can you tell me about the status of things in that case?"

"You've got to be kidding. That's an open case." With that Lane picked up his phone and dialed another extension. "Max. Got an attorney here who says he's working for Alex Vincent. Thought you might want to talk to him."

Lane hung up his phone. "Sit tight, Hawkins. Max Pace wants a word with you."

"Good. I hear he's running this anyway, and you're just his gofer."

Lane bristled but said nothing. Max showed up, grabbed a chair, pulled it over near Wade, sat on it and pointed a finger in Wade's face.

"This isn't like you, Hawkins. You don't usually get your nose in police business. Listen to me, Hawkins. You tell that mad scientist that he might well need an attorney. You tell him to stay away from his ex-wife and her private affairs."

"If you want him to hear that, you need to tell him yourself. I'm not like young Lane here. I'm not your messenger boy," Wade said, watching Luke Lane's reaction.

"Hey, wait a minute," Luke Lane protested, but Max motioned for him to hush.

"This is an open case. If anyone's getting nervous, well maybe they have a reason to. Alex Vincent is on my list to question about his whereabouts when that baby disappeared. I've several other things to ask him also."

"What are you waiting for? It's been six months. Maybe you should send one of your errand boys to fetch him for you. I came here for some simple information. You're making a federal case out of this. I'll get what I need elsewhere." With that, Wade got up to leave. However, he purposely left the manila folder he'd carried in with him leaning against the leg of Luke Lane's desk. He pushed it under the desk with the pointy toe of his boot as he rose. "Good day, gentlemen. I've work to do." Wade started to walk away from Luke Lane's desk.

Out of the corner of his eye, he watched Max Pace stomp back toward his office. Luke rose and headed for the coffee pot. When Max was out of sight, Wade turned around and went back to retrieve his folder. Luke Lane stared at him curiously until Wade lifted the folder to show him what he was after. Lane nodded his approval, though he did it with a nervous look on his face. Wade then walked up the same aisle Max had. When he approached Max's office door, he overheard Max yelling at someone on the phone.

"An attorney! Why does your ex have a new attorney? It's that kid of yours. He knows too much, I tell you. You ought to send him to live with that nut at the lab. Ever since you took over—" At that Max apparently noticed Wade's shadow outside his glass office door. He slammed the phone down and jerked open the door.

"What do you want? I thought you left."

"I needed to ask you a couple of things in private," Wade said. "I didn't want young Lane to be party to this. Tell me, the rumor around town that you're a member of the Saints of Seven, is there any truth to it? Furthermore, is your lady friend Evelina Vincent really the high priestess of that group?"

Max's face instantly turned pale. His hand shook when he pointed at Wade. "Get out of here before I have you arrested."

"Have a good day, Chief Pace. Good ones may not last forever," Wade said, and then he smiled and turned to leave.

Wade left the police station and drove his old pickup truck over to the Taos Street Elementary School where Evelina Vincent taught kindergarten. He waited for her to come out for lunch recess. Wade recognized her from his previous case. Every time he'd seen Evelina, she'd acted as if she was the one really in command, but somehow she always hid behind others. Like Max, she had others to do the messy work. Once out in the play yard, she quickly got on her cell phone and seemed to be very agitated. Wade waited until she took the children back inside, then he drove toward his office. Once there, Wade buzzed Nita.

"Yes, Wade."

"See if you can get Sonny Horn on the phone. What's his class schedule these days, you know?"

"He's got three classes today. He'll be in Albuquerque all day. Now tomorrow he's off all day."

"Call him, please, and leave a message. Tell him I need him to gumshoe some for me if he can. He can call or see me early tomorrow morning. Better yet, call Doli at work and have her give Sonny the message when he gets home. Ask her about that paint pony of hers. It was under the weather last week. I offered to trailer it to the vet, but she said she could doctor it just fine."

"That Doli has surely made Sonny a fine wife," Nita said

"She's a good woman."

"She's not the only one out there, you know. If you'd start looking—"

"Mother!"

"Well, I'm just saying—"

"Just call Doli, leave the message for Sonny, and find out about her horse."

★★★

Well before three, Alex Vincent called Wade.

"I stirred things up really good over at the police station," Wade said. "They're hiding something, maybe lots. Patience, Doctor. Sometimes one just has to have patience."

"That would be easy if it was just me, but it's my son—"

"Sometimes we need to add a dose of faith in with our patience."

★★★

Wade was sitting in his favorite chair reading his book when the late night local news came on the TV. When they started with their lead story, breaking news from the east side of Santa Fe, Nita gasped and pointed at the TV. "Wade! Look."

"An all too common story these days again hits the Santa Fe community tonight. This time there is a big question, and the answer may have a gruesome twist," the newscaster started off. "With another child tragically missing, we ask: Does this disappearance have any connection with one about six months ago? To date, the case of baby Melissa Vincent has not been solved. Tonight we learn that the two-year-old son of Mrs. Vincent's housekeeper and baby sitter, little Kreg Browning, has disappeared. He apparently was abducted from the Vincent home around sundown this evening. His mother, Sally Browning, was in the kitchen when she heard a door close. When she went to investigate, her son was gone. With us now is chief of detectives, Max Pace…"

Wade didn't need to hear any more. His mind tuned the TV out. Alex Vincent was right. He had to get Tucker out of that house quickly. How? Searching deep into his memory, Wade remembered a tape he'd listened to and filed away several years ago. What was the name of that organization? It was an underground railroad system for kids and their parents caught in legal entanglements. Kids in danger, kids the law couldn't do right by. Kids like Tucker Vincent.

Well past midnight, Wade remembered the name: Lollypop—yes, it was called the Lollypop Railroad. This might be the only way to protect Tucker—to save his life. Then too, it might well do just the opposite for Wade. What would happen if he helped put this father and son into something as radical as an underground system? Just how much legal trouble, and outright danger from this crazed cult, might he have to face?

Chapter 4

Wade Hawkins sipped on his third cup of coffee since arriving at his office more than two hours earlier. He'd gone to bed late, very late, then tossed and turned for hours. When he did lie still, he stared at the ceiling, only dozing off for a few minutes at a time. He finally got up when the living room clock struck four. Now, without warning, the front office door opened.

"Hey Wade. You in here Wade?"

"Come on in, Sonny," Wade said, recognizing the voice. When Sonny entered his office, Wade nodded toward the old cassette recorder. "I'm just sitting here listening to this over and over. Must be a dozen times by now. You're up early yourself."

Sonny looked at the tape jacket on the desk beside the cassette player. *Lollypop Railroad,* the handwritten title read.

"I remember this, Wade. I got it for you. Yeah, I'd heard this interview on that radio talk show and thought you might want to know about it. Why now?"

"I started down here last night—Mom stopped me. Might as well have spent all night here though. When I wasn't wide awake thinking about all this stuff, I was dreaming weird things and not resting anyway. You see the news last night? That missing child story?"

"Bad stuff. You think there's any tie in with that other little girl?"

"Dr. Alex Vincent came to see me the other day. That's why I want you to help me. You in?"

"Does a reservation dog ever pass up a bone? You know I need all the money I can get until I graduate and pass the bar exam. I've only got classes two days a week this semester. What's the deal?"

Wade was hesitant about getting Sonny involved in this. With this latest twist, he feared things might get ugly.

Sonny was a tenacious investigator, as good as there was in Santa Fe. Wade believed his being half Apache gave Sonny his sharp, detail-grasping mind. Sonny was working hard at becoming an attorney. Wade was toying with the idea of taking him in as a partner, something he'd never had. Wade kept Sonny on a monthly retainer, as much to help pay for his schooling as for his services. Sonny's wife, Doli, was a member of the Cochiti Pueblo tribe, so they lived out on that quiet little reservation south of Santa Fe.

"Alex Vincent wants to get his son out of that house," Wade finally said. "I'd say he's right, but no judge will agree. Besides, he's super busy on some hot project up at the lab now, something real time consuming."

"Vincent—he's the ex-husband of the mother of that other missing child, right?" Sonny asked.

"Yeah. They split up about two years ago. That little girl wasn't his. Nobody is ever mentioned as the father. Mrs. Vincent, Evelina, she's a kindergarten teacher. On paper, she looks like mother-of-the-year. Behind all of that though, she's a member of that Saints of Seven group."

"Wow, that's a big red flag. Yeah, I'm forever hearing some really scary stuff about that group. Hey, you don't think they've done in these little kids, do you?"

Wade shrugged his shoulders.

"That's heavy, Wade. What am I looking for?"

"I think Evelina Vincent is one of the leaders, maybe the top one. I'd like that confirmed. I suspect Max Pace, chief of detectives, is on the inside of this too, maybe others on the force. I'd sure like a list of who's who."

"I doubt if there's anything in writing. What about that woman you got out of that group? Could she help?"

"They never let her know much. She might be some help, but go easy on her. I hate to bring back memories of that time to her. She's doing fine now, don't mess her up."

"Yeah, I'll see what I can find elsewhere."

Wade closed his eyes and leaned his head back. *By late afternoon, I'll be ready to crash.* After a minute he opened his eyes, leaned forward and toyed with his coffee cup.

"So, what's with all this and the Lollypop Railroad?" Sonny said while he poured himself a cup of coffee, then started making another pot. "That's desperate stuff, you know."

"I've got nothing but the word of a twelve-year-old boy to his father that his life is in danger. Tucker claims he's overheard his mother talk of killing his sister."

"Wow. You've heard this?"

"Actually I haven't, only from the father. Dr. Vincent's not the type to make things up though. I did call a friend at the Los Alamos lab and confirmed that he told the truth about working on some major project. There's something really big going down. Something about national security, apparently. The lab's in a frenzy. If this wasn't real, Alex Vincent wouldn't pick this time for a custody fight. Still, I need to hear all this from Tucker before I go much further." Wade again leaned back and closed his eyes.

"Tell you what, Sonny, any time you have in the evenings and on the weekends, stick like glue to Evelina Vincent. I want to know what she does, and with whom," Wade said without opening his eyes.

Sonny nodded, and then pointed to the tape jacket. "You actually thinking about this?"

Wade glanced at what Sonny pointed to. "Up until last night I didn't have any idea of what to do. Maybe this Lollypop group is out of business by now, or they've had to change their contact system or something. Sure won't find them in the yellow pages. Heck, they could all be in jail. Anyway, I don't know how Alex Vincent could leave his work, and I don't know of anyone else who could take his son into something such as this. Still, I don't know anything else to do. Listen to this again, tell me what you think."

Wade hit the rewind switch, then the play button.

"Welcome back, this is the Hank Stutter show. This hour's guest is going to be controversial for sure. Some of you might be intrigued, others enraged. Without further set up let me introduce to you, by phone somewhere in Mexico, she claims, a lady who calls herself Lollypop."

"Thank you Hank. Thank you for giving me this opportunity that may help save some lives."

"Save some lives?" Hank asked. "Do you really believe you do that?"

"Every day we have children and their parents in our system that might otherwise be harmed or even killed."

"Why don't they just go to the authorities?" Hank asked. "I pay good tax money for the police, the child protective agency and who knows what else. If my kid was in trouble, if someone threatened him or something, I'd go to the cops."

"In most cases that's the right thing to do," Lollypop replied. "But what if there's a nasty divorce going on and one parent knows their child is in danger but can't prove it? The police can only work inside the law. They investigate crime after it's happened and have little to do with stopping things before they happen or without hard evidence and court orders. There are times, fortunately not too many, when to save a child they must be removed from where the law puts them and taken to a place of safety until the law can catch up with the facts."

"The law catches up with the facts? You admit what you do is outside the law. The real fact is you're criminals, in your own words, right?"

"We save children who might otherwise perish. We value life over law."

"Life over law—that sounds so noble, but you're in the same class as those who bomb abortion clinics in the name of life, aren't you?"

"I'm talking about living, breathing, yet crying and desperate children. What if your wife left you for another man, a man who you knew was molesting your child. However, this man was able to hide what he was doing from the law? What if he turned things around and accused you of

28

being the molester? What if the law then banned you from any contact with your child? Would you just let the law handle things while your little one was being brutalized by some psycho? Wouldn't you want someone to care enough to provide a safe place for you and your child? Would you care that they were violating the law?"

"Good story, but I still don't buy it. What about money? Money has to play a big part in all of this. How much does it cost to whisk away a parent and child into your fairytale system?"

"We're well funded. We work on donations only. It costs you nothing to be put into our protection. At any time anyone can donate what they can. Some donate money, others time."

"People do get out of your system then?"

"Sure, that's our goal. Many times our action makes the system take a deeper look at what's gone on, and then they make the necessary corrections. No one wants to live on the run for long."

"You call yourself an underground railroad?"

"Yes. We're like the resistance movements during our Civil War, the Nazi movement, and even our own revolution. Yes, we operate somewhat outside the established law, but we save lives. In our case, it's the lives of endangered children. I'd go to jail myself if it would free just one more child who really needs it."

"You make that sound so honorable—saint like. This toll free number you use, is it a direct line?"

"Of course not. It's routed into Mexico, then through some sophisticated transfer equipment, eventually ending up on a recorder. There's more to it than that, but you get the gist. This is our sixth year, and we haven't lost a child or parent yet. We're a lot more than a secret hole in the wall or dark corner of the basement."

"Well, you make up your own minds, folks. I'll give you the contact number, the one that goes to Mars and back, or something like that, then you can call in here and talk to Lollypop yourselves on our regular Hot Talk line. Her Lollypop number is 800/555..."

Wade hit the stop button. Neither he nor Sonny said anything for a minute. Sonny then broke the silence.

"You gonna call, Wade? Is this that desperate?"

"You saw that news last night. You want your kid living in a house where two others have disappeared?"

Sonny finished his coffee, took the cup to the small counter sink, then walked to a window and looked out at the desert as the morning sun brought it alive.

"You know enough for now. I'll handle everything I can," Wade said. "I'll keep you out of all but what I need your help on. You best get going and I need to make this call before Mother comes in. I don't want to have to explain this to her—not yet. She'll remind me of the time Dad came against the crooked District Attorney and spent a month in jail for contempt. She always forgets that when he got out, he had more business than ever. Sometimes you have to put people, especially kids, ahead of all else. Mom knows this well. It's just that she still puts her kid ahead of all else."

"Speaking of kids, talk to Tucker, Wade. Don't get too far into this before you talk to him yourself."

"Yeah, I'll do that, as soon as I can."

★★★

For nearly an hour, Wade went through making calls and receiving calls. Finally, he was connected to Lollypop.

"Mr. Hawkins, I apologize for all this delay in our getting connected, but I live some distance from this office and well, anyway, this gave us time to check you out. You have quite a bio as someone willing to go all out to help the hurting family. How can we help you today?"

Wade heard Nita come in the front door. "Just a minute, please, I have to close my door. I'm no longer alone in the office." Wade quickly shut his back office door and returned to the phone. "Sorry. My mother is my secretary and, well, she watches over me just like a mother."

"You know, you should be thankful," Lollypop said.

"Oh, I am. Now, here's my situation. I have a client who's desperate to get his son out of his ex-wife's house. I truly believe that this child's life is in danger. There are some strange things going on here in Santa Fe."

"We monitor the types of things you're talking about as best we can, and I see a new video marked 'Santa Fe' on my desk for my viewing. It's most likely a collage of news reports on some of what we're talking about. I remember a case some months back of a missing child from there also."

"Yeah, I believe they're tied together. I may need to move quickly on this. Talk to me about how we'd set this up for someone to enter your system."

"This may sound harsh, but we won't tell you much at all. We'll work out a time and place for the pickup of parent and child, and then we take it from there. The less you or anyone else on your end knows, the better."

"I see your point. I've got to sell this to my client though. Maybe this will be easier. It's so simple—just jump in by faith."

"Faith is a powerful thing, don't you agree Mr. Hawkins?"

"Sure, but I'm thinking of what I know of my client."

"Let me view this tape and do some other research. When can I call you back?"

"Anytime today, really. However, I'd like to leave early, mid-afternoon, if I can."

"I'll be in touch later. There will be time then to discuss more details of your situation. I'll know more on my end what I need to learn from you. Good day to you, Mr. Hawkins."

With that she was gone. Wade sat in his chair in silence. Minutes later he jumped when Nita buzzed him.

"Wade. The phone light is out. I know you're no longer on the phone. You closed the door on me. I remember what that meant when your father used to do that to me."

"It's nothing to worry about, Mother. I'll be right out."

Later that day, while sitting alone in his office, Wade popped the top off a can of iced tea. He'd appeased his mother as best he could, but he knew she smelled trouble ahead. Lollypop had called him back about an hour ago and informed him they were just waiting for word from him. Once he gave the go ahead, they could facilitate a pickup in a matter of a few hours notice. Wade finished his drink, tossed the empty can in the trash, and then called Dr. Vincent.

"Hello."

"Doctor Vincent? This is Wade Hawkins."

"I've been hoping you'd call. Wait a minute."

Wade heard footsteps and figured Alex was moving to get out of earshot of the curious. "OK, what do you have for me?"

"Maybe the answer. We've got to talk. I need to talk to Tucker. When do you get him next?"

"Saturday morning. I can get him about eight. Do you want us to come to your office then?"

"Can you get him before then?"

"Not without arousing suspicion—no it wouldn't be good to try."

"Then Saturday morning, come out to my ranch. Go out the old Turquoise Trail through Cerrillos, then…" Wade gave him directions, and added a warning. "Keep an eye out in case you're followed. If you are and can't shake them, call me. You have my card. It has my home and cell numbers on it. Call me anytime."

"Sure—you think someone might be following me?"

"Maybe. Look, we may have to act quickly. Give some thought to your work, how you could do it from a remote location."

"Remote location? What are you saying?"

"Just think about that. See you Saturday."

★★★

Luke Lane sat nervously in Max Pace's office.

"Come on Lane. You've got to have something by now. We've got to get acting on this."

"Look Max, the guys on Dr. Vincent say he hasn't even sneezed. He's spending twenty hours a day in that lab. What's going on up there anyway?"

"Never mind that. This is a whole lot more important," Max said. "What about that attorney?"

"About the same. These must be two of the dullest men around. The only thing is, Hawkins was at his office real early the other day, you know, the day after little Kreg—"

"Yes, yes. What else?"

"Well, that wanna be private eye from over Cochiti Pueblo, Sonny, uhh—Sonny Horn, yeah, he was there too, but left soon after my man started his watch."

"Where'd Horn go?"

"Ahh, we didn't have anyone to follow him. I guess I should put a man on him."

"He's probably in the parking lot right now, tailing you! He's the outside man, the one who's going to be snooping around and making trouble. Get a man on him now!"

"Yeah, sure Max. Right away," Luke Lane said, then he rose to leave.

"Wait! Vincent will be in Santa Fe to get his kid Saturday. Keep an eye on him."

"Sure Max. I got it covered."

★★★

Alex Vincent picked Tucker up at 7:45 Saturday morning. They headed for the nearest McDonald's for breakfast. Alex noticed a blue Ford sedan pull into the parking lot seconds after he did. Alex got a quick look at the driver when the car drove by them. He noticed it had government plates. Once seated at their table, Alex noticed the same man sitting at a table, sipping a cup of coffee. The man had positioned himself where he could easily watch them as he read the morning paper. No sooner had Tucker started eating his pancakes when the other man laid his paper on the table and quickly headed for the men's room.

"Come on. Leave your food, we need to get out of here." Alex said taking Tucker by the arm.

"But—I've just started. Can I—"

"No time now. Come. We'll eat later." Father and son ran to the car. In seconds Alex sped out of the parking lot. When he stepped down on the throttle and turned up the street, he looked back in the mirror and saw the other man running toward the blue Ford. Alex put his foot down to the floor and the BMW raced toward I-25. In minutes, they were on it heading for the exit to Wade's ranch.

"Dad. You OK?" Tucker asked as he studied his father.

"Yeah. We had someone tailing us. When he went to the restroom, I knew we had to make our break. Sorry. We'll eat later. I'm too nervous now to eat."

"Yeah, me too. Wow. This is just like the movies. What's gonna happen, Dad? Is Mom doin' this?"

"We have to do something, Son. I need you to be ready to do whatever I tell you, whenever that is, understand?"

"Sure Dad, anything. Me and you."

★★★

When he'd set up the Saturday morning meeting at the ranch, Wade knew Nita would be in town doing her weekly shopping. When Alex and Tucker arrived, Wade was in the barn feeding Kicks.

"Everything alright?" Wade asked Alex after he was introduced to Tucker.

"I was followed. We ducked out on him when he went to the men's room at McDonald's. I'm still shaking inside."

Wade nodded. Time was not on their side. Out of the corner of his eye, Wade watched Tucker pet Kicks. The horse pushed his head down against Tucker, wanting it rubbed.

"He's spoiled," Wade said. "Once you start rubbing him, he'll follow you around all day begging for more. He likes you or he'd push you away."

"I like him too, but he's so big. I never saw a horse before, 'cept on TV or the movies. He's a whole bunch bigger than any horse looks on TV."

Minutes later the three sat in Wade's study and listened to the Lollypop Railroad tape. When it was finished, Wade turned the recorder off and waited for a reaction from Alex. After a moment of silence Alex spoke.

"I know I need to do something. This just seems so radical. I guess it has to be, or I'd get caught the first day. However, there's my work…. I'm immersed in this big project. Keeping all of that secret…"

Wade waited a minute, then he turned to Tucker. "Tell me, Tucker. Just talk to me. Tell me all about what's going on. Everything you can think of."

Wade clicked on his recorder on a blank tape when Tucker began. "Well, Mom got real weird about a year before me and her left dad. I think that's when she joined that secret church thing, as she calls it. I read about that, just a little, but then I got too scared. I put the little book thing back up on the shelf." Tucker paused for a moment. "Back when little sis was born…"

Tucker talked on for over half an hour. Just when he finished, Wade heard Nita walk in the back door. Wade rose and looked at Alex Vincent.

"This is all up to you. It will take some legal and financial doings, but I can do it all in a day or so. Let me know what you decide." Wade paused for a minute, looked at Tucker, then he looked deep into Alex's eyes. "Don't wait too long."

When they started to leave Nita yelled at them. "Just a minute, Wade. You're not going to let these people out of here without breakfast. Not in my house. Little boy, what's your name?"

"Tucker."

"Tucker! Now that's a good name. How do you like your eggs, no, I can see it. You're a pancake fellow, aren't you?"

Tucker looked at his dad and smiled.

"Yeah. I love good pancakes."

"Then you sit right down, your father too. You haven't eaten pancakes until you've had mine. Wade, over in the freezer, get me a pound of those good sausage links."

Sonny had kept his eye on Evelina's black Hummer for several nights, but so far nothing had happened. Tonight though, people were coming and going at her house. When Max Pace showed up, Evelina turned off the house lights and she and Max got into the Hummer. Sonny followed them from a distance. They got on the interstate and headed north, getting off at the Pecos Wilderness exit. Sonny held back. Apprehension gripped him. Should he try to follow them around this desolate area? Deciding to try, he turned off the lights on his jeep, and then eased forward slowly.

About a mile into the forest, he came to a tight bend in the road. After making the turn, from behind a large bolder a hundred yards or so up the road, a vehicle lurched out in front of him and headed toward him with high, bright lights and a spotlight shining in his face. Sonny slid to a stop, slammed his Jeep into reverse and started backwards. Suddenly, he heard shots being fired and bullets whizzing over his head. Sonny whipped the Jeep sideways between two trees, slammed it into low then reached for his shotgun. When he pointed the gun at the approaching vehicle, it slid to a stop, then quickly backed up the way it had come. Sonny stepped on the gas and headed back toward the interstate. He held his shotgun across his lap until he was half-way up the entrance ramp. Then he put it down, picked up his cell phone and called Wade.

The next evening, Wade sat in his rocking chair, reading his mystery book. Moments later the phone rang. Nita answered it.

"Yes, he's right here," she said, then brought the phone to Wade. The worried look on her face told Wade who it was. "It's that cute little boy's father," she whispered while handing the phone to Wade.

"Yes."

"Mr. Hawkins. The police were here. They threatened me. I think they're going to set things up and charge me with the disappearance of both of those children. I—we must move quickly."

Chapter 5

The next morning when Wade turned his pickup truck into his office parking lot, there sat Luke Lane waiting for him. Wade saw the detective quickly make a call—to Max Pace, he assumed. Wade parked his truck, then he walked over to Luke's car. He put his hands on the car's roof, then leaned down and talked to the young detective through the open window.

"Up early, aren't you?" Wade asked. "Getting some overtime?"

"Cut the funny stuff, Hawkins. You get under my skin real easily."

"Guess that gives me and Max something in common, right?"

Lane pursed his lips to respond, then didn't. Instead he asked, "You going to invite me in?"

"Shouldn't we wait on Max? You did call him, right?"

"He'll be here. Look, Hawkins, this stuff is sort of personal for Max. You'd do best not to rile him on this. Just go easy and it'll all go away."

"Or get lost in some cold case file down in the basement. What's your part in this, detective? You part of Max's secret society, or are you just trying to be big enough to get in? Now that's something you should go easy on. It's not what it seems, trust me."

"Trust you? Who are you—"

Luke Lane broke off his conversation as Max Pace's car sped into the parking lot, and with tires squealing, Max braked the car to a stop. Luke Lane instantly opened his car door and got out as Wade stepped away.

"Max will want to go inside," Luke said.

"I'm enjoying the fresh air," Wade said.

Max hurried over to the other two men. "What are you waiting for? We need to talk to you, Hawkins. It's about you and this Dr. Vincent thing."

Wade didn't move. He noticed Luke Lane was looking down with his eyes closed as he awkwardly tapped one foot.

"That's an open case. You know I can't discuss that with you," Wade said after a few seconds of silence. "What else do you want?"

"Look, Hawkins, don't get cute with me," Max said. "What's this crazed Doctor Vincent up to?"

"He's working hard at the lab," Wade said.

"Yeah, yeah, I know that. What else? What's he up to that involves his ex-wife?" Max asked.

Wade shrugged his shoulders. "What's going on with the missing Vincent girl case? How about the Browning boy? Have you tied them together yet?"

"Hey! I'll ask the questions," Max said. "I came here to get some answers. Maybe you'd like to come downtown with me."

"You have something planned to charge me with?"

"Don't get wise—"

"Some wisdom would be good for you, Max. Unless you have an arrest warrant, and it better be legit, stay away from my client. If you want to talk to him, call me, and I'll arrange for a meeting. With his schedule these days, it may have to be at two in the morning, but I'm sure you can fit it into your life to be there. That is, if you're not up in the Pecos. Now, if you have something of substance to discuss with me, let's have it. Otherwise I have important things to do." Wade waited a few seconds. "Well?"

"I'll be seeing you around, Hawkins, you and that nosey breed friend of yours. I suggest you go about those important things you just mentioned and forget all about anything to do with Dr. Alex Vincent."

"That almost sounds like a threat. What do you think, Detective Lane? Did your boss just threaten me? He did insult the Apache blood that runs in my veins when he slammed Sonny, don't you agree?"

"No! No, of course not. He's just—"

"I'm just giving you some advice, Hawkins," Max cut in. "Just giving advice. See me in my office, Lane. Bring some donuts—the good ones."

With that, both officers got into their cars and left. Wade opened the front door to his office. He went in and sat at his desk. He flipped through his rolodex. Lollypop… Lollypop… There it was. He picked up the phone.

★★★

Sonny sat in his Jeep a few hundred yards down the road from the little, single-story house at the outskirts of Santa Fe. He observed the cracks in the stucco, the pealing trim paint and some loose boards in the cedar fence. Shortly before sundown, a young woman drove up and parked an older Toyota in the driveway. Sonny started his Jeep and pulled it in behind the car while the woman opened her car's trunk and took out several bags of groceries. She turned and gave Sonny a worried look.

Sonny got out, smiled, and then addressed the woman.

"Hi. You're Sally Browning, right? I'm Sonny Horn. I'm an investigator working on a case that involves your son. May I talk to you for a few moments?"

"I thought everyone had given up on Kreg. Sure, I'll talk to you. Come on in."

Sonny handed Sally one of his cards, then reached for the groceries. "Allow me, please."

Sally said nothing, but handed over the bags, then she turned and started for her house. She unlocked the door and led Sonny to the kitchen.

He set the groceries on the table. Sally quickly put several frozen things in the small freezer compartment in the top of her refrigerator.

"Come in here and sit a spell," Sally said, moving to the family room area. She sat on a threadbare, sagging-cushioned chair with mismatched pillows, and Sonny chose an old wooden rocker across the room from her. Sally closed her eyes, leaned her head back, and then turned it from side to side.

"Excuse me, I've got such a headache," she said. "Have one nearly all the time now since Kreg—well, I just can't seem to get rid of it. You're not from the police, are you?"

"No. I'm working for an attorney, Wade Hawkins. He's Alex Vincent's attorney. You know Alex, right?"

"Oh, yes. He's a nice man. Tucker worships the ground he walks on. If only he wasn't so busy…"

"What do the police tell you about Kreg?" Sonny asked. "What do they think happened?"

"How do I know? All Max Pace tells me is to sit tight, that he's got everything under control. Sometimes I wonder…" Sally again seemed to let her thoughts drift off.

"You were saying?" Sonny asked.

Sally shook her head. "No, I best not say what I was thinking. Sometimes I think some awful things."

"What do you know about Evelina Vincent's involvement in that Saints of Seven group?" Sonny asked.

"It's her whole life. How she can ignore that little boy of hers for such foolishness, I'll never know. That baby girl of hers—she never even held her. I know it's only my opinion, but something just ain't right. There, I went and said something. I really shouldn't be talking like this. I do work for Mrs. Vincent."

"You still work there?"

"Tucker needs me. If something ever happened to him…"

"You think Tucker is in danger?"

"Oh—no, I best not say that. I don't have any proof, I mean, I really don't know of any danger."

"You've had some tough things happen in the last few years, haven't you?" Sonny asked.

"You know about my husband then? Buck was so very good. Oh, I need him now. Why was he killed? Why was Kreg taken away from me? Am I such a bad person? Is God punishing me for something I've done? I wouldn't know what it would be. Still, I think God's mad at me—I'm sure mad at him. I'm mad at everyone, really. The police, they're lying to me. The Army, I get little from them. If Buck hadn't taken that leave… Kreg…

Will you help me Mr. Horn? Oh please, find my boy before I go completely crazy."

★★★

"This is great Alex. You'll really have your program ready to start testing tomorrow? I knew you'd come up with something that would work. How'd you do all this so quickly?" Kurt Stein asked.

"Slow down, Kurt. I've given all of this my best guess and thrown things together without any testing. That will come tomorrow. Tomorrow is just a test."

"I know this Code Dog is your baby," Kurt said. "It's got to work. We need something to show when Secretary Kingston gets here. I hear President Daugherty is planning a big Fourth of July announcement. He's betting we'll have a breakthrough by then."

"That's going too far out on a limb. Even if this program can start to decipher all these codes, it might take weeks, or longer, to pull it all together. I don't want to have someone promise what I can't deliver."

"I agree with Alex," Carla said. "These politicians need to come down to the real world. If they say we've broken this code, then if we really haven't…"

"Ah, you two. It'll work," Kurt said. "We've beaten this thing. We'll be heroes. I can smell a Nobel Peace Prize already."

"Easy, Kurt," Alex said. "This is only the first part. Even if this works and we translate this code, someone then has to take this raw data and solve whatever threat faces us. Thankfully, that will fall on someone else's head."

"You two can mope around all you want, you doom and gloomers," Kurt said. "I'm going out to celebrate."

"I'm going home to get some sleep," Carla said. "My kids won't know what to do with me home for the evening."

Kids. That word echoed through Alex's head. Early in the morning he was to meet with Wade Hawkins to finalize his and Tucker's departure. If his Code Dog program started breaking down the strange lines of code, maybe Kurt could take over. That way leaving would be much easier. Being a realist, he'd been making some radical preparations should he need to keep working on his program. He'd know late tomorrow after he'd run this first test.

★★★

"Mom, can me and you go over to the ball field so's I can watch some guys play and maybe we can talk some?" Tucker asked his mother, looking at the floor, unable to look her in the eye.

"Oh Tucker, not tonight. It was a hard day at work and, well some other night, Actually, I have a meeting with some of my Saints friends here a little later. You'll have to go to bed early. You know how important this is to me." Evelina said, flipping her long hair, now kept constantly in a braided ponytail, over her shoulder. As she often did around the house, and even around town, she wore a headband. This one was made of Aztec print cotton. Though she tried to walk some and eat well, she carried that heavy look. Being a good three inches taller than most women, and two inches taller than her ex-husband, she was somewhat uncomfortable with her body. Sometimes she tried hard, but she never could look very feminine. These days she would usually be found, when anywhere but at work, in a loose, flowing robe of some sort.

"So what's so important that you want to tell me?" she asked Tucker.

"Oh—nothin', Mom. Just thought we could talk some. I understand you're too busy. We'll do it some other time. Just wanted to talk."

Dad's work at the lab... Mom's work and all her Saints of Seven stuff... Sure wish little sis was still around... Maybe Dad will come through—but he never has.

★★★

"This general power of attorney will give me the authority to run your personal affairs until you get back. I'll have your mail forwarded here. Did you bring that list of financial information I asked for?" Wade asked.

"Yes. Everything's in this folder. All my payment schedules and so on are listed. There's a dentist appointment for next week that needs to be canceled, but I didn't want to cancel it and arouse suspicion."

Wade nodded. "I'll take care of that. They may be watching your bank accounts; do you have any cash anywhere else?"

"Yes. I sold about $10,000 in stock last month at the advice of my broker. I never got around to re-investing that. That money is in my brokerage account."

"This is him?" Wade asked, pointing to a name listed under a Los Alamos brokerage house."

"Yes. I guess with that power of attorney you can get that money."

"I'll get it and forward it however Lollypop tells me. That might take a week or so to get to you. I'd take whatever money you have at home with you. You won't be able to use your bank card or anything like that. In fact, make sure you leave your wallet in your car when you drop it off. Taking it with you won't do anything but get you into trouble. Your cell phones too. I'm sure Tucker is like most kids, and he can text a mile a minute, but using your phones would be like sending out a come-and- find-me signal.

"Then there's your jewelry. That's an awfully nice ring, your watch and that gold bracelet are all very high-end. In your real life, that's well appreciated. However, I'd say that where you're going, most likely to very common places, all of that might really clash. I'd leave all things such as that behind. Those shoes also. Fine as they are, they won't help you hide. If you have any walking shoes, something rugged and casual, that's what I'd wear. Maybe buy yourself an inexpensive watch also. Something a poor person would wear. Remember, you're trying to not look like yourself. If you still have your last glasses' prescription, I'd go to one of those fast eye places here in Santa Fe and get a pair that's vastly different from those gold frames you have now. Maybe something plastic—something you'd never wear. Again, trying to be different from the real you. You're a classy guy, but the man on the run must appear to be of a much lower class to draw the least suspicion."

"Yeah, right. All of that makes sense. I've got a little stash set back. I'll be alright as far as money goes," Alex said.

"You know you'll have not only the Santa Fe police after you, but the Feds will be on your tail too. They might make you feel like John Dillinger."

Alex responded by slowly nodding his head.

"If this underground thing is as good as they claim, that shouldn't matter," Alex said. "I'm more afraid of Evelina and her group. The FBI would just arrest me and bring me back. That group, after what they've done to those two children, I shudder to think what they'd do to Tucker and me."

Wade nodded. He took a deep breath. Was he sending this desperate man and his son into safety, or would they just disappear off the face of the earth? "What about your work?"

"I've cobbled together a bunch of stuff that I've been working on. A new approach to decoding, a bunch of theories all put into one program. I'm running the first test on some new code as soon as I get to the lab. If it's successful—oh do I hope it's successful—then I can leave things in the hands of my two primary assistants. They can take things from there. If not, then I've got to take drastic measures. I'll have instructions for you if that happens. I don't want to drag you into a national security thing, but I'll have to have someone as a contact who can't be made to talk."

"Too bad you won't be around to celebrate if things go well," Wade said.

"I'll celebrate with Tucker," Alex said. Then he looked hard at Wade. "Did you have a father in your life, Mr. Hawkins?"

"Very much. He started this law firm. I guess I owe him just about everything I am."

"That must have been really wonderful. I didn't. My dad would show up occasionally. I had several stepfathers, and Mom had other boyfriends. Nobody ever acted like my father though—like I really mattered to them. After I went off to school in Massachusetts, I rarely went back home, even for Christmas. Several times I went to friends' homes—friends with real fathers—and I always felt so empty, so abandoned, like I'd missed so much. I swore I'd be a real father to any child I ever had. However, I haven't kept that promise. I need to make that up to Tucker. I just wish it was under better circumstances. Tucker's been hurt a lot. Guess I've been a big part of that."

For several seconds Wade pondered what Alex Vincent had just said.

"I'm sure you and Tucker will have to depend on each other a lot during this ordeal. He'll never forget this. He may not understand all you're doing for him now, but someday he'll fully understand the sacrifice you're making for him."

"I don't know what all we'll find out there," Alex said. "My world has been very narrowly focused. I don't mind telling you that I'm scared."

"I'm sure you'll be fine. You might be surprised what you'll find out there, and inside yourself. You'll probably find people who have opinions based on their life experiences that are very different from yours. The very foundations of your core beliefs might get challenged."

The two men sat in silence for several minutes, and then Alex Vincent asked Wade a question.

"You're one who believes in God, aren't you?"

"Absolutely."

"Carla does too. That's Carla Hunter. You know her. Sure, she gave me your name. I never can figure her out. With all her education—yet she believes so strongly. That's what intrigues me—sometimes even angers me. How one can believe so adamantly in something not provable by science. If it was anybody else but Carla..."

Wade remained silent for a moment, and then addressed what Alex was contemplating.

"The way I see it, God is backwards from about anything else. In science, you prove something in a lab first, and then you believe in it. With God, you have to believe in him first, that's the faith element, then he'll prove himself to you. Maybe now with a new lifestyle and some free time you can search this out for yourself. That's the way it has to be—each one of us and God."

"That's just so—so unscientific. So against everything I've been taught and believe. I guess if there is a God, maybe I'll find him out there somewhere. I'll have to have proof though. I don't buy into any of that faith stuff."

"Alex. What are you doing? There's nothing we can do now," Carla Hunter said to her despondent boss. "It didn't work. So, we start over tomorrow. Kurt's already gone home, or somewhere. I'm going home now. You need to do the same."

"I needed it to work. I really needed it to work," Alex said. "I failed. I let all of us down."

"We'll analyze that tomorrow. Look, we gave it our best. Maybe it's only one little thing. Please go home now. I'm leaving." Carla turned from Alex's office doorway and started to leave.

"Carla. Come back. I have to talk to you, please."

Carla returned to the door. Alex felt her inquisitive stare as he sat with his eyes closed. Then she stepped back into the office, closed the door and sat in a chair.

"So talk, Alex. It's more than today's test, isn't it?" Alex slowly nodded his head.

"I'm—I'm leaving. Tonight. Tucker and I. You can't tell anyone, please. I'm going underground with Tucker. I have to do this. His life…" Alex paused for a moment. Carla said nothing.

"I've got things set up to keep working on Code Dog from wherever I am—some work anyway."

"Alex, you're not stealing a computer, are you?" Carla asked, looking at his briefcase.

Alex shook his head. "No, not really, but—I've got to do this, Carla. I don't care about the law. I know I've somehow got to help decode Aba Saad's documents, but if something would happen to Tucker…"

"How are you going to do all this?" Carla asked.

"You'll find out in a few days. It may be a week or more until I'm in touch, but I will be."

"Can I do anything?" Carla asked.

Alex shook his head. "No one can do this for me. Tucker's my son—he needs me. I just needed to tell someone how I feel. Kurt won't understand. Maybe you don't either. It could well be that no one will. I don't want to be branded a traitor, but…"

Carla slowly nodded her head. "I understand, Alex. You're not a traitor. I'll not tell anyone until tomorrow. Will that be alright?"

"Yeah, tomorrow will be fine." Alex looked around his office. He looked at his briefcase, his briefcase that now held his computer hard drive stashed among a handful of CD's and thumb drives. He'd hidden them between two slices of bread in a crumpled, brown lunch bag, knowing that Lester, the guard on duty, rarely looked in his things at all, and if he did it was only a cursory opening and closing of the case. He hoped tonight wouldn't be any different.

"Tucker's out in the lobby with Lester. Evelina dropped him off there several hours ago. Walk out with me, please. I…"

"Sure, Alex. Let's go."

They walked out into the lab area, then down the hallway to the lobby.

"Little fella be all tuckered out, Doc Vincent," Lester said. "He surely is one fine boy. It must make you one proud daddy every time you see him."

"Sure does, Lester. Let me wake him. Hey, Tucker, time to go."

"Uhhh—ahhhh. Can't I stay here? Me and Lester been talkin' and—can't I go back to sleep?"

"Not tonight. Up on your feet. Time to go." Tucker slowly got to his feet. He yawned, and then stretched.

"Hi, Mrs. Hunter," Tucker said. "I hear things didn't go so well today."

"We'll fix it tomorrow. You go on with your dad now."

"Yeah, OK. Hey Dad, can I carry your briefcase?"

Alex's hand jerked and clutched the leather case to his chest, then let it loose. "Ah, yeah. If that's what you want, here. Say goodbye to Lester."

"See you Lester. You sure do tell a good story," Tucker said.

"You're a good listener. Be careful with your daddy's briefcase. I'll let you, assistant guard Tucker Vincent, be the one to check it tonight to make sure it's all OK. I 'spect you're carrying some mighty important stuff there."

Alex's breathing was short and forced as they exited the building and started for his car. Carla was parked in another row. She started in that direction.

"Be careful, Alex. I'll be pra—"

"Yeah, sure, I know."

When Alex and Tucker reached their car, Alex turned and looked around. In the dark he couldn't see much. Still, he took a good look.

This might well be the last time I ever see any of this.

★★★

Wade sat staring at the clock. He hadn't told Nita anything. There was just too much to explain until it was done. Wade walked out on his porch. Off in a distance he saw approaching car lights in the black, nearly moonless night. They slowly came closer. Wade looked at his watch. Not a minute too soon. The lights came closer, and finally illuminated the front yard. Wade walked over to the BMW when it pulled to a stop.

"Pull it behind that big garage," Wade said. "I'll put it inside in the morning. Then come and wait inside."

Wade walked back over to the porch and waited for his visitors.

"Wade. What is going on?" Nita asked when she joined Wade on the porch. "What are you doing? Who's out there?"

"Sorry, Mother. I couldn't tell you about this before. I can't right now either. I'll tell you a little when they're gone. Go back inside. Don't worry. Everything will be all right."

"If this was on the up and up you'd be doing this in the light of day, not like some criminal out here in the middle of the night," Nita said. "I should have known," she said when she saw Dr. Vincent and Tucker. "Let me get some water on for hot chocolate. I'll make coffee too."

"No time, Mother," Wade said, hearing the flailing drone of a chopper off in a distance. He flipped on the outside barn lights and picked up the red-beamed flashlight he'd bought to guide the chopper in. In minutes the chopper hovered overhead, and then it cautiously set down.

"Come on!" Wade yelled to Dr. Vincent. "There's no time to dally. Go!" he yelled as Dr. Vincent crawled into the tiny bubble. Wade handed Tucker up to him, then slammed the door and motioned for the pilot to lift off. The engine raced and the blades blasted sand in every direction, then the little craft was off and speeding through the air.

Wade stood there watching it go. Nita came over to him.

"Oh, Wade. Tell me. Tell me what you've just done."

Chapter 6

Alex Vincent clenched his fingers tightly around the handgrip on the dashboard of the little chopper. His heart punched at his ribs. Breath came in short, harsh bursts.

"Hey. Loosen up. No need to be so tense. I can fly this in my sleep. Been flyin' these birds since 'Nam. Call me Bacho. How about you?"

"Al—Alex," Dr. Vincent said, his tongue sticking to the roof of his mouth. "This is my son, Tucker."

Bacho nodded. "Sit back and get that seatbelt on. There's a sidesaddle seat in back for the kid. Get them belts on."

Alex looked back at Tucker. His son's eyes were wide open and his little hands were shaking.

"Can you get into that seat?" Alex asked Tucker. Grabbing the back of the seat, Tucker pulled himself up onto the small, black vinyl seat.

"Yeah, that's it," Alex said. "Now put the belt on… good."

Alex tried to force a smile at Tucker. He knew his attempt at assuring his son that all was well had failed. He reached down at his right side, grabbed his thick, black nylon belt, and snapped it into place across his body. He took a slow, deep breath, then timidly looked out into his blackened surroundings. They'd already gained considerable altitude and were moving along at what seemed to be a rapid rate of speed.

"Where are we going?" Alex asked.

"The first lesson you learn in this outfit is not to ask questions. The less you know, the less chance of you getting into trouble. We've got about 300 miles ahead, so just sit back and relax. Like I said, nothing's going to happen. There'll be plenty of time for questions later. On the floor back there you'll find a Thermos of coffee, that little one has hot chocolate. Help yourself to the donuts in that box too. There's a can there if you have to—well—you know. Maybe you shouldn't drink too much coffee."

Alex swallowed hard. He closed his eyes. Did it have to be this way? Would the whole experience be like this? He looked back at his son. Tucker, seeming to have relaxed somewhat, gave a half-smile.

"Want some hot chocolate?" Alex asked.

"Sure. Can I have a donut too?"

Alex handed him the green and white box along with the smaller of the two insulated bottles. Looking out the window again, he tried to figure which direction they were going and how fast. The few scattered lights below told him nothing. Three hundred miles… they could end up in

Colorado, Arizona, Texas or even Mexico. If they were going south, they'd probably soon see the lights of Albuquerque. Going near a controlled airfield wouldn't be smart though. If they were going south it would surely be in a roundabout way. Most likely, they were headed for some other state.

Alex looked out at the stars. Back when he was a child he'd been fascinated by the mysteries of outer space. He'd dreamed of becoming an astronaut. Now he realized it had been years since he'd taken time to look up and enjoy the beauty of the host of stars a near moonless night afforded. Looking out the window to his right, he quickly spotted the dippers—thus the North Star. So, north was out the right side window—they were heading west into Arizona. Alex glanced over at Bacho. Sure, he was Native American, probably Navajo. They were heading for one of the reservations—either the big Navajo one or maybe Fort Apache. It was only an hour or so until daylight. By the time they got to where they were going, to it would be light. Planned to arouse less suspicion than a chopper flying into a remote area in the dark of night, Alex surmised.

Alex looked back at Tucker. A half-eaten donut still in his fingers, his head was slumped forward, and he breathed deeply. Children could be so trusting. Alex closed his eyes, but that only made him more nervous.

"Relax, Alex. You can unwrap your fingers from that bag of yours. It's not going anywhere," Bacho said.

Alex looked at his hands. He did have a white-knuckle grip on his briefcase. He lowered it to the floor, then let go completely.

"I've never done anything like this before," he said.

"The important thing is, I have, many times. You'll be safe, so will your boy. These people are the best. Tomorrow you'll start a re-programming regiment, and in a few weeks you'll almost forget who you really are. I've seen some who, after only a few days of reduced stress, don't want to go back to their old life."

I'll not be one of them, Alex thought. *The first opportunity I get, as soon as it's safe, I'm going home.*

Carla Hunter sat alone in the lab. She'd been there since well before sunup. She sipped on yesterday's warmed-over coffee. She didn't have the ambition to make fresh. Where were Alex and Tucker? What repercussions did she face for being Alex's willing accomplice? What would she tell the others here, the authorities? How would they ever crack all that crazy code now without Alex? On and on her mind went with all questions—no answers.

From out in the hall she heard footsteps. Kurt—of all people she'd have to tell first about Alex.

"Morning," Kurt mumbled while he headed straight for the coffee pot. "Ugh! What are you drinking? How could you?" He started making a fresh pot. Carla said nothing.

"So, Alex is sleeping in again. We were totally embarrassed yesterday when his pet project wouldn't even start to do what it was supposed to, and Alex doesn't see fit to show up early. He's got to go, Carla. He's just got to go."

"He's gone."

"What do you mean?" Kurt said, setting down the coffee pot he'd been filling with water. "You mean he's really gone? He just bailed out on us? This got something to do with that kid stuff?"

"A minute ago you said he had to go."

"Yeah, but heck, you know what I meant. I meant, well, it was his attitude that had to go, not really him. Wow, what a mess we're in now. You call the cops? When did you find out?"

"He told me last night when we left. I haven't called the authorities. Who should I start with? Security here? The FBI in Albuquerque?"

"Did he take a computer? Don't tell me you let him walk out of here with his computer?"

"Of course not. I asked him about that. I was just so confused. I didn't know what to do."

"You should have done something," Kurt said. "Why didn't you call me? I'd have done something."

Kurt walked over to Alex's computer and turned it on. Nothing happened.

"He didn't take his computer, just the hard drive and external USB drives," Kurt said as he opened Alex's top desk drawer and looked at the empty space usually filled with drives containing his personal code solving projects.

"Oh no! I never thought—"

"That's right, Carla, you surely didn't think. I'd say you start with security here. Let them bring in the Feds. You've really stuck your neck out this time. If it gets chopped off, you've only your feminine psyche to blame—maybe your do-gooder religion too. You walked right out of here with a man who stole our whole project and who knows what else. How do you know he didn't make up all that about his kid to throw us off? What if yesterday's failure was a setup? What if he's dealing off our work to some contact of Aswad Hamal right now? I can't help you with this, Carla."

Carla stood in silence, staring out a window; the same one Alex often looked out. She stared out into the vast, empty canyon.

Alex Vincent couldn't believe what he saw. The sun was rising over the horizon behind them as Bacho set the chopper down in a canyon, near a cluster of a half-dozen adobe and stick buildings. Several children and a mangy dog ran to greet them. Alex looked back at Tucker and saw fear in his son's eyes. While the rotors wound to a stop, Bacho looked at Alex.

"This ain't so bad, really it's not. Hey, you're safe. What's more important than that? Besides, it's only for a few days, until the original heat's off. Come. We've got some new clothes for you two. There's all you'll need while you're here. When you move on, you'll be taken care of again. This is cool. Just relax and live. No phone, no TV, no trouble. Come, meet my family."

★★★

Carla sat at a table across from two FBI agents. Huck Miles, the lead agent, had drawn all he could out of her. Now, agent Sig Simpson started in on her, repeating everything they'd already gone over many times.

"He told you he was taking classified material," Sig started.

"No, I've never said that. I asked if he was taking a computer, and he said no. I just wasn't thinking about anything else. I was worried about Alex and Tucker and about how we'd complete our project here without him."

"But you didn't stop him," Sig said, leaning forward, pushing himself closer to her.

"No, I—"

"You know where he went, right?"

Carla closed her eyes. How many times had she answered this question?

"You need to come with us, Mrs. Hunter. We're taking you to Albuquerque," Huck Miles said an hour later when Sig seemed to tire of getting no new answers.

"Where? Are you taking me to jail? Are you arresting me?"

"Holding you for questioning," Huck said. "Arrest may come later. It depends on if you decide to start cooperating,"

"But I've told you everything I know."

"Hands behind your back," Huck said while Sig reached around his back and produced a set of cuffs.

"You're going to handcuff me? Like I'm a criminal or something?"

"Don't make this any more difficult than it needs to be, Mrs. Hunter. Just cooperate," Huck said. "You'll have plenty of time on your ride to Albuquerque to remember all the things you seem not to want to now."

"I can't leave here—our project. At least let me call my husband."

"I'd call an attorney, if I was you," Sig said as he put a hand on Carla's shoulder, and half shoved her toward the door. Carla walked out of the lab building and across the parking lot to the gray Ford with Federal plates on it. She could feel the dozens of eyes staring at her through the office windows as she was pushed into the back seat.

Sig started the car and drove toward the street. Just when he reached it, another car sped down the street toward them. The driver braked hard and cut in front of Sig.

"What the—" Sig punched the window button. "FBI, pal. Outta my way."

"Sorry," the tall man who'd exited the other car said. "Deputy Secretary Blake, Homeland Security. Mrs. Hunter is needed back in her office. You're not taking her anywhere. Move! She's in our custody. You're off this case."

"But—" Sig protested.

"No buts, this is our jurisdiction."

Sig looked at Huck, who shrugged his shoulders, then nodded back toward the lab building.

★★★

"Hey, Joey. What are you doing?" Tucker asked his new friend when Joey went to a rack of wood and grabbed several logs. Joey was a good inch taller than Tucker and had told him he was thirteen.

"Building a fire to cook lunch. Grab a couple of logs, will ya?"

"Yeah, sure," Tucker said, and then he picked out two of the smallest ones and quickly caught up to Joey.

"Don't you have a stove? Doesn't your mom cook inside?"

"Too much heat. Besides, food tastes better if it's cooked out here over wood."

"I never—"

"You city kids are all alike. You come out here and you ain't never taken a bath in the river or built a fire or killed and skinned supper or anything. Where do you think things come from?"

"Most things are just in a store, or the like. Other things, well they're just there," Tucker said.

"You mean like electricity and running water and the pipes for dirty water and all that?" Joey asked.

"Yeah, I guess. Whoever thinks about any of that?"

"Out here you will, 'cause we don't have any of that."

"You ever see a TV, Joey?"

"Yeah, sure. We have a place in town too. Most of the time though, we live out here. Especially when we got a kid like you. Nobody knows you're here. What are you running from anyway?"

"Ah—my mom, I guess."

"Your mom! She a witch or something?"

"I guess she might be. I don't know."

"She cast spells and all that?"

"I don't know, Joey. Let's talk about something else."

"Yeah. Hey, after we eat, I'm goin' out after some quail. I shoot them in the head with my 22 rifle. You ever shoot a gun?"

"Nah, I don't know if Dad would let me."

"Let you? My dad makes me. I've gotta get us all dinner for tonight. It's fun though. Ya gotta come with me."

"Yeah, sure. I'll come. I don't know about the gun thing though."

From under a tree by one of the out buildings, Alex watched Tucker and Joey. He wished he could adapt to such a drastic change so quickly. Tucker seemed to have lost all his fear. It was as if he knew his dad was going to make everything all right. However, who would make it right for him? Could he trust this Lollypop Railroad to keep him safe? Looking around, at this point he had great doubts—but no options.

Bacho and his wife—her name so full of letters Alex did what Bacho said most visitors did; he called her Mrs. B—the two of them came over to Alex along with their two younger children who seemed to speak little English.

"Tucker, your son's name, that's good for a last name," Bacho said. "That makes it easy for him. He's now Danny Tucker. Think he can handle that? If he slips up and uses Tucker, it still fits."

"Well, yeah, if we have to. So then, who am I?"

"Alex becomes plain old Al—Al Tucker. That's who you are until, well until you go home, or it becomes necessary to change it again."

"Guess we can handle that."

"Good," Bacho said. "There'll be much more, but that's it for today. Get this much into your head."

Bacho and Mrs. B left and went back to their little house.

The yellow dog that seemed to be everywhere came up to Alex and nuzzled against his leg.

"Ah, go on, you filthy mutt. I don't have time to be your friend. Go—go play with the little kids."

★★★

Max Pace sat alone at the end of the poorly lit bar. He'd been there for several hours. His phone had rung at least six times before he turned it off. He couldn't talk to her now. He had to think of a plan first. There had to be a way to draw Alex and Tucker Vincent back home. Suddenly, he felt a hand on his shoulders. It felt icy cold and sent chills down his spine. He shuddered.

"Max, it won't do you any good to try and hide from me. You've obviously had your head in the sand for weeks now. I told you Alex was up to something. You couldn't even stop him from snatching my own kid. And to think, we're trusting you to keep the lid on so many things.

Sometimes you scare me. Anything is only as good as its weakest link, and I think you're ours, Max dear. Now with Tucker gone, Sally won't be around my house much, so I can't keep her under control. Did you ever think of that?

"That young detective of yours, Luke Lane, he's way too curious," Evelina continued. "You've got to cool him off. Now the Feds are snooping around. Then there's that attorney. Snap to it, Max. We have the power now. Remember how it was? The power you felt—the jolt that shot through your body—when you dipped your fingers into that warm, oozing blood. Once should have been enough, but you've been privileged to partake in the service of power twice. You have that special power in you, Max dear. Don't let your mind fool you. Look at me. I'm on a higher level than ever. You should be too. Just let your mind go. And accept what the spirits have for you. Be free. Rise above normal humanity."

Max pushed Evelina away and rushed to the men's room. Her so casually, so coldly, reminding him of what they'd done, her bringing it up the way she did caused him to slump to the sticky concrete floor and bury his face in the stained, putrid toilet bowl.

Wade Hawkins and Sonny Horn sat at a table in a back room at the Roadrunner Grill having a late lunch.

"That Sally Browning, she's having it real tough, Wade," Sonny said. "When she gets the word that her boy is dead, I don't know if she can handle that without some help, and she doesn't seem to have any. Taking care of Tucker kept her somewhat occupied, but now without that, I just don't know."

"Keep an eye on her. If there's something we can do to help, let me know. Maybe Mom could talk to her."

"Is Nita still mad at you?"

"She's worried. Can't blame her. Who knows where this will take us? From the lab side, I'll have to fend off the FBI and Homeland Security. From here I'll have to outwit the Santa Fe Police. I don't know what to expect from the Saints of Seven."

"Speaking of the Saints of Seven, I'm not having much success coming up with a list. One person in it for sure is Rhea Thatcher. She teaches with Evelina Vincent, and they're best buds. Thatcher is the nervous type though. She went to her doctor several times last week, and she carries around enough pill bottles to choke Kicks. She may be one who'll crack."

"Keep an eye on her when you can," Wade said. "Has anyone gone back up to the Pecos?"

"Not that I can tell. I haven't."

"I still think you're making that up. You're just afraid to be out in the dark. It's that old Apache-thing."

"I'll Apache-thing you. I told you what happened, and it did, exactly as I said."

The smile on Wade's face faded. "They're a dangerous group. Don't get boxed in."

Sonny nodded as he toyed with his eggs. Minutes later, when Wade and Sonny pulled into Wade's office parking lot, there sat a blue Ford at the far end of the parking lot.

"You've got company," Sonny said.

"Yeah, no surprise. Just drop me off, and then get out of here," Wade said. "No sense of you being in on this until they find you."

"Call me later."

"Might be my one call from jail," Wade said. "Naah. Keep the faith, Wade."

Wade walked into his office to find two men sitting in the lobby. Before Nita could introduce them, Sig Simpson jumped up and got in Wade's face.

"FBI, Hawkins. We need to talk with you."

"Soon as I go to the restroom."

"That can wait," Sig said. "I've been here over a half-hour already."

"As I started to say—I'm sorry, but I don't know how to address you. You haven't introduced yourself. I'm going to the restroom. Then we can talk in my office."

"That—"

"That will be fine," Huck Miles cut in. "I'm agent Huck Miles. My partner here is Sig Simpson. We'll be waiting for you."

Wade nodded and went back to his office. His use of the restroom was mostly to let these two stew a little longer. After a minute, he rang Nita and had them sent back down the hall.

"As you surmised, I'm Wade Hawkins. That was agents Huck Miles and Sig Simpson, correct?"

Huck nodded, "Correct. I'm sure you know why we're here."

"Suppose you tell me."

"Dr. Alex Vincent. I believe he's a client of yours. I also believe you sent him somewhere. We need to know where."

"Are you sure you're supposed to be here?" Wade asked. "I heard Homeland Security is heading this up and you boys have been run out of the lab. Let me make a call to see if you're not lost by being here."

"Easy, Hawkins. I don't know what all is going on at the lab, but we have an interest in bringing back Dr. Vincent," Huck said.

"I can't help you."

"Listen, you," Sig cut in, "if you don't tell us where he is, we'll haul you in."

"I can't because I don't know," Wade said. "I have no idea where he is."

"You helped him get away," Sig said.

"But I have no idea where he was taken to."

"Why did he go?" Huck asked.

"The details are privileged of course, but it's a child custody thing. Hardly what your boss wants you spending your time on. I'd find a new case, guys."

Sig started to say something but a raised hand by Huck cut him off.

"If we find out you're lying, well, that wouldn't be good," Huck said.

"No, that wouldn't be good. That's why I truly don't know the answer to your question."

"We'll talk again, Hawkins," Huck said, then he rose from his chair and, without so much as a look or wave, he started for the door. As Sig rose, he opened his mouth as if to speak, but then he closed his lips and clenched his jaw. He turned and got in line behind Huck.

Nita came back to Wade's office when they were gone.

"Oh, Wade. Now you've got the FBI haunting you. Wasn't there another way?"

"None that I could think of."

Alex Vincent lay awake looking out the open window at the host of stars in the sky. *Al Tucker* he kept repeating over and over. His body was exhausted, yet he couldn't sleep. Beside him lay Tucker, now Danny, out cold. Tucker, rather Danny, was so proud that he'd helped Joey hunt down the quail they'd had for supper.

So primitive.

All day long, thoughts of the lab had been on Al's mind. Had Carla gotten into trouble? How could he do anything out here in this deserted hole? He had about four hours of battery power on his computer. He'd use that tomorrow.

Should have brought several extra computer batteries. Who knew?

His mind wandered on. Near dawn, sleep finally came.

Al slept until the sun was up considerably the next morning. When he got up, he read a note from Danny telling him that he and Joey were off somewhere fishing. After eating some fresh corn tortillas with honey on them for breakfast, Al opened up his briefcase. He opened the bottom of his empty personal computer he'd brought, then carefully installed the hard drive from the lab. He started it up. Everything seemed to work fine. Bacho walked by him carrying a bucket of water.

"I've got a little solar charger and a bank of deep charge batteries we use in the winter time when light gets short. 'Spect you know how to wire them up for twelve volts so you can rig up your adapter, and that should keep you going all day, night too if you need it."

"Hey, that would be great," Al said. "I've been wondering how I could make things work out here."

"There's usually more than one way to do something," Bacho said. "Out here you learn to find that other way. That boy of yours, now he sure has taken to this life quickly."

"Yeah, Joey seems to do well teaching other kids. He should look at making teaching a career."

"I hadn't thought of that, but you're right," Bacho said. "Anything you need? I've got to go fuel up my bird."

"No—how long will we be here?"

Bacho smiled—showing his white teeth. "When the next stop is ready, away we go."

"Don't suppose you know where that next stop is."

"Got a pretty good idea, won't tell you though. Can't spoil the fun." Bacho again smiled, then headed for his helicopter.

★★★

Carla Hunter looked out her kitchen window. She was back home with her family. Out on the street sat a dark sedan. She was under twenty-four-hour surveillance, but at least she wasn't in jail. Kurt was furious and had chased her out of the lab earlier. She knew that behind all his hard ways Kurt was insecure. He was scared without Alex here to lead him, and he was scared of failing. And most of all, Carla believed, he was scared of himself, his limitations, that he couldn't live up to the expectations he'd set for himself.

Then Carla thought of Alex. Where was he? How was he? Was Tucker safe? Could Alex do the work they so desperately needed him to do from wherever he was?

★★★

Out in the eerie silence of the remote canyon on the Navajo reservation, Al rose in the middle of the night. He'd slept fitfully in the hot, calm air. He slipped his sockless feet into his shoes, opened the door of the little hovel given to him as home here, then he walked outside. He stood in awe of the multitude of stars in the blackened sky for several moments. After a moment, he slowly ambled down the path toward the wood rack. His mind was buried deep in thought when instinctively he sensed something move at his feet. *Tat-tat-tat-tat*, the distinct buzz of rattles cut through the silence of the night as startling as if it was a bolt of lightning.

Chapter 7

Al froze. His legs felt like bungee cords attached to feet of led.

You get bit out here, you'll die!

He closed his eyes. His breathing was short and hard. His heartbeat seemed to match the pace of the snake's rattle.

Don't pass out now!

The staccato of the rattle again cut the silence of the desert night, sending more terror through every cell in his body.

Then, from up the path in front of him, Bacho's mangy, yellow dog leaped upon the coiled viper. Instinctively trying to get out of the way, Al started to back-peddle, but stumbled. Falling, he cracked his head on the hard, rock-strewn earth.

"Oooooh!" burst from his lips. Then he quickly came to his senses and scrambled away, crawling across the dry earth as rapidly as his dysfunctional body could. The dog, with the snake grasped in a death hold in his jaws, was violently shaking his head from side to side. Hearing the commotion, Bacho, with kerosene lantern in hand, quickly rushed toward the scene.

"Good boy Dog. Break his back! Don't let go," he yelled when near enough to see what was going on.

As Al scrambled to his feet, Danny and Joey both came running to his side.

"Stay back!" Al warned. "That dog's got a snake."

"Ahh, shucks," Joey said. "That ain't nothin'. He does that all the time. I was hopin' it was somethin' real excitin' out here. Old Dog keeps all the snakes out of our yard, the buildings too."

Al looked at Joey, then Bacho.

"Joey's right," Bacho said, his usual smile across his face. "Times like this old Dog here is worth more than a mine full of silver. Got him from a native brother over at Window Rock. Most of my folks really hate snakes. Some of them have trained and bred their dogs to free their homes and grounds of those creepy things. Watch now! Old Dog's about got the better of this one."

In the dim light of the kerosene lantern, Al strained his eyes to watch the flailing and thumping this dog was giving the snake. With a violent shake, the dog tossed the snake aside, then grabbed it again and started all over.

"Might as well go back to bed," Bacho said. "The fun's over for now. What were you doing out here anyway?"

"I—I just wanted some fresh air, I guess," Al said. "I walked out to think, that's all."

"You should have thought before you walked out," Bacho said. "Be careful out here in the dark. We're not like the back streets of some big city, but we have our own dangers."

"Guess I'll be staying inside once the sun goes down," Al said. "I'm not used to things like this."

"You owe Dog a good hug in the morning."

"Yeah, suppose I do. Doesn't he have a name? You just call him Dog?"

"That's good enough for me. I know most folks go and name their animals, but then you get to thinking they're talking about a kid or something when they talk about them. I always figured names belonged to people."

"Yeah, I see what you mean," Al said. "I'll ah, I'll see you in the morning. Come on Son, let's get back to bed."

★★★

Wade Hawkins leaned back in his chair and studied the man sitting across his desk.

"There's nothing but trouble for you if you don't come clean, Hawkins," Detective Max Pace said. Wade looked hard into the other man's eyes, but Max wasn't looking back at him. He lightly tapped one foot up and down as he folded, and then unfolded his hands. He cleared his throat, then spoke again.

"Look, Hawkins, I'm leveling with you. You have a good record. Why do you want to go and mess that all up over this case? Think of your future. I could be a big help to you, you know. I don't know what you think was going on. That kid was in no danger here, really. He's just a kid. You can't believe what he says. What do you say, Hawkins?"

Max finally looked into Wade's eyes. After a few seconds of silence his shoulders slightly twitched, his eyes blinked, and then looked back down at the floor. Wade remained silent while he watched Max agonize over his dilemma. When Max finally looked up at him again, Wade smiled and spoke.

"Relax, chief. This is your lucky day. I'm going to tell you all I know about where Dr. Vincent and his son are. Yes sir, I'll tell you all I know."

"Oh good, Hawkins," Max said, sliding back in his chair. "I knew you'd see how things have to be. Look, maybe once this is over, I mean, well, we could use a good attorney, I…"

"Listen to me, Max. Write it down if you have to," Wade said. "I don't know where Dr. Vincent is. I don't know when he'll be back. I don't want to be part of your little group. I'll fight you to the end over this. Why don't you go back up into the Pecos and rummage around the blood and bones up there, maybe you'll find your conscience. Maybe you'll realize how dirty you've really become, and then you'll come back to me with a story to tell. That's all I want from you, Chief Pace. I want to see you walking through my door, confessing and begging God for forgiveness. Until then, don't bother coming back. Go on, now. Go do some soul searching."

Max Pace jumped to his feet and leaned over Wade's desk.

"Who do you think you are!"

"Just a man with a conscience. A man bent on doing what's right. The question is, Chief Pace, who do you think you are? You think you've become someone really important—powerful. Someone's got you believing you're above it all. You're not. Come clean now before anyone else gets hurt. You're carrying a big load, too big for you. I see it in you. This will kill you, if not your body, most assuredly your soul."

Max Pace took a step back, looked at Wade for a minute, then turned and exited without saying another word.

Danny stood by his father's side while both watched the little chopper wiggle in the gusty wind as it set down on the small, flat-rocked pad Bacho used for its port. After exiting the craft, Bacho waved to them, and then he walked toward his house, a brown envelope in his hand. Half-an-hour later, Bacho walked toward the rough-sawn log table where Al sat beside the little solar setup he'd been using to operate his computer. Al glanced at Danny, who watched from the doorway of the barn where he and Joey had been playing. Reaching the table, Bacho sat down and dumped the contents of the envelope out on the table.

"Here's your new identity. This should be everything needed to validate who you are. Things that should be so, like your social security card, are aged and worn to look old. There's an Arizona driver's license. Should you need to, there's everything you need to get one in another state or a job—get in and out of Mexico too." Bacho then looked away, seeming to stare aimlessly off into the miles of openness. "Read the paper while I was waiting to fill up. You sure have things shaken up."

"I had no choice," Al said. "I'll get this all solved, really I will. I'm no traitor."

"Didn't think you were. It's code you're working on right?" "Guess that's no secret now."

"Bet old Charlie can help," Bacho said, staring intently off toward the distant mountains.

"Old Charlie?"

"Yeah. Charlie Begay. He was one of those code talkers back in the big war. He got to studying code so much he became an advisor to the CIA. He's been called back to Washington several times. 'Course that was years ago, during Nam and such. Lately, he's—well, we'll go see him. If everything is in that computer of yours, best charge up your battery. I don't know if Charlie ever saw the likes of that before, but what the heck."

"I really don't think I can show any of this to someone without proper clearance," Al said. "I mean, what if he talks—"

"Charlie talk? Mister, wait until you see where Charlie lives. There's nobody to talk to. Besides, he had a Q clearance at one time, still might."

"I'm working on this new program and—"

"Hey, you're going to be here for a few days. Tomorrow we'll go see Charlie. What's to lose?"

Al leaned back in his chair and looked at Bacho.

"Can't do that. I need to stay right here, right where that railroad group sent me. I'm not going running all over this reservation like some coyote or such. I'm sure old Charlie was a true hero back in his day, I respect that. There's nothing he can do to help me develop my program or be of any help breaking some code written in multiple foreign languages. Please, you've got to understand."

"Yeah, I understand. Actually, I was just looking for an excuse to go visit my sister. Her Hogan is on the way to Charlie's. Charlie's nearly blind and can hardly hear thunder. Guess I was just thinkin' of myself, not what's best for you guys. It's hard for me to sit tight. I'm the nervous type—have been since 'nam anyway."

"Going to the village mercantile," Bacho said after a few moments of silence. "Need anything?"

"Not really," Al said. "I think we're pretty well settled in here and will be for as long as we're here."

Bacho nodded, then started walking toward his old pick-up.

Several hours later, Bacho drove back up to his house. He walked over to where Al was working.

"How's it going?" he asked.

"Nowhere. I'm getting nowhere. I've been working on my program but everything just goes in circles."

"We leave tomorrow at midnight," Bacho said quietly without looking at Al.

Al swallowed hard. Time to move on already? Just a couple of days ago, when he first saw it, he'd hated this place. Now he felt at least a little secure here. What was ahead?

"You'll do alright, really you will," Bacho said, still not looking at Al. "You've caused quite a stir in the news, though. I don't know what you're working on, but there are all kinds of rumors on the TV news channels. I know you wouldn't be doing this unless your son's life depended on it. I wish you the best."

Al slowly nodded his head. He could think of nothing to say. He looked over at his son, and then closed his eyes.

Yeah, this is worth it. Whatever lies ahead, as long as it works out in the end, it'll all be worth it.

★★★

Sonny Horn sat in the small living room of Sally Browning's home. Moments ago, when walking through the kitchen area, he'd observed how different, how much more cluttered the home felt than the last time he'd been here. Sally had talked constantly to Sonny since they'd sat down, but nothing made sense. Then suddenly, she shuddered slightly, then lowered her head into her hands and burst into tears. She sobbed openly, her body quivering while the tears flowed. After several moments, she somewhat regained her composure.

"I'm so sorry, Mr. Horn. I—I don't seem to be able to control myself these days. First my husband, now my son. Am I really that bad of a person?"

"Mrs. Horn, I don't think either of those things have anything to do with what kind of a person you are. You're beating yourself up needlessly."

"Why then? Tell me, Mr. Horn. Why? My Kreg's dead—I know it. The police tell me nothing. They'll never solve this— they don't want to solve this. Now this with little Tucker…" Sally again started sobbing.

"Have the police talked to you about Tucker?" Sonny asked when Sally again gained control of her tears.

"Detective Lane told me they think Dr. Vincent is responsible for all of this. They say he's the one who took little Melissa, my Kreg, and now his own son. Do you believe that, Mr. Horn?"

Sonny cleared his throat, and then breathed deeply.

"I don't know what information the police have. But no, I don't believe that. Have you seen Evelina Vincent lately?"

"She told me not to come back, to stay home and rest. She said the police will solve this. They won't though—they'll just push this case into some dark hole. At least with my husband the Army sent me something to bury and mourn over. How can I ever get over Kreg, never really knowing what happened?"

"Don't give up yet, Mrs. Browning," Sonny said. "Something might force the police to come through."

"So I just sit here and watch the news until then? Hoping to hear something to bring peace to my tormented soul?"

Sonny didn't know what to say.

"Care to have a drink with me, Mr. Horn?"

"No—no, maybe that wouldn't be the best for you either."

"I don't care, Mr. Horn. Why should I care?"

★★★

Wade Hawkins sat in the back room of the Roadrunner Grill reading the newspaper while he waited for his lunch. Out in the front he heard a waitress talking with someone.

"Yes, he's here, in the back."

Wade heard footsteps coming towards him, and then the waitress spoke again.

"Sir, sir, your cigar? You know all of this is non-smoking."

"It's not lit, lady. This old world's gotten so bad a man can't have a good smoke anywhere anymore. I don't even bother to light them up, except at home. I just chew on them for whatever good that does. Saves me a lot of money though, so it does."

Wade recognized the voice. He started to fold the paper when the visitor came closer.

"Long time, Wade."

Wade grasped the outstretched hand his visitor extended toward him. The other man dragged a chair away from the table with the point of his boot and when seated, tossed his hat on another empty chair. He pointed to the folded paper.

"Reading some good stuff, I see. Looking for your name? I've tried to keep it out of there, at least off the front page."

"I appreciate that, J. Quinton. You've got lots to fill up the pages, I'd say. How's circulation?" Wade asked.

"Record month last month. Tell me Wade, how'd you get sucked into the middle of this anyway? Your father would turn you over his knee if he could."

"He did that a few times, maybe not enough. You and dad were often at odds. Why the concern now?"

"Ahh, we were at odds a time or two, but we liked each other. Back when I bought the paper, I had all these idealistic ideas, you know. Heck, I was from Missouri. I didn't know how folks out here thought. Your dad helped me a lot. We sure could use more men with his kind of thinking around here now. How's your mother?"

"Good. Still mother-henning me," Wade said. "I'll tell her you asked."

"Good woman, so she is. Your dad was lucky. I tried three times, you know. Never could find one that wasn't just after a free ride. Kids all turned out like their mothers. Your dad was lucky, so lucky to have you take over his business. I'd give…" J. Quinton Sedwick cut his sentence off and stared aimlessly across the room for a moment, then looked back at Wade.

"So, Wade, what's this all about?"

"I know very little. That's the way I want it. I can't tell what I don't know."

"You bucked that Saints of Seven group awhile back. Is that who's behind all this? Are they capable of some of the things people are saying?" J. Quinton asked.

"Maybe to both questions," Wade answered.

"Max Pace. Something's not kosher there. Is he involved?"

Wade shrugged his shoulders.

"Come on, Wade. You know I won't quote you."

"I'll square with you, J. Quinton. I truly believed that little Tucker Vincent was in danger. I found someone who could help Dr. Vincent and take him to safety. That's really about all I know."

J. Quinton nodded. "I checked everything out I could. This wasn't easy on Dr. Vincent. He was in charge of something really big up at the lab."

"The FBI is watching you, Wade," J. Quinton continued. "Your phones are all tapped. Homeland Security is behind this. I think it's something to do with terrorism. I won't chase after that angle for now. The FBI put the heat on me for that. The cops here, well, I'm going after that angle with both barrels. I never did like that Max Pace. That weasel's lied to me for the last time. I know you've got young Horn out snooping around for you. Look, if he comes up with anything—you know what I mean—how about it?"

"I can't do anything that might endanger my client."

"Wouldn't ask you to. That's not what I mean," J. Quinton said. "Look, I've got my best man on this case, Jake Bonner. You ever meet him?"

Wade shook his head no.

"Ex-cop from San Francisco. Got shot up pretty badly and had to take an early retirement. He's got that cop's nose. I got a hunch he's going to break this open for me. I just thought maybe you could help."

"When this is all over, I'll give you an interview then," Wade said. "I doubt if I'm much help until this is finished. I'll say this much, the sooner this is over, the better for everyone."

"All right, Wade. Keep reading though. You just might find some mighty hot copy." J. Quinton Sedwick picked up his hat, slid back his chair and, after again shaking Wade's hand, he turned and left. When he did, the waitress brought Wade's green- chili and onion laden cheeseburger and refilled his iced tea.

"I kept this hot for you, Wade. I didn't think you'd want this while Mr. Sedwick was here," the waitress said.

"Thanks, Vicki. Yeah, it's hard to eat and talk."

Just when Wade started eating, he again heard footsteps coming towards him. He looked up and saw Carla Hunter. He rose to greet her. While he did, she turned and looked about.

"Being followed?" Wade asked.

"I feel like a crook," Carla said. "I came down here and have been to six different places but haven't shaken them yet. I called your office and Nita told me you were here."

"My phones are bugged," Wade said.

"I didn't use my real name," Carla said.

"Good, but they'll still figure you out soon enough," Wade said when they were seated in opposing chairs.

"Any information from Alex?" Carla asked.

"Nothing. In some ways that's good."

"I'm worried sick," Carla said. "With all the stress—you know the FBI had me in cuffs and on the way to Albuquerque when HLS stepped in?" She again looked around. "I've some questions for Alex. He has his notes with him. Time is running out for us. It's bad, Mr. Hawkins. I can't say much, but we're up against the impossible. I don't know how I'll handle things if we fail and—"

"You have lunch yet?" Wade asked.

Carla shook her head. Wade motioned for Vicki.

"You can't do anything now. You need to eat and relax. If I remember right, you have two boys. Tell me, how are they doing?"

★★★

Evelina Vincent sat in the hard wooden chair across from Red Conners. She stared at the slender, graying man.

"I'll get right to the point, Mr. Conners. You know who I am. You know about my son being missing. It's been all over the news. I'm told you're the man I need. That you're the best in town."

"Seems to me, you also have a missing daughter, your housekeeper's son too," Red said.

"Listen, I'm not hiring you to do anything about them. It's my son who I need you to find. If you're not up to the job, well, maybe Santa Fe's best isn't good enough. Maybe I need to go to Albuquerque."

"Whoa! I didn't say I wasn't interested. I just need to get a handle on what you want me to do. All right, we forget the other two and concentrate on your boy. Why'd your old man take him anyway?"

"My *ex-husband*. Look, I came here to hire you, not be treated as if I'm on trial. Here—here's a picture of Tucker. Listen, Alex is a geek. He can't last long out there. He has trouble remembering to eat regularly. I just don't want some out- of-town police department or the FBI finding him."

"Afraid of something he'll say?"

"Look, I'll pay you good money—your usual fee up front. You find them and there will be a big bonus—how about $5,000.00?"

Red leaned forward as his eyebrows raised. "This is an open police case. I don't like to work on them. The cops hate it."

"The cops? Trust me, no one there will bother you," Evelina said.

"Yeah, I hear you've got the inside track with old Max."

Evelina jerked back in her chair.

How did Red Conners know about her and Max? Who else knew?

"Well? You got the grit for this or not?" she asked.

"Any idea where they are?" Red asked.

"Iowa. That's where Alex was born. Other than his time in school in Massachusetts, that's the only place he's ever been. Here's a list of relatives of his that I remember, some addresses too. Here's my card. I expect to hear from you daily. We have a deal then?"

Red nodded slowly. "Yeah, if you've got the money—"

"We have all we need."

"We?" Red asked.

"The Saints of Seven, Mr. Conners. You should know by now, we own this town."

It was dark, several hours before daylight, when Al and Danny stood on a ranch road, high up in a cedar-forested mountain in southern Arizona. Bacho waved to them when he lifted his little chopper into the darkness of the night. Standing there alone, neither father nor son said anything until the drone of the engine could no longer be heard. Al clutched his computer case in one hand, and an old, cotton, duffle bag containing a change of clothes, and a few other things for each in the other.

Danny held a plastic grocery bag that contained a small loaf of outdoor baked bread, some strips of elk jerky, and a small jar of pear-cactus jelly, all given him by Mrs. B.

"I'm scared, Dad. There's nobody here to help us. Nobody's here at all. I think maybe we're gonna die out here. Then the bears and wolves will eat us, and nobody will ever know what happened to us. Thinkin' maybe we should have stayed home."

Al was silent for a moment. He had to show strength to his son. His mind said the boy was right—but his mouth spoke otherwise. "We'll be fine Son. It will soon be daylight, and help will come."

Then a coyote howled, and it wasn't very far away.

Chapter 8

Red Conners sat on the edge of the motel room's bed. With his elbows on his knees, he held his head in his hands. For at least the twentieth time he looked over at the clock on the badly scarred and stained nightstand. It was still ten minutes before five in the morning—long before daylight.

This room fit right in with the rest of his trip so far. The bed sagged in the middle, the mattress was lumpy, the pillow was hard and smelled much like a wet dog. All night long the neighboring room's TV had blared through the thin wall behind him. He walked over to the window and pulled back the edge of the curtains. In the darkness of the night, he could hardly make out the cars in the parking lot.

He'd taken a late night flight into Des Moines, picked up a rental car, then checked into the first motel he'd come to. Letting go of the curtain, he reached over to a switch and flipped on a light. After sitting on a tattered and stained chair, he leaned over the wobbly table and again looked at the list of names and addresses Evelina Vincent had given him. Laying that down, he picked up the map he'd grabbed at the rental car counter. *Fertiland, Nitra Creek, Black Meadow...* None of these town names were on the little map. He hoped there would be a detailed state map in the lobby, maybe some coffee too.

Red reached for the pants that he'd flopped over the back of his suitcase last night. He'd shower later. First, he needed a plan.

"Easy boy," Wade said to Kicks. "I know you want to get out there and stretch your legs, but you know you've got to let me get this cinch tight first." A minute later, Wade led his horse out into the early light of the new day. The sky behind the easterly mountains was taking on a yellow cast and the scattered, puffy clouds over that way now had a pink hue on their bottom sides.

Wade pulled himself up into the saddle and then nudged Kicks forward, letting him head up the trail at his own pace. This was a common event. Wade tried to work in a sunrise ride at least once a week. It always brought back memories of the times he and his father started their day this way. Sometimes they'd talk—nearly all of their most intimate conversations had taken place in the saddle out on this rocky trail. Other times they just rode in silence, taking in all that nature offered them. Out here that was plenty.

Reaching a point where the trail crested a little butte, Wade pulled Kicks to a stop. He dismounted and led his horse to a patch of course grass, then dropped the reins. Wade walked to the edge of the rise and looked out over the cedar-strewn valley below. He climbed up on a boulder and sat on its cool, hard surface. If only his father could be here to give him some of that carefully thought out, rock solid advice he'd given so often. Wade reached up and took his hat off, then lay back and looked up at the now vast azure sky while the early rays of the morning sun touched his face with a hint of warmth.

"I'm in a mess this time, Lord. Got myself in a good fix for sure. I feel it—I know it—things are going to get a whole lot worse before this is over."

★★★

"There, over there, Dad," little Danny said, pointing to a tumbledown shack near the entryway to a heavily-timbered mine shaft opening.

"Yeah, that's got to be what Bacho told us to look for. I guess we just go over there and wait." They'd been walking for an hour or so, ever since the sun had produced adequate light to show the trail. Al saw now that Bacho was right, as dark as last night had been, there was no place open enough to land the chopper any closer to the mine shack than the meadow they'd touched down in.

Al wished Bacho had stayed until their contact arrived. He remembered Bacho's words as he and Danny had crawled through the tiny chopper door.

"You'll be just fine. Someone will be along later in the morning. You've got plenty of water and enough food, so don't worry," Bacho had said, flashing one of his big smiles. With that, he'd lifted off, leaving them alone out in the wilds.

Now, they cautiously walked over to the long-abandoned shack. Remembering his experience of several nights ago, Al searched the ground with eager eyes looking for anything that might bring them harm. Reaching the blackened board and batte building, he first looked into it through the hole where once a window had kept the elements out. Seeing nothing to fear, he walked to the door and gave it a shove. It swung open with a screech of rusted hinges. He glanced over at Danny, who stood back several yards. Al shrugged his shoulders, peered inside, then walked through the doorway.

"Come on in, Son. It seems safe. There are some chairs in here. I'll find something to brush the dust off them."

Looking around for something to clean the dust from the chairs, Al went back outside and gathered up a large handful of dried grass. He tipped one of the old wooden kitchen chairs over, bumped it hard on the rough, plank floor, then brushed off what dust was left with the grass. He then pushed it toward his son, and then he repeated the procedure on a second chair.

"Gee. That's pretty cool, Dad. Where'd you learn to do that?"

"Just seemed like the best thing to do. I guess that's what Bacho meant when he said you learn to make do out in this kind of country. I guess you have to use your creativity if you want to survive. Maybe these country people who I've always made fun of as being simple are really very creative. Think about it. Some raise much of their own food, build their own buildings, use animals and simple machinery to help them. I never thought about anything like this before. Guess I never had to."

"Yeah, but I still don't like it. I'd sure like to be watching TV or playing a video game in my own room instead of this. What if no one comes? We'll die out here, won't we Dad?"

"Oh, I—no, we'd find our way out. This trail has to lead somewhere. We've got enough water for several days. We can't be that far from life." Al spoke these words to console his son, but they did little to console his own knotted stomach and pounding head.

"So, what did Mrs. B give us? Any surprises?" Al asked.

"Nah, I already looked."

"Well, are you hungry?"

"Not really, Dad. You?"

"Well—no, I guess not. Sure could go for a good cup of coffee though."

"Any bears around here, Dad?"

"Bears? I—I don't know. I don't think so. We haven't seen any animals and I don't think there's anything to worry about. That coyote that howled away earlier never came close. I'll bet he was more afraid of us than we were of him. I don't know if there are bears anywhere for hundreds of miles. I wouldn't even think of anything like that."

Bears... what if there are bears or the like around here?

"Oh, there's bears around alright," Danny said. "Joey said he and his dad hunt them all the time. They even eat them. Joey said his dad could track a bear as good as any dog. How do dogs track things, Dad?"

"They smell the scent left by whatever they're tracking. We can't smell things the way a dog can."

"Yeah. Those bears can smell too. Bet they could smell us, Dad. We ain't had a bath since we left home. Back home I wouldn't care, but I sure don't want some bear smellin' me now."

"Let's talk about something else," Al said. "Where does Joey go to school?"

"Come school time they go and live in some town, some little place up there, and he goes to school. He doesn't like school much. He's a smart kid.

He sure knows lots of stuff, but he's kinda dumb too. He can't even run a computer. Really, Dad, they didn't even have a telephone out there. No cell phone. He says they don't work out there. I'd sure like to text all my friends and let them know I'm still alive. I wouldn't tell them much."

"Hey, listen. What's that?" Al asked. "Listen, it's an engine. Someone's coming!"

"Yeah. What if it's some bad guy, Dad? Whata we do then?"

★★★

Sonny Horn sat in his Jeep. He glanced at his watch—she should appear any time now. He'd parked up the street from Taos Street Elementary School, the same way he'd done for the last three mornings. Each day Evelina Vincent and her assistant, Rhea Thatcher, brought their kindergarten class outside for a short recess time at ten o'clock. Right on schedule, out came the children. Sonny quickly dialed the school's number.

"Taos Street Elementary School, how may I direct your call," came the answer.

"I know it's the middle of the day, but I really need to talk to Evelina Vincent. It's important."

"Well, she should be at recess now. Whom should I say is calling?"

"Ah—tell her Red." *Yeah, Red for Redskin.* Red Conners had called Sonny before he left town, fishing for any information Sonny would give him. Red was good at his job. He had a way of intimidating other investigators, but Sonny carefully rebuffed all of Red's attempts. Evelina would be expecting calls from him—she'd answer any call from anyone called Red, no matter what the Red stood for.

"Hold on please," the operator said.

Sonny closed his phone, stuck it in his pocket, then got out of his Jeep and started walking toward the playground. The door opened and a young lady motioned for Evelina to come to her. When she did, Sonny picked up his pace and quickly walked up to the fence. Rhea Thatcher saw him and came over to him.

"Good group of kids, I'd say. I guess someday my son will be going here," Sonny said. "You the teacher?"

"I'm just the assistant," Rhea said. "Teacher's aide, really."

"That sounds like fun. I don't know much about things here, but someone told me there's been trouble here, that one of the teachers is into some witch-type thing. You know anything about that?"

Sonny watched Rhea Thatcher flinch at that. She suddenly got very nervous.

"I—I, that's just not true. People say all kinds of things. Mrs. Vincent is a very nice lady and—"

"Yeah, Vincent, that's the name," Sonny said. "Her two kids were part of this. Rumor is they've been sacrificed to the devil. You say that's not true?"

"The devil! It's not the devil—I mean. Who are you?" Rhea asked. "You better leave. I have to go be with the children. Go, or I'll call the police. Get out of here!"

Rhea's voice had risen to a feverish pitch, and her hand shook when she pointed a finger toward Sonny. Her face had gone pale.

"Don't ever bother me again," she said, turning her head back as she walked away. "I don't know who you are or what you want, but you're wrong. Don't ever come here again."

"I'm not bothering you. That's your own conscience doing that," Sonny said as he started backing away. "Look, Miss Thatcher, it's not too late. There's still hope for you, but don't wait. The truth is going to all come out. You can be part of the solution, or you'll be one who receives the full wrath of justice. You decide."

"Get out of here! Go!" Rhea yelled again.

Sonny turned and quickly walked to his Jeep. When he pulled around the corner he looked back at the playground and saw Evelina rush from the building toward Rhea who had dropped to her knees in the sand and appeared to be sobbing uncontrollably.

You're gonna crack, lady. When you do, I just hope you come to the right people before those others do you in.

★★★

Al Tucker stood to the side of the open window hole and looked through it with one eye, trying to see the approaching vehicle. He searched down the trail to see what kind of vehicle was coming. Danny had gone to the far corner of the building and pressed his back against the wall. The engine noise steadily grew louder. Where the trail rose up out of a canyon, Al saw the form of an older, tan colored pickup truck moving through the trees.

"It's a pickup truck, Son. We'll just wait and see if it stops here or goes on by. They wouldn't know we're here, unless they've been told. So if they stop…"

"Good thing it's not a bear. Hope they don't think we're like stealing their gold or whatever's in that old mine. They still hang thieves from trees?" Danny asked.

"It's turning toward us. It must be our contact. It's gotta be," Al said.

"I don't see any rope in here. Think there's a rope in that truck?" Danny said.

"Quiet, Son. Nobody's going to hang you."

"Betcha they got a rifle. Maybe they just shoot thieves today."

The truck stopped where the road ended, about a hundred feet from the shack. The engine shut off. The driver opened the door, stepped out, and then slammed the door shut.

"Anybody here?" they called out.

"Goodness, it's a woman. Come on, Son. She has to be for us."

"Bet she can still shoot. She's one of these wild women like Mrs. B. You should see Joey's mom shoot, Dad. If this woman can shoot a gun like Mrs. B—"

"Hush up that talk. Come on. She's calling for us." Al stepped to the doorway and waved to the woman. She waved back.

"Come on," he said to Danny, then he picked up his bags and started toward the truck.

"Hey, wait for me," Danny hollered. He grabbed his bag of food and water, then he ran to catch up.

The woman moved to the front of the truck and seemed to stare inquisitively at the two people coming rapidly towards her. Al was more nervous than inquisitive.

"Hi, I'm Al. My boy Danny," he said nodding his head toward his son, who'd caught up to him and was now at his side, tight as a shadow, when they reached the truck.

"Call me Alice," the lady said with a smile. To Al, she presented quite a sight. Her faded jeans and large tattered straw hat somehow fit with the rugged setting they were in. The hand she extended to Al gave a firm grip and a solid shake. She reached down and tussled Danny's hair.

"Welcome to the Circle B.," Alice said. "Woke up to a sick horse, so I did. It just came in from California yesterday. It had proper papers and all that, so I don't know what to think. I sure hope she didn't bring in something that'll be catchin' to any of the others. Couldn't wait on the vet. He'll probably have been here and gone by the time we get back. Though that would be a good sign. Hope you all didn't worry yourselves too much 'bout my comin'."

"I'm just glad you weren't a bear. I was gettin' a bit scared some bear would smell us and hunt us down," Danny said.

"My—my," Alice said. "Ain't any bears around here, Danny. Plenty of mountain lions though. Then the fool government turned them wolves loose up north of here… I 'spect it's just a matter of time before they start their killin' here 'bouts."

"Mountain lions! And wolves you say? Wow, and I feared of an old bear. What's worse anyway?" Danny asked.

"Well, I wouldn't want to have to face down any of them without a good gun. Then there's them darned snakes," Alice added.

"Yeah, we've already run into one of them," Danny said. "You got a dog that kills snakes?"

"Got a couple of red heelers we keep down around the animals. They're supposed to kill snakes, but I ain't never really seen one do it. We don't have many snakes down around the headquarters though. Maybe they do keep them away. Hey, get in. We can talk while we ride. It takes quite a spell to get down off this old mountain. Toss your gear in the back and jump in."

★★★

Carla Hunter and Kurt Stein sat at a small conference table across from Homeland Security Secretary, Clayton Kingston. Carla noticed Kurt's right foot tapped a staccato pace on the carpet. Just the same, her own hands trembled slightly. Secretary Kingston leaned back in his chair.

"When? When are you going to have contact with Dr. Vincent? Surely, he'd have contacted you by now if he intended to. I say he's defected. He's taken his son and he's sitting in some plush palace in some Arab land somewhere. He ever talk about becoming a Muslim?"

"He doesn't believe in any God," Carla said. "He's an avowed atheist. Alex hasn't defected. We'll be hearing soon. I'm sure."

"Based on what?" Secretary Kingston asked.

"Just—just Alex. I know how he is. Any day now he'll be in contact," Carla replied.

"How is he going to get data to you?" Kingston asked Carla.

"He didn't say. We're to e-mail him everything we think will help him, and he said we'd be getting data back from him. I don't expect he'll be opening his own e-mails until he gets settled somewhere."

"Shut off that e-mail immediately," Secretary Kingston said. "Until we know Dr. Vincent's not gone-over, we surely don't want Aswad Hamal to know where we're at with this. If we'd get close, he might just move up his timetable. Are you making any headway? Can we help in any way?"

Kurt cleared his throat. "Nothing is jelling. I'm running out of ideas. Alex is the one who always came through in times like this. I used to get so mad at him when he seemed to be way out in left field, but in the end, he'd find the solution. Maybe if we locked up Alex's ex-wife and some of her friends, he'd feel safe bringing Tucker back home," Kurt suggested. "Of all the times—"

"That's a thought. I'll put someone on that angle," Secretary Kingston cut in. "Don't know what charge we'd use," he paused for a moment. "Well, get back to work. I don't have to tell you that we don't want to have to shut down all mass transportation. I shudder to think what that would do. It would cripple our economy—everything. We might never recover. Still, we just can't let some bomb or something spread death to millions— that would be even worse." Secretary Kingston looked at Kurt, then Carla.

"Call me the instant you hear from Dr. Vincent, or come up with a solution yourselves," he said. Then he rose to leave.

★★★

Several hours later, down in the foothills near a small wet- weather wash, Alice drove her pickup toward one of the half dozen buildings at the ranch headquarters. Al looked out over the row upon row of white painted pipe corrals. Each had its own sun shelter, hayrack and water tank. Though he knew nothing about horses, he could see this was a class operation.

"What are they used for?" Al asked.

"Ahh, what used for?" Alice asked.

"The horses," he said.

"They're all rodeo stock. We used to do a lot with the broncs, but now we gravitate toward the mounts for the barrel racin' gals, ropers and steer wrestlers, some cutters too. Business has gotten huge. As I said up on the mountain, we get horses from all over this here southwest.

"This here's your home tonight, Alice continued. "Don't get too comfortable. We pull out in the morning. You can shower up and change now if you'd like. I'll have your laundry done up. Lunch is in about an hour. Anything else you need?"

"Yeah," Al said. "I really need to get internet access. I think they'll be expecting me to use my satellite connection, but they might be able to track that back to where it's sent from. To be safer, I think, I'll use a public wireless connection to a new address I had set up just for this. I hope that will slip by them for a while."

"Some of the guys have gone over to the truck stop down on the interstate. I can't go with you. Everyone around here knows me, so you gotta go alone."

Al caught sight of the fear that shot through his son's eyes when he heard they needed to separate for even a short time.

"It'll be all right, Son. I'll go after lunch. You'll be fine here."

"Ahh shoot," Alice said. "You and I can check on that sick horse. We'll spend a spell with a new colt we had just last week. Your pa will be back before you know it."

"We're leaving in the morning, then?" Al asked.

Alice nodded. "Tell ya all about it then. By now you got an idea how all this works."

After he'd had a good long shower and a quick lunch, Al followed Alice out to an open barn where she pointed to an old Ford sedan.

"We got the title to this old car when some drug runners abandoned it down on the lower end," Alice said when she gave him the keys. "We seldom use it. However, it's the only thing around here without the ranch name on it."

Al drove down the sandy ranch road slowly. Then he headed up a two-lane stretch of asphalt for some time. Reaching the interstate, he turned up the ramp. He drove for several minutes, following a line of semi-trucks. Then, seeing the truck stop ahead, Al pulled off the interstate and drove into the busy parking lot. He grabbed his computer case and went inside.

He found an empty booth and slid in. He quickly made the connection with the network and connected to his e-mail box. He retrieved the data Carla and Kurt had sent him several days ago. Just when he finished that and was about to start sending a message to Wade Hawkins for him to pass on, he looked up and saw two police officers. They were walking directly toward him.

Chapter 9

When she left the school that afternoon, Sonny Horn tailed Evelina Vincent across town to her home. When she drove up her driveway, Sonny spotted a government sedan already parked in the turnaround. Sonny stopped across the street and watched FBI agents Huck Miles and Sig Simpson quickly exit their car and greet Evelina before she could close the garage door on them. He watched what appeared to be a reluctant Evelina lead the two FBI officers into her home. Sonny then turned around and parked half a block up the street. He'd no more than shut off the engine when he saw Luke Lane's city car pull up several car lengths behind him. Minutes later, Luke Lane got out of his car and walked up to the curbside of Sonny's Jeep.

"Loitering, aren't you Sonny?"

"I've got a good reason to be here, do you? Max know where you are? Does he know his lady friend is entertaining two very desperate feds?"

Detective Lane didn't answer any of Sonny's questions. He seemed to be caught off guard.

"Get in, if you want," Sonny said. "You're sticking out like a hawk in a chicken coop." Lane opened the door and slid into the Jeep.

"That you who put the heat on Rhea Thatcher?" Luke asked.

"Who?"

"You know who," Luke said. "Hear you've been loaning your shoulder for a cry towel to that crazy Browning woman also. Take my advice, that one's dangerous."

"Why? Is she about to go public?" Sonny asked.

"She's got nothing to say."

"She can say plenty. Thatcher can too. Those are two time bombs for Max and friends. This one in here," Sonny said, nodding toward Evelina's house, "now she's the real deal. She knows all the pieces. She not only has blood on her hands, she's clear up to her elbows, neck maybe."

"That's all talk. You don't really know Evelina. She's actually a sweet lady," Luke said.

"Then why are you tailing her?"

"You ask too many questions, Sonny."

"My boss wants lots of answers."

"Your boss—now there's someone who should look out. He's gone way over the line. Taking that boy—he'll pay for that," Luke said. "If there wasn't something big going on up at the lab, the Feds would have their hands on him."

"Get real, Luke. If it wasn't for what's going on at the lab they wouldn't even be here. They're not working any of the missing child cases very hard. Ask me, I'd say the heat's on them from above to let Alex Vincent alone. Apparently, whatever he's working on he can still do from wherever he's hiding. Ever think they may well have him under surveillance and be happy to let him stay wherever he is? His son's in no danger with him. It's here," Sonny again nodded toward Evelina's house, "where he's in danger. You any part of that little cult thing?"

"It's not a cult. It's a—I don't know. Whatever it is, Max keeps that shut up tight to anyone else on the force. I'm not sure it's really all that big a deal. Sometimes I think it's just a bunch of these uppity types giving themselves another opportunity to look down on the rest of us."

"It might well have started that way, but it's gone down the line a long way from that now," Sonny said. "You know that's true, Luke."

"You don't really believe they're involved in the likes of baby killing?" Luke asked. "Surely not."

"Things get out of hand quickly in that kind of group when someone, usually the leader, tells of exhilarating experiences in other places and all the power others have derived from them. Talk becomes a frenzy, and then there's a plan. Often things start with something like cats or goats, then before you know it, the worst has happened. Then once isn't enough because they need more power to protect themselves, so on and on it goes."

"You really think she'd do the likes of that?" Luke cut in as he looked toward Evelina's house.

"I understand Evelina got real involved in the religions of some of the old native Indian tribes around here. That led her to some radical New Age stuff that's not really new at all. Most of what's called new has its roots in old Babylon and other ancient pagan religions."

Sonny paused for a moment, then continued. "It seems that about that time Evelina muscled her way into control of this pretty benign little rock-worshiping, tree-hugging, group here. Then she brought in the right people to protect the group, and then pushed it to this."

"You can't prove any of that," Luke said. "I've known Max for five years now. He's no killer. He's—"

"He's changed a bunch in the last year or so—admit it. He's got the hots for Evelina, and he craves power. Look, I know how you guys on the force have to stick together; your life may depend on it. However, Luke, you also know that when one goes bad—especially when it has nothing to do with his job—you've gotta step back and find the right side and move to it," Sonny said.

"So, this Saints of Seven thing, what's it stand for anyway?" Luke asked. "There are more than seven people in the group. The word Saints sounds like a good thing. Where's the seven part of it come from anyway?"

"I don't know for sure. I do know that the number seven, when used by some group like this, often has its roots in the biblical use of the number where it usually means perfection, or being totally complete, like God himself. However, it seems that many of the things that refer to God are eventually taken by someone who wants to be some kind of god themselves. These things are often used in just the opposite way God intended.

"Look Luke," Sonny continued. "I'm no preacher or Bible scholar, and I've not really studied this in depth, but I learned a few things when Wade worked on another case involving these guys a while back. Some in this group claim they get their use of the word seven from some old Middle East writings that claim there's seven demons represented by the seven points of the constellation Pleiades. How these people go from that to their group, I don't have a clue. People often just make up their own connections and creeds. If they're persuasive enough, soon they have a following— sometimes a following so desperate to fit into something they'll do anything they're told or led into. You know, the Charles Manson thing. It's all about power. It's about becoming some kind of god themselves. It all gets very weird."

"Too weird for me," Luke said. "Max would never be into something like that. That just can't be."

"Hey, come on Luke. For Max it's all about Evelina. She's obviously one persuasive babe. It wouldn't be the first time a good man lost it all over some woman. Just keep your eyes open, your mind too."

Both men sat silently for a minute, then the front door of Evelina's house opened and the two FBI agents came out and quickly got in their car.

"You going to follow them?" Sonny asked Luke.

"Better not. I'll stay here for a while. I've got a spot up around the corner where I can see anyone who comes, but they don't pass by me," Luke said.

"Be hard to explain sitting out here to Max, huh?"

Luke didn't say anything as he opened the door and stepped out. He then turned around and lowered his head and spoke back through the open window.

"Hey, uh, keep me in the know, alright Sonny? And, uh, thanks for the info." Luke stepped back, straightened up, then headed for his car.

Sonny started his Jeep, and then drove down the street after the two agents. He caught up with them after several blocks. Instead of turning toward town, they made a turn that would take them to Wade Hawkins' office. Sonny grabbed his phone.

"Nita, it's Sonny. Wade in?" Nita connected him to Wade. "Hey Wade, those two feds just left Evelina's house and sure seem to be heading straight toward your office. You've got four or five minutes if you want to get out of there."

Wade said he'd just wait for them and asked Sonny to be there too. Sonny turned left at the next intersection, bounced his Jeep across several back streets, and was already parked in Wade's parking lot when the other car rounded the corner.

Sonny hurried inside and was sitting in Wade's office when Nita escorted the agents to Wade's door.

"Agents Miles and Simpson, what brings you back so soon?" Wade asked, and then continued on without waiting for an answer. "Oh, if you fellows don't know, this is Sonny Horn. Sonny does some investigative work for me. I figured it would be good if he was part of this, whatever it is you have for me today. Sit down, sit down. Coffee or water?"

"No, no thanks, Hawkins. This shouldn't take too long," Huck Miles said when he and Sig were seated in two chairs across from Wade's desk.

"Talk to me, Hawkins. I've got missing kids, a missing code guy, local cops who won't cooperate, you won't help either. On top of that, Homeland Security seems to want to keep us out altogether, but I've got orders from my boss to do something. Can't you help me at all?"

"How about Evelina Vincent? Did she give you any help or did you just have tea and cookies? You weren't there very long," Wade said.

The two agents glanced at each other, and then Huck spoke again.

"She's the key, right? She got a call from someone when we were there. She went into another room, but we still heard some of her side of the conversation. It sounded as if she was talking to an agent she'd sent out somewhere. She reamed him good."

Wade just shrugged his shoulders.

"Come on, Hawkins. Tell me where they are," Huck pleaded. "This can't be good for the kid being on the run like this."

"No, it's not good. However, it's keeping him alive. Two children in that house haven't been so lucky."

"You don't really know what's going on with those kids. I can see why the father might think that, but—what about his job? I'm told the lab needs him in the worst way."

"Do you have any children?" Wade asked Huck.

"Yeah, I've got two."

"Your job or your kids—what do you choose?" Wade asked.

"Alright," Huck said. "Look, the locals are out to get you, Hawkins. I can't help. If you'd tell me where they are…"

Wade shook his head. "How many times do I have to tell you? Truly, I don't know. That's the truth. I don't want to know."

"There's a group, an underground thing. Lollypop is what the dame who heads it calls herself. You involved with them?"

Wade looked at Huck, but gave no response.

"Someday we'll crack that little group wide open. They're good. They must have a lot of money, or something. Nobody talks. Even when people come out of that, nobody talks."

"Look, honest guys, I'm not trying to be rude, but I don't have anything to say that will help you. I'm helping to save a child's life. I'm at peace with what I'm doing. That's all I can say."

"Yeah, alright Hawkins. Look, I don't want to be at odds with you on this, but so many things don't add up. I don't want to do anything to hurt that kid for sure, but I don't believe it's best for him to be where he is. I'm still going to try and bring him in."

"And be a hero?" Wade asked. "A feather in your hat if you bring back the lab boss the whole government is looking for? A promotion? A raise?"

"All right—all right. I'll see you around, Hawkins." At that Huck rose, looked over at Sonny and nodded. "Good day, Mr. Horn."

Sig rose and stepped toward Sonny.

"I catch you tailing us again and—"

"Simpson!" Huck Miles growled.

Sig pointed a finger and shook it at Sonny, then turned and followed Huck out the door.

★★★

Al's eyes were glued to his computer screen. Yet in his side vision he watched the two policemen continue to walk toward him. They reached his table, and then stopped.

"This all right?" one officer asked the other when he motioned toward the booth directly across from Al.

"Yeah, wherever. You see what the special is?"

"Wasn't looking. I think I want that chile-verde burrito anyway. I see young Lopez back in the kitchen. He does a good job, the best here. You ought to try it."

"My wife has me spoiled. Nobody makes better Mexican food than Lisa."

"Well, this is a lot better than that frozen stuff I buy down at the Quick Market."

"Ah—the joys of the single life."

"Hey, it's not so bad. At least I can still do whatever I want."

"What do you want to do that you couldn't do with a good wife?"

"Ah, don't start on me now. I suppose you've got some lonely cousin or the like for me to take out."

"Well…"

The two officers talked on. Al looked down at his table, and then slowly started dancing his fingers across the keyboard. In mere seconds, he had the entire folder of data on its way to Wade Hawkins. He started to slide the screen's curser up to the close the file box.

"Hey—more iced tea?"

Al jumped, startled by the young waitress. "Ah—no. I've got to go. Thanks anyway."

"You're not a truck driver—you're someone important, aren't you? So, Mr. Important, what do you do?" she asked.

Out of the corner of his eye, Al nervously watched the two police only a few feet away.

"Ah—" Al said while he closed the program on his computer, turned off the power, then closed the screen to the keyboard. "I'm just a salesman, you know. Hey, I gotta go. An appointment. I'll be late."

"Yeah, sure. What do you sell anyway?" "Ah—paper," Al said.

"Paper?"

"Yeah, computer paper. Hey, my ticket? I'm in a hurry," Al said while he kept watching the two officers. So far, they were too involved in their own conversation to mind what was going on at his table. Al slid to the edge of the booth, and then stood up. "Please, my ticket."

"Sure," the waitress said, and then she tore off the green sheet from her pad. "Paper, huh. Sure is a bunch of that sold, I'd say. I'll bet you're rich. Hey, you married?"

"No—please," Al said grabbing his ticket. He reached into his pocket, pulled out a handful of change and pushed it across the table.

"Thanks," he said, turning quickly, then he walked toward the cash register.

"Hey, when you comin' back?" the waitress asked while she followed Al across the tiled floor.

"Just passing through. Don't expect I'll be back," Al said. "Oh—yeah, well maybe I'll see ya," the waitress said as she followed right behind Al, trying to get up beside him. "You get back through here, you ask for me, will ya? Star. Ask for Star."

"Sure," Al said while he hurried toward the register.

"See," the young waitress said as she pulled up her uniform sleeve over her shoulder, exposing a multi-colored star tattoo on her upper arm.

"Got some other ones. They like to come out at night. Wanna see them twinkle in the moonlight?"

"Please," Al said, afraid the police would be attracted to this commotion. "I can't—"

"I get off at eight. Come back then."

Al turned his back on the young waitress. He quickly paid for his tea, and then he hurried through the door. He glanced back at the two officers still sitting at the table. Outside he wiped the perspiration off his forehead, and hurried to the old Ford. He eased out of the parking lot, then got back on the interstate and headed towards the Circle B.

Danny came running towards him when Al parked the car and turned off the ignition. He grabbed his computer and opened the door.

"Dad! Dad! You gotta see this little baby horse. Never saw anything like it before. We gotta get us a ranch, Dad. I just gotta have me a baby horse."

"Hey—this is awfully fast. They don't stay babies, you know. In no time it'll be as big as one of these," Al said, nodding towards a stall with several full-grown mares. They'll grow up faster than you will."

"I know, I just never saw anything like it," Danny said. "He likes me too. I fed him some sugar and he licked it right off my hand. Maybe someday, huh?"

"Yeah, maybe. Hey, why don't you stay out here and see what else you can learn? I've got to check over the things Kurt and Carla sent me."

"Sure, hey, I forgot all about them," Danny said. "They OK?"

"I'm sure. Look, I really need to spend some time working, maybe later—"

"Sure Dad. I'll run back down and see what Alice is doin'. Catch ya later."

Al sat studying the data from the lab. Kurt and Carla weren't having any more success than he was. He was still deep in thought when Danny burst onto the patio.

"Hey Dad! Alice said the steaks are on the grill. How do you want yours? I'm supposed to find out," Danny yelled through the screen door. Al looked at his watch. Four hours had passed.

"Oh, tell her medium, no wait, I'll come with you. I'll tell her myself. Al closed things out, then shut off the computer.

★★★

Wade Hawkins opened the e-mail box he'd set up to receive data from Dr. Vincent. He'd been doing this faithfully each day after Nita went home, but each day had been a disappointment. Bingo! He had a note from Alex. Not much, but at least now he knew his client was safe. He grabbed a CD and quickly made a copy of the e-mail. Then he erased the message. He slid the disc into his pocket. He went to his desk, pulled open the top drawer, took out a card with a phone number written on the back, then dialed it.

Wade listened to the ringing of the phone. Just when he started to hang up, he heard the usual "Hello" greeting.

"Bill? Wade here. Just checking to see if you'll be at the church down here at seven tonight. I know these meetings are easy to forget about.... Yeah, I thought I'd best call you since it's not on the regular schedule.... OK, see you then."

Wade hung up the phone. He pushed back his chair, leaned back and put his boots up on his desk. He closed his eyes and thought about all that was going on. The people at the lab were desperate. The FBI was desperate. And Alex Vincent surely was too. The one group that concerned him the most though was this crazed cult. Yeah, they were desperate too, and dangerous enough to do anything to anyone.

Wade drove slowly into the parking lot about a half hour before his appointed time to meet Bill Hunter. They'd previously set up a church at the edge of town for their contact point to pass on messages from Dr. Vincent to Carla. Wade had watched a car following him across town and now saw that same car park up the street, turn off its engine, but no one exited. After about five minutes, Wade started his truck, then quickly drove up the street and stopped right beside the car. He lowered his window and looked over at the other man who had his head slumped off to the side with his eyes closed, pretending to be sleeping.

"Come on Red, you can do a better job of surveillance than this," Wade said. "I'd say you wanted me to see you. You trying to scare me?"

Red Conners turned and faced Wade.

"Guess I'm just tired and off my game. I should have listened to my gut and never gone to Iowa. I'll never go back there. No sir, not for money nor love. Something going on at church tonight, Hawkins?"

"Yeah, just the usual choir practice at seven. Worked late, then came straight over here. Want to join the choir, Red?"

"Sure. I'm gonna come right in and sing them do-goody songs with a bunch of old women. Tell me, Hawkins, what's this all about anyway? Man, there's more feds buzzin' around town and up at the lab than I've ever seen. What in the world is going on?"

"A whole bunch of stuff," Wade said. "Something big is going down at the lab, real big, but I don't know what. Add to that Dr. Vincent's personal problems. However, the real one to watch is that group you're working for. You need to check out your clients a little better, Red."

"I'm not working for a group. Only one person hired me."

"Yeah, Evelina Vincent—same thing," Wade said. "She runs things— she runs you too now I'd say."

"Hey, nobody runs me," Red said, quickly straightening up in his car seat. "I'm looking for that lab guy and his kid. That's all I'm getting paid for, and all I care about. Your hands aren't so lily-white on this. For a man so pious and all, you're right in the thick of this."

"Yeah, but I'm on the right side. There's nothing wrong with being in the fight—just make sure you're on the right side. You're not, Red. Things go your way, another kid might die. How'd you feel about that? You're working for blood money, Red."

"Ahh—you're making too much out of this," Red said. "Yeah, here you are, all goody-goody at church on a Tuesday, and you're judging me. That ain't right."

"Why not? What you're doing could well endanger little Tucker's life," Wade said. "How else am I to feel?"

"Move that truck outta my way! Let me out of here. I can't take any more of this crap. Look, there comes someone else, some old lady ready to sing with you. Go on, get back to church. Let me outta here."

"Think about what I've said, Red," Wade said when he started his truck and put it into reverse.

"Get outta my way!" Red yelled when Wade slowly backed down the street.

Wade pulled into the church lot and parked over beside the car that had driven into the parking lot. It was Bill Hunter's car

"Hi, Bill. Glad you knew what I was talking about. I'm pretty sure my phone is bugged."

"Who was that?" Bill asked, nodding up the street. "He sure left in a hurry."

"Yeah. I was tailed here. Anyone following you?"

"Following me? Gosh, I never thought of that. I don't know. I've not noticed anyone."

Wade got out of his truck and walked over to the passenger side of Bill's car. He got in and handed Bill the CD containing Dr. Vincent's e-mail.

"Alex must be somewhere safe to send stuff out. I'll call you when I get more. Give my best to Carla. How's she holding up?"

"Hardly ever see her. I've never seen her so stressed. Even when she is home, she can't sleep. She won't talk about anything. I know it must be something really important to security, or she'd not be putting all of us through this."

Another car pulled into the lot.

"Looks as if some of the real choir members are coming," Wade said while he looked at the clock on the dash.

"Yeah. I best get home to the boys," Bill said.

"Somehow this will all work out, Bill. I gotta go too, before these gals try and get me to sing with them. Now that would be something you wouldn't want to hear." Wade got out of the car and walked to his truck. He watched Bill Hunter drive away, then he started his truck and slowly drove across the lot, then up the street.

Chapter 10

The sun was just starting to lighten the sky when Al heard the clatter of a diesel engine starting. He pulled back the sheet, dropped his feet to the floor and groggily moved to the window. Alice was backing one of the big dual wheeled pickups under a gooseneck horse trailer.

"What's going on?" Danny asked while sitting up on his cot.

"We best get ready. Looks as if Alice means early when she says early."

By the time Al and Danny were outside, Alice had hitched up the trailer, and backed it down to one of the pipe stalls.

"Morning. How'd you fellas sleep?" she asked when they approached her.

"I ah, I don't remember anything, so it must have been good," Al said. "How can I help you?"

"Got things in hand. Just gotta get these two mares in here, then we can get breakfast and go. Fixin' to travel a long piece today. Be 'bout dark when we get there, I 'spect. By the way, all the hands here think you're my cousin from Dallas. That's why I came down off the mountain the way I did. That way I came up the road into here as if I'd been out on the highway. They're all too afraid of tryin' to talk to someone like you. It works best that way."

"Oh—I just thought most of them didn't speak much English," Al said.

"They don't, but they're all legal and good hands. Some have been here a long time. Just thought you might be curious, not that it matters. Go on up to the house. Maria should be ready to start breakfast by now. She understands 'nough English to figure out how you want your eggs, or what you want in an omelet. I'll be along in a jiffy."

After a quick breakfast, Al and Danny grabbed their bags and met Alice when she drove the truck up to the little guest house. She jumped out and motioned for Al to get into the driver's seat.

"Get in. You ever drive the likes of this before?"

"No way. I've never driven anything bigger than a car. I've never even ridden in anything like this. Are you sure you want me to do this?"

"When we get around the border checks it would be best if you were driving. That way we'll look like a normal ranch family. No sense attracting unneeded attention."

"Oh, yeah. Wow, I've never imagined myself doing something like this before."

"Nothin' to it. Get in and strapped up, that attention thing again, and I'll talk you through it. Out here on these back roads is the best place to get started."

Al looked over at his son, who'd crawled up into the small back seat of the extended cab. He felt somewhat embarrassed that a woman was teaching him how to drive a truck. But then, Alice wasn't some frills and lace kind of woman.

"I'll tell you what my dad told me. Look out on that hood out there, OK? Now pretend there's a big glass of water sitting out there, and you have to drive without spilling it. You drive like that, those horses will be just fine. I see people today who seem to forget that they've got precious cargo in their trailers behind them. They just go a flying down the road with horses bouncing all over in their trailers."

Alice then changed the subject. "All right, these diesels got lots of hump right off the bottom, so easy on that throttle, use regular drive, not overdrive. All right. Now take it to the interstate."

About five hours later, at Alice's direction, Al pulled off the highway into the parking lot of a small truck stop near Las Cruces. Alice directed him to a pump on the auto diesel section.

"Watch back there at the trailer," Alice warned.

Al looked in the mirror. He spiked the brakes when he saw that the long trailer was going to crunch into the end pump.

"Time for a lesson in backing up one of these," Alice said. "Anybody behind you?"

"No."

"Alright, take the wheel, one hand on either side. That's it. Now, turn the wheel in the opposite way you want the trailer to go. Watch your front end, don't cut into the pumps. Now slowly move back. That's it. Now swing way out away from the pumps, and then cut back toward them."

It took Al two tries, but he got the trailer around the pump island while getting the truck close enough to get fuel in its tank. When the fuel tank was full, they parked the truck and trailer off in a gravel parking area. Alice got out, and then looked around as if she was looking for something. Seeming satisfied with things, Alice led the way inside where they had lunch. Danny toyed with his burger and hardly ate any of his fries. When walking back to the truck, Al led Danny off to the side as they slowly crossed the lot.

"So, why so quiet? You feel OK?"

"Oh yeah. Don't know if I'm gonna like it where we're going. It's kinda spooky not knowing what's up. I mean I like Alice. I liked Joey too. What if I don't like things where we're going?"

"Well, we'll still be together. It seems the people who've gotten involved in this thing really care about us. I'll bet whoever we end up with will be just like Alice and Bacho."

"Hope so, Dad. Been thinkin' about home. Missin' things I guess."

"Me too, Son. Me too."

Al looked over to the truck and saw Alice talking to another woman. The two were laughing and Al surmised they knew each other. The other woman handed Alice a McDonald's food bag, then walked away toward another pickup truck.

What's going on? What's in that bag? We just ate—there's no McDonald's here.

"I'll drive around El Paso," Alice said after they caught up to her at the truck. The three got into the truck and once Alice got back on the interstate she started telling them what was ahead.

"If you're wondering about that woman back there and that bag, she's part of the system. That's your money from your attorney. I 'spect I don't need to tell ya to keep it hidden well."

Alice then nodded back to the trailer. "These two four-legged girls in the back belong to a fella named Duce Duval. He's got a big spread, the Lost Lucy Ranch is the real name, but most folks now call it the Double L. It's way out on the far side of Alpine, Texas. It goes quite a piece down south too, so it does. Duce is one fine man. I've been breedin' stock for him for many a year now. You'll be in good hands with Duce. Lots of things to do there, Danny. I 'spect you'll be there a fair spell, unless something, be it good or bad, comes along and changes that.

"Duce is hoping you can help him work out the bugs on a livestock management software program he's been working on. Somehow he's gotten word you know a thing or two about computers, Al. The Lost Lucy has some fine horses and a whole lot more cows than I have."

A short while later Alice got off the interstate.

"We'll take the loop around the city. No sense draggin' this trailer through downtown El Paso."

★★★

Sonny Horn sipped on the last of the large black coffee he'd gotten at the corner store an hour ago. The strong liquid was now barely tepid, but he tipped up the cup one last time to get out the final few drops. He then tossed the foam cup to the floor on the passenger's side of his Jeep. It was nearly midnight. Where was Max Pace? He'd checked out Evelina's house. Max wasn't there—neither was she. Rhea Thatcher was gone also. The Pecos Wilderness? Were they all up there and up to no good? Was this some kind of sacrifice night?

Sonny quietly slipped out of the door and pushed it closed. He had the Jeep's interior lights rigged so they didn't come on when the door opened.

He stood beside a cottonwood tree and looked around. No one seemed to be paying any attention to the street. Not even a dog barked. He walked slowly down the sidewalk then stepped inside the adobe wall at Max's house. He stared at the darkened area around him, letting his eyes adjust to the shadowed area. After a few minutes, he cautiously walked back around Max's driveway. Reaching the back of the house, he stopped again.

Just when he started to move toward the back patio, he heard a car coming down the street. Sonny froze. The car stopped. The driver shut off the engine. Sonny moved to a large cottonwood tree and hid in the shadow behind it where he waited for at least five minutes. Just when he was about to go toward the nearest window to look inside Max's house, the car door opened, then closed quietly. Sonny watched the entryway of the driveway. Among the shadows, he saw the form of a man stepping around the wall. He heard faint footsteps coming towards him. Sonny looked around, and then stepped under the carport, away from the house and to where he'd make no shadow.

The other man moved rather quickly, seemingly at ease, as if he knew the terrain. Reaching the back door, he flicked on a mini-flashlight and flashed it up to the top of the security door, then flicked the light off and started back to the driveway. Suddenly, he stopped. He looked around slowly, methodically. Sonny knew this guy sensed his presence. The average man wouldn't. Only one with lots of training and experience would feel the presence of another human at a time like this.

"Who's there?" the man asked. Sonny didn't recognize the voice. "Who are you?" The man then asked.

Sonny cleared his throat. "Who wants to know?" It was dangerous to admit he was there, but it might be worse not to.

"I'm a friend of Max's. I was just checking to see if he was home. Thought we'd play some cards or something."

"Looked to me as if you were checking to see if that little leaf you'd put above that door earlier was still there. Just how long has it been since Max has been here anyway?"

"I don't know what you're talking about. I told you—"

"Yeah, I know what you said. I also saw what you did. Look, it seems to me, we're both looking for Max. I'm not on the force, are you?"

"No. I—ah, I'm not carrying. Come out and let's talk. You must be Horn, the guy working for the attorney. I've seen you around. That you?"

"Alright," Sonny said while he moved out into the faint moonlight where he could be seen. "And who are you?"

"Bonner. Jake Bonner. *Santa Fe Gazette*."

"Yeah. Heard you were out here too. Let's talk," Sonny said, and then he cautiously moved toward the other man. "Let's get out of here though. I don't want to be here when Max comes home. My Jeep is off to the right. Let's go somewhere."

"Yeah, that house across the street has a dog. I'm surprised he hasn't started barking yet. Let's keep it quiet until we get out of here."

The two men walked in silence, then got into Sonny's Jeep. Sonny started it and slowly eased down the street.

"So, when did you put the marker in the door," Sonny asked.

"Right at dark," Jake replied. "I didn't have all night to stay here. We got wind that there was some kind of meeting with this group tonight, but didn't know where or when. I tried to tail someone but they all just seemed to fade away. I don't know where they went."

"The Pecos, I'd say. I tailed them up there once," Sonny said. "Got shot at and run out of there too."

"No kidding. Did they know it was you?" Jake asked.

"Had to," Sonny said. "I don't scare easily, but they didn't come at me easily."

"Who?" Jake asked.

"I'd tailed Max and Evelina in her black H2. It wasn't the Hummer that came at me though. It was a pickup. Sounded like a Ford. I was blinded by the lights; they had a spotlight on me. I had no intentions of sticking around once the bullets started flying."

"Weird bunch, huh?"

"Beyond that, Jake. Dangerous bunch. Deadly I'd say."

"Yeah. Didn't mean to scare you back there," Jake said. "You know how it is once you feel somebody's watching you."

"Military or big city force?" Sonny asked.

"Both. Marines and San Francisco PD. How about you?"

"Semper fi," Sonny said. "Couldn't do the other part. Too many people in those big cities. I know I've missed some good training, but—"

"You're doing alright without it. 'Bout got myself killed there," Jake said. "Took four slugs in my hide one night—two more in the vest. Got me off the force though. Ain't slept more than an hour or two at a time since. Pain, all the time, it's the pain. Looking back now, it wasn't worth it."

Sonny pulled the Jeep off to the roadside by a city park. "So, you seem to know the players. Who's going to be the one to roll over first?"

"Good chance it'll be Rhea Thatcher," Jake said.

"She's stressed," Sonny nodded his agreement. "How about Luke Lane turning up something? What would he do if he found proof that implicated Max?"

"He's loyal to Max, but looking out for Luke first. With Max out of the way, he'd likely take his place. He's one we can try to use."

"Yeah. You ever talk to Sally Browning?" Sonny asked.

"That's what really kicked me into high gear on this," Jake said. "That woman's about to go over the edge. She can't take anymore. I think that's what Max—Evelina really—wants. If she goes mental, then they can bury that case. No one will care."

"You talk to the feds?" Sonny asked.

"Nah," Jake said. "Heard they're hot for your boss though."

"They could be trouble. Seems those FBI guys are at odds with some of the boys at Homeland Security—some kind of power struggle."

"I'm about ready, well J. Quinton and I really, we're about to launch a series on this. We'll shake some heads and minds. It's gonna start Sunday. Front page, unless we go to war or something. Some people are really gonna be mad. You think Max is on the sauce now, just wait."

"I'll be watching for that," Sonny said.

"Yeah. Hey, Sonny, I'm tired. Let's go back to my car. I'm ready to go home."

★★★

Al cautiously drove the truck and horse trailer down the two lane road out of Alpine. It was nearly dark, and he'd turned his lights on several minutes ago. He crested a hill and instantly saw a county sheriff's car sitting over near the bar ditch.

"Don't often see the sheriff out this far. Usually it's the border patrol hiding in these bushes," Alice said.

Al looked back in the mirror. The sheriff's car rapidly pulled up on the road. Dust and gravel flew. In seconds the top lights started flashing.

"I don't know what he wants," Al said nervously, "but he's coming after us."

Chapter 11

Wade Hawkins was out by his barn, sitting on a bale of hay, deep in thought, when he heard a car driving in his road. He looked up and saw J. Quinton Sedwick's Suburban at the head of the tail of dust as it rapidly approached. Seeing Wade in front of the barn, J. Quinton drove right up to him, then got out and for a few seconds stood by the car door.

"Howdy, Wade," he said when he started toward the barn. "Figured you'd be here. Don't mean to bother you none."

"You know you're always welcome. I might throw you out a few minutes after you come, but you can always come."

"Heh, yeah, there has been that kind of day back yonder, hasn't there? Not this time, Wade," J. Quinton said. "I 'spect young Horn told you that he and Jake had a good jawin' about things last night. He tell you we're fixin' to run a front page story tomorrow?"

"Yeah," Wade said as he nodded slowly. He then reached over and grabbed a bale of hay from a stack and dropped it to the ground across from the one he'd been sitting on. "Have a seat. Not much for accommodations out here. Mother's in the house though, so—"

"Just like bein' a teenager, right? Hiding things from your mother?"

"Sometimes I do feel that way," Wade said.

"Anyway, I brought you a proof of the story. Thought I'd see if you had anything to add. It's mostly about the cops stonewalling the Browning boy's disappearance and them keeping the lid on anything about the little Vincent girl."

Wade quickly read the story, then handed it back to J. Quinton.

"Max Pace is going to come after you with guns blazing. Evelina Vincent will be goading him to shut you up."

"Been itchin' for a good fight," J. Quinton said. "Haven't had one for a while. In the old days—"

With a slight squeak, the side door of the house opened and Nita stepped out onto the patio.

"My, my. Now that's just about the finest woman in all of Santa Fe," J. Quinton said. "How's she doing?" "Ask her yourself. She's coming this way."

Once she saw who was with Wade, Nita walked over toward the two men. When she got about twenty feet away she started talking while she continued to approach them.

"J. Quinton Sedwick—where have you been?" Nita asked. "Don't tell me you're too busy to get out of the city once in a while. When my husband was alive, why you were out here all the time. If you two weren't cooking up some political scheme, you were arguing about something going on around town.

"Now here you are with Wade," she continued. "I 'spect it's not politics you're a talkin' about. Maybe you can talk some sense into this boy, J. Quinton. I'm too old to take care of this place if they throw him in the hoosegow."

Nita changed the subject when neither man responded. "You still like you're steak with the hair still on while it's a hollerin' moo and the blood still sizzlin' inside?"

"Don't know 'bout that hair and moo, but you ain't had steak 'till you had it good and rare," J. Quinton said. "Just the same—"

"Ain't no excuse will do," Nita said. "You ain't gettin' away from here without a steak and some fresh greens from the garden. Got some early green chile all pealed up and a pecan pie for desert. Now tell me you ain't stayin'."

"Umm. Nita, you should have been the attorney in the family. You do present a winning case," J. Quinton said. "The pie did it. As I remember, yours is the best in town."

"Don't stay out here too long, this heat will get to ya—if it hasn't already. Shadows are getting long. Be sunset before you know it. No breeze, so it's still mighty hot out here. Ain't nothin' you fellows can't talk about in the cool of the house—nothin' good anyway."

"Slow down first out on the pavement, put your blinkers on, then pull off on the side carefully, watch out for that bar ditch." Alice said. "Let me do most of the talkin'. Don't know what this fella wants."

With knuckles white and his mouth like hot cotton, Al did what Alice said. Then he opened the windows and shut off the engine. His hands trembled more with each step the young deputy took, growing larger and larger in the side mirror.

"Arizona—ya don't say," the deputy said when he ambled up to the driver's window. "Lost out here or something?"

"Delivering a couple of breed mares for the Lost Lucy. Been breedin' for Duce for years. Workin' stock for the Rodeo, ya know," Alice said. "We was wantin' to get there by dark, but guess we didn't quite make it."

The deputy turned and walked back to the horse trailer and looked at the horses. He came around the other side, to Alice's window.

"Got Double L brands on them, alright. Don't know why Duce would have to go outside of Texas to get them bred up good. Didn't know y'all had much but snakes and big cactus out in Arizona."

"Why you boys from Texas come a hoofin' our way all the time to try and take back some of our money," Alice said. "Got us first class rodeos in Prescott, Tucson, and Phoenix, local ones all over the state. Then there's a whole passel of our boys always a comin' over here bringin' home some of your Texas money every weekend too. Got some of that myself loopin' barrels in my girlie days."

The deputy, seeming unimpressed, nodded toward the trailer.

"Got no lights on the trailer. You plugged in?"

"Oh fiddle sticks," Alice said. "You know how that is. Ya gotta fix up them wires every time you hit the road. Our roads ain't much different than yours for rocks. Being's, we got more mountains than flats, we probably bounce around even more. Got a test light right here in this door pocket, some black tape too. We got it all, officer, spare fuses and bulbs. We'll get to work findin' the problem."

Al pulled the parking lights on in the truck, and then took the test light back to the connector. He pulled out the trailer plug and stuck the test light into the socket, touching each prong until he got a light. He then shoved the trailer plug back in and instantly had trailer lights.

"Just a loose connection," he said. "Want us to check the brakes and signals?"

"Nah," the deputy said. "I'm sure they'll be OK now. If you're only goin' to the Double L, you probably won't meet up with anybody else anyway. Hey, when ya see old Duce, tell him Sparky said howdy."

"Will do. Thank you, Officer," Alice said when she crawled up into the cab. She looked at Al. "You alright?"

"Sort of. I really didn't need that."

"Let's go," Alice said. "It's still a good half an hour to the ranch headquarters."

Later, after arriving at the ranch headquarters, Al stood on the rough plank porch of the small guesthouse that sat a hundred yards down the road from the main ranch house. He looked around at what he figured might be his home for some time. All signs indicated that everyone had already turned in at the main house. Alice let out the two horses, then led them into a pipe stall and gave them some hay and water. The door of this small house wasn't locked, so they went in and made themselves at home. Alice made a pot of coffee, then found some cheese and rye bread in the refrigerator.

"Not much here, Danny," Alice said. "You like cheese? There's some eggs here too."

"I just wanna go to bed," he said. "I'm not hungry."

"You and your pa can take the big bed in there," Alice said, nodding toward the one bedroom in the little house. "I'll sack out here, on this sofa. 'Spect you'll hear things startin' up early 'round here. Get all the sleep you can."

Minutes later, Al went into the room and found his son already sleeping. He lay down beside him and tried to do the same, but sleep wouldn't come. He thought of how he'd felt when he saw the police car coming after him—how he wanted to take his son and run. What awaited him way out here on this ranch? When would this be over? Should he just give up?

He turned his head and looked at his son. No, giving up wasn't an option. They'd gone too far.

★★★

Max Pace pulled into his driveway well after midnight. He'd been up north fly fishing all day. Then he'd hit a few bars on the way home. He walked into his house, picked up his phone and saw that he had twenty-three messages. He ignored them all. He'd purposely left his cell phone home, craving some uninterrupted time to think about all the things going on. He'd picked up the paper on his patio when he'd come in and now sat down to read some of it. He was jolted to full attention when he read the front page headline: *Police Investigations—Inept or Corrupt?* He started to read the story, and then his phone rang.

"Yeah."

"Max! Where have you been?" Evelina asked. "Have you read the paper?"

"Sorta—I just started. Who gave them all this anyway?"

"Why are you asking me? It's your job to steer these things the way we need them to go. You've got to get Luke Lane off any of this now. He's too curious—besides, he wants your job. Hush up that Browning lady also. I'll take care of Rhea, though I don't think she's said much. What about this reporter? Have you talked to him?"

"Jake Bonner? No! I never heard of him before," Max said. "Old J. Quinton Sedwick has to be behind all of this, though. I can handle him, Evelina. Trust me; I've kept a lid on him for years."

"Do you understand how serious all this is, Max dear? Remember, you're the one with the most to lose. Use your power. More power runs through your psyche than all these schmucks put together. Meditate. We've too much going for us. We've gone too far. There's no reversing now. You knew—"

"Yeah, I know. We all listened to you," Max said. "You do your part—I'll hold up my end. I'm tired now. I'll talk to you tomorrow."

"Wait, Max, you haven't told me where you were all day. Where was your cell phone?"

"I was fishing, up north fishing. Not that it's any of your business. Had no phone, no friends, nothing. I did some deep meditating—my own kind. I had to get away from all this stuff here, including you, Evelina. A man needs some time alone."

"No you don't, Max. You only need what I tell you. Don't do anything like that again," Evelina Vincent warned. "I mean it."

"Look, I'm still a man. I can make my own decisions."

"No Max, you can't. Just submit—it's easier that way."

★★★

Carla Hunter sat at her desk, staring at her computer screen, when Kurt Stein walked in. Engrossed in what she'd been studying for over an hour, she made no acknowledgement of Kurt's arrival.

"Hey, I took a shower, brushed my teeth too. Why the cold shoulder?" Kurt asked.

"Sorry, Kurt. Come here. I've something for you to see."

"Someone e-mail you some wild party scene?"

"Kurt—keep that part of your mind to yourself," Carla said. "No, come here, I've got a message from Alex."

"Alex!" Kurt said, and then quickly stepped to Carla's desk. "How did you get this? What's he say? Let me look."

"Easy, Kurt. It's just a note. He got what we sent him. He's working a lot, but with no more success than we're having."

"How'd you get this? It didn't come UPS."

"It doesn't matter, if you don't know, you can't be made to tell, remember?" Carla said.

"Like the feds are going to hang me by my thumbs or something. Where's he hiding?" Kurt asked. "What's he say about what I sent him? He think I'm on the right track?"

"He just got it. He'll get back to us."

Carla looked at the clock. "It's nearly eight at HLS headquarters. I'm going to call Secretary Kingston and tell him Alex has made contact. I've got to get the ban lifted so I can send some things off to Alex."

Carla picked up the secure phone and dialed Secretary Kingston's direct line. In a moment, his secretary answered. "Please tell him that Carla Hunter is calling, and that it's important. I'll hold on, thanks."

In a moment Clayton Kingston answered. "Give me some good news. Tell me you've got all of this figured out, and we can go forward. Make my day, please."

"Well, not quite, but I've got the next best news. Alex has contacted us. He's going over our work and continuing to work on his code program. I feel a lot better now. We'll get this soon."

"I wish I shared your exuberance. I'd still feel much better if he was right there with you. However, I'm relieved he hasn't turned on us—but we still can't really be sure. This could be a ruse to get us to open up. How did he get you the message?"

"Well, ah, he got it to us through a safe contact.... There's total confidentiality, I assure you...."

"He still could be playing us," Secretary Kingston said. "We don't really know where he sent that from. Or, he could have done it with a gun to his head. He could be off on an island, laughing at all of us as we stress over all of this."

"I don't believe that," Carla said. "Alex isn't the type. We have to trust him."

"I suppose so. None the less, I'll have someone monitor and proof anything before you send it. Just a precaution, you understand. Someone will be in contact with you by the end of the day. Well, maybe this is the beginning of a good day. I'll be in on Monday. Maybe you'll have some really good news by then."

"Fine, we'll see you then," Carla said.

With that Secretary Kingston hung up. Carla sat motionless for several moments. Kurt got up and went to the coffee pot.

"How could he put his personal interest ahead of the nation?" Kurt asked. "If we fail, I hope he's caught and tried for treason, if there's anyone left to try him. Of all times for him to become a babysitter. You know neither he nor his ex-wife wanted that kid. Too bad they didn't have an abortion."

"Kurt—how could you? That's cruel," Carla said. "Tucker is such a sweet little boy."

"Too bad. Maybe if he was a little monster Alex would be here," Kurt said. "Maybe then he wouldn't care."

"Careful who you call a monster," Carla said.

"Hey—we're surrounded by monsters. They're trying to take over this country. Don't you get it? Sometimes I think I'm the only one who sees how serious all this is," Kurt said. "We could all die, then what?"

"Well, that depends on you, Kurt. You know—"

"Not now, not now with your religious imagination. How do you do it? How do you look around and believe any of that God stuff?"

"How do you look around and not see God? Everywhere I look I see the hand of God, Kurt."

"Cut it! No! Not now I said. Get to work on something, something real, all right? We're counting down the days to doom, and you see God everywhere. You drive me crazy. Don't ever talk to me like that again. Not now, not ever. I only care about this life—my life."

"That's sad," Carla said.

"Hey, that's the way it is. So tell me, is Secretary Kingston coming Monday?" Kurt asked. "Is that what I heard? You better be ready to tell him all about how you got this."

"Or what? He'll throw me in jail? Maybe I could use the break. You can do this all alone."

"Wow. You must need a nap or something. Chill out, will ya? All right, we stick together," Kurt said. "Look, you bail out of this, I'm on the next plane to Mexico City until all of this is over. Hey, maybe we both need a nap—no, make it a good long vacation."

"We need to solve this, Kurt. That's what we really need. Somehow we just need to solve this."

★★★

Max Pace sat in his office drinking coffee. Every time he looked out across the rows of desks he found at least one of his people staring at him.

"Lane!" he called out. "Hey Luke, come in here a minute."

Luke Lane stepped into Max's office and started to sit in a chair across from Max.

"The door," Max said. "Close the door."

"Sure, Max," Luke said. He turned and closed the door, then sat in the chair. "What's up?"

"I'm taking over both the Vincent and Browning missing children cases. Bring me the files. You're off them—totally. I don't want to see you snooping around anything to do with either of them. Got that?"

"Max! You can't do this. I've got a lot of things going on both of them. I'll break them; give me some more time, just a little."

"Just bring me the files," Max said without looking at Luke. "Didn't you read the paper yesterday? I've got to take over myself. I'm protecting you, don't you see?"

"No, I don't see," Luke said. "I don't need your protection. I'll solve all of this. I'll get that boy back too. Don't do this to me, Max. How will it look?"

"How did I look yesterday?" Max asked. "My mind is made up. I'm putting you on that rigged gambling machine thing."

"Ah, Max. Anyone could do that. Man, don't bust me to the bottom," Luke protested.

"Outta here, Lane. I want those files, the complete files, pronto."

Luke walked out of Max's office and back to his desk. He returned with the two files. He handed them to Max, then turned and started to leave.

"Luke—stay outta this. Someday you'll thank me."

★★★

Carla Hunter toyed with the pen she'd been using to make notes. Her mind was adrift this morning. Kurt seemed to be in a like mood. The Secretary of Homeland Security would be in their office anytime now, and they'd have little positive to talk about.

The silence was broken by the distant flailing of chopper blades. That would be the secretary coming up from the Albuquerque airport. She looked over at Kurt. He sat staring out a window. Carla got up and started to make fresh coffee. When the water started gurgling, Kurt looked her way.

"Real cream. Remember, Kingston likes real cream."

"Yeah, I stopped and got a little container this morning," Carla said. "What else?"

"I don't know. We surely don't have what he wants to hear. Do you think he'll take the project away and give it to Livermore or someone else?"

"I don't know. If we can't do it…"

Neither one said anything for several minutes. Kurt finally broke the silence.

"I couldn't sleep last night, so I got on the internet. Got to looking at things in Mexico, you know. I'll bet I could get a good job down there. Sure could live cheaply. You ever been there? Mexico City way?"

"No," Carla said. "I can't believe you're thinking like that. That's not you."

"Neither is failing—and that's what I'm doing now. This is personal, Carla. I know you'll think I'm a chump for saying this, but I really don't give a rip about all those faceless people we're supposed to be saving. I don't know them. I can't seem to get up any real feelings for them. What I do feel is that I'm letting myself down. That's what bugs me. I'm failing. I'm going to be looked at as one who couldn't come through when really needed. That's what I can't face."

"I can't believe you said that," Carla said.

"I knew you'd feel that way," Kurt said. "Tell me you really care about people you don't know, people who have no direct effect on your life."

"Of course I do," Carla said. "We're talking about little children, young parents, and old people. So what if you don't know them personally. Does that make them any less real? Are they any less valuable just because you don't know them?"

"Just telling you how I feel," Kurt said. "I knew you wouldn't understand."

"I don't. You continue to amaze me, Kurt. Maybe it's because I came from a big family, and you're an only child—no that's not it. I know better. You're just totally self-centered."

"Yeah, I am. So what?"
Then there were voices, followed by footsteps out in the hallway.

Chapter 12

Al didn't know what time he fell asleep; there was no clock in the room. He'd dreamed meaningless nonsense, awoke and tossed about, then dozed and dreamed some more. He was towing a horse trailer down the freeway—with his BMW. Next a police car passed him, and the horse trailer was behind the police car. Then horses were running by him, their hoofs pounding. Then there were lots of men on the horses. Then…

"Hey Dad. Wake up Dad. Look, there're guys outside on horses! It looks like in those old movies you watch. Can I go out and watch 'em?"

"Huh—what time is it?"

"It's morning. It's gotta be. Boy, this is cool! What are they gonna to do with them big ol' horses?"

"I have no idea," Al said as he sat up, dropping his feet to the floor. It was still more dark than light. He picked up his watch, and then shook his head while he read it's indicated time of 6:15. Being summertime, and with Arizona not changing to daylight savings time, it was now only 4:15 where he'd been yesterday morning. He slowly rose, then looked out the window just in time to see three mounted riders head up the road.

"Someday I'm gonna do that," Danny said. "Bet those fellas are gonna have fun all day long."

"Fun? They'll work hard all day and come home wishing they had a city job," Al said. "No man should have to start to work this early."

"Ah, Dad; you used to stay all night at the lab."

Al nodded his head. "Remember, careful talking about the lab."

"Sorry, I forgot," Danny said.

Al heard Alice rummaging around the kitchen, then he smelled coffee brewing. He pulled on his clothes, then opened the bedroom door and went straight toward the bubbling coffee pot.

"Short night," Alice said. "That's alright. I gotta get on the road. I want to be home by dark. Going with the sun will help well over an hour. I'll beat it home before it gets down in my eyes."

"You going back home today?" Al asked. "That's a lot of driving in two days."

"Yeah, well, I've got things to do at home. You boys will be fine here. I'll go take care of my business with Duce in a few minutes, and then I'm sure he'll be down and get to know you some. Like I said before, they don't come much better than Duce Duval."

Alice diced up some jalapeños she found setting on a window sill. Then, along with some jack cheese and eggs, she made up some tasty omelets.

"What are those guys doing on the horses?" Danny asked Alice.

"'Spect moving cattle to another area where there's more water or grass," Alice said. "It's been dry as last year's hay here- a-bouts and the summer storms haven't kicked in yet. They'll come, though. They'd better."

"How big is a ranch like this?" Al asked. "How many acres?"

"Acres? This is west Texas. They usually talk more in sections rather than acres out here. An acre ain't worth talkin' 'bout. As I recollect, the Lost Lucy has about 180 or more sections."

"And just how big is a section?" Al asked.

"One mile square—that's 640 acres."

"You mean each section has 640 acres, and the Lost Lucy is 180 sections?" Al asked. "That's—that's over 100,000 acres! You mean one man owns that much?"

"Shoot yes. There's bigger spreads than this in these parts, much bigger. Look out there. You know how many acres each cow has to cover every day to round up its food? It's got to compete with the deer and antelope, the goats and the like in some places. Then there's the predators, lots of big cats, after the young and the weak. It takes a heap of land to eke out a modest life at best."

"Never thought about anything like this. Guess I've been awfully sheltered working and living as I have all my life," Al said.

"You'll leave here, even if you hate it, you'll leave with a respect for this kind of life. Who knows, you might even like it," Alice said.

Al walked over and stared out the window. He sipped his coffee while Alice started to gather up the few dishes.

"I'll clean up, Alice," Al said. "If you've got business with Duce, then that long drive home, you best get going. I think I'll sack out for a few minutes. I'm not used to doing what we did yesterday."

"Can I go outside, Dad?" Danny asked.

"Best wait on me, Son. It wouldn't do you any harm to rest a little more too."

"But I ain't tired. There's a bunch ta see here."

"Yeah, and trouble to get into since you don't know what anything is. No, we best wait on Duce to talk to us first."

"Yeah—OK. Hey! Where's the TV?"

Alice laughed. "Duce has one on satellite over at the big house. I'm afraid there's none here."

"No TV! You serious? That's—I—they that poor?"

"Not that poor, just that far from any signal. The nearest stations are too far to reach on an antenna, and the nearest cable line is fifty miles away. You'll learn to live without it."

"I don't know," Danny said. "I once saw a thing about some people in Africa or there-a-bouts that didn't have any TV, but here? I don't know."

"Be glad the generator works, or you wouldn't have lights, or cooling," Alice said.

"Generator?" Danny asked.

"Forget it, Son. Let Alice get going. How can we thank you, Alice? What can we do?"

"Get your troubles fixed up so's you can go home. What'll make this worth it to me is when I get the word that you're back home."

Al nodded. He knew Alice wasn't doing this for any gain, not money anyway. Maybe someday he'd find out what went so wrong in her past that she now tried to make things up through the lives of others.

Carla sat stunned. On the other end of the conference phone, over the speaker came the voice of the President of the United States.

"Mrs. Hunter, I understand you've gotten correspondence from Dr. Vincent," President Daugherty said to her.

"Y—yes. I—I, it was just a note letting us know he's working hard. However, Alex is very good. I'm sure he's on to the solution."

"I'd like to believe what you just said, Mrs. Hunter," the president said. "In all honesty, do you believe you will have this solved quickly?"

"Ah—Mr. President—I can't give you a time. We're doing all we can."

"That's not very decisive or comforting. I know I'm being redundant to the point of annoyance, but we need this. For the sake of the nation, this is on your shoulders. I'll be in touch in a few days. Good day, Mrs. Hunter."

Carla cradled the phone, then stared at her notes on the table in front of her.

"Let's talk again in the morning," Secretary Kingston said from his seat across the table from Carla. "I'll be spending the night in Santa Fe."

"Sure," Carla said. "Maybe we'll have something by then."

Carla looked over at Kurt. He'd positioned himself well away from the phone.

Thanks a lot. You stuck me with sounding stupid to the President.

★★★

When Alice started her truck, Al awoke up from his short nap. He went out on the porch and waved to her as she started pulling away. Danny rushed to his side.

"Bye Alice," he yelled. "Betcha I'll see you again. Be good to that baby horse."

Al and Danny then stood in silence until Alice was out of sight. Just when he was about to turn back to the door, Al heard footsteps on the gravel trail coming from the big house. He turned to see a slightly shorter than most, slender-built man walking toward them. His hat was out of shape and sweat stained. His skinny-legged Wranglers bunched up at the underslung-heels of his rock-scarred boots. Only the oversized, silver, rodeo- champion buckle on his harness-leather belt hinted of class— cowboy class. Though he'd never before paid any attention to this type of life he'd now been thrown into, Al knew he was looking at the real thing. This was a true, modern day cowboy.

"Howdy," the man said when he reached the old wooden porch. "I'm Duce Duval. Reckon you figured that. Sorry I wasn't up to give you a fittin' welcome last night, but I got tuckered out 'bout eight and turned in. Knew Alice would fix y'all up right anyway. 'Spect this here'll be a bunch different than you ever lived like before. I don't know nothin' else myself. Shucks, if it weren't for horses and cows, I don't know what I'd do with my life. Guess that ain't all true. I could think of lots of things to do, I 'spect."

"I'm—I'm Al Tucker. This is my son Danny. It's good to meet you, Mr. Duval."

"Make that Duce. Had that handle since I was a little toad. You're safe here, Al. Nobody in these parts will do you harm. Folks here-a-bouts are plumb good at minding their own self. The best I can say now is for you to do what you can to make yourself at home. I got lots to keep you busy. You look like a fella who might know his way around all this computer stuff— heard ya was anyway."

"Yeah, I guess you'd say I'm pretty computer savvy," Al said.

"I'm tryin' to get all my books and records on a stock management program. I'm having a devil of a time with some of it. I just don't get how to do some of the things so they work right. Figure if I had someone show me how to do it all the right way, why, I'd be ahead of the herd."

"I'll help you anyway I can. I've got lots of work I need to do while I'm here, but I expect to carry my weight, as I've heard people say. More than likely I'm in worse shape in how little I know about your business than you are with your computer knowledge. Back when I was a kid, I was around some Midwest farms, but from what I see here, this is like being on another planet for me."

"Alice says you'll make it. She's never led me wrong yet. I know ya need some time for yer own project, but I got an easy, but important, job for ya to do. Let's hoof it over to my office in the big house, and I'll give ya the whole skinny."

As they all walked over to the main house, Duce talked on about the ranch and about the drought that had him moving cattle from pasture to pasture looking for a little grass and enough water.

"We're in survival mode now. The rains will come, someday they will. 'Till then we work like dogs to keep some meat on them critters' bones. Here, take a look see at this map on the wall," he said once they'd moved into his office. "This shows all the wells and tanks, the pipelines too. Got nine wells. Two of them are bone dry. A spell back they all had windmills on all of the wells, but I've put solar systems on two of them in the last few years—these two over here," he pointed to two of the wells on the map.

"Now these two down here," he pointed to two others shown to be down in low wash-bottoms, "they got diesel generators on them to run submersible pumps hung below the windmill cylinders. These two wells have never let us down. When we need to, like now, we tie off the windmills and run them generators night and day. See these pipelines? They push water for miles. All said, we have nearly fifty miles of pipeline going from tank to tank. We can fill some of those tanks from three different wells. These tanks down here are just clay tanks," he pointed to one area of the map, "but the others are all concrete or steel-rim.

"There's enough floats and valves to give one a headache, but it all works—when nothing's broke."

Duce walked over to a chair at a large table and sat down. He motioned for the others to join him.

"I need you fellas to ride herd on all this. When something breaks, we do the little stuff ourselves. I have a windmiller, a pump guy I guess they call themselves now, who does the heavy work. I surely can't afford to wait until something is down a week before I react. I've got another map like that one up there I'll give ya and I've got all the well GPS coordinates on it. All the wells and tanks got names—they're on the map too. I need you to take that pickup out there with the fuel tank on the back and keep those fuel tanks on the generators full. The oil checked and filled too. Then I need you to make the rounds and check on all the water tanks and wells. If a windmill is torn up, I need to know right away. If a tank goes dry in an area where we're running cattle, why that's life or death for them. Think you can do that?"

"I—sure, I mean, it seems easy enough," Al said.

"It'll take you several days to make the rounds. I'll tell you which ones need daily attention and which ones you can see once or twice a week. You'll still have time to do your own thing—help me with my computer too, I hope," Duce said, then went on in his slow drawl. "Before you leave in the morning, I'll give you that map, the GPS thing too. Make sure you fill the truck tank and the bed tank every night when you come in. That way you're ready to roll come daylight.

"Take a lunch—we'll fix that for ya here. I'll have that little 'fridge down in the other house stocked for ya with some snacks and what all. That runs on LP and the lights are on solar and generator fed batteries—24 volt. If you need to use your computer, I got 12 volt adapters that'll take those cigarette lighter things, ya know? Anything else ya need, we might have it, and then we might not. Someone goes to town about twice a week. Stop back up after a spell. I'll have everything you need to make your rounds. Truck keys and all. Just take it easy today. You had a long day yesterday. I don't know how Alice does it."

Duce rose, so did Al and Danny, who then followed him through the house. They walked out into the hot wind blowing up from the south.

"Use that cooler in the window when you have to, it'll get hot after awhile. It'll run out of power at night though. Need new batteries I guess. Oh, and keep the screen door closed. Don't want to let in any scorpions or rattlesnakes."

Al and Danny glanced at each other.

"Yeah, watch out for snakes around the tanks and wells," Duce warned. "They love the shade and moisture there. There's an old 22 on the truck window rack to kill them demons. Kill them so's they don't kill my stock. Lose a handful of curious calves every year to them. Well, I gotta go see how the boys are comin' along in findin' the south herd. I'll see ya'll later."

Al and Danny walked back to the little guesthouse in silence. Once inside, Danny spoke first.

"Whatcha think, Dad?"

"This is all so bizarre I don't know what to think. A few days ago I was working on the most secret government work, and tomorrow I'm going out in the middle of nowhere to look at pools of water and ancient windmills. One day I'm trying to save the country—a few days later I'm saving a bunch of thirsty cows. I've got to lie down, Son. I need to think about this whole thing."

★★★

In the middle of the afternoon, Al heard Duce's truck pull up to the front of the ranch house.

"Let's go see Duce, Son. We'll get the keys and fill up the truck tanks and check out that GPS locator. Surely he has some kind of a water container for us. Maybe he's got some groceries too."

When Al knocked on the front door, a squat, weather-worn, gray-haired man greeted them.

"Ah, the new guests, Señor Al and Señor Danny. You come in, sí. Me Pablo. Cook for la rancha. My Messis, she do thee laundry and clean. Each day you come early in thee morning. Pablo have you breakfast. Burrito for you lunch too. You need mucho water too. Sí, the Messis, she make very good water jugs," Pablo said picking up a plastic gallon jug jacketed with heavy wool.

"Sí, you dip thees in thee water at thee tanks and set it in back of you truck. The air, she blow by and dry thee wet wool. Thee water in thee jug, she get nice and cool. You will like."

"Oh, yeah. Cooling by evaporation. That's simple. Well, that answers most of what we came here for," Al said. "Ah—is Duce here?"

"Sí. Señor Duce be in hees office. You go and knock on thee door."

Al started to go down the hall.

"One momento, Señor." Pablo went to a small desk in the dining area and pulled out a tape measure from the top drawer.

"You work for Señor Duce, you need hats. Thee sun here, she will bake you. Make you loco. Pablo go to town tomorrow for supplies. Bring back hats for you." He took the tape and wrapped it around Danny's head. Danny's eyes opened wide while looking at his dad. Al just shrugged his shoulders. When Pablo had measured both of their heads, he grasped Danny by the upper arm.

"Pablo see you be one smart young fella. You do good in school, no? Need more muscle, though. Work be good for you. Señor Duce, he help you get strong. Then you be smart and strong."

"Here," Al said pulling out several hundred-dollar bills. "Get us what we need, please."

"Sí, gracias, Señor. Will bring you back mucho change."

Al nodded, and then knocked on Duce's office door.

"It's open," Duce called from inside. "Hope we're not bothering you," Al said.

"Not at all. Come on in and sit a spell," Duce said. "It's cooler here than that old shack down there. You get settled in?"

"Well, that didn't take very long," Al said. "I think I got caught up on my sleep also."

"Good. You met Pablo. I heard him tell you he's going to town tomorrow. I'll have him get you some clothes, some ranch clothes. Write down all your sizes and all and he'll take care of it from there. There're gloves in the truck. Here's the map, GPS, and truck keys. I told you about the gun on the window rack. There're plenty of shells in the glove box. You do know how to shoot, don't you?"

"I do," Danny jumped in. "I shot rabbits and quail out on the res… well, with a friend of mine."

"Good. It's an old bolt action with a clip feed. Button safety on the trigger guard. You'll figure it out if you need it. We keep the chamber empty for safety.

"Hey, how about a soda?" Duce asked. "We've got some cold ones here. 'Course when we say soda out here we mean Dr. Pepper. That's 'bout all you'll find in these parts, at least by us old timers."

"I'll take one," Danny said.

"Sure, I will too," Al said. "Tell me, Duce, where'd the name of this place come from?" Al asked while Duce went to the small refrigerator and came back with three sodas.

"The Lost Lucy? Yeah, strange name, huh. It seems that back about 1850 a fella named Sly Hamner first settled in these rocks. He had him a daughter named Lucy that he thought the sun rose and set on. Story is she was the prettiest thing in west Texas. Seems one day Lucy went for a short ride and was never seen again—not hair nor hide. Horse never came home so it's always been assumed the Comanche got her. Old Sly went crazy over this and had to be sent away. My great-grandfather bought this spread then and it's been in Duval hands ever since. Through the years, we've added a bunch to it."

"Still got any of them Comanche today?" a wide-eyed Danny asked.

"Not wild ones, none to be afraid of, not for years," Duce said. "No, only the land and the animals are wild now. A few of the illegals, the ones smuggling drugs or the coyotes with their people, they can be mighty dangerous. Avoid them at all costs."

There was a soft knock at the door. "It's open," Duce yelled.

The door opened and in stepped a man in khaki slacks, golf shirt and loafers. He obviously wasn't a ranch employee. Al's interest peaked to find out who this was.

"Hey, Rev, what brings you out here?" Duce asked. "Meet Al and Danny Tucker. They're helping me for awhile. Fellas, this here is Ty Jackson, preacher at my church in town. Best preacher in all of west Texas, I like to say."

"Good to meet both of you," Reverend Jackson said. "If you're going to be here awhile, maybe I'll see you in church sometime."

"Ah, maybe," Al said. "Yeah, maybe."

"Missed you last week Duce, here's the message tape," Ty Jackson said. "The real reason I came out is to give you this new drawing on the addition. I wanted you to have time to look it over before we have that board meeting after church the Sunday after next."

"Oh, good," Duce said.

"Listen," Al said. "We'll get going. I want to fill up the fuel tanks and—"

"OK, just be back around six for steak," Duce said. "Preacher will be stayin' so come early and hungry."

"Sounds good," Al said. "I haven't eaten much for awhile. Thanks for the sodas. We'll see you later then."

Dinner was informal, and after not having much to eat for two days, the steak tasted extra good. At first Al was concerned that Ty Jackson would start asking questions. He soon figured out that the preacher knew enough not to ask anything about the new ranch guests. While Ty Jackson taught Danny how to play checkers, Al browsed through a ranching magazine. When the sun started to go down, Ty Jackson rose to leave.

"As usual, Duce, I've enjoyed myself. I'll see you Sunday. Maybe see you fellows again if you're here a spell."

"Maybe, Reverend Jackson, just maybe," Al said. "Come on Son, we best get going too. That sun comes up early. That's one thing we could use, Duce, an alarm clock."

"Look in the medicine cabinet. That's where Gloria, that's Pablo's wife, always puts it when she cleans up after someone leaves. Don't know why. Someday I'll get around to asking her. I'll see you in the morning. Bring the map with you. I'll tell you where to go tomorrow."

"Sure. Thanks for everything, Duce," Al said. "Thanks a lot."

★★★

The next day Al and Danny followed the route Duce laid out for them and were back mid-afternoon. Al went to work on his computer. Soon a knock came at the door. Al went to see who it was.

"Pablo, come in."

"Sí, new clothes, and hats. Now you no burn in thee hot sun, Señors,"

"Thank you, Pablo," Al said while he took the smaller hat and pushed it down on Danny's head. Danny laughed.

"Ah, no good," Pablo said. He went to the cupboard and got out a tea kettle, put some water in it and set it on the stove burner, struck a match and turned it up on high. In minutes steam puffed out the spout. Pablo then proceeded to shape the hat to blend with the shape of Danny's head.

"Yeah," Al said after a few minutes. "That sure looks better. Hard to believe it's the same hat."

"Now you, Señor." Pablo worked on Al's hat for some time, then nodded his head in approval. "Now, with your new clothes you look right, the way a man should look—if you only had some boots. Sí, when you get to town you must get you some boots. Pablo cannot do that for you. You would have to lend me your feet."

Danny laughed at that and Pablo seemed pleased.

"Pablo go fix supper. You come eat at six."

"We'll be there. Thank you, Pablo. Thanks a lot," Al said. The rest of the week, father and son checked on wells and tanks. Duce was pleased that they found everything working properly and that no more wells had gone dry.

"Tomorrow's Sunday. I'll be going to town early and won't be back 'til late afternoon. I figure you'd like to go along, but I don't think that'd be best. You're safe out here. Maybe next week. Take the day off though. Rest up as best you can."

"I'll need to find an internet hookup soon," Al said. "I've got to check my e-mail and send in some work. Any idea where I can do that on a public connection?"

"The university. They've got a computer area with public wireless there, I believe. You can slip into the library and do your business. Just give me a day or so's heads up."

"I'll need all day tomorrow and two or three more evenings before I'm ready," Al said.

"Why don't we figure on going in Friday then? There's a rodeo at the college. We'll take that in and make a night of it. You two can do your own thing so no one will question you bein' with me."

"Sounds good," Al said. "We'll go to town Friday then. Now, let's take a look at what you've got going on with your stock management program. Maybe I can work some on that tomorrow too."

★★★

Monday morning Al pulled up to the first tank and shut off the truck. He and Danny got out. Al started to pull himself up on a large rock to look inside the huge, concrete storage tank when from around back he heard someone yell.

"¿Quién es usted?"

"Get in the truck, Son. Get that gun ready."

Chapter 13

Danny ran and yanked open the truck door, then jumped up on the seat and took down the little rifle from the back window rack. He stuffed the loaded clip up its channel, cycled a round into the chamber, and checked that the safety was in the safe position. Al slowly backed up to the truck.

"What was that, Dad?"

"Someone's over there. It sounded like a woman. She may not be alone. Hold onto that gun. I'm going to drive around back and see what's going on."

"Yeah. I don't wanta walk back there and find some crazy woman. Maybe it's one of them Comanche types Duce talked about."

"She spoke Spanish," Al said as he started to back up. "She probably slipped in from Mexico." He then slowly drove around the tank to the back. There on the ground, stretched out on the rocky sand, her head propped up against the watering tank, was a young woman. She held a rock in her hand, as if she was ready to use it to defend herself.

"What's she doing, Dad?"

"Look at her foot. She's got a broken ankle, most likely. I'd say she was with a group of border crossers and when she got hurt, they left her here." Al opened the door and slowly got out.

"¿Habla usted Inglés?" Al asked her.

"Sólo hablo español," the woman said, slowly shaking her head no.

"She only speaks Spanish. You've learned a little of that from some of your friends in school, right? I haven't used what little I learned for many years. Let's see if we can figure out what happened to her."

"What's she doin' here, Dad?"

"People from Mexico come here to work and send money back home. That's what many of them are doing anyway. Others only come to cause trouble, but I'd bet she came to work. She probably has family here somewhere, and they sent her money to come also."

"Why come here to work?"

"Money. Much of Mexico is nothing but poverty."

"What are we gonna do?"

"Let's try to talk to her."

"Me llamo Al," he said, then pointed to his son. "Danny." "Me llamo Ramona," the girl said, lowering the rock.

"How do I ask her how she is?" Al asked Danny.

"I don't know. I never learned that."

"I think it's something like, ah, ¿cómo está usted?" Ramona pointed to her ankle. "Roto."

"Yeah, she says her ankle is a problem. I'm sure it's broken. I wonder how long she's been here." Al looked at Ramona and pointed at her. "Uno day? Dos days?"

"Sí, dos."

"I think she's been here since Saturday night," Al said. Then he asked, "Usted hambre?"

"Sí, mucho."

"She's hungry. Get out our lunch sack. It's a good thing they left her here by the water tank, or she'd be about dead by now."

Al gave Ramona one of their burritos, and she devoured it in what seemed like only seconds.

"What do you think, Son, give her the other one?" "I ain't hungry, Dad. Least not like her."

The second one went down nearly as quickly. When she'd finished, Ramona started pointing off to the north and trying to tell them something. She kept using the words, "el coyote tom'o mi hijo."

"I think she's telling us her son was taken off to the north, up that trail. Let's check up that direction for a ways, and then we need to take her back to the ranch house. She needs help."

"They took her boy and left her here?" Danny asked.

"Probably."

"That's sure mean."

"If they thought she was going to die, they couldn't leave her son with her."

"This is bad. I ain't never seen anything so bad. Nobody better ever take me away from you, Dad."

"Mi hijo," Ramona softly said with tears running down her cheek. Al didn't know how to console this poor woman. What was she really doing here? Was the risk of stealing across this deserted desert worth some menial job in the country's heartland or northeast? Were things really that bad in Mexico?

Al looked around at the tracks in the sand. There appeared to be multiple sets of adult tracks and at least one set of small child footprints. He figured the child was Ramona's son.

"See the tracks, Son? Look, here's some that probably are her son's. They're going north. Let's take the road here on out east and see if there's one going north soon. Maybe we can see where this group was picked up and which way they went. I'm sure this all happened two days ago, so we won't find much. I'd like to make sure no one else was left behind out here."

Al helped Ramona into the truck on the passenger side. Danny jumped in the back. As he figured, after going east for only a mile or so, there was a road, such as it was, that crossed and went north. Following that for a mile or two, another one then crossed again. He took this road back west. When he reached the point where he was north of the water tank, he saw where a vehicle had pulled off into the side. Once he stopped, he saw the foot tracks, from those who'd left the tank, leading right up to the side of the vehicle's tire tracks.

He got out and looked around. "See the tracks?" he asked Danny. "They got into a van or something and over there it turned around. It went back out the way we've just come in. At least there are the footprints of the little one mixed in. I don't know where they took him, but at least he's not out in this desert, wandering around dying of thirst. I don't know of anything we can do now."

Al got back into the truck and started back towards the ranch. This road, like all the others out here, was a two-track, rock strewn trail that took about an hour to cover the first fifteen miles. When about six or seven miles from the headquarters the truck started losing power. Danny felt something was wrong and leaned over the side and yelled in at his dad.

"Why are we going so slowly?"

"Something's wrong with the truck," Al answered. "We've got a few miles to go. I hope we make it."

They dropped down into a sloped bank, dry wash, and as they reached the upper bank on the other side, the truck died. Al tried to start it again but nothing happened.

Danny jumped out of the bed and stood by the driver's window.

"What now, Dad?"

"Let me look," Al said, and then he got out of the truck and opened the hood. "Ahh, these diesels—I don't know where to begin. It felt as if it was starving for fuel. There's no ignition system, so it almost has to be fuel."

Al took off the air cleaner lid and saw that the cleaner was dirty, but not plugged. The manual showed a separator to bleed off water, and he opened the valve on that. Nothing came out. He tried to start the truck again, but nothing happened. Getting frustrated, and hot, Al slumped to the ground. Danny sat beside him.

"We gonna die out here? We ain't where we're supposed to be. Nobody's ever gonna come lookin' for us down this road, will they Dad? We've never been here before."

"We're not too far from the ranch house—two or three hours walk I'd guess. However, it's too hot to start walking now. If no one comes by around midnight we'll start walking. I think I know where this road meets the main one to the ranch. It's not but about four or five miles, maybe. Then it's only a couple more to the ranch. It should be a pretty good moon tonight. We'll be fine. Maybe someone will find us before that. They won't know we're in trouble until late this afternoon and probably not start out looking much before dark."

"Whata we gonna do 'bout Ramona?"

"We'll leave her in the truck. She'll be alright until someone can get back to her. I'm sure that ankle hurts like the devil, and it needs to be set, or operated on, but she's not going to die from it. I'm sure she's more concerned about her son."

"She ain't never gonna see him again, is she?"

"Hard to say. She's most likely going to have to go back to Mexico. If her son ends up with a relative, maybe they will send him back to her. More than likely, once she's healed up, she'll try to come over again."

"I don't wanna live in Mexico," Danny said. "That don't sound like fun at all."

"I guess we're spoiled," Al said.

"I kinda like bein' spoiled. I'd sure like to be sittin' in a nice air-conditioned room drinkin' a cold soda right now. Maybe I ain't really so much a cowboy as I was thinkin' I was."

It had been dark for several hours. The moon was rising high into the sky and Al knew it was soon time to start walking. When the sun went down, Danny fell asleep and rested peacefully against the back wheel of the truck. Al hated to wake him. Al's stomach growled. He knew Danny would be hungry too when he awoke. He looked in at Ramona. She was obviously in pain, worried, and scared. Things were bad for him, but Al knew it was a lot worse for this poor young woman. Off in some distant canyon, a coyote howled. It was answered by another one, seeming to be farther away.

Duce had mentioned the other day that he'd seen what he called a panther at the ranch house a few weeks back. He'd learned that was what the locals called a cougar, or mountain lion as it was called back home in New Mexico. They'd take that little gun with them, but he knew it would be little help if one of those big, hungry cats looked upon them as an easy meal.

Al had been for eliminating private ownership of guns for years. Now he wished he had a great big one. He chuckled to himself. It took something this drastic for him to realize how a few people, well educated and well intentioned, such as he was, could get organized and try to force their opinions upon everyone, even those who they didn't know or understand.

He pushed himself up and stretched his legs. Ramona looked out through the window at him. He walked over to her.

"We," he pointed at himself and Danny, "go rancho for socorro, sí? Usted quedarse, sí?" Ramona nodded that she understood. Al hoped he'd told her they were going for help, and she was to stay here. He made a mental note to brush up on his Spanish once all his current demands were over.

Danny woke up and came over to his dad.

"We goin' now?"

"Guess it's time. Take a drink of water, I'll take one also, then we'll leave what's left for Ramona. It's cool now and we shouldn't get too thirsty. As Al handed Danny the jug, he noticed the far off flashes of light to the north seemed to be getting brighter. That probably meant the storm was moving somewhat their way. He knew the area drastically needed rain, but he hoped none came tonight.

Al went over to the window by Ramona. He looked at her and smiled, then handed her the water jug. He didn't know what to say. She gave what appeared to be a forced smile back. Al nodded, and then turned away.

"Come on Son. Let's get help," he said as he reached out and took Danny's hand.

They'd walked for about an hour when Al stopped and took a good look at the approaching storm. Clouds now covered the moon and the only time they could see the road well was when the lightning flashed. That was becoming every few seconds. The wind had kicked up, and its gusts blew stinging sand against their faces and into their eyes. Then the first raindrops hit; big, cold, skin-stinging drops that felt like little knives of ice.

"Let's find a place to get some shelter," Al said as he looked around. They'd just crossed an arroyo, a deep dry wash with steep sides. Al turned back to that, and as the lightning flashed, he saw a scrub tree growing out of the bank on their side.

"There, under that little tree down in that wash. Let's go." Danny silently followed his dad as they stumbled and slid down the loose gravel bank and huddled under the tree.

"This is wild, Dad. We don't have storms like this at home."

"Maybe we do. We just don't stay out in them. If you were inside your nice home right now, you'd not really know all of this was going on outside."

"It's kinda cool. I think I'll go outside and check things out sometime."

"These hats are coming in handy," Al said. "It's like a roof on your head."

"Wish we had a real roof."

The storm raged around them for about fifteen minutes, with most of the rain staying to their north. When it had obviously moved off to their east, Al stood up.

"Back on the trail, I guess."

"Yeah," Danny said with little enthusiasm.

"What's that?" Al said as his ears picked up a gurgling, rolling sound. The lightning flashed and sparkled off the wash upstream to their north.

"Water's coming, Son. Let's go. Hold onto my hand tightly. Don't let go." Al threw the gun sling over his shoulder and grabbed Danny's hand. He frantically started climbing up the loose gravel bank. On the third step his foot slipped, and they slid all the way back to the bottom. The rushing water was now sounding like an approaching truck.

"Come on!" Al cried as he grabbed at a root growing out of the bank. He pulled on the root with one hand, Danny with the other. He kicked into the bank to get a solid foothold, then thrust with his leg and pulled with his arm at the same time. Seeing a large rock at the rim of the bank he quickly released the root and grabbed the rock. It held. He felt Danny grab his pant leg with his free hand. One more thrust and Al was able to lean over the top of the bank. A deeper grip on the rock and he crawled up over the edge, pulling Danny with him. The wall of water was now rushing by them, sloshing from bank to bank and ripping away anything loose in its path.

Al looked at his son. Neither spoke for a minute. Al crawled over to the edge and looked down to the tree they had been huddled under. He could only see the top of it swishing back and forth in the rushing water. Where they'd huddled moments ago was now chest high in water. Al pushed himself back, and again looked at Danny.

"That wasn't a good idea. I used to think I was about as smart as anyone alive. Guess out here I'm pretty stupid."

"We just don't know. Betcha we won't do that again. We're smarter now. Right Dad?"

"Sure are. Well, the rain's let up. Let's get going. We've got a long way to go."

Danny walked over closer to the edge and timidly looked down at the water. "This is kinda cool, Dad. I'd like to be on a floater and be riding that water just as far as it'll go. Wouldn't that be neat, Dad?"

"Only if you wanted it to be the last thing you ever did."

"Oh. You could do it, Dad. Me'n you could do just about anything."

They walked on for about another hour. Al could tell Danny's pace had slowed. Surely soon they would reach the main road to the house. With luck, someone out looking for them would come by and give them a ride. He was starting to get thirsty and his stomach was growling often. The clouds had moved off and the moon was back lighting their path. Al saw a large rock off to the trail's edge.

"Let's take a break and sit on that rock for a minute."

"Good deal, Dad. How much more? When we gonna be there?"

"Oh, I figure it's a ways yet."

They sat on the rock and rested their tired feet and legs.

"From now on we'll always carry a second jug of water, and throw in a box of crackers or granola bars if Duce has any," Al said. "We'll stay on the roads we're supposed to be on also."

The night had gotten quiet. Even the coyotes had apparently gone to sleep. Then, from up the road ahead of them, Al thought he heard something. He studied the sky that way and soon saw lights on the horizon bobbing up and down. By then he could hear the hum of an engine.

"Someone's coming."

"What if it's some bad guys? What if it's the guys who took Ramona's boy?"

Al didn't know what to say. Yes, this could be someone running an illegal immigrant van, but was more likely someone from the ranch.

"I think we have to take our chances. I'm tired and we need to get help for Ramona." Al leaned the little 22 rifle against the back side of the rock, then he stood up. The vehicle came closer. Danny held his father's hand. Then the lights broke over the horizon line ahead. It appeared to be a truck with a light bar on top. The whole area lit up.

"I think it's the Border Patrol. They have trucks like that. Remember who we are. I'll have to cover for us. Don't say anything you don't have to." Al felt Danny's squeeze harder on his hand.

The driver saw them and pulled up near them and stopped.

"Who are you?" he yelled to them.

"We work for Duce. I'm his water guy, you know. I check the wells. My truck broke down back the road, and we're walking back to the headquarters."

The agent then pulled up closer to them and got out.

"Mighty dangerous out here sometimes. There's illegals crossing through these parts all the time and with the panthers and, heck, you don't even have a gun."

"Little 22 over against that rock," Al said, pointing that way.

"A 22? Like I said, you don't have a gun. That would just make anything bigger than a snake mad. Where's your truck?"

"Back there about three hours walk. There's a woman in it, an illegal I'm sure. Found her down at what Duce calls Four Points well. She's got a badly broken ankle. It seems as if they left her there, but took her son on with them. I found where they got into a van—way down where this road crosses the first draw—but of course they were long gone. I think they left her Saturday night."

"There goes my night. That wash'll be runnin' hard back yonder. I'll take you boys over to Duce's first, then go get the woman. Jump in here. Bet your feet could use the break. Al grabbed the gun then lifted Danny up into the raised truck. He got into the passenger's side.

"You're new," the agent said once they were turned around and going down the road.

"Yeah, I'm Al. This is Danny. We're just here for the summer. I was off for the summer and, since my wife left us awhile back, well, I decided to take my son off to do something different. Some adventure, I guess."

"Everyone out here calls me Rocky," the agent said. "Sounds like you've had some of that excitement you were looking for today," Rocky said. He was quiet for a moment, and then started talking again.

"I know that wife leaving thing. Mine did the same about a year ago. Tore me up so it did. While I was out here chasing bad guys, she was chasing a bad guy of her own. They got married right after the divorce. They up and moved out to San Antonio. Took my boy with them. Hardly ever get to see him anymore. But that's all changing. This is my last week out here. I'm moving out to San Antonio myself. Still, I'd like to do just what you're doing now. Just me and Cody, my little guy, off by ourselves for awhile. Mister, you got the right idea."

Al was glad the agent went on to talk about himself and his troubles and never got around to asking anything about him. It only took fifteen or twenty minutes to reach the ranch headquarters. Duce came out to meet them.

"Sure am glad to see you fellas. Got all hands out lookin' fer ya."

Al told Duce what had happened. After a few minutes Rocky finished the cup of coffee Duce had given him, and then he stood up. "That draw oughta be crossable by the time I get there. I'll go get that girl. It'll be daylight before I get her to the emergency room at Alpine. Hopefully, someone else can take over from there."

"What will happen to her?" Al asked. "What about her son?"

"Oh, we'll fix her up, send her home, and then find her out here again someday. We might send her back several times, but eventually she'll get through. The boy's probably already up at a packing plant in the Midwest or somewhere. They'll take care of him until she gets there. You ever play hide and seek as a kid? That's about all this is. At the end of the game, everyone goes where they want to. Hey, you take care of your boy. Have a good summer." He smiled at Danny, then turned and left.

"You boys must be beat. See the storm got ya too," Duce said, looking at their wet and muddy clothes. "Sleep in tomorrow. We'll go get your truck. It's that darned rear fuel pump again, I'm sure. Put three or four of them on that thing already. I've got a spare. We'll have it on tomorrow so you can get back at it Wednesday. Now go raid the kitchen, then go on and get some sleep."

Friday evening Duce dropped Al off at the university library while he and Danny picked up some supplies. The library was nearly empty and Al quickly settled in and went to work. It only took a few minutes for him to send and receive his data. He then sat at a table where he could watch the driveway in front where Duce would be pulling up to the building. He started looking over the notes Carla had sent him. After a few moments, he looked up and saw Duce drive up. Al closed his computer down and hurried outside to the truck.

"Over there's the rodeo arena," Duce pointed down the valley. "We'll go over to the church first, and I'll go over there with Ty. You can take my truck and be by yourselves. Meet me at the parsonage by the church when it's over."

Al and Danny sat in the midst of the crowd and found themselves getting into the spirit of the competition. Not knowing the objective of each event was a handicap, but they figured out much of it as things went along.

After ice cream and Oreo cookies at the Jackson house, while Al and Duce talked with Ty and his wife, Paula, Danny fell asleep sitting in a chair.

"Better get these fellas home. Me too," Duce said. "I've not been out this late for months."

"Come see us sometime, Al," Paula said as they left. "Bring Danny with you."

"I'd like that," Al said. "Thanks for your hospitality."

"They seem like regular people," Al said as Duce drove out of town and toward the ranch.

"Sure are. Just regular people," Duce said. "Good people," he then added.

At least they didn't preach at me, Al thought, but said nothing.

★★★

On the fourth ring of her phone, Evelina Vincent picked it up. The caller ID showed a 432 area code number.

"Hello," she said.

"Hello, Mrs. Vincent?"

"Who's calling?"

"It's Julie Gomez—is that you Mrs. Vincent? I used to help you at school."

"Yes, of course, Julie. How are you?"

"I'm fine. Doing very well really. I ah… I thought I best call you. Mom sends me the Santa Fe papers, so I know what's going on back home. Look, I'm out here at Sol Ross University, you know in Alpine, Texas?"

"Yes, your mother told me."

"Yeah, well, like I said, I thought I needed to call you. It was the strangest thing—scary really. Yesterday in the school library, I saw your ex-husband."

Chapter 14

In the shade of his open center, horse barn, Wade Hawkins sprayed a soft mist of cool water on Kicks.

"Feels good, right old boy? Had us a great ride out there. Got too hot though. I guess I should have come home earlier." Wade then walked Kicks to an old wooden trough and scooped in a helping of oats, with a little dried molasses, into the box.

"Eat up—then I'll put you back in the corral for water," Wade told his horse while he gently rubbed the white blaze that ran down its face. Hearing a vehicle coming in his road, Wade looked up and saw Sonny's Jeep approaching.

Sonny parked in the shade at the north side of the barn, and then quickly walked over to Wade. Wade could tell something was up.

"Howdy, Sonny. What's going on?"

"Doli was down at the market and bumped into an old friend of hers who works the breakfast shift at the Eagle's Nest Grill. This gal told Doli that early this morning Red Conners was having breakfast there when he got a phone call and left in the middle of his meal. I started listening to the scanner and overheard talk about preparing the police chopper to take Max Pace to Alpine, Texas. I called Jake Bonner, you know, that guy over at the paper who's been on this, he told me that one of the Albuquerque TV stations has already sent a gal out that way and the others are talking about it. Jake said J. Quinton is talking about sending him also."

"What's it all about?" Wade asked.

"According to Jake, the local radio station out there got word that one of the students at their university, a girl from here in Santa Fe, this girl claims she saw Alex Vincent yesterday. That radio station called a station here about mid-morning, and that's what's got all this stirred up.

"Red Conners must have gotten a heads-up from Evelina or something," Sonny continued. "He fled the restaurant about three hours before the radio here knew anything. That'll be a zoo out there—I've been there. There's a nice little airstrip— one over at Marfa too—but not a rental car for a hundred miles. Some enterprising college students should make some spending cash chauffeuring these guys around. What do you think about all of this, Wade?"

"Could be this girl called Evelina herself. If she did, I'd say the FBI has that phone tapped, and they'll be out there by now too. I'll have to make a call to Lollypop. Maybe she can head off anything, if this is for real. You know how stories get twisted and stretched. Hopefully, it's nothing. From the way the Homeland Security Department is handling things at the lab, they may run everyone else out of this and protect Dr. Vincent at all costs. Maybe if he's picked up, they'd believe him and keep Tucker in their protection."

"You can't count on that, Wade," Sonny said. "Too many bodies are in this. What if some local sheriff senses his fifteen minutes of fame, jumps in, and we have another Ruby Ridge?"

Wade slowly nodded his head.

"I've got to go to a pay phone and call Lollypop to leave her word of all of this."

"Yeah, sure. Come on, jump in my Jeep, I'll take you into town."

"Gotta go to the office first and get the number. Let me put Kicks in his corral so he can get some water.

An hour later, Wade had been to town, made the call to Lollypop, and had returned to his ranch. Sonny drove up to the barn, where Wade got out.

"Got classes most of tomorrow, but I'll get an eye on something tomorrow night," Sonny said.

"I'll let you know if I hear of anything," Wade said. "Maybe all the attention will be out there in Texas, and things will be quiet around here."

"Yeah, and it could be this'll just open a can of worms, get this back on the national scene," Sonny said. "If we get CNN and FOX and those other guys crawling around…"

"I'm told the fly fishing is good up below Navajo Lake this time of the year," Wade said. "Might be you and I need to check it out."

"Now you're talkin', Wade. Just say when."

"Say howdy to Doli."

With a wave, Sonny started out the road. Wade took out his bandana and wiped the sweat from his face, then started back to the barn.

★★★

The next day, Sunday, Duce Duval pulled into the small church parking lot, then he walked toward the building only minutes before the service was to begin. Ty Jackson met him at the door and motioned for him to come to his office.

Duce followed him and once inside Ty closed the door then walked over to a window and looked outside. He started speaking without making eye contact with Duce.

"You come straight in?" Ty asked.

"Yeah—why?"

"Then you haven't seen them yet. We're crawling with FBI, New Mexico news people, Santa Fe police, and I don't know who else."

"What?"

"Duce, they're looking for a man and a young boy. They're showing pictures all over town. A girl from Santa Fe, who goes here to Sol Ross University, claims she saw the man—he's that missing code man from the lab over there—and word got out and well..."

There was a moment of silence.

"I'm going to cancel the board meeting on the building expansion—that can easily wait another week. I'll announce that you're going to the orphanage in Chihuahua this week and ask for donations. I'll take up the usual special offering we do for your trips there. Don't be surprised if you're stopped and questioned before you get out of town. Someone said they saw this man and boy in a white pickup at the rodeo."

"Good thing half the vehicles in the area are white pickups," Duce said.

There was another moment of silence, and then Ty turned and started for the door. "I've got to get the service started. Let me know if I can do anything."

"Thanks—thanks for understanding also. We've never really talked..."

"It's best that way, Duce. I trust your judgment."

Duce sat near the back of the sanctuary and only mechanically joined into the numerous worship songs the congregation sang. His mind was on Al and Danny and how he had to get them out of this area to safety.

When it came time for announcements, Reverend Jackson announced the rescheduling of the board meeting. He also announced that in the morning Duce would be making his monthly trip to the orphanage that the church supported down in Chihuahua.

"Last time they said they needed white T-shirts and socks. Of course they can use food items. Duce will be going to the store after lunch, so we'll be taking up an offering to help with that. Anything else you want to give, you can see Duce after the service."

Reverend Jackson stood in silence for a moment. He contemplated what to say, and then he spoke from his heart to his people.

"You've all heard about the excitement around town today. Let me just say that we need to be slow to judge what we don't fully understand. The police are looking for a man who they claim is a fugitive who's taken his child illegally. They want to catch him and take him back and return the child to the mother.

"However, as always there is another side. I don't know which side is right—maybe it's some of both. I've read extensively about this story, and the father claims his son's life is in danger, that the mother is involved in a satanic cult where two other children have turned up missing.

"This much I do know. We need to pray for the safety of this father and son. We must pray that they won't be harmed either while on the run or when they return home."

Duce heard this plea of Ty's, but heard little, if any, of the sermon. He'd had children at the ranch before. The emergency plan had been in place for years—but there hadn't been a need to use it until now. He dared not call Lollypop. No, he must follow the plan just as it was laid out. How many FBI agents were around anyway? What about at the border?

When the service ended, Duce went to lunch at the Rifleman's Grill with Ty and Paula Jackson. They were sitting in the small room off to the east side and had just been served their food when the front door opened and Duce saw the color in Ty's face drain.

"What's wrong?" Duce asked.

"It's that FBI man I talked to yesterday," Ty said in a near whisper.

"It's alright. Just relax," Duce said. He knew they needed to be talking to not be suspicious, so he started talking about the church addition.

Duce unfolded his napkin and started drawing.

"I looked over the plans you left out at the ranch. Is there any way we can cut down on the hallway space going back to the new Sunday school rooms? What about laying that part out like this? See, if we move the entryway over here, then we just have a small foyer with all the doors coming together right there."

"I see," Ty said. "By adding a second door, we could also pick up space over here," he pointed to the new kitchen area.

Duce felt someone behind him. Ty looked up at the man who'd come to their table.

"Officer Miller, isn't it? We met yesterday. I'm Reverend Ty Jackson."

"Sure, Reverend, I remember. I'm still out showing these pictures and asking questions. I hate to interrupt your lunch, but—"

"Oh, that's fine. This is my wife Paula and one of our board members, Duce Duval. Duce lives on a ranch way out yonder and we don't get to see him that often. We're just brainstorming some ideas for a new addition."

"Mrs. Jackson, Mr. Duval," agent Miller said nodding to each. "I see. Napkin architecture," he said, looking at Duce's drawing. "Many a good idea has had its conception on a napkin or placemat." He then laid the pictures of Dr. Vincent and his son on the table.

"Don't suppose you've seen these two?"

"I've heard you're here looking for them. Are they in town?" Duce asked.

"A girl at the college, she's from Santa Fe, she claims she spotted the father at the library. Nobody else there is sure it was him, but then nobody else knows him either. Couple of people think they might have seen them at the rodeo Friday night."

"Lots of strangers at rodeos," Duce said. "There were people from Oklahoma, New Mexico and I even saw one truck from Colorado. Cowboys come in, so do their friends. In a crowd, they all look alike. I'd notice the regulars, people I know, but I'm not one to mind strangers, unless they need help or something."

Agent Miller picked up the pictures.

"Pretty hard to hide around here. You're right. If that really was Dr. Vincent this girl saw, he could have come here from miles away and be back there now. Still, there's a bunch of rocks around here we haven't turned over yet. Best get going. Thanks, folks."

Duce kept his eyes on his plate for a moment, and then he picked up his pen and pointed back to the napkin.

"Where would you put that other door?" he asked Ty. "Code requires that we have two." Out of the corner of his eye he watched agent Miller at the table next to them. Duce and Ty aimlessly talked on while Paula sat in silence. Duce knew she was troubled. When agent Miller left, Duce balled up his napkin and pushed back his chair.

"Gotta get over to the Dollar Store and get those T-shirts and socks."

After paying the bill, they walked out to Ty's car. Riding back to the church where Duce had left his truck, Duce spoke to Paula.

"Don't be so stressed, Paula. I'm sorry you know anything—though you know very little. Everyone will be fine."

"I know you will, Duce. It's that little boy. He's so precious. I knew something was up, but…." She was silent for several minutes.

"He seemed so happy to be with his dad. If his mother is in that cult…."

When she didn't go on, Duce spoke to her.

"The authorities only have the law to follow—that's their job. There are times when the law and real life conflict. That's when I believe we have to move in the higher law, the law of loving our neighbor and helping those in need, even at risk to ourselves. Maybe I'm wrong, but I don't believe so."

"I don't either, Duce," Paula said. "But isn't there some other way?"

"I don't know. Sometimes you just have to stick your neck out."

★★★

While filling his cart in the children's clothing section of the small discount store, Duce overheard two men in the next aisle.

"Hey, Red Conners, what are you doing here? Don't tell me—Evelina didn't send you, did she?"

"Who else, Max? Who else would be so interested in this they'd send me here? I didn't even take time to pack right. Gotta buy a toothbrush and paste, razors too. I thought the FBI was handling this. The city send you?"

"I, ah—it was my decision," Max Pace said. "The heat's really on this case."

"Seems to me the heat is more on the other two kid cases. Surely, you've been reading the newspaper," Red said.

"I think old J. Quinton will zip up on this now," Max said, while he looked at the shampoo. "Anyway, this kid is still alive, the other two—"

"Sounds like you know something you've not made public, Max."

"Watch it, Red. I'm only saying—"

"You're saying plenty, Max. No wonder Evelina's afraid you'll crack. You're getting on her bad list, Max old boy. That's not a list I'd want to be on."

"Look, I don't know why you're here. I can handle anything that comes up," Max said. "It's my job—"

"What happened to Luke Lane? Thought he was on this case."

"None of your business, Red."

"Speaking of business, what are you doing for wheels here?" Red asked. "I drove out, but I saw the city chopper coming in. I assume that was you."

"Had to buy a car," Max said. "The guy promised he'd buy it back for a grand less than I paid. That's mighty close to extortion, but what could I do?"

"I'd like to be a mouse in the corner when you present that bill, or are Evelina and company going to pay it?" Red asked.

"Just because you're on her dole—"

"Ya, got me on that one Max. Hey, I gotta go. Probably see you around."

Duce slowly filled his cart with all the T-shirts and socks in the children's section. He waited until both Max and Red were gone, and then went to the candy aisle.

For the next hour, rolling slowly down the many miles of pavement, then gravel road, back to the ranch, Duce's mind was occupied with what he had to do. He rationalized doing nothing. What chance was there that anyone would ever make it out to his ranch? Little to none—but still, if they did, well, no way was the risk worth it. What about the crossing? With several ways to do it, which one would be best? He was still deep in thought when he pulled up to his headquarters.

Al heard Duce's truck come in the road. He watched him park it in the shade and go inside his house. In only minutes, he heard Duce's boots thumping on the wooden porch at the front of their bungalow. When Duce knocked on the door Al quickly went to answer it.

"Hello, Duce—you made it back from town. We were just playing checkers. You know, with no TV or such."

Duce said nothing but walked right in and sat at the battered old kitchen table. He put his elbows on the table and held his head in his hands. He reached up and took off his hat and set it brim up on the table, then leaned back in his chair. Al waited for Duce to begin the conversation.

"Well, might as well cut to the chase," Duce finally said. "Someone spotted you at the university Friday. Some girl from Santa Fe."

Al reached out and took hold of a chair. He pulled it out from the table and slumped onto it. He looked over at his son, who'd crawled up on a rocking chair.

"There're more FBI and strange cops in town than anyone's ever seen—news people too. The FBI questioned me at a restaurant. At the store, I ran into someone named Max, who was talking to another fella named Red Conners. I've never had this happen before. Don't know what's so all fired important that the FBI is here."

Red Conners! Al knew him to be a celebrity private investigator in Santa Fe. He'd cracked a kidnapping case involving the child of one of the Hollywood actors who lived there. *Evelina must have hired him. He's good. If he's around here...*

"It's me," Al said after gathering his thoughts. "It's what I'm working on. They want me back at work very badly. I'm doing all I can out here, but..."

All were silent for several minutes. Then Al started asking questions.

"So, what do we do? Do we have somewhere else to go to? Is it safe to move?"

"Yeah, there's a plan in place to move you. Safe? I don't know what's worse, hiding you here or moving you on. No, that's not right—I've got to move you. It's nearly four hours to the crossing. We need to be there before daylight. That's about six. We need to leave about two o'clock to be safe. They're watching white pickups. I'll take my gold Suburban."

There was another moment of silence, then Duce pushed back his chair and spoke again. "I've said 'bout enough. Don't leave anything behind that might tell on you—like notes or anything else with handwriting. Well, rest up now. Get anything of yours out of that truck you've been using. I'll have food and water for our trip. Guess that's all. See you at two then."

Al nodded, rose and walked Duce to the door. When he'd left, Al went over to the sofa and dropped to it. He felt his son looking at him, but didn't feel like talking. Duce was going out on a limb for him. This man could lose everything, even go to jail. Yet he did all of this willingly. What was it that led, pushed or even drove a man like Duce to care so much for strangers? Finally, Al looked at his son.

"What do you think, partner? That's how they'd say it out here, isn't it?"

"Think so, Dad. Don't know nothin'. I just get to liking things, and the people, and—we gotta move on. I wanna go home. Can't we just go home?"

"No—no we can't. I guess I love you too much to put you back into that."

"Yeah. It's OK, Dad. Guess really I'm havin' the best time of my life. You're my dad, for real. I don't miss mom—it's just other things."

★★★

They'd driven for nearly four hours and the hint of yellow on the horizon behind them indicated daylight was soon approaching. Ahead, the lights on the horizon announced they were nearing a town. Danny had slept most of the way—at least since they'd been on pavement and not bouncing over the rough ranch roads. Duce and Al had said little, but now Duce started talking.

"It's best if Danny stays sleeping, or at least pretends to be asleep. The line should be short. I know most of these guys. Hopefully, we'll go right through. Things have gotten a bit more intense lately, with all the drug turf wars and all in the areas west of here. Juárez and El Paso crossings are a mess. The same over in Arizona, too. There hasn't been much of that trouble here— not yet, anyway.

"Here's our story," Duce went on. "We're on our way to an orphanage in Chihuahua, which we are. If asked, you're a doctor, a physician. You're going to help these poor orphans. All those bags back there have things for the orphanage. I do this about once a month, but usually alone."

Duce drove across the streets of Presidio towards a bridge and group of large lights ahead.

"Well, this is it. God help us."

The line in front of them was six cars deep. One car went through. They inched forward. Then another one was waved through. Suddenly, a car came around them and quickly pulled into the official parking lot. The man got out and looked back across the line of cars.

"No!" Duce cried out. "That's Miller, the FBI agent I met in Alpine."

Chapter 15

"Dad! What's goin' on, Dad?" Danny quizzed from the back seat.

"Stay down, Son. Pretend you're sleeping. It's really important," Al said.

"These windows are heavily tinted. It's still pretty dark outside. Be hard to see anything in here," Duce said. "Maybe he'll go—oh no, he's coming this way. I'll stare at the agent ahead. You read this." He tossed Al a Texas Cattleman's magazine that had been lying on the seat between them.

Agent Miller moved over to the line of traffic, then started walking back, right toward them. A car pulled through the checkpoint. Duce let his foot off the brake, and the Suburban slowly inched forward. He had to stop just when agent Miller reached Al's door. At that instant, the FBI agent stopped, then turned toward the guardhouse. One of the Mexican agents had yelled something to him. Al watched Miller reach into his inside coat pocket and pull out his badge, then flash it at the border agent.

"FBI—agent Miller," he yelled.

The border agent nodded, and then went back inside to his desk. Miller put his badge back in his pocket. He turned and looked back at the line of waiting traffic. He started on back the line. Al breathed easier as he watched agent Miller in the side mirror. Reaching a white pickup truck, Miller started talking to its occupants.

"Thank God for that white truck," Duce said. "Otherwise he might have started at the front and gone right through the line." Another car went through the gate—Duce drifted forward. Now only one car and one pickup were ahead of him.

Al watched agent Miller in his mirror.

"Miller's gone on back," he said once the agent left the white pickup.

"Yeah, two more—now one," Duce said when the pickup was waved on through. He eased up behind the car ahead.

"Oh no," Al said. "Miller's coming back up our way."

"Come on! This is no time for a friendly chat," Duce said while he watched the border guard and the driver of the car laughing about something. One of the cars at the back of the line blew its horn. The border guard looked up, and then motioned for the car to go on through. Duce pulled up to the gate.

"Good morning, Señor. You all United States Citizens?"

"Yes sir," Duce said, Al nodded, and then looked back into the mirror. Miller was only two cars back and coming right toward them.

"Your business in Mexico today?" The border agent asked.

"Going down to the orphanage in Chihuahua. I go every month."

"Sí. Me know you, Señor. Theese is a mucho good thing you do. Geeve my best to the poor leetle ones. Bless you, Señor." With that he stepped back and looked at the next vehicle. Duce eased on the gas and pulled away just when agent Miller reached his back bumper.

"That was close," Al said.

"Too close," Duce replied. "I wasn't expecting that."

"So that's all there is to it? Just like that we're in Mexico?" Al asked.

"Well, if we were going to stay here in Ojinaga, yes. For us, there'll be another checkpoint about an hour down in. That's where you need your paperwork. That one could be some trouble."

"Trouble?" Al asked.

"Yeah, your computer. You'll have to convince them that it's coming back out with you. You can't take in a used computer and leave it."

"Oh, what do I do?" Al asked.

"You're a doctor and all your resource books are in there." "Ah—" Al stammered. "I guess that might work. As I see it though, that's not quite true, I thought, well, you being a church person, a God believer and all that—"

"Look, here's the way I see things like this," Duce cut in. "God commanded man not to bear false witness. That means I'm not to tell an untruth that would in any way hurt you, or anyone else. You know, something that would wrongly get you into any trouble or cast you in a bad light to others. It wouldn't matter if I was out to harm you or out to help myself get out of some wrong I've done. Either way, telling something to hurt someone else is wrong. There's more to it than that; however, that's the general intent, as I see things.

"The Bible is full of people being less than totally honest while doing something good, doing something to help someone in need, and I can't think of any reprimand from God. King David feigned lunacy, Moses told Pharaoh he wanted to take the people out to the desert for three days to worship. Then there was Rahab, who hid the spies and lied about it. Paul's friends hid him and lied also.

"Then think of all those in Europe who hid Jews from the Nazis. They saved thousands of lives, but often had to be untruthful to do it. Was that good or bad? To me, God's a whole lot more practical than many people think. If I'm wrong, well, I reck'n he'll forgive me. He hasn't given me any one-on-one instructions, just a mission to get done. I'm doing the best I can. I'm a rancher try'n to do the Lord's work. Ain't some fancy preacher or Bible scholar."

"I never heard anyone talk like that before, at least not one of you God people," Al said. "I thought you'd say that telling a story like this would be something that would send someone straight to hell. I see what you're saying though. Guess I've got some false ideas about what all of you people really believe."

"Well, not everyone would agree with me. However, most who'd argue the loudest ain't doing nothing but talk. I'm out here doing all I can. I don't know how else I'm to protect you and your son from harm."

Al said nothing more while he pondered this. It made sense— it just wasn't what he expected. Would Carla feel the same way? He'd have to ask her if he ever got back to the lab.

"Tell, me, Duce—maybe I'm getting too personal—but I'm curious what you get out of any of this? Whatever got you started?"

"Ain't too personal," Duce said. "'Spect you got a right to know. Just remember though, you asked, so don't go and accuse me of preaching, or the like. It goes back to when I rodeo'd full- time. Money was rolling in and we had us one constant party. Vicki—she was my wife back then—she tried to get me to settle down, but I was on top of my world.

"Then late one night we lit out of Durango. Vicki begged me to let her drive. It's strange, when sober I'd let her drive. When I was drunk, nobody drove but me." Duce said nothing for a moment, and then continued. "Missed a curve and rolled that truck and trailer all the way to the bottom of that canyon. Buried Vicki and little Bradley three days later." Again Duce was silent for several moments. Al then asked another question.

"So that's when you started your God thing?"

"I'd never thought about God much up 'til then," Duce said. "Never thought I needed him. I'd been a success at everything from football to bulls. I sure thought about God after the accident. I hated him so much that if I could have gotten my hands on him, I'd have killed him barehanded. Guess it was denial that it was really me to blame. God was an easy target to hate."

"What changed that?" Al asked after another spell of silence.

"I was drinkin' more than ever. Only then instead of being the life of the party when drunk, then I just got mean, and wanted to strike out at whatever or whoever got near. Some weeks I slept more nights in jail than home or anywhere else. One morning I woke up out in the desert outside of Tucson. I had no idea how I'd gotten there, or at the time even where I was. I was sick— sick and fed up. Guess I'd reached my bottom.

"I lay out there in that hot sand all day. I decided I wasn't leaving there until I decided once and for all whether I wanted to live, or if I just wanted to give up and die. I'd been halfway between living and dying for nearly two years at that point. I lay out there until the sun went down that night. I'd gotten mighty thirsty by then. All I had was half a six-pack of warm beer. The beer was on the back floor—right beside my shotgun. Finally, I took one of those cans and popped the top, turned it over, and watched it empty out on the sand. Then I did the same to the others. Took that shotgun and pumped out the shells. I got in the truck and started following my tracks out of the desert. Out there, all alone and broken, I'd made my peace with God—I've never looked back."

"Just like that?" Al asked.

"Yeah. 'Spect you know how it is. I'd had a dozen or more people talk to me about God and Jesus through the years, but I only half listened. It never seemed important—wasn't for me. Must have heard enough though that some of it stuck somewhere in my mind. Through the years, I'd seen several guys radically change, but I never believed they really wanted to live like they were then. I figured they still missed their old hell-raising, and they were just being martyrs, trying to fix their guilt or something.

"But something happened, deep down inside me out there," Duce went on slowly. "Before I got to town I had to stop and cry like a baby for what must have been an hour or more. I'd held so much inside that had to come out. Some things took a long time to let loose—others were gone that night."

Al looked out the window while they climbed up the side of a mountain. The drop was several hundred feet and there was no guardrail. He closed his eyes. What Duce had told him kept rolling through his mind.

It's all emotions. It's only God in Duce's mind. Yeah, he had some radical experience out in that desert. That doesn't give any proof it was God. Duce is just like all the others; he's deceived by his own thoughts and desires, that's all.

"Hey, Dad. Can I sit up yet?" Danny asked from the back seat.

"Oh, yeah, sure Son. You have a good sleep?"

"Long time ago. Just been layin' back here listening. When's that next check point thing?"

"It's just ahead," Duce said. "Maybe it won't be open yet this morning, and we can go right through. If not, be prepared to hand over some money."

"Money? You mean bribe money?" Al asked.

"Call it what you want. In the States, when you think about it, we tax nearly everything a man does. You pay taxes and permit fees daily to the big government and they then filter a little of it down to the guy on the street— the guy making it all work. Here in Mexico there isn't nearly as much legal money confiscation, as I like to call our tax system. Of what there is, almost none gets to the little guy doing all the work, so these guys come up with their own compensation. I think it sounds a lot worse than it really is. Maybe our system is better, maybe not. At least here you see who's getting your money, and you know what for."

There was another period of silence, then Duce rounded a bend, and there up ahead was the checkpoint—it was open. No one said anything while he drove up to the line. Only two cars were in front of them. The agents walked around. Each checked inside the trunks then waved each on. When Duce pulled up the agent looked at him.

"Sí, Señor. Ah, the orphan gringo, no?"

"Your memory is good, Officer. That's where I'm going. The young one back there wants to visit it, and this is a doctor who is to examine one of the children at the hospital," Duce said, nodding toward Al.

"What have you in those bags today? What you take today to the children?"

"T-shirts, socks—some candy of course," Duce said. "One of the ladies sent some towels and sheets."

The agent nodded and looked casually in the bags. He reached into a bag full of candy bars, tore open a package and took out a Snickers bar.

"Mucho good," he said as he ripped open the wrapper and took a bite. Then he pointed to the computer case. "Computer?"

"The doctor's. His notes and things. To help the sick boy."

"No computer, Señor. You know you can't take that."

"I must have it—all my notes—all my work," Al said.

"Then you take it back home?" The agent asked.

"Yes, I have to. I can't leave all this down here," Al said.

The agent nodded. "Then what you need is a permit, sí, Señor?"

"Sure, I just need a permit. Where—"

"Permit will cost you $50.00, American. Being a doctor, you should be able to afford that permit, sí?" The agent reached his hand out. Al looked at Duce, who nodded affirmative. Al took out his wallet and removed a fifty-dollar bill, then handed it to the agent.

"You now have your permit, Señor Doctor. Make sure you make good use of it."

"Gracias," Duce said as he quickly got back into the driver's seat and started the engine. "Let's go," Duce said softly. "He could have asked for a lot more. I don't want him to change his mind."

★★★

Early Monday morning Wade Hawkins pulled into his office parking lot where he found FBI agents Huck Miles and Sig Simpson waiting for him. He got out of his truck, leaned against it, and waited for them to come to him.

"Morning, Hawkins," Huck said. "If we ask really nice, can we go and talk in your office?"

"Since you asked like a gentleman, yeah, come on."

Wade led them back to his office where he motioned for the two agents to have a seat. He went around to all the windows and opened the blinds, letting in the bright sun. Sitting in his chair, he picked up a pen and laid it on top of a pad.

"What's up, guys?"

"Ya gotta help us, Hawkins," Huck Miles said. "This has gone on long enough. You've made your point. Bring that code- man back, and we'll investigate his claims with his child."

"That's not a federal case," Wade said. "Since when is child endangerment on your agenda?"

"We'll go at it from a Civil Rights angle, or something," Huck said. "We'll work that out."

Wade looked at his visitors. He sensed they were under a lot of pressure.

"Why aren't you two out in Texas?" Wade asked. "I hear that's where all the action is. You afraid someone else will get the glory on this—the promotion?"

"Come on, Hawkins," Huck Miles said. "You've got a bad attitude toward the Bureau."

"You guys have brought that on yourselves," Wade said. "Through the years there have been too many broken promises, and too many botched cases. Look, with this case I don't know what else I can tell you. I've been straight with you. I don't know where they are. I don't want to know. I don't want to know anything about it."

"You can find out. You've got the contacts who will tell you," Huck said.

"I don't think they would. Secrecy is the name of their game. You play it their way, or you don't play."

"Look, Hawkins, you know that with us you'll be safe. I don't know about anyone else around here. You know as much about some of those involved as we do. They could be dangerous. For your safety, come in with us."

"I share and appreciate your concerns, Huck. I'm committed to the safety of young Tucker Vincent. If I caved in to you on this, my reputation would be ruined. I'd face ethics charges by the bar and everything else."

"You make it sound as if helping us would be worse than what you've already done." Huck said.

"It would be."

"All right, Hawkins. You've got a point. I don't like it, but you got your point. Look, if they don't find them out in Texas and Max Pace gets back here, well, I think he's going to be desperate," Huck said.

Wade nodded his head. "Like you are?" he asked. "Pressure can lead to poor decisions. Be careful. Look, someone's got to tie those other two missing kids into one case and solve whatever happened to them. Otherwise—"

"Ain't going to happen, Hawkins," Huck cut in. "Nobody's working that angle. Unless someone stumbles onto something, that's all buried and forgotten."

"Don't give up, Huck," Wade said. "I've got a feeling the truth is all going to jump right out for all to see someday. You don't want to miss it."

★★★

Several hours after leaving the last checkpoint, Duce drove the Suburban up the dirt drive to a cluster of mud and stucco covered adobe buildings. The corrugated steel roofs were rusting badly, and there were several open holes in the crumbling walls where windows had once been.

"What's the story on this?" Al asked.

"It's not much. A local church started it about thirty years ago, but couldn't keep it going. One of the members up at our church in Alpine has some family here. We got word of the plight of these kids, and we've been helping for many years now. A few years back several of us dumped quite a chunk of money into drilling a new well and putting in enough bathrooms for this crowd. Last year we put in a new kitchen. Windows and roofs are next. Not much English is spoken here, so I'll have to keep you up to speed on what's going on. Look at that," Duce nodded toward the string of children running towards them. "We've been discovered."

The children swarmed around them, jumping and screaming happily, Al saw Danny point to a child in a wheelchair being pushed by another boy.

"What's his story?" Al asked nodding to the wheelchair bound boy.

"That's Pedro. Every time I come here, I wonder if I'll still find him here. Poor little guy's in so much pain. He's all broken up inside. His liver is diseased and his kidneys are about gone. Who knows what else? The doctors don't seem to care much about treating these kids, even though we pay all the bills. Dialysis would most likely help, but—

"He's not the only one with a debilitating illness here," Duce continued. "In fact, you'd be hard pressed to find one of these little ones who doesn't have something seriously wrong with them. They're throw-a-way kids. Take Pedro. His father stabbed his mother and threw her off a second story balcony. He then threw Pedro off there too. He might well have died if he hadn't landed on top of his dead mother. His father was sent to prison where he got killed in a fight. No one else wanted Pedro.

"Come on, let's get out those new shirts and socks," Duce said. "Looks as if they surely do need them."

Al sat somewhat dazed even after Duce got out.

"Dad—Hey Dad, am I gonna have to live like these kids?" Danny asked.

"I don't know Son. I really don't know what to expect. Whatever, it's better than jail."

Al and Danny helped Duce carry the bags of clothes and other things over toward the small office building. A woman, apparently hearing the commotion, came out when they got near. She ran and hugged Duce, then moved to Al and threw her arms around him. Then she dropped down to one knee and hugged Danny, kissing him on the cheek. Her excitement equaled that of the children.

"This is Rosetta, guys. She is the nuts and bolts of this place," Duce said. "There are lots of people who help her, but this was her idea. Vision may be more like it, and she makes it all happen. Come on, we've got a little trip to make."

Leaving the bags of things with Rosetta, they walked back to the Suburban. Some of the children followed, laughing and shouting with happiness neither Al nor Danny understood. Once inside the Suburban and driving toward the road, Al asked Duce a question.

"Are they really that happy for just getting those T-shirts and socks?" Al asked. "That can't be."

"Mostly. Of course they know we're on our way to the local McDonald's here—a little bit of the states. We'll bring each one back one of those special kids' meals and a chocolate shake. That's a big deal to them."

"That's no big deal," Danny said. "You mean they don't ever get to go there themselves? We're near a town, right? Then they've gotta have TV and video games. It's not like out at the ranch."

"'Fraid not, Danny. Most of them have never seen a TV, or even know what an electronic game is. We're talking poor kids here. I had plans of really doing something here, and then the drought wiped out most of my grass and I had to sell most of my herd. What I make on my rodeo horse stock hardly keeps my ranch going these days. It's going to turn around, though. Then I'll be able to make this a first class place."

Driving through the streets of the city, Al looked around for a public building where he might find internet access. He spotted a library. On down the street he saw the familiar golden arches of the McDonald's.

Must have been thirty kids there. Meals and shakes for all of them?

Once back at the orphanage and sitting in the noisy mess room, with all the kids behaving as if it was Christmas, Al looked over at his son. He saw that Danny was watching Pedro. The wheelchair bound boy was doing his best to eat his burger and drink his shake. Soon the others had finished eating and were outside playing. Pedro sat alone in his wheelchair at the end of a table. Danny walked over to him and sat down. Neither boy said anything. Pedro handed his little bag of fries to Danny. Danny shook his head no.

"It takes Pedro a long time to eat, Danny," Duce said. "I hear he's a good checkers player. You want to play checkers with him?"

"Sure," Danny said. "Where's the board. I'll get it set up."

Duce got the game out of the closet, and by the time Danny had the game setup, Pedro had finished his meal, all but some of his shake. The two boys started playing, and soon they were laughing as if they'd been doing it for years.

Al moved a chair outside to a spot of shade on the north side of the building. Duce walked over to the office with Rosetta. He came back to Al in a few minutes.

"I'll get us some rooms over at el Sonora motel. It's a good safe place. I need to call Lollypop and let her know what's happened. She's most likely heard of the scare in Texas. I'm sure she'll be greatly relieved that we're here. I'll stay with you until your contact picks you up. That shouldn't be but a day or so," Duce looked out over the playground for a minute.

"I'll be back for supper. It's tacos tonight. I'll bring out ten dozen, and I'll bet not a one is left."

"Ten dozen?" Al asked. "You need help? How about some money?"

"Things aren't quite that bad—not yet. Thanks anyway. Hey, Pedro might get tired before long. He usually takes a nap after lunch."

"I'll keep an eye on him and be here when you get back," Al said. *I couldn't go anywhere if I wanted,* he thought while Duce walked away.

Al sat on his chair in the shade and watched the kids kick an old ball around in the dusty play lot. Inside, Danny and Pedro continued to play checkers. Al leaned back against the wall and closed his eyes. Last night's few hours of sleep and the long drive this morning were catching up with him. Just when he dozed off, Al was startled by a cry from inside the building. Several of the older boys came running toward them. Al jumped up and rushed to the door. Inside, Pedro sat with his head down on the table, cries of pain flowing from his mouth.

"I didn't do nothin', Dad," Danny said. "He just dropped his head and started cryin'."

"He's in pain, Son. It's got nothing to do with your playing with him."

"Señor, we take. We take to his room," one of the boys, the only one who seemed to know any English, said as they lifted Pedro's head and started pushing his old wheelchair toward the door.

"That was scary, Dad," Danny said while watching the boys push Pedro toward one of the old buildings. "Pedro's real sick, isn't he?"

"I'd say he's very sick. There's no free care down here for the really poor, not like we have. Being sick like he is, no one could get him into the states—not legally. I guess they just let poor, sick people die."

"Even kids, Dad?"

"Yeah, I guess even kids."

"That ain't good," Danny said.

"Actually it's this way in much of the world, Son. America is very special."

★★★

Duce was right. Half an hour after the tacos were carried in, the boxes were all empty.

"I don't know about you guys, but I'm about ready to call it a day," Duce said.

"Me too," Al said. "I hope tomorrow I can do some work. I saw a library up the street from the McDonald's. Maybe tomorrow afternoon you can take me there."

"The motel is just over on the next street. You can easily walk there. As far as I know, it's safe to walk the streets here yet. So far no one's killed any Americans here, or attacked the police like some of the other towns. I 'spect you'll be going west and up into Arizona. You best keep your head down and eyes searching for trouble when you get out that way. Darned shame what's come over this country. Won't be long until it spills over the border, I 'spect."

Duce was silent for a moment, then he got his mind back to the orphanage. "While you're at the library, I'll come over here and fix a few things in the morning, so that will work out good," Duce said, then changed the subject. "I heard Pedro got sick. Poor little fella. I'll try to get a doctor out here tomorrow."

"Can't anyone do something?" Danny asked.

"I've tried, but I can't get him to the states. Last month I contacted several of the big TV ministries, ones that have medical units. Maybe one of them will come through. I'm afraid I've waited too long. Maybe I missed what I was supposed to do. Maybe I wouldn't face the obvious soon enough. If I'd have gotten serious back a year ago…"

"Look, Duce, I'd say anything you could do would be only a short term extension. I think there's damage inside that poor boy that nothing can fix. Maybe if he'd have been operated on right away—"

"It was over two years after his beating when he showed up here. I guess in my heart, I know there's no hope, nothing but a miracle."

A miracle? Come on Duce, you're smarter than that.

★★★

The next day Al rose late. Danny sat looking out the motel window.

"Morning, Dad. You sure were sleeping. You hungry?"

"Huh—don't know yet, but I'd say you were. What do you have in mind?"

"That McDonald's is just over on the next block, remember? I could go for some pancakes."

"OK, I guess they have the same breakfast menu down here. We'll find out anyway."

An hour later they were back at the room. Al got out his electric adapters for his computer and found the right one for the local current. Danny turned on the TV, and lay on his bed watching it, even though all the programming was in Spanish. Duce showed up late in the afternoon.

"I'm hungry. How about we go over to this little cantina I know and get something to eat?" Duce asked.

"Sounds good. I'll come back and work some more later, then go over to that library in the morning," Al said.

"We won't be too late. I promised Rosetta I'd bring ice cream out to the kids tonight," Duce said. "That won't take long though."

"How's Pedro," Danny asked.

"Not good, unfortunately. He's in a fit of pain much of the time. Rosetta tells me he's rapidly getting worse. This is extremely hard on her. She's really taken to Pedro—everyone has really."

The two, three gallon buckets of ice cream were nearly empty—the chocolate one was scraped clean and the vanilla one had less than a pint in it, when Duce suggested they go back to the motel.

"I'm tired and really need to get to bed," Duce said when he rose from the table.

Al and Danny followed him to the Suburban, and by the time they got to the motel, Al had to carry Danny to the room.

Al worked until midnight, then, not able to think clearly, he had to turn in. He rose at daylight the next day and was working away when Danny awoke.

"Beat you up this morning," he said to his son.

"Yeah, Dad. I sure got tired last night."

"Give me about an hour, and I'll be ready to go to the library—breakfast too."

"Good, Dad. I'll just turn on this TV. Maybe I can figure out some of what they're saying."

Back at the motel around noon, Al took a break from studying the data he'd gotten earlier from Carla when he'd been at the library. He closed his eyes and was nearly asleep when there came a knock at his door. He sat up quickly. He looked at his son and saw fear in his eyes.

"Who is it?" Al asked while he walked to the door.

"Open up, Al. It's me, Alice."

"Alice!" Danny screamed. Al opened the door and she stepped inside. Danny wrapped his arms around her and held on tight.

"We goin' back to the Circle B?" Danny asked.

"'Fraid not, but I am your ride out of Mexico," Alice said. "I don't see any of Duce's vehicles. Guess he's over at the orphanage."

"Yeah," Al said. "He's working over there."

"Let me get a room," Alice said, "then we'll go see him."

Half an hour later, Alice drove out to the orphanage. When she pulled up to the office, she pointed over to the row of bunk-rooms.

"There's Duce. He's carrying someone."

"It's Pedro," Danny said. "Why's Duce carrying Pedro, Dad?"

"Oh no," Alice said. "Not now, please."

Chapter 16

An hour after Nita had gone home for the day; Wade Hawkins sat alone in his office. The door opened and Sonny stuck his head through the opening.

"You in here Wade?"

"Come on in and sit a spell, Sonny. Want a soda or something?" Wade asked.

"I'll just get some water, thanks," Sonny said.

Glass in hand, Sonny sat on one of the client chairs at the front of Wade's desk, then he stretched out his legs. "What do you hear from all that excitement out in Texas?" he asked.

"Not much," Wade said. "I hear Max Pace is back home. J. Quinton called and told me the trail, if it ever was anything, had gone cold. Most likely all the dogs will be back sniffing around here all too soon. What do you hear out and about?"

"Not much here either, Wade. I did park across from Rhea Thatcher's car the other day. When she came out after work she looked at me and shook her fist. Then she got into her car and buried her head in her hands. I think she was sobbing. I left.

Maybe I should have gone over and talked to her, but with us being on school property, I didn't want to start anything."

"When she's ready, she'll come around," Wade said. "What about Sally Browning? Is she doing any better?"

"No. She won't let me in her house. The last two times I've stopped it's been late afternoon, and she's still in a robe—looking much like a ghost. I've asked if I can do anything, but she just seems to be in a fog. She scares me Wade. She's so fragile. You know, she's one I really feel sorry for."

"Mother says the same thing," Wade said. "The last time she went there she was sure Sally was inside, but she wouldn't answer the door. Why don't you talk to some of her neighbors? Maybe someone can help keep up some contact with her. Surely, she has family somewhere she could turn to."

"Yeah, maybe someone else will care. Her husband was a veteran; you think they might have something for a widow like her?" Sonny asked.

"Good idea. I'll have Mother check that out tomorrow. Maybe county mental health would make a call."

"Yeah, maybe. I just hate to get any local government involved. Ya just don't know who's who," Sonny said.

"It's really easy to get cynical, isn't it? Maybe some of the younger ladies at church would go see her and break through that wall she's built up. I think tomorrow's the woman's mid-week, morning meeting. I'll mention this to Mother tonight. I can't think of a more worthy project right now," Wade said.

Sonny drank the last of his water, then got up and refilled the glass. When he returned to his chair, he changed the subject.

"I'm thinking about heading up to the Pecos while things seem to be in a lull here. Might even spend a night or two up there. There aren't that many roads and places where a large group of cars can get into."

"The Pecos? Be careful," Wade said. "Maybe I should go and take care of you at night."

"Ah, Wade. You'd have run just as fast as I did if you had bullets flying over your head. It's got nothing to do with any fear of dying at night. That's just old Apache bunk. You know I don't believe any of that."

"No fear of wandering the hereafter in darkness forever, never finding the way into Apache paradise?" Wade asked, with half a smile.

"How'd any group of people start to believe a wacky idea such as that? What could have happened to start that belief?" Sonny asked.

"It's hard to figure," Wade said. "Study that stuff too much and one can end up like Evelina Vincent. I'm told that's how she first got interested in the supernatural, the dark supernatural. Look where she's ended up."

"I've heard that too, but then I've also heard that her mother was into Satanism out in the corn fields of Iowa. I read a book once that claimed there's more of that junk out there than in most any big city. The lady who wrote it had lived there for several years. Some of her stories and claims made me shiver," Sonny said.

"I think it's everywhere," Wade said. "It's just the times we're living in."

Sonny nodded. "Hey, you hear anything about the Homeland Security Department offering a bunch of money to anyone who stops some new terrorist thing? I hear that's what Dr. Vincent and his group are working on at the lab. Someone said Secretary Kingston is going to go on TV real soon and make some announcement."

"Yeah, J. Quinton mentioned he's been told that's coming. That doesn't sound good. That will put panic into a lot of folks. I know Dr. Vincent was, still is I guess, working on something really sensitive," Wade said. "Bill Hunter says Carla's never home. He's worried that with Dr. Vincent being gone, she's taken on too much responsibility. Whatever is going on, it must be really serious."

"Well, I don't think I'll be able to stop any terrorist thing, so I'll get to work and see if Red Conners is back from Texas," Sonny said. "I'll check on good old Evelina, and drive by Max's house too. Maybe I'll find Luke

Lane there. He sure seems worried about his boss. You know Lane's been yanked off all of this?"

"Yeah," Wade said. "He can't be too happy."

"He's only inches from being on our side. Just a little nudge. When the right time comes, I'll give it," Sonny said, and then he rose and took his glass to the sink. "See you tomorrow, unless I go to the mountains. I'll call you if I do."

"Careful, Sonny," Wade said. "Things seem a little calm now. That can be very dangerous."

"Yeah. I've thought the same myself."

★★★

Several hours after Duce had brought Pedro's body down to Rosetta's office for the other children at the orphanage to have a final goodbye; Al was back at the motel trying to work. He couldn't stay focused. He turned to his son.

"What are you thinking?" he asked Danny

"Oh, nothin'."

"I thought maybe you were thinking about Pedro."

"Yeah. When Duce put him up on that table, with all the other kids crying, I cried too, Dad. I don't know why he died. I just met him, but I know he was a very good kid. How could he be anything else in that wheelchair? Why'd he die, Dad?"

"I don't know, Son. I don't have any answer."

"What now, Dad? Once Pedro's dead, where is he? Some people believe we go to another place, but I don't know. Do you know, Dad?"

Al leaned back and closed his eyes. "I don't think anything can be proven. I don't know how anyone could. What test would you use to know if some intangible part of a person went somewhere in another realm? Yet, the belief of some of these people is so strong…

"I sometimes think they know something I don't, but they can't prove it," Al went on. "Some of these people talk as if they actually know what they believe is real. I usually have an answer for you, Son, this time I'm pretty vague. I never before cared to know what these people believe. Guess now, as part of all this strangeness we're living, I'm getting curious, a little anyway."

"You're as mixed up as me," Danny said. "Don't know if I should be feelin' sorry for Pedro. Ya know, him bein' always in that wheelchair and sick and all. He couldn't do like the rest of us. If he's in some new place, and he's like everyone else, then he's better now. I was thinking, sorta pretending I guess, that maybe Pedro is now playing with Kreg and little Melissa. Could he be Dad?"

"That's deep thinking for a little guy. Why don't you try to think of something else? Something more normal," Al said.

"OK. I'm hungry. Let's walk over to McDonald's. That's normal, right Dad?"

"Too normal—but OK."

★★★

Al and Danny stood at the rim of the tight crowd of children and the few adults at the grave site. Rosetta talked to the children, read some from her Bible and raised her hands to the sky and prayed, but with it all being in Spanish, and she spoke so fast, neither Al nor Danny figured out much of what she was saying. Soon, with the men helping, the older boys lowered the wooden casket into the hole. They started shoveling dirt in on it while they sang a song. Some of the children were crying too hard to sing, but with Rosetta's leading, the singing went on until the grave was filled in. Then some slowly started drifting away, back to the buildings.

Alice and Duce soon joined Al and Danny, and they all followed the scattered group down the path.

"Well, I guess this is the time we must all get on our way," Duce said while he walked beside Al down the trail off the mesa, back toward the orphanage buildings and his Suburban. "After I say goodbye to Rosetta, I'll take you to the motel. I'll stop by the undertaker and order up a small stone. Don't know what I'll put on it."

"Got an idea, Duce," Danny said. "I'd just met Pedro, but he was my friend as quick as we met. I'd just say he was everybody's friend."

"Why, that sounds just right, Danny," Duce said. "Yeah, that was Pedro—everybody's friend. That's how he should be remembered."

Back at the motel, Al shook Duce's hand.

"You've helped me so much, Duce. I hope things go really well for you. I surely hope your helping us never becomes known."

"I've enjoyed knowing you. You take care of that boy. Maybe you can go home soon. From what I hear, that would be a good thing for all of us."

After Duce left, Al and Danny put their things in Alice's truck. They checked out of the motel. Alice started the engine and Al and Danny climbed into the truck, then they headed across town toward the road north.

"I don't know about you boys, but I'm fixin' ta get me a good mess of grub before we head out," Alice said. "It's a long time 'til we get fed again. I know just the place."

"Yeah," Danny said. "I was sure thinkin' about eatin' myself." "I'll buy," Al said. "Anything but McDonald's. Please, there's got to be something else."

"You'll like where we're goin'," Alice said. "You'll get enough to hold you all day long, so you will."

"I'm thinking it might not be good to stop much until we cross the border," Al said. "Duce said there's lots of trouble out where we're going, with all this drug war stuff."

"Yeah," Alice said. "They've killed a bunch over in Juarez and such. They've sometimes just moved into a little town, killed off all the police who won't side with them, and just taken over. We won't stop until we get to Douglas. I filled up with diesel here when I got into town yesterday. I've got enough fuel in both of these tanks to get us home. Just in case something happens, I've got an extra ten gallon in those jerry cans in the bed."

"You might have noticed the Sonora plates on my truck," Alice said. "Having Arizona plates, any state really, down here now is just adding to the possibility for trouble. Took these plates off a van abandoned on my ranch. They often run illegals up what is usually a dry wash. Guess they got caught in a storm, and the water caught them before they knew what was happening. They must have all run off on foot."

Once out of town, they drove northwest, toward Arizona. Hours later, with the sun high, they were on a two lane road that climbed around a canyon wall. Suddenly, a bus came careening down the middle of the road.

"Look out!" Al yelled.

"Hang on! We're goin' over the edge!" Alice jerked the steering wheel to the right as she jammed the brake pedal. The tires screeched as they slid on the course pavement. The truck went over the edge. After dropping, bouncing, and sliding on loose gravel they came to rest on a ledge about ten feet below the road. The bus driver just blew the horn and kept on going, never even slowing down.

"You alright?" Al asked Danny.

"We stopped? Boy, Dad, I thought of Pedro when that bus was a comin' and figured I was gonna be right with him."

"Alice? You alright?" Al asked.

"No! The only thing that would make me alright would be if I could get my hands around that idiot bus driver's neck. These fool drivers just think they own the whole road. If this little bench wasn't here, we could have tumbled all the way to the bottom—that's a hundred feet or more. Well, let's see if we can get this thing back up on the road."

Alice tried everything she knew to do while Al and Danny pushed, but the canyon wall back up to the road was too steep. Having given up, the three of them stood at the road's edge. A man with a truckload of watermelons came slowly up the hill. The driver stopped. He got out to see what the others were looking down at.

"You trucka, she go over, sí?"

Alice nodded. "You pull it out. I'll give you $20.00." "Twenty dolla? To pull up you trucka?"

"Sí," Alice said.

With a smile on his face, the man got in his truck and pulled it to the edge of the road. Alice took a rope, and with one end threw a hitch around the tow hook on the pickup's back frame, then tossed the other end up to Al. "Let me know when he's ready," Alice said. "I'll help from down here." She got in and started the engine.

The produce truck driver tied the other end of the rope to his front bumper, then got back into his truck. He started backing up and Al motioned to Alice when the truck drew the rope tight. In mere seconds the pickup truck was back up on the pavement.

Alice coiled up the rope and Al took out a twenty-dollar bill and paid the man.

"Ah, gracias, Señor. Me pleased to help. Must be mucho careful on dees road. She have many fool drivers."

"So we learned," Al said. "You be careful, too."

"You go now. Me trucka, she very slow. You go mucho fast." "Thank you again," Alice said when she started to pull away.

Just when she started to move, a local Policia car came down the hill and pulled over in front of Alice's truck. The young officer got out and approached the pickup. He motioned for the produce truck to move on. The policia looked in the window at the three passengers.

"Ah, Señora, you have problemo, sí?"

"A bus ran us off the road. It's no problem now. That truck pulled us back to the road."

"A bus, Señora? I see no such bus. I see dees skeed marks from you truck. Know what I think? I think you drive you trucka too fast. I theenk you are mucho reckless driver, Señora. Sí, you could have hurt dees fine leettle boy, no? Ah, Señora, you follow me to town. Careful you not run into me car. Sí, me thinks you be one very lucky, reckless driver, Señora. So, a fine you must pay. We cannot let go unpunished those who come here and make danger to our poor people.

"These license plates on you trucka," he said, pointing to the front plate. "When me check them, they be yours, sí?"

"You know why I have them on there," Alice said. "No they're not my plates. One of your people abandoned a van on my ranch. I'm only trying to protect us from being a target. You know that."

"Ahh, stolen plates too. You be in mucho trouble, Señora. Mucho trouble. Follow me. You be safe with me."

With that the officer turned and went back to his car.

"Reckless driver," Alice said. "I should show him what a reckless driver I can be and run right over his car. I hope that's all this is. If those plates on that van were stolen before they were left on my ranch… trouble, trouble, trouble. This guy may think of some other things by the time we get to his office. I don't want to spend the night in jail."

"Jail!" Danny said. "I don't wanna go to jail."

"Don't worry, Danny, we'll be alright," Alice said.

"I ain't never been in jail, Dad."

"Relax, Son. We'll just follow Alice's lead. I don't think he wants to feed us or anything like that. I'm sure all he wants is money."

Alice didn't say anymore. She stared straight ahead. Hands clenched tightly on the steering wheel.

They pulled up to the little adobe building that appeared to serve as police station, jail, courtroom and anything else governmental in the village.

"I'll let you do the talking to begin with," Al said to Alice.

"I'll motion to you if I need help," Alice said. She raised the windows and locked the doors.

"Ah, Señora, I must have your key," the officer said. "Must inspect for contraband, sí?"

Alice handed him her key. He unlocked the truck door and rummaged around their bags and came up with Al's computer case.

"A computer? Yours Señor?" he asked as he looked at Al.

"It's a very special computer," Al said. "You can't mess with it."

"Ah, Señor, my son, he say he want a computer. He say it make him better in school, sí? He would have the only one in his school, Señor. I think he would like this very special computer, no? I think you will show him how to make it work. He is very smart boy. You, you are mucho rich, sí Señor? We, as you surely see, are mucho poor. You can easily buy a new computer, but me—I cannot use my pittance of compensation to buy such a fine thing for my son. Is it fair you son have and me son no have? Come inside Señor, we talk about me son's new computer."

Danny grabbed his father's hand as they went inside the dusty little building. The officer put the computer case up on the table and opened it. He took out the computer and set it in front of Al.

"You show me Señor, show me how to make it work."

Al looked at Alice, who shrugged her shoulders. He was on his own. If he let this computer get into someone else's hands, he knew he might just as well stay here in Mexico forever.

"Go on, Señor, show me how to turn it on."

Al lifted open the screen. He reached up and pushed the start button. The operating system started to load, and then a flashing message in bright red came across the screen.

"Now, you look at this," Al said to the officer, pointing to the screen. "See what this says? See it? See it? It says that this computer is the property of the United States Government. I'm a special agent for the United States

Government. I'm here undercover on a special anti-terror mission. This computer will only work with my password. If I don't enter that within one minute from the time I turn it on, a call for help goes out. A GPS signal will tell our agents waiting for me across the border that someone unauthorized, someone like *you*, Señor, has turned this on. If I don't enter my password within a matter of seconds now, the CIA will be down here in helicopters within minutes. They will land right out in your street and need I tell you what the CIA will do to someone who steals one of our top secret computers?"

"Señor, me deed not know. Por Favor, you enter password now, then you go. I beg you. Thees is not the computer for my son. I know he would not like theese one. We forget we ever talk about that, sí?"

Al turned the computer away from the officer, pretended to enter his password, and then shut it down, closed it and put it in its case. He rose and started for the door, Alice and Danny at his heels.

"Señor, forgive me. I am honored to have one so important in my office. We are so small and so poor, I—"

"No harm done. However, not a word of this to anyone, understand?" Al said, stopping and staring hard into the other mans' eyes. "Remember, I know where to find you."

"Sí. I shall talk to that bus driver. He should be more careful. He must not harm such important Americanos as you."

Al waved to the officer when Alice pulled away. No one said anything for a minute, and then Alice broke out laughing.

"That beats all. I never saw the likes of that. What did your computer screen say anyway?"

"Oh, it really doesn't matter," Al said.

★★★

When evening passed into night, just before full dark, they pulled into a yard with timber and tin buildings that appeared to Al to be a ranch supply yard. Alice backed under a large stock trailer filled with bales of grass hay.

"I buy a lot of this down here. They bring it up from down along the coast. I figured it might be late when we got back so I paid for this when I left the trailer. I don't like to spend the night on this side of the border— not here."

"Why buy hay down here? I see green hay fields along the river basins all over Arizona and New Mexico," Al asked.

"That's usually all alfalfa. That's mighty good feed for cattle, but I'm one who believes it's too hot for good horse hay. You might say I'm from the old school that believes horses do much better on good old grass. I get some out of Colorado, but that usually costs me a bunch more. Usually, when I can get a whole trailer load down here, I let them bring it right to the ranch."

"Ain't we there yet? How much longer we goin' tonight?" Danny asked.

"Town of Douglas is right across the border," Alice said. "We'll get us a couple of rooms there. I'd go on up to the Circle B, but I don't have a good explanation on what you two are doing with me again. Besides, I'm mighty sleepy-eyed. Don't want to end up in a ditch somewhere."

Alice walked around the trailer to check the lights. She stopped at the back and stared at the strap going over the top of the load. After a moment, Al joined her.

"Something wrong?" he asked.

"I strapped this load myself," Alice said. "That's not the way I tied up the end of the strap. Somebody's loosened it, then retightened it."

"Why would they do that?" Al asked.

"I can't tell in the dark, but I'd bet dinner that someone has removed a bale of hay and replaced it with marijuana—maybe something else. Might even be people hidden inside this load now. They'll be watching the crossing, waiting for me to cross, then follow me into Douglas and stop me for their goods. Could just take us all out to eliminate any witnesses. Dang, this is scary. I hope they're not watching us now. Let's get this trailer unhitched. I'll come back tomorrow and straighten this all out. Got a friend who's a judge here. Good man. I'll come back with him."

In minutes, Alice pulled the truck away from the trailer and out on to the street. Al looked back at Danny, but no one said anything.

Suddenly, a pickup truck parked up the street turned on its lights, and pulled across the street, blocking Alice's path.

"Lord help us," Alice muttered as she pulled to a stop.

The driver got out of the truck. He held what appeared in the dark to be a shotgun. He started toward Alice's side of the truck.

Alice slipped the truck in low gear. "When I take off, get down and stay down," she said. She waited until the man was halfway between the two trucks, then she floored the throttle, jumped the ditch and spun through the yard of the house only a few feet away. She smashed through a cactus patch and bouncing back onto the gravel street on the other side of the man's truck.

Caught off guard, the man didn't fire his gun until the truck was tossing gravel his way as Alice raced up the street. Just as Al pushed himself upright, there was the crack of the shotgun, and the clatter of its pellets ripping through the tailgate of Alice's truck.

"Get down," Alice yelled, jamming the shifter from second to third, then mashing the throttle back to the floor. A second shot again peppered the rear of the truck. Alice slipped the truck into fourth gear, its speed rapidly increasing.

"You OK?" Al yelled back to his son.

"Yeah. What's going on? Is someone shooting at us?"

"Yes. Stay down. We'll be safe in a minute, I think," Al said, looking up at Alice and seeing total fear in her eyes and tight cords up her neck. He wanted to help, but was clueless as to what to do.

"The border's only a mile or so away," Alice said. "If we can make it there…" She glanced into the mirror. Suddenly, the lights of the pickup flashed at her as its driver spun it around to chase after her. Having a start of several hundred yards, and being able to maintain that distance, once the lights of the border crossing came into view, the pursuing truck backed off, then disappeared down a side street.

Pulling up to the gate, Alice jammed the parking brake, opened her door, and jumped out. The border crossing guard recognized her.

"Trouble, Señora Alice?" he asked as he walked around to the rear of her truck and observed the damage. "Eeeeh. Me hear the shots. What for someone shoot at you?"

Alice leaned against the side of her truck and breathed deeply. Al opened his door, and as he got out, Danny called out to him.

"Can I come, too? I wanta see, too."

"No. Stay back there. We may have to get out of here quickly. If that other truck went to get others…"

Alice quickly told the guard all that had happened. "I'll come back tomorrow and get my trailer. I'll contact Judge Garcia and get his help. Guess this is the last time I'll be buying hay down here until this violence is over. Dirty shame. Ain't never been so scared," Alice said. Suddenly she thought about her passengers. "You alright, Al? Danny, how's Danny?"

"We're fine, Alice. You sure were brave," Al said as he noticed the slight quivering of Alice's hands. "You saved our lives. No doubt about it. You're one brave lady, Alice. How much damage is there to your truck?"

"Ain't worried about the truck. We best get out of here," Alice said. "You're not going to let any of those guys cross over and look for me, are you Alfredo?"

"The crossing, she be closed for the night. No one will cause you anymore trouble tonight, sí."

"If a bunch of them come rushing up here, how will you stop them?" Alice asked.

"I will call for extra help right now. We have plated this wall. I will be safe inside these building. I will park that truck over there across the entrada," Alfredo said, nodding to a pickup truck parked off to the side. "No one will get through. You go and get some sleep now. Me so sorry this happen to you. Mexico, she be a good country. Many bad people here now though. Someday you come back. Someday you be safe again."

As Alice drove across the streets of the Arizona border town of Douglas, all in the truck were quiet for some time. Al broke the silence.

"This is all my fault. You nearly lost your life on my account. Your truck is all shot up. Now you can't go back for more hay... it's all my fault."

"Shucks no, Al. It's not you. It's those low life drug dealers. It's all their fault. This evilness has got to stop. As an American you can't even take a gun there to protect yourself. It's got to stop. It's just got to stop."

Alice drove over to a small motel, then Al went to the office and got a couple of rooms. Alice backed her truck up against the building so that it couldn't be easily identified by its damage in case anyone on this side was sent to look for it. Al practically had to carry Danny into their room.

He set his bags on the dresser, and then turned on the TV. He was stunned when Homeland Security Secretary Clayton Kingston's face came on the screen. Secretary Kingston had apparently just explained the threat of some unknown attack on our transportation systems in early September. Al listened intently while the secretary continued.

"Based on the credibility of our sources, we take this threat with total sincerity. Let me assure you we have some of the country's best minds working on deciphering our extensive information and have the cooperation of the entire peaceful world community behind us.

"Now I call upon you—the American citizen. I ask that each of you be extra aware of any unusual activity around you. Maybe you see a strange container someone is carrying. Maybe you know of someone who's been away for awhile who returns with no good explanation for where they've been. Pay attention to anything that looks out of place.

"Remember, we believe we're looking for American citizens of any race or background, men or women, who've been recruited by terrorists such as Aswad Hamal's group to bring destruction to our country.

"We believe the greatest threat is planned to happen sometime around the next remembrance of the Twin Tower attack. That's several weeks away yet. However, we believe that we need to give you sufficient notice to prepare yourself for how this may affect you and your family. Furthermore, we want to ask for your help at this time.

"To show our seriousness in involving you, the fine citizens of our country, and the entire peace loving world, really, we are offering a reward of one million dollars tax exempt. This will be to any person, except those government workers who are directly working on this project, anyone who provides us with credible information that leads to the capture of these destruction-planning agents or who in any way stops this terror threat. Simply put: You stop this terror disaster, and you get a million dollars from us. With a smile, I might add.

"As of right now I'm raising the terror alert to severe. We will remain at this level until we are sure we've deterred this evil scheme. We've set up a massive phone bank fed through one toll free number. That's the number now shown on the bottom of your screen. I've asked that all TV networks, regular and cable, show this number in a corner of their screen for at least 25 percent of each broadcast hour. I will personally address you, our nation of vigilant, loyal citizens, whenever there is any new development. For tonight, I thank you, and God Bless America."

"There you have it…" The news reporter then started into his analysis of what was going on. Al sat stunned in the chair he'd slumped into. Seeing this on TV made it all more real. He looked over at his son. After a minute, Al looked back at the TV. He leaned forward to try to release the tightening knot in his stomach. He closed his eyes, then cradled his right hand around the back of his neck. He felt the rapid pulse against his clammy fingers.

Why now? Why did all of this have to happen right now?

"There is a stunning report from the Los Alamos National Lab, another twist in this story, really," the reporter said, drawing Al's attention back to the TV. "It's reported that the code project leader, a long time employee and one of the most respected people at the lab, has gone missing. Reports say he's kidnapped his son and has fled the country. Information is tight on this, there are many twists to this story, but it does appear the man in charge of DAD, that's the Decoding and Deciphering unit here, has gone missing and has taken a massive amount of data with him.

"There's some signs also that this man may well have been a spy—a long time mole, and he's derailed our solving this project," the reported continued. "That's the story around Los Alamos and Santa Fe. Of course there's no comment by the FBI, but our sources are solid. We'll break in with details anytime we get them on this bizarre side of this whole scary scenario.

"Our panel here tonight…" The reporter went off on evaluating this information. Al looked over at his son. *Good thing he's already asleep.* Al turned off the TV then walked to the door, opened it and stood in the doorway looking out at the night.

I should go back to the lab. They need me. My country needs me. If millions become infected and many die…. I'm endangering everyone out here who's helping me.

Al looked up at the multitude of stars in the sky. He closed his eyes then slowly nodded his head. He turned and looked at his son asleep on the bed. Tears slowly trickled down his cheeks. He wiped them away, but more came.

Chapter 17

"Oh Wade," Nita said after she and Wade had listened to Secretary Kingston's address on TV. "So this is what all that's about with little Tucker and his father. How could you get yourself so involved in something this complicated?"

Wade hit the mute button on the TV remote. "What would you have done? If this was the only way you could come up with to save little Tucker, what would you have done? I couldn't let anything happen to that kid. He reminded me..." Wade didn't say anymore. Nita didn't respond for a moment, and then she spoke softly.

"You can't bring them back, Wade. It's been a long time now. I wish you'd go on and build a new life. You're young yet—you could get married and have—"

"Mother, please. I'm not ready."

"I won't be here forever, Wade. I just thought—"

"I'm sorry, Mother. I just can't stand the thought of being hurt so much again."

"Oh Wade. You can't let the pain of the awful past kill your love in the future. Remember the good times."

"I do, everyday. I can't do anything that might take away from those memories."

"Son, memories are in the mind. You need more than that. I have great memories too—memories of your father. But I'm old—you're still young. Won't you try?"

"I can't, Mother. I just can't."

Wade punched the mute button and the TV sound came back to life. He started flicking through the channels.

★★★

Al stood in the doorway of his little motel room watching the sun rise the next morning. He'd been up most of the night. Much of the time his mind was on Wade Hawkins. If he was going to turn himself in, he needed his attorney's help. Alice opened the door to her room and stepped outside. She waved to Al, and then walked over to the motel office. Moments later she came walking toward Al with two cups of coffee.

"Figured you could use a cup," she said. She nodded to a picnic area with a table. "Let's go sit down."

Al followed her to the table. He sat down without looking at her.

"Thanks for the coffee."

"Sure. Look, Al, I try not to get involved with the people who come through me on the railroad. It's best that way—the way it's supposed to work. So don't think of me as being duller than a butter knife when I say I had no suspicion of who you were. However, when I turned the TV on last night it jumped right out at me. Guess you weren't making much up yesterday about your computer. What you're doing with taking your son is always hard for anyone, but it must be doubly hard on you with all this other weight on your shoulders."

Al just stared at the ground. Neither one said anything for a moment. Then Al looked at Alice and spoke his heart to her.

"I'm giving up. I'm going to turn myself in. I nearly got you killed. They're calling me a traitor and—"

"You can't do that! Land sakes, what if you still can't make the right thing happen at the lab? You'll be a traitor then for sure. You're too far into this now. You're working on things from wherever you are, right?"

"It's not quite the same. Being right at the lab, maybe—but I really don't know what more I'd do. I don't think we can do this. It might be possible if given a lot more time—but with only days left…"

"That boy needs you," Alice said. "He's a gift from God, especially for you. God hasn't put you in command of the whole country—if he wants to save the country, he'll work that out somehow—but God has put you in command of your son."

"You too, huh? Everybody talks about God as if it's a given he exists and has some magical power over things. Sometimes I wish I could accept the principle of a God. That would make life simpler. You people use God to help carry some of your load. Me, I've got to carry all of mine. I don't think I can carry all of this any farther."

"Land sakes, Al. I ain't no saint, or even the likes of one, you know that. Guess I just grew up knowing God was watching over me. I made that decision to put him in charge many years ago. I don't always understand how things go. I surely don't agree with many things as they unfold, but in the end, I always see how things work out for good. Maybe not always mine, but always good for someone. I don't know how a body makes it any other way. You're right about him carrying the load when I can't." Alice was quiet for a minute, and then she spoke again.

"Look, give this until the end of the day. We don't have far to go to your next stop. Those folks there seem to be a whole lot smarter than I am. I'll bet they can give you some good advice. When Danny wakes up, we'll get ready and move on. Think about this some more before you make such a final decision."

151

"Yeah, that would be final all right," Al said. "OK. I'll go take a shower and get Danny going. We won't be long." Al rose and started for his room. He stopped and looked back at Alice.

"Thanks. You're not God, but you've taken some of my load. Just being able to talk to someone has really helped."

★★★

Late that morning Alice pulled the truck into the drive of the Oak Canyon Inn near the old mining town of Patagonia. "This is it, guys. You'll like Maria, her father Anton also. Come, let's see if she's here or off to one of her other businesses. She's about the busiest person I ever did meet."

Al caught Danny looking at him with wide eyes. He smiled back at his son, trying to relax him.

"How close to the border are we?" Al asked Alice.

"Only a few miles the way the crow flies. There're some old mines out yonder—long ago abandoned. There's a handful of horse ranches out and about, a few cattle roam the land, too, but that's about all there is between here and Mexico. It's safe, though. Nothing like last night is going to happen to you here."

"See that I get the bill for fixing your truck. I'll have it no other way," Al said.

"Insurance will cover most of it," Alice said. "I'm just glad no one got hurt. That could have been the end for all of us."

They all walked over to the office. The Inn was an old mission style building. Something about the place gave Al a sense of peace.

"Lots of history hereabouts" Alice said. "The Apaches, and the early Spanish missions and settlements, with all that fighting that caused. Then there was the capture of John Ward's stepson, who years later became a famous scout for the cavalry. Out yonder, like I said before, there're the mines. There was the confederate takeover of this whole area and—why, there's 'bout as many ghosts here wanting to tell their tales as anywhere. If you like to hear stories of times past, Danny, old Anton here will talk to you from sunup 'till sundown. He ought to write a book, so he should. 'Course I don't know how much of what he tells is actually true, but it sure is mighty good listening."

Alice reached the office and started to open the door. Al reached over and grabbed it then held it open while Alice, then Danny entered. He followed them over to the counter.

"Well if you aren't a welcome sight," the woman who came through a large archway behind the counter said to Alice. "I expected you yesterday. You don't look none the worse for wear. Everything OK?"

"Well, a couple of distractions that held us up, and we're all kinda saddle sore from a long stretch of highway miles, but fit other than that,"

Alice said. "Maria, this here fella is my little partner, Danny Tucker. That big one is his pa, Al. Me and Danny, now we've doctored sick horses, fed a baby colt, and have ridden more miles in my truck than I care to remember. His daddy has every right to be proud of him. He's a keeper. These two can tell you about our adventure yesterday. I don't have time now."

"Well, Danny, I'm Maria—Maria Cortez. You might see the name Dugan around here at times, but that's old history. A big welcome to you too, Al. I hear you've been scurrying like jackrabbits in a cactus patch with a coyote nipping at your tails. You boys must be worn out. Got a room fixed up for you that's way down at the end of this building where it'll be quiet and cool. Now that you're here, I've got to run over to town for a while. Dad can handle things here. I'll wake him up. Alice, you know the room I have for these fellows. Can you take them over there?

I'll see you two when I get back. We'll have dinner tonight."

"I've promised Danny that Anton will tell him some stories," Alice said when she picked up the key Maria had laid on the counter.

"I think Dad would rather lose his sight than his voice," Maria said. "If he couldn't spin a yarn to anyone who'll listen, I think he'd just dry up and die. Well, later then."

Maria turned and went back through the archway. When she did, her eyes caught Al's and locked there for a second. Al watched her until she was out of sight. Even then he stood there for a second, staring at where she'd disappeared. After a few seconds, he realized Danny was tugging at his hand. "Hey Dad, Alice asked you if you were ready to go? You OK?"

"Sure. Guess I need to catch up on my sleep. Must have been daydreaming."

Al and Danny retrieved their meager collection of belongings from the truck and followed Alice to the room Maria had made ready for them.

"Well, it's goodbye again," Alice said. "The way things are going, 'spect I might be seeing you again someday."

"I hope, Alice. You and me really are partners, aren't we?" Danny asked.

"We sure are, Danny. However, don't forget a much more important partnership—that's you and your dad."

"Yeah, me and dad's having the best time ever, aren't we Dad?"

"Ahh—yeah. Sure are. You and me anyway," Al said, and then he turned toward Alice. "I can't think of any words that would be adequate to thank you for all you've done for us, Alice. I think you know though. Maybe someday we can talk again."

"I 'spect we will. Be careful now." With that she reached down and gave Danny a hug, then turned and started for her truck.

"Gonna miss her, Dad. Just like all the others. Only you're forever, right Dad? All the others are just gonna have to walk away someday. Good thing I can trust you're not gonna walk out too, Dad."

Alright. I'm forever. I'll not walk out on you, son. Somehow I'll stick this out until the end.

★★★

Wade Hawkins had his desk piled high with case-law books, stacks of files and several legal pads. He had an in-depth computer file on case law on his computer, but preferred books. He could have several open at the same time and believed he often saw things the computer screen inadvertently hid. He heard the phone ring, and then Nita buzzed him.

"Wade, there's a lady on the phone named Rhea Thatcher. She doesn't want to tell me what it's about."

"Oh, yeah. I'll take it." Wade pushed back the clutter in the middle of his desk and picked up a pen, then found a pad. "This is Wade Hawkins."

"Mr. Hawkins—I'm Rhea Thatcher. I—I work with Evelina Vincent. I'm—I can't go on anymore. I got your name from the newspaper articles. You're connected with Alex Vincent and Tucker, right?"

"They're clients of mine."

"Yeah. I need help. I've got to talk to someone—you seem to be the right person. I'm in real trouble. So are others. I've got to tell it all." Rhea was quiet for a moment, then continued. "I'm too scared to come see you—not at your office anyway."

"Where can we meet? When would it be normal for you to be somewhere?" Wade asked.

"Oh, well, this is Wednesday—this is the night I usually go out to that casino north of town. I must wait until it gets dark. Yes, I'll meet you, say about nine? In the back. Let's meet in the back parking lot of the casino. I think I'll just die if I don't confess what I've done. I don't know how I ever got into such a mess. I'll never forgive myself—I can't. It's just been too much—too much."

"I'll see you at nine tonight then," Wade said. "Look, if you want to start to make amends, the town deserves to know what's going on. I don't think the police—"

"No police! Not the police here," Rhea cut in.

"I know. I was thinking of bringing the editor of the local paper," Wade said.

"Oh, yeah. That would be good. Maybe I can get some redemption if I tell the whole community how sorry I am. OK. Bring that newsman."

"I'll be there. I can't promise what will happen to you," Wade told her.

"I don't deserve anything—nothing but what I've done to others. I guess really I deserve to die and burn in Hell for what I've been a part of."

Wade closed his eyes. "Sometimes, Miss Thatcher, redemption begins with confession. We'll talk tonight then. Goodbye now." Wade hung up the phone. He sat in silence. He couldn't push that conversation out of his mind. He looked at the stacks of things for the project he was working on, but couldn't clear his mind to get back to it. Wade picked up his phone and dialed J. Quinton Sedwick's number.

Max Pace sat at his desk studying next week's duty roster. His cell phone rang.

"Pace," he answered.

"Max. That little bug you put in her phone paid off. She just made a call to Hawkins. She's going to roll. They're to meet at nine tonight in back of the casino. I'll have someone call her and pretend to be Hawkins' office and change it to 8:30. You know what to do."

"Listen, Evelina, I never—"

"No, you listen. This is your part of the deal. She talks—you hang. It's her or you, Max. Oh, and if it's you, then it's also me, that can't be, so you have no choice. Go to Albuquerque and get a rental car. Park your city car in one of those off airport parking lots and take the shuttle over to one of the rental car counters.

"You've got to have several throw-a-way pieces stashed around—every cop does. Make it good," Evelina said. "I'll say she told me she was to meet Hawkins there," Evelina continued. "Do it right, we implicate Hawkins and get rid of him as well— that nosy investigator of his too. Leave the gun at the scene. We'll pin its ownership on Hawkins later."

"What are you saying? Things don't happen that way. You've been watching too much TV," Max pleaded. "Not in the real world…"

"Call me when it's done, Max dear."

"Evelina! Evelina!" She'd hung up. Max closed his eyes and took a deep breath. He couldn't think about this—he just had to do it. It was a long way to Albuquerque and the rental car lots. He slid open his bottom drawer, removed a bottle and poured two-fingers of the dark liquid into his coffee cup. He slowly sipped this and let it burn all the way down his throat. When the cup was empty, he pushed himself to his feet and then sauntered out the back door.

★★★

Al refilled his glass from a pitcher of iced tea while Danny finished the last of his milk and pushed the glass up to the front of his empty plate. Al saw Danny looking inquisitively over at Anton, who sat across from him. Danny had been quiet during the conversation of the adults while they dined on carne asada, ranchero beans and homemade corn tortillas. It was obvious that his son was inquisitive, as was he himself, why this jolly, gray-haired man rolled up to the table in a wheelchair.

Anton pushed himself back a few inches from the table and patted his stomach. "Ah, she's done it again. My daughter fixes me meals as good as her mother used to. Maybe where you come from there's something better, my little friend Danny, but to me the chili, ahh, she is the best thing to add to any meal. I cannot imagine having a meal without having something flavored with the pod of one of the Good Lord's many types of chili plants."

"This was very good," Al said while he looked over at Maria, who sat across from him. "You do have a way with food, I mean, it seems you like to cook—do you?"

"We operated a cantina when I was growing up. I was always at mother's side. Cooking brings back good memories. Having someone appreciate what you make always helps. Father never empties his plate without giving me a compliment for dessert."

Anton leaned over the table and looked into Danny's eyes. With a twinkle in his own, he asked a question. "Danny—you like ice cream? Chocolate ice cream? How about a bowl of good, cold ice cream with marshmallow and cherries on top?"

"Wow! I mean—can I Dad?"

"Do you have room? It seems you've eaten a lot already." "Yeah, but chocolate ice cream—I haven't had that since—well, it's been a month or more." "Alright, Son."

"How about you?" Maria asked Al.

"Maybe just a little," he answered. "It seems I have lost a little weight lately. Maybe ice cream wouldn't hurt."

"Come on, Danny. Let's go out on the patio. Maria will bring our dessert out there. Let me guess, I'd say you like to hear stories about how things were in these parts when it was controlled by those wild and daring Apaches. Did I tell you I have some of that blood running in my veins?" Anton pushed his chair away from the table, and then started wheeling it toward a wide door in the back of the kitchen.

"Really?" Danny asked while he jumped up and scooted to Anton's side. "You really part Apache? You related to Geronimo?"

Maria laughed while she walked to the refrigerator. "Dad sure enjoys telling his tales to young boys. It keeps him young, I guess. A little bit anyway."

Al wanted to ask why Anton was in a wheelchair. He wanted to ask so many things, but this didn't seem to be the time. As he watched Maria move about the kitchen, he thought of more questions. Maria took the two bowls of ice cream out to Anton and Danny, then brought two more over to the table and sat back down across from Al. She looked at him with her deep brown eyes but said nothing while she took a spoonful of ice cream and slid it into her mouth. Putting the spoon back to the dish, she swallowed.

"Ohh. Sometimes that hurts my teeth. I don't know why I do this. I guess it's because Dad likes it so much—he loves chocolate ice cream."

"With chili on it?" Al asked, and then felt his face flush.

"That's about the only thing he doesn't like hot," Maria said, and then smiled. She looked at Al while she took another spoon of ice cream. "This must be hard on you. I'm told you have work you must do, so I'll try not to expect much from you around here. I've got things well covered for now anyway. We rent most of these rooms out by the week, or even longer. We're mostly booked up into November." She went back to eating her dessert. Neither one said anything until she'd finished. Then she pushed her empty bowl off to the side and spoke again.

"I have several other businesses over in Nogales. That's a half hour west of here and a big crossing for produce, other things too, of course. There're dozens of refrigerated storage places around here. Anything to do with moving perishable food is big business there, well, big for us. Of course we're not New York."

Al had paid little attention to what Maria was saying so when she stopped, things went silent. He realized he needed to say something.

"So, you're into moving fruit and vegetables?"

"Well, not exactly. We move other things," Maria said. "This is a good place to move many other things around also. There's the auto plant over there and so much else on the other side of the border."

That left Al a little puzzled, but he didn't want to pursue that answer, he didn't think Maria wanted to give any more details. Suddenly, a beeper in Maria's purse went off.

"Oh dear," she said when she quickly grabbed it and checked the number. "Looks as if I've got to go over to town. I'll have to finish these dishes later."

"I can do them," Al said, then again, felt his face flush.

"Thanks, but I won't be long. You've got to be tired. Why don't you get settled in, and I'll see you for breakfast? I'm sure Dad will keep Danny going until one or both get tired." Maria grabbed her purse then she and Al started for the main door of the living quarters. At the door, she stopped. "It's good to have you here, Al. If I can help you in any way, I mean, I know you're under quite a load—"

"I—I'm not sure how things are going to turn out for me. My world had always been so small and secure. Now—well I don't even know if I'll be here tomorrow. Sometimes I think of curling up like a baby and crying. I mean—well, I shouldn't have said that. I don't know what I mean. I've never needed anyone to do anything for me, but now I have to rely on someone else for my basic existence." Al lowered his head, then looked away, embarrassed he'd said anything.

"You sound much like Dad when he ended up in that wheelchair. Only difference is, someday you'll pull through this and get back to normal. Actually, you'll probably be better than you were before. With Dad…" After staring into Al's eyes for a minute, she turned and walked toward her car.

Al started toward his room. When he heard the car pull away, he turned to watch it. Was Maria right? Somewhere out ahead, out where he couldn't see or understand now, did he have a future?

★★★

At breakfast the next morning Danny and Anton kidded and verbally jabbed at each other, as if they'd known each other all their lives. Maria seemed quiet and Al couldn't think of any way to open a conversation. He heard voices outside, and then there came a knock at the door.

"Come in fellas," Anton motioned to the young boys at the door. "Got someone here you need to meet. This young man here is Danny. He's fixin' to be with us for a spell."

Three boys came through the door and over to the table, all the while eyeing up Danny.

"Danny, these here young men are Troy and Tony and Mike," Anton said, pointing to each of the boys. "They've listened to a book full or more of my tales. Some they've even heard often enough they could tell them themselves."

"We heard there was another kid here. You play baseball?" Mike asked Danny.

"A little," Danny replied.

"Well come on then. We're gettin' up a game over at the park. We need all the players we can rustle up," Tony said.

"Can I, Dad? Can I go play ball?" Danny asked.

Al looked at Maria. She smiled a reassuring smile that Al took to mean Danny would be safe with these boys.

"As long as you only go to the park. I'm sure Maria knows where that is. Be back for lunch," Al said. "I'll be in our room."

"You got a glove, kid?" Tony asked when they headed for the door.

"Not here," Danny replied.

"Come on anyway. We'll fetch up somethin' for ya to use," Tony said.

When the screen door slammed shut, Maria nodded toward the boys. "They're good kids. They'll take care of Danny. He'll have fun."

"Good. He's grown up a lot these last few weeks," Al said. "I don't remember when he last played with other kids. I know we had a lot of time to make up together—maybe by now we've gotten through a big chunk of that."

Al looked out through the door at the mountains to their south. He felt Maria staring at him. He wanted to gaze into her magnetic eyes and ask her if they could do something, anything, together. Something deep inside, pushed way back into corners of the mind and heart where he'd never before dared to go, there came this need for touch. Touch of body. Touch of soul. Touch of spirit. Touch in a way he'd never ever experienced. Touch where you give and touch where you take. Touch where your weaknesses meld with the strengths of another, and you give in return. Al closed his eyes—he couldn't stand this. This was no time to get involved in any way with someone—especially someone like Maria.

"Guess I best get to work," was all he could say as he pushed these emotions back into their tiny, well protected compartments.

"I'm going out on the patio and do some reading," Anton said.

"I've got some work around here," Maria said. "Of course you never know when I'll have to go over to town. If I do, do you need anything?"

Al shook his head and mumbled "Not really—not today." He pushed back his chair and rose. "Hey, that breakfast was as good as last night's dinner. I'll ditto what I said about your cooking last night."

"You're more than welcome," Maria said. "I'll see you later—lunch right?"

"Sure. Look forward to it," Al said, then left for his room. *Get to work— you gotta get to work. Get focused—stay focused.* When he walked across the walkway, Al heard a noise coming from the office parking area. He stopped and turned around to see Maria walk across the lot to a car that had just pulled in and parked under a tree. U.S. Customs, the decal on the door said.

What does she have going on with Customs?

★★★

Danny rushed into their room just before lunchtime. "Hey Dad, I had three hits. These kids like me. They want me to go with them to some church thing tonight. It's a kids' thing they have every Wednesday night. Can I go, Dad? Can I?"

"Ah, gee, I don't know. Let's ask Maria. I'll bet she knows if it's a good thing or not."

"You like her, don't you Dad? I think she's cool. Anton said Maria likes you. He said he can tell."

"Whoa," Al said, caught off guard. "Let's not talk about that. That could get way out of line. Come on, it's almost noon. Let's see if Maria has lunch ready, or if we have to make our own."

Walking over to the residence area behind the office, Al noticed Maria's car under the carport—so was an old pickup that seemed as if it had seen many a hot, desert summer. Anton was at the table waiting for them. "How was the ball game?" he asked.

"Fun. It's getting too hot out there now though. Be stayin' around here for awhile," Danny said.

"Hey, you play checkers?" Anton asked Danny.

"Sure. I learned out in—" he cut himself off. "Yeah, I'll play with you," he said, glancing at his dad.

"Well, wash up now and dig in here. I hope you'll like this salad; it's got lots of things in it. I can't stand a salad that's all lettuce," Maria said. "Sit down, Al. I hope things are quiet enough here for you."

"Oh, this is wonderful. The place is just fine. I'm actually relaxing some."

After they'd eaten, Danny looked at his dad. "Can I ask Maria about goin' with the kids?"

"Oh, yeah," Al said. "She'll know all about it. I'm sure."

"The guys asked me to go with them to their church thing tonight," Danny said. "That kids' thing they do every Wednesday, you know? Dad and me was wondering if it's an OK thing or what."

"I think it would be good for you. From what I hear they have their time at the church, then they all go somewhere, usually Wal-Mart. We don't have a mall here, so I guess this is our version of big city kids hanging out at the mall. They have a snack at the snack bar, then go look at things. Some of the kids, those whose parents don't get out much, do some shopping for their parents. It seems to be something the kids all like."

"Sounds alright," Al said to Danny. "Remind me to give you some money. Someone going to pick you up?"

"Big old bus, I guess. That's what Tony said. Gee thanks, Dad. I'll stay here and play checkers with Anton this afternoon, then go with the guys tonight, and—"

"Just make sure you're up to the room in time to take a shower before you go with the guys. I need to get you, both of us really, some more clothes. Maybe someday when you're going to town," Al said, looking at Maria. "Maybe I can hitch a ride to that Wal-Mart or somewhere and get us some things, so we have more than a couple of changes of clothes. I found the guests' laundry room earlier and did up our dirty stuff, but don't want to do that every day. Besides, a few more choices other than these ranch type clothes would be a welcome change too."

"Tomorrow morning would work for me," Maria said. "I'll drop you off there, and then go about some business."

"I need to get to some internet access also—something public. I don't want to use anyone's personal location."

"There's a truck stop down by the border. Would that work?" Maria asked.

"Should. I'll check it out."

★★★

When the kids boarded the bus after the youth meeting, youth pastor Hec Ramos made it a point to take a seat beside Danny.

"So, you're staying out at the Inn for awhile," Heck said. "That Maria, she's one fine lady."

"Yeah. I like her a lot. She sure can cook. Anton and me play games, checkers mostly. He tells stories too."

"I've heard he's quite the story teller. What did you think of our story tonight? I could see you were paying close attention."

"I don't know nothin' about God, or any of that. Dad's not sure about any of this God stuff. He's—well, he says he needs proof. That's the way Dad is. If Dad would believe in God, then I would too."

"I'll bet he's a smart man," Hec said.

"Oh yeah. He's about the smartest man in the whole country. That's why he's—well, he's real smart."

"Hey, here's the store. Let's go raid the snack bar. Their burgers are great," Hec said.

"Bet I can eat two," Danny said, then he took off running with the others.

After the group had finished eating, Hec got everyone together. "Remember the rules, OK? You don't cause any trouble. You don't break anything. You stay in groups. We meet back here at eight o'clock, alright?"

Everyone nodded and responded with "yes's" or "OK's" then took off. Danny went with Troy, Tony, and Mike. "Let's check out the baseball stuff. Maybe they got some new ball gloves in," Tony said. They took off in that direction.

Going back the aisle, they passed the electronics section. Danny was curious if there were any new video games out. "Hey, guys. I want to go in here first."

"Ah, there's nothin' in there. You go if you want. Come on back to the baseball gloves when you're done," Tony said.

Danny walked back to the aisle into the area with the TVs and videos. There were at least a dozen TVs on, all on the same channel. Being the top of the hour, there was a change of programming. The first words out of the new announcer's mouth grabbed Danny's full attention.

"Here's our first story tonight," the announcer said excitedly while the camera zoomed in on him. The headline at the bottom of the screen read: *Fugitive Father.* "We're hot on the trail of a man on the run from Los Alamos, New Mexico. Join me folks. I'm Buck Stacy and this is *Catch Me If You Can.* Tonight we want you to help us catch this man, Dr. Alex

Vincent—" the screen was suddenly filled with a picture of his dad. Danny stood there frozen. The picture was old, but it still looked like his dad.

"Why?" Buck went on. "You've heard the rumors on the news. This man from DAD, that's the Decoding and Deciphering unit at LANL, the famed Los Alamos National lab, is our top fugitive from justice. He's on the top of the FBI's ten most wanted. He's reportedly taken a top secret, computer hard drive, maybe some disks and thumb drives along with copies of all the related test material regarding that serious threat Secretary Kingston told us about last week. And because he's also kidnapped this boy, his son Tucker—" At that the screens all went to full face on him. Danny jumped back and stumbled into a rack of videos. Then he, along with the videos, crashed to the floor.

Chapter 18

Wade Hawkins sat in the passenger side of J. Quinton Sedwick's Suburban. They'd parked well out in the center of the parking lot in a space where they could see everyone who entered and exited the casino. The old newsman looked at his watch, as he'd done every few minutes since they'd gotten here. They were early. Wade knew it wasn't even 8:30 yet. J. Quinton opened his briefcase and checked his hand held recorder and pocket sized digital camera for the third time.

"I tell ya, Wade, this gets my blood going. I need to get out on something like this more often. I'm drying up in that office. Maybe I'll sell the paper and go back to being a street reporter—that's where the action is. This is good old fashioned fun. Running that darned paper is all business. With all these new electronic gizmos and the nice cars today, why, this job's a dream. Back when I started—hey, isn't that her?"

Wade looked at the woman who'd just left the main entrance. He held up the picture Sonny Horn had taken of Rhea Thatcher in the schoolyard. Yes, this was her.

"She should get into a green Subaru. Yeah, that's it. She's leaving early. Hope she hasn't changed her mind," Wade said when Rhea got into her car. After starting the car, she drove it around the back.

"She just might be anxious to get started talking. I say we give her a minute to find a place where she's comfortable, then we'll go have our talk," J. Quinton said, as he felt for his recorder again. Just as J. Quinton reached up to turn the key, there was a muffled popping noise.

"What's that?" J. Quinton asked. "Was that a gun? Where'd it come from?"

"I don't know, but I don't like it," Wade said. "She left early and—"

A silver Buick suddenly sped around the side of the building and started across the parking lot straight for the exit.

"Get a picture," Wade said, leaning forward. "Zoom in on that!" J. Quinton already had his camera in hand and in seconds was clicking away at the fleeing car.

"Got a good one of the plates, caught the driver's face too. You know it looked like—"

"Forget the car! Get back there," Wade pointed to the back where Rhea Thatcher had gone and from where the other car had come. J. Quinton started the Suburban, then squealed the tires as he slammed on the gas and headed for the back of the building.

"I don't like this," Wade said. "We were set for nine. She came out at eight-twenty-something. Hope I'm wrong, but I'd say someone changed our time and—there!" Wade pointed to the green Subaru parked over by the dumpster. J. Quinton slid to a stop right in front of Rhea's car, then he and Wade jumped out and both ran to the driver's window.

"Oh Lord no!" J. Quinton cried when he quickly looked at the carnage the pointblank range blast had left. "Ugh!" he said, but then he quickly snapped several photos.

"Come on," Wade said grabbing J. Quinton by the shoulder. "I'm being set up. I'm supposed to find this a little later and be caught here. We've only got a few minutes to get out of here. The reservation police will be getting a call in minutes."

The two men got back into their car, slowly drove around to the front, then out on the road.

"Take me back to my truck. We'll hang around there for awhile," Wade said, and then he pulled out his cell phone.

"I've got the sending number blocked on this, so I should be able to make a call without them picking up my number." Wade dialed 911.

"Yeah," he said when the operator answered. "Hey, I just heard what sounded like a gunshot coming from the casino up here on the reservation. Sounded as if it came from the back of the building." Wade flipped the phone shut.

The two men rode in silence for a few minutes. J. Quinton spoke first.

"She was really young, wasn't she? Kindergarten helper, right? What a waste. Did you see who was in that car? Was it who I think it was?"

Wade was too deep in thought to answer. Yes, he thought he knew who was driving that car. Had things gone this far? Would this be the beginning of massive bloodshed, or the last gasp of this group of sick, sadistic people?

J. Quinton pulled out his phone and hit one of the speed-dial buttons.

"Bonner—got some hot photo shots you'll want to blow up big for detail. I don't care what you're doing you'll want this right away. Meet me at the Roadrunner Grill parking lot. You'll see Hawkins' truck there. If I'm right, this may blow all of this wide open."

Half an hour later, Wade and J. Quinton were drinking coffee and talking about things Wade's dad and J. Quinton had done both as partners and opponents. Wade looked up and saw Luke Lane stride across the floor of the back room, right toward the two men.

"Here comes Luke Lane," Wade said to J. Quinton.

"Welcome, Detective," J. Quinton said when Lane reached their table. "Have a seat, want a donut? Some hot coffee?"

"No time to be cute, guys. Seeing the two of you together seems as if something was planned for tonight. What have you been up to?"

"We're just reminiscing about old times. I remember Wade here when his mama pushed him in a stroller. His daddy and I sat right here in this room and smoked us many a cigar—you could do that in those days. Where's your boss tonight?"

"Why do you ask? You been listening to a scanner?"

"No scanner—just a gut feeling, maybe," J. Quinton said. "You know the feeling, right? You know things are going on around you, but you just can't quite get a grip on them. I think things are about to unravel, what do you think detective?"

"Were you two up at the casino earlier?" Luke asked.

"Casino?" J. Quinton asked. "My boy, you were here when I editorialized for years against those things. Wade, why he headed up one of the committees studying the moral detriment of letting them in. Still say we were right. Those things just steal from the poor, giving them false hope. Then the crooked tribal leaders and their rich, east coast management companies take out all the money."

Luke Lane slid back an empty chair then dropped into it. "It's been a rough night. Someone shot Rhea Thatcher. She was Evelina Vincent's assistant. It happened out behind the casino. I can't find Max. Guess he's up among the trees in the Pecos or somewhere."

"Vincent lady up there, too?" J. Quinton asked.

"Nah, she's sitting at home, alone."

"Then you know, Detective, that there's little chance Max is up there. I'd say he was on another errand. I've got some feelers out. Check the paper tomorrow. We just might solve this whole thing for you."

"I've been pulled off all the missing kid stuff," Lane said.

"You were getting too close," J. Quinton said.

"That's not it. I—I don't know why, I guess."

"The blood might get worse, Detective," J. Quinton said. "Once I start printing some of the things we've turned up today, some of your friends might get desperate. You need to step back and put everything and everyone on the table for scrutiny— everyone. That's why my paper is ahead of you—we don't have anyone to protect going into this. I say they're all guilty, make them prove otherwise."

Luke Lane sat in silence for several minutes. Then he nodded to Wade.

"You're awfully quiet, Hawkins. I hear the feds are going to turn up the heat, and you're going down."

"Could be," Wade said.

"Aren't you worried? You could go to jail."

"I considered that possibility when I started into this. I've done nothing I wouldn't do again. I know Max would like to shove the Tucker Vincent case under the rug with the other two missing child cases, but he can't cover up what he doesn't know. And I can't tell what I don't know."

"I gotta go back to work," Luke Lane said while rising to his feet. "You guys enjoy your little trip down memory lane."

"Yeah, you have bad guys to catch and oh yeah, a boss to find," J. Quinton said. Luke's only response was a halfhearted wave as he walked away.

No sooner had Luke Lane gone when Jake Bonner came rushing in carrying a large manila envelope.

"Saw the city car in the lot, so I waited. Luke Lane nosing around?" he asked as he sat down.

"He won't face the facts. He knows, but he just won't act," J. Quinton said.

"Well, maybe this will push him. Look at these. You got some great shots, Boss. That license plate is easy to read, and look at that face shot. Maybe you couldn't bet your life on it, but if that's not Max Pace in the driver's seat, I'll shine his boots everyday for a year. I've got a friend on the force down in Albuquerque. He's running down the rental agencies to see who rented this car. I think by print time tomorrow we'll be set to run this. You going to write the story yourself?" Jake asked J. Quinton.

"I just might. Might be just what this old warrior needs. Well, I've had enough for tonight. What do you say we call it a night, Wade? Say howdy to your mama."

★★★

"Hey, young fellow, you alright?" the store clerk asked Danny while the youngster scrambled to his feet.

"Ah, yeah. Oh—sorry I knocked all this stuff down. Oh my," he said while he started picking up videos, with the TVs all blaring his story only a few feet away.

Keep this man busy picking these up so he won't look at the TV sets!

"You didn't get hurt, did you?" the clerk asked when he set the rack back in place.

"Nah. I just wasn't lookin' where I was going," Danny said. "Hope I didn't bust nothin'."

"Oh no. You can't hurt these things just by dropping them. Well, there, that's the last of them. If you're alright—"

"Yeah, I'm fine. Hey, thanks Mister. I gotta go find the other guys," Danny said, then he took off for the ball gloves.

Just before 8:30, Danny got back to his room. His dad was still working on his computer.

"Hi, Son. How'd things go? Have a good time?"

"Yeah," Danny said.

"That wasn't real strong. You didn't like it?" Al asked.

"Oh sure. It was fun. Guess I'm maybe tired or something."

"Not sick, are you?"

"No, just tired I'd say."

Danny kicked his shoes off, and then crawled up on his bed. He stared up at the ceiling. After a few minutes, he looked over at his dad. "Got a dictionary, Dad?"

"No, no I don't. Why do you want a dictionary? Didn't know you knew how to use one."

"Oh, I was just thinkin' about something. That's all. That's where you find what words mean, right?"

"Well, yeah. If you tell me what it is you're looking for, maybe I can help you."

"Oh, no, that's alright." Danny lay there in silence for some time. Then he spoke again. "What does fugitive mean, Dad?"

"Fugitive?" Al turned his chair around and looked at his son. "Now what in the world makes you ask that?"

"Oh, I was just thinkin'."

"And you just happened to think of the word fugitive and said to yourself, hmmm, I wonder what fugitive means."

"Well, no."

"So where did you hear this word?"

Danny was silent for a moment. Then he started to cry. After another minute he started talking.

"It was awful, Dad. I—I was by the TVs and a picture of you came on. I—I got scared, Dad. This guy on the screen called you a fugitive father, Dad, and it was written there in like great big letters and, ah—then they showed a picture of me. Got so scared I started to run and knocked over a rack of videos and then—well, the man at the store helped pick them up. Then I ran off to find the other boys. What was he sayin' about you, Dad?"

"Oh, I see. On TV huh? Well, fugitive means someone on the run, someone you can't find. Someone in hiding or being hidden by someone else. That's what they were saying about me."

"But they don't know, Dad. If that's what fugitive means, then they got it all wrong. That's more like what you used to be. You were never around for me. I never could get a hold of you or find you when I needed you. Those TV people got it wrong, Dad. The old dad was kinda like a fugitive. Now you're the best dad anywhere. I wanta tell everyone to stop looking for us 'cause me'n you are doin' better'n ever."

Al sat looking at Danny for a few minutes before he commented. "I'm glad you feel that way, Son. We didn't have much before, did we?"

"I don't want them to find us, Dad. If we go back home, I'm afraid things will go back to the old way. I don't want the old way, Dad."

Al thought about that for a minute, and then he made his son a promise. "Things will never be the old way, Son. I don't know what is in our future, but it won't be the old way—I promise."

Wade Hawkins read the local paper that next morning while he ate breakfast at the Roadrunner Grill. The headline was a question: RECOGNIZE THIS DRIVER? Underneath was a picture of the driver's area of the silver Buick as it sped out of the casino parking lot. The story went on to show the car's license plate and a copy of the lease agreement with the rental agency in Albuquerque for that car earlier in the day.

The story of the brutal shooting of Rhea Thatcher seemed secondary to the paper's implication of who perpetrated the crime. Wade was reading the last of the story when Sonny showed up.

"Heard you were in on this last night," Sonny said to Wade. "Jake Bonner called me early this morning. It's going to be hard for him to wiggle out of this, isn't it?"

"I just wonder how wide a loop this will cast," Wade said. "Will this crater the whole thing, or will Max be the fall guy for it all?"

"I think I'm going to stay close to Evelina today," Sonny said. "She might be ready to do something drastic. What do you think?"

"That's what I'd do—though the police station might be an interesting place about now."

"Jake's going to hang out there. I'll let you know if I hear anything. Nothing happens, I'll talk to you tonight."

Max Pace walked into his office, hung his hat on the coat rack, and then headed for the coffeepot. Once seated behind his desk, he noticed the office seemed to be unusually quiet. He looked out across the rows of desks and caught several of his men staring at him. He looked down at his desk. The morning's paper lay there opened up with the front page spread out on his desk. He glanced at it, then grabbed and drew it close to him. His hands started to shake. He felt beads of perspiration pop out on his forehead. His breath got short. He looked out over the paper at the outer office. All eyes were now on him. Then his phone buzzed.

"Y—yes," he stammered.

"Max, the chief wants to see you in the mayor's office ASAP," his secretary said.

"T—tell him I'll ah—I'll be there in a few minutes."

With trembling hands Max folded his paper and put it under his arm. Then as calmly as he could, without making eye contact or saying anything to anyone, he walked out of his office, then out through the door to his car.

He started the engine, and then headed for the interstate. Seeing a convenience store ahead, he instinctively pulled in. He got out, entered the store, and walked straight to the liquor counter.

★★★

That morning Al rode over to Nogales with Maria. Neither said anything for the first few minutes. Finally, Maria asked Al how he was getting along.

"Oh, we're doing great in some ways," Al said. "The business thing—I don't know."

"It's got to be tough, living the way you are," Maria said. "Maybe it won't be much longer."

"Well, there's no going back, really," Al said. "I don't know what I'll do when this is over, but I'm sure I've lost my position. Besides, I don't know if I could ever go back to my old life after this. Looking back, it now seems things were so lifeless. I really didn't have a life. No wonder my wife left me and got all involved in some weird group."

"Would you like to have her back?" Maria asked.

"No—that I'm sure of. Not after all that's gone on. I can't tell you much really, but things with her are really scary."

"Danny's such a sweet boy. You're fortunate to have him."

"Yeah," Al said, "but I'm just learning that. I see now that I've wasted so much time. You know, if this hadn't happened, I might have gone on to be an old man and never discovered what life can be. Not that this is that good, it just shows me over and over how totally ignorant I was about so many things in life."

They then drove on in silence for several miles. Al wanted to ask Maria all about herself, but lacked the nerve to ask any personal questions. Maria then started talking about her plans for the morning.

"I'll drop you off at Wal-Mart. I have to run over to one of my offices. Sometimes things come up that take hours to solve. I really don't know when I'll be back."

"It's going to be a nice day," Al said. "I'll just hang around until you come back. Remember, my computer is in your trunk."

"It'll be safe. I've got important things in there, too, not as important as yours, I'm sure."

"Oh," Al said, "sometimes I'm not so sure how important what I do is. I'm trying to do something really important now and can't get it done. Maybe some average guy who's always had to solve problems and fix things the hard way could do a better job than I'm doing."

They drove into town and headed north to the store. Pulling up to the front entrance, Maria stopped and looked over at Al.

"It's been nice to have someone to talk to. Sometimes I—" She cut herself off, then shrugged her shoulders. "I didn't mean anything by that. I'll be back as soon as I can."

Several hours later, Maria picked up Al with his multiple bags of new clothing.

"I've got a closet full of things at home, but we've been living like rabbits out here. Maybe this is a sign we'll be here a while," Al said while he put the bags in the back seat. He got into the front, and Maria drove toward the truck stop.

Moments later, circling around the pumps at the truck stop, Maria broke the silence.

"I'd like that," she said while she parked the car.

"What?"

"Oh, I was still thinking of what you last said; that you might be here for awhile."

"Oh, yeah," Al said. "I'd like that too."

An hour later they were back at the Inn where Maria fixed lunch. Just when they finished eating, there was a knock at the door. Maria went to answer it.

"Hi, Hec," Al heard her greet the guest. "Come on in. We're just finishing lunch, can I get you something?"

"Glass of water. That would be great."

"Hi, Pastor Ramos," Danny said when Hec came into the dining room. "This here's my dad."

"Hi, Mr. Tucker. I'm Hec Ramos. I met your son over at the church last night. Thanks for letting him come," he said to Al.

"Oh sure," Al said, shaking Hec's outstretched hand. "Danny had a good time. Just call me Al, please."

"I hope you don't mind Al, but I brought Danny something. Hec handed Danny a plastic grocery bag. Danny looked at his dad who nodded his approval.

"It's not new," Hec said while Danny took out the baseball glove. "A fellow gave it to me, so I could pass it on to someone who needed one. He'd cleaned out his garage after his last son went off to college. He gave us all kinds of sports stuff. I heard the boys saying last night that you didn't have a glove, so—"

"Wow! This is neat. Thanks a lot. We've got a game planned for later, once it starts to cool off. This'll make the guys happy."

"Good," Hec said. "Maybe I'll see you next week. Sure like to see you Sunday too, if you can make it. Hey, thanks for the water, Maria," Hec said. "You're awfully quiet today, Anton," he said looking across the room.

"Just savin' my voice for all those stories I'm set to tell young Danny here this afternoon."

"That sounds like fun, but I've got to run. We'll see you all later," Hec said, and then he started for the door.

Al rose and followed him. When they reached the door, Al reached his hand out to Hec.

"Thanks for being so good to my son."

"I'm the luckiest guy around, Al. I get to do what I really like to do— help kids. I'm just passing on what someone once did for me."

"Thanks anyway," Al said as Hec opened the door.

Wade took the call from Sonny shortly after coming back from lunch.

"Evelina isn't around. There's a break in the summer kindergarten program and no one's seen her. It's hard to keep up with this year-round school thing anyway. Jake says Max got a call to meet the chief at the mayor's office, but nobody's sure that's where he went. I've looked everywhere for that black Hummer of Evelina's, but I can't find it. I'm going back up to the Pecos. I'll call you tomorrow."

"Be careful."

"Yeah," Sonny said. "I'll be fine."

"Call me."

"Yeah, later."

That night after dinner, Danny took off for the ball game and Anton pushed himself outside. Maria started clearing off the table.

"I'll help you," Al said.

"Oh, well OK," Maria said. After a moment of silence, she spoke again. "I've never had a man help me before."

"There must have been a man in your life before. You said something about using the name Dugan."

"That was my husband. That was a long time ago. Yet, sometimes it only seems like yesterday."

"That sounds like good memories. Was he killed?" Al asked, and then wished he hadn't.

"No and no. The memories aren't good and he's still alive. He's serving life in prison."

"Oh—I didn't mean to pry. I—"

"It's alright. It's been over ten years now. I should be able to talk about it. Hank had me fooled. I thought the world of him. We had a little girl— Julie. She'd be a couple of years older than Danny is now, if—" Maria was quiet for several minutes, then continued. "I'll give you the short story. Without digging up all the details, Hank killed our little girl. He hid her body, but Dad found the grave. Dad wouldn't wait for the police. He went after Hank alone. Hank shot Dad six times—one went through his spine. Hank left Dad for dead. When the sheriff found Dad, they quickly airlifted him to Tucson, and as you see he pulled through—such as he is."

"I'm sorry. That sure must have been tough. I see now why you became part of this Lollypop Railroad," Al said, then started off in a different direction. "I don't know if any of you know how much someone like me appreciates all you folks do. What you all do makes me ashamed of my self-centered life up until now. Maybe someday I can do something back in return. It seems each day that I feel more led to pass on to someone else what's being done for me. Maybe when this is all over for me…"

Al didn't finish his thought. Neither one said anything for a minute, then Maria looked through the window at her father and spoke to Al.

"I hope yours get over. I hope you never have to live with something that never gets over—something that haunts you every day. I love Dad greatly and he's given me so much…" Maria was silent for a moment, and then she went on. "Maybe when he's gone—maybe then I can finally forget and move on. It's not Dad I'm upset with. It's just that seeing him always reminds me… I can't believe I said that to anyone. Forgive me, please."

Early the next morning Sonny cautiously drove into the Pecos Wilderness area. He eased his Jeep across one road, then another and another. When the sun started to lower, Sonny pulled into an area that showed signs of often being used by campers. He turned off the engine and stepped out of his Jeep. He walked over to a tall ponderosa, dropped to the ground, took off his hat then lay back in the shade and soft needles.

He awoke sometime later to find a scraggly looking man standing at his feet. A beat up old .45 Colt automatic was in his hand, and Sonny was looking right up its barrel.

Chapter 19

"Easy there, Mister," Sonny said. "I'm not out to do you any harm. Let's just point that old shooter away from my head. My name's Sonny—Sonny Horn. I'm not here to hurt you, trust me."

"Seen ya driving 'round and 'round. Your eyes was a lookin' back and forth, a lookin' hard for somethin'. Ya saw a lot, but ya didn't see me, no sir, I kept my cover, good soldier that I am. Nobody sees me les'n I want'm to. I followed ya here and been watchin' ya sleep." The bedraggled man slowly slid the big Colt into a scarred up holster. "You don't fool me—Mr. Sonny Horn. I know what you want to see. Ain't none of them to see today. If'n you come a lookin' 'round here in the light of the full moon night—oh, I know their place alright—I even know their faces. They ain't never seen me, though. But I see what they do when they dance to the moon. The owl and the coyote, they know too. I see the devil himself join in their folly. I know him. Sometimes he comes to me at night...."

Neither man said anything for a moment, and then the stranger continued on.

"What they do in the light of the moon, no man can do without the help of that evil one who takes over their minds. I know him. I know what he does to a man's mind. You best scat, I warn ya, Mr. Sonny Horn. Scat before they come."

For no logical reason, the man started spinning around and screaming.

"Leave me alone! I never wanted to kill them. I had to. Leave me alone!" He pointed his old gun as if he was pointing at someone attacking him. "Leave me alone!"

Sonny started to push himself up to his feet but stopped when the man swirled around and pointed the gun at him again.

"They're all gone—all but you. You saved me. You saved me."

"Yeah, I'm your friend. I saved you. Go ahead, put that gun down." The man slowly lowered the gun, slid it into its holster, and then he reached down to help Sonny up. Sonny took his hand and rose to his feet.

"Who are you?" Sonny asked. "What's your name?"

"Tito Lightfoot, sir." The man snapped a salute while he stood at attention, though he seemed to look right through Sonny.

"Sergeant First Class, Tito Lightfoot, Sir," he repeated, then closed his eyes, breathed deeply, then he seemed to relax some. It looked to Sonny as if he was coming back to reality. He dropped his salute, then took a step back. He opened his eyes and spoke slowly.

"Nobody saved me. Why'd they all leave me? I wasn't dead. Then those Charlie-devils came and took me—" At that Tito spun around and pointed his gun all around again.

"Tito, Tito, things are OK. I'm here with you now. No one's going to hurt you," Sonny said. After a few seconds, Tito seemed to relax again.

"Yeah, OK. Who'd you say you were?" Tito asked.

"I'm Sonny. Sonny Horn. I've heard about you. You're the Mescalero Apache fellow, from down Cloudcroft way. You were a POW for a long time—a real hero. Hey, I'm part Membriño myself. We're of the same blood, Tito. That sorta makes you and me family, Tito. Brothers-like, you know?"

Sonny tried to assess his situation. Tito could lead him to what he searched for. It wouldn't happen tonight though. If he spent the night out here in the wilderness with Tito...

"Hey Tito, I'm going to spend the night," Sonny said after a minute. "If I stay here, will you come back and talk to me in the morning?"

"Come on, Sonny. I'm only crazy when something unusual happens around me—something out of the ordinary, ya know? I'm OK now, honest. Come, I've got a good camp, a cave really. I just get nervous around people, but—I've never hurt anyone— except back in Nam. Ahhh—if I'd never had to go there I'd be OK. Now, well, I know I'm a crazy. If someone doesn't shoot me some day, I'll just die out here all alone."

"Hey, get in my Jeep. You can lead me as far as I can drive."

"Yeah, I'll be OK. Didn't mean to scare you, Sonny. I act like a nut, don't I?"

"You seem pretty regular to me now," Sonny said.

"I'm a nut. That's why I live out here. I don't want to hurt anybody— never again."

With that, Tito picked up his old mountain bike and put it in the back of Sonny's Jeep.

"Come on, Sonny. I'll lead you to my place."

★★★

Wade Hawkins sat at his favorite table in the back room of the Roadrunner Grill, eating breakfast and reading the top story in the morning paper. "Pace Arrested" read the bold headline. The story quickly went into the basic details. Max didn't show for his meeting at the mayor's office. A notice went out to the state police to be on the lookout for him. Later in the day, Max was found passed out at a rest area in southern New Mexico. A nearly empty bottle of Kentucky Bourbon lay at his side. He was being held in the Santa Fe city jail without bail.

While Wade read on through the story, J. Quinton Sedwick walked up to his table, pulled out a chair and sat down.

"What's next, Wade? Cops gonna cover this up or hit the floor running to get this all out and cleaned up?" he asked.

"Don't know. Is the whole force polluted or is Max the one bad apple?" Wade asked.

"From all we can find out, he's in this alone, on the force that is. There may be others scattered through the city government though. I've got Bonner hunting down Evelina Vincent. It'll be interesting to see who pops up as Max's attorney. Think any of your colleagues are in that clique?"

"Haven't heard of any. There's a judge on the list that we've compiled though," Wade said.

"Yeah, we've got that too. You think he can manipulate his way into handling this?" J. Quinton asked.

"Surely not. I think we can prove he's connected to Max through this group. I'm sure we can stop that."

"Well, gotta run, Wade," J. Quinton said as he rose and slid his chair back under the table. "This'll be a busy day for sure."

★★★

Maria had just joined the others for breakfast when a phone started ringing in her large brief case. She looked perplexed when she jumped up and rapidly dug out the right phone. She quickly walked toward the patio door, and then went outside to answer it.

A Satellite phone? What is Maria doing with that? Why did she rush outside? Just what is this woman into anyway?

Maria came back to the table in a few moments. No one asked her anything, and she volunteered nothing. After she finished her breakfast, she turned to Al and got real serious.

"I really hate to ask, Al, but I need a favor. I know how busy you are— but you could take your computer with you—can you help me today?"

"Ah, yeah sure. What do you need?" Al asked

"The lady who's been managing one of my offices is sick. I just need to have someone there. I planned to do it myself, but something very important has just come up. I've got to go to Mexico today and don't have any idea what time I'll be back. If you could baby sit that office for me, I'd be most grateful. There's very little you need to know, I'll explain it all on the way into town."

"That sounds like it will work out just fine," Al said.

"Don't worry about young Danny here," Anton said. "I've got a few things around here that I see need done. I'll keep him out of mischief here, and I'm sure his friends will be around later. We'll be just fine."

Al looked over at Danny.

"Yeah, Dad. Me and Anton'll do OK."

"Let me get my computer then," Al said to Maria. "I'll see you in a minute."

On the way into town Maria explained to Al that he'd be collecting packets of documents involving freight that customers wanted shipped into Mexico. There was a form for each to fill out to start the process. She'd take it from there when she got back.

"That's easy enough," Al said. "Most of these are regular customers?"

"Probably all," she said. "I have a very loyal group of shippers."

Late in the morning, after only a few customers, the door opened again. It was a Customs Agent, the same one who'd been out to the Inn last week.

"You're a new face," the agent said. "Maria out?" "Yeah. I'm Al. Maria's not sure when she'll be back."

"That's Maria, alright. You're that new long-term guest out at the Inn. Yeah, you're a researcher she said. I heard Becky here was sick. Maria talked you into this, huh? I'm Corky Cortez, Maria's cousin. She sorta acts as an extra set of eyes and ears for me out here. I watch out for her things, her too, really, so we sorta help each other. I'll check back later." Corky started for the door. "Hey, my number is in that rolodex on the other desk if you need me."

"Thanks," Al said. That explained the Customs car at the Inn. It only clouded Maria's sat-phone and sudden trip to Mexico though.

★★★

Sonny watched the sizzling slices of Spam that Tito fried up for breakfast. Tito had quite a setup here. Being well hidden, one could walk by within a few yards and not notice the cave entrance unless you were looking for it. He had a small cook stove hooked up to a large propane bottle and chests full of canned and boxed food. Tito had talked a lot to him last night. Around his comfort area, Tito acted very normal. He'd told quite a story.

"My sister from down in Ruidoso brings me a new tank of fuel, clean clothes and a mess of food each month," Tito had said. "Takes away my trash too. She's my guardian, ya know. She gets my check and all. I go live with her some in the winter. It gets cold up here then. After a month or two though, I'm back up here. I can't be around people or any noise or the like. I was in that VA home over there, I don't remember where it is now, but I couldn't stay. I took off one day and got out on the interstate and the police grabbed me and put me in the hospital in Las Cruces. Sis got me out and we went camping up here. I found this place. It's been home ever since."

Sonny sat here now and watched Tito make breakfast. He thought of the father he'd never known. He thought of asking Tito if he'd by chance known his father, Captain Jackson T. Horn, but then thought it best not to drudge up old war thoughts. Things were going well this morning. Sonny needed to find the altar, or whatever, used by that cult. Besides, he'd spent way too many hours wondering about his M.I.A. father back when he was younger. None of that really mattered now.

When they'd finished eating, Sonny rested and waited until Tito seemed ready to go.

"What do you think, Tito? You up to leading me to that altar?"

"Told you I can." Tito didn't seem any too anxious. "Why should I?"

"I'm trying to end that whole thing. There's a bunch of us who don't want any more of this to go on. It's not good what they do. You know that."

"It's evil. They scare me. I don't sleep for nights after they've been here. When I do sleep, I have, ahh, they called them flashbacks in the hospital. It's a good thing I'm here alone." Neither man said anything for a few minutes, and then Tito spoke again. "You think you can stop these people?"

"Yeah, I really do. It might take a little while, but we're gonna shut this down."

"OK, Sonny. I'll show you where they meet. I'll show you, but I'll not go there. I'll hide until you're done."

"It won't take me long. I just want to see if I can get any samples of, well, I'll see what's there," Sonny said.

"Let's go then," Tito said, and then he started walking off toward where Sonny had left his Jeep.

Nearly an hour later, Sonny parked the Jeep in an area large enough for a dozen cars or so. He shut off the engine. This was well hidden from the main road, yet easily accessible by any passenger car. Tito said nothing for a minute, sitting in silence with his eyes closed. Sonny waited until he was ready to talk. Finally, he spoke, yet kept his eyes closed.

"Off to the north, over behind that outcrop of boulders. That's what you're looking for. I'll stay here."

Sonny slowly got out of the Jeep and started walking to where Tito had said. Rounding the boulders he froze in his tracks. There lay a flat, rock slab, blocked up level. The grass around it was all worn away and a circle of stones surrounded the altar. Sonny slowly moved forward. He slipped a handful of poly bags and a pair of tweezers from his pocket then started picking up fragments of charred bone. He took out his knife and scraped off dried scabs that he assumed were once small pools of blood. He flinched at the thought that some of what he was picking up might be the remains of children. He took out his camera and snapped about a dozen shots of the altar and everything around it.

He carefully closed and marked the various bags and, after looking around one last time, started for his Jeep. It was empty. Where was Tito?

"Tito? Where are you?" There was no response. "Tito?"

This crazy man with a 45 is hiding somewhere. Being around this has set him off again. Where is he?

With eyes scanning all around, Sonny slowly walked toward the Jeep. As he reached it, he yanked open the door. He slid into the seat, then quickly jammed in the key and turned it to start.

Like a gopher popping from its hole, Tito jumped up from the other side, opened the door and climbed in. He said nothing. Sonny started out the two track trail toward the road. Reaching the sand and rock roadway, he turned back toward Tito's cave. In a few minutes, the other man seemed to relax, and then he started talking.

"You get what you wanted, Sonny?"

"Yeah, I think. Hey, thanks a lot, Tito. I'd have looked a long time before I'd have found that place."

"You'll stop this now?" Tito asked.

"Soon. Real soon," Sonny said. "You OK?"

"'Bout like usual. I'm scared of the devil, Sonny. He's all around. I never know when I'll see him. He's gonna be after you now too, Sonny. Be careful."

"Sure. Hey, if I come back up here sometime, once all this is over, could I spend some time with you?" Sonny asked.

"I 'spose so. Why would you do that?"

"Oh, I'd just like to talk with you, that's all. Beings we're both Apaches, I'll bet we could have some fun together. I know there's lots you can teach me about living like this."

"Come anytime, Sonny."

"You won't shoot me with that 45, will you?"

"Shoot you, Sonny? I can't shoot you. I don't have any bullets. Sis won't let me have any."

Sonny took Tito back near his camp and dropped him off, then headed for the interstate. He took out his cell phone and checked it every few minutes to see if it had service. Finally, when he was only a mile or so from the pavement, several signal bars popped up. Sonny punched in Jake Bonner's number. On the third ring Jake answered.

"Jake? ...Sonny here. I've got it. I've got it! I've got bones and blood. Get ready to send all this stuff to your friend at that lab in California... yeah, I've got it with me now. I'm just ready to leave the Pecos. Have I got a story for you."

Maria finally showed up at the office where Al had spent the day. It was nearly five o'clock.

"I'm sorry, Al. I never expected to be all day. Sometimes— well, what good will excuses do? Hey, let me call Dad, and he can pop in a pizza for Danny and himself. Then you and I can go somewhere and have dinner."

"Oh, yeah, that sounds fine to me. Danny probably will be fine—I'm sure he will be," Al said.

Maria called the Inn and talked to Anton. Al talked to Danny, who thought it was "cool" that Anton would make dinner. Maria slouched into a chair and looked at Al once he'd hung up the phone.

"You know what? Rather than going somewhere with a bunch of noise and people, why don't we just get a pizza ourselves also and head out to the old mine?" she asked.

"The old mine?" Al asked.

"Yeah. When I was a kid that was my favorite place to go. Dad leased it for a while and tried to get it back open. For years, I'd go out there to find peace for my spirit. It always seemed to be the place for me that was closest to God. You know, where I could feel his presence when I talked to him?"

"Ah, well, that's something I don't really understand," Al said. "I never had anything like that."

"Oh, well, if you don't want to—"

"No, I do want to. Pizza and a country sunset sounds perfect," he said.

Maria ordered a pizza, then they drove across town to pick it up. Leaving town, they started out on the road toward the Inn, then turned south toward the border when they reached the Santa Cruz River—now a dry basin waiting to catch the runoff of the coming summer afternoon storms. It seemed Maria drove forever until she pulled up into a road obviously seldom used. After only a few yards she stopped.

"Over there," she pointed. "There's an old wall we can use as a bench."

Al followed her and set the pizza box between them. They ate pizza and drank soda in silence for some time. The sun dropped low in the western sky and the heat of the day started to lift off the dry, baked earth.

"Let me show you around," Maria said when she rose and started walking up the side of a large mound. She spent nearly an hour telling of things she'd done here and there. She laughed when she remembered some of the things in her childhood.

"Look at all this old concrete everywhere. I was just six or eight years old, but I helped Dad mix a lot of it. Three, two and one, three, two, one— I'll never forget that formula. Three shovels of gravel, two of sand, and one of cement. Dad used to say the best things in life, the ones that will last the longest, all had simple formulas. Guess he was right on the concrete. It's still here."

Three, two one... A simple formula. What if you ran that through...?

"Hey, you still here?"

"Oh, sorry," Al said. "Just something you said made my mind slip to what I'm working on. I just let my mind get away from me."

"Well, if you want to go home and get to work—"

"No—no I'll just try something later. It's probably nothing. Just one of those things that pop into your mind when you hear something, know what I mean?"

"I guess." Maria was quiet for several minutes, and then she spoke softly. "I haven't been out here for a long time. I've subdued this along with my other bad memories. See, it was here, over there really," she pointed to a pile of old tailings, "that's where Dad found Julie buried. Of all the places for Hank to do such a thing. He not only stole Julie, he stole all these good memories I had here. I haven't been here since all that happened. Maybe this is the first step in my getting over, I mean really getting over, all of that."

As they stood there a cool breeze blew up from the mountains to the south.

"Come," Maria said. "This is enough for one time." They walked back to the wall and the empty pizza box. Maria stopped and turned to Al.

"Hold me, please. I just need to feel someone's arms around me. Let me pretend I have someone to care about me. Sometimes I think I'll lose my mind. I'm so tugged at, yet pressed upon, both at the same time. I can go so long. I can be the strong one for so long, then…"

Al reached out and put his arms around Maria when she came to him. She wrapped her arms around him and buried her face in his chest. Something in him wanted desperately to tell her that he would protect her, that he would care for her forever and ever. Instead of saying anything, he just stood there holding her, his body quivering like a nervous teenager.

Al went back to his room that night and turned on his computer. *Three, two, one… the simple things…* He started reorganizing a line of the code in these simple sequences. Suddenly weather data for the month of September at DFW airport started filling his screen.

Chapter 20

The next morning, Wade Hawkins sat in his office while Sonny sat across his desk, excitedly telling about his experiences in the Pecos while Wade looked at the pictures of what he'd collected. They'd overnighted the bone and blood samples to the lab where Jake Bonner had connections. Now it would take days, maybe weeks, for definitive results.

"This guy, Tito Lightfoot, you should see him, Wade," Sonny said. "He's smart enough to stay out of people's way. There's a lot of do-gooders around who'd try to put him back into a hospital or mental home type place. Others might harass him enough he'd flip completely. I think he's OK out there— physically anyway. He knows his fears and limitations. As long as his sister checks in on him, I think he's alright. He's tormented by the devil. Claims he actually sees him. He probably does see evil spirits, or such. He needs to be set free of that spiritual captivity."

Sonny was quiet for some time. "He needs a true miracle, so he does," he then said softly. "That's what it would take to restore the likes of Tito Lightfoot."

Wade nodded. "Let's hope nothing happens to his sister."

"Yeah. I'm going to go down and look her up when I get time. I'd like to do something to help this guy."

"Did Jake have anything to say about Max?" Wade asked.

"Max isn't talking. I'd say he's more afraid of Evelina than the law. I think he believes he can beat this. I'd say his mind is really twisted."

Nita buzzed Wade.

"Yes?... Alright, send them in," Wade said.

Wade shook his head and pushed back his chair. "It's our two misdirected FBI agents," he said to Sonny. "Sit tight. This shouldn't take long."

Agents Huck Miles and Sig Simpson walked through the door and up to the side of Wade's desk, ignoring Sonny.

"Wade Hawkins," Huck Miles said, "you're under arrest for obstruction of justice and assisting a fugitive in interstate flight. You have the right..."

★★★

"You alright?" Maria asked Al when he walked into the inn's dining room the next morning.

"Yeah, great, really. Been up all night, though. I finally cracked a big chunk of all that stuff I'd been working on. There's only one section that still stumps me. I've got to burn CD copies and get them to ah… well; I can't risk any kind of electronic transfer. I just don't trust that. Besides, there's a security thing on the other end where I've been sending my notes. Sending notes there is one thing, all this data; well, it might get someone in trouble. Someone besides me that is. I've got to put this in one of my assistants' hands myself. Can you make contact with Lollypop and see what she can set up?"

"Ahh—yeah. I can do that. What do you have in mind?"

"I thought maybe Bacho could fly me up somewhere close to where he picked me up originally. Somewhere where I can meet one of my assistants. Kurt would be best. Lollypop knows how to reach him. She has a contact number of someone who will see him in person and arrange our meeting."

"Kurt you said. I'll see what she thinks of that. Does this mean this whole project is solved?"

"Not at all. This is just raw data. At least now someone can start to make some sense out of it. There's still that last section though… it's just so different."

"You alright to go to the office today?" Maria asked.

"You might catch me napping on the job. Guess you'll just have to fire me."

"Fat chance. I'll make that contact after I drop you off." Al looked at Danny. "You're awfully quiet."

"Oh, just thinkin'."

"About what?"

"We ain't gonna have to go home now, are we Dad?"

"No. This might take some of the heat off me though."

"So this might be a good thing?" Danny asked.

"It's a great thing."

"All right, Dad. That's cool. Maybe we can stay here forever."

★★★

Late that afternoon, Maria showed up at the office Al was attending.

"Alice will pick you up in the morning and take you back up on the Circle S. All goes as planned, you'll be back here the day after."

"Don't suppose you'll tell me any more details."

Maria slowly shook her head.

"Alice said to make sure you read today's Phoenix paper. Said you'd figure out what she was talking about. I got a copy for you." Maria handed Al the paper. He opened it and there on the front page, below the fold, was a story title: *Santa Fe attorney jailed in missing DAD case.*

Al walked over to a window and looked out. Wade was in jail. This was all his fault. An innocent man, a good man, one who spent much of his time helping those in need, was in trouble over him.

This has got to end soon. That's just not fair at all. He doesn't know anything.

"You OK?" Maria asked.

"Yeah. Well, I'm thinking about tomorrow. You got this covered tomorrow?"

"Yeah. Don't worry about a thing. Just be careful."

"Careful? As I see it, in this outfit you just sit back and go for the ride. Especially if Bacho's involved."

About dark that night, Sonny Horn and Jake Bonner sat drinking iced tea in the back room of the Roadrunner Grill.

"J. Quinton is going to make this stink all the way to Washington," Jake said. "Just what do they think they're going to get out of Wade?"

"Beats me, Jake. Maybe they think Dr. Vincent will hear about this and give up. Wade's serious, though. He doesn't know where the Vincents are, and I doubt if they're reading the *Santa Fe Gazette*. Look at this," Sonny said, looking across the room, "here comes Luke Lane."

"I wonder if this is official or a fishing trip," Jake said, soft enough that Luke couldn't hear.

Before Sonny could answer, Luke reached their table and pulled out a chair. "I know I'm butting in, guys, but I promise I won't be here too long. I heard about Wade—only after it happened, though. I don't know what's going on with the feds, honest."

"You got a plate full as it is, right Detective? Are you taking over this whole enchilada?" Sonny asked.

"I want to. It appears as if I'll be appointed acting Chief of Detectives in the morning. Look, I know I stood up for Max when I should have cut and run, but I want to get this all out and clear. We've got to find out what happened to those kids. Don't think we'll like what we find, but we got to do it. If Max will talk—"

"He's more afraid of Evelina than anyone. Speaking of her majesty, have you seen her since the Rhea Thatcher thing?" Sonny asked.

"She's keeping a low profile," Luke said. "I was over there tonight. She was out. I think I'll cruise by again when I leave here."

"Might do the same myself," Jake said. "We might see you over there. J. Quinton would surely like to have me talk to her."

"She's not going to give you anything but some story. She's good at that. Max believed them all. I don't know how he could—" Luke cut himself off.

"He was lonely; she was exciting," Sonny said. "Things didn't start out to be so far out. She's a kindergarten teacher, remember? That's how these things start out. They seem good, then they get a little off and before you know it you're on a roller coaster ride."

"Hey guys, I've got to go," Luke said. "I'll talk to you tomorrow after I meet with the big chief. Maybe you can get a good story in the paper? A positive word about the department in the paper might be a big help."

"Yeah," Jake said. "Call me tomorrow. Hey, good luck, Luke."

Luke nodded to Sonny who'd nodded his agreement with Jake. After he left, the two finished their tea, then went out into the parking lot.

"Without old Max to keep a tail on, I'm gonna be bored," Jake said.

"Let's take a cruise past Evelina's," Sonny said. "Be interesting to see if there are any strange cars there."

They drove in Sonny's Jeep across town. Nearing Evelina Vincent's neighborhood, when they turned a corner, they faced two patrol cars with light bars flashing.

"Looks as if someone ran off the street into that cottonwood," Jake said. "Hey, look Sonny, isn't that Luke Lane's car? How'd he—" Sonny stepped on the gas and sped up to the scene. Jake jumped out and walked up to the yellow ribbon. One of the officers, a man called Flint, came over to him.

"Howdy, Jake. Things are getting mighty weird around here. First, all that mess with Max, then the Hawkins thing, now this."

"What happened, Flint?" Jake asked.

"Looks as if someone pulled up beside Luke and shot him while he drove along. That kid over there by my car claims he saw it happen from down the street," Flint said. "I don't know if I believe him or not. Could be he's covering for someone else— one of his friends. You know how that is."

"What's he say happened?" Jake asked.

"He doesn't really know much. He can't identify the other car exactly. All he can say is it was big and black."

Jake and Sonny looked at each other.

"Hey thanks Flint. I'll catch you for the rest of the story at the shift change, OK?" Jake asked.

"Sure Jake, just spell my name right."

Sonny drove past Evelina's house. Finding it dark and lifeless, he turned back toward the grill to drop Jake off at his car. Neither one said anything for several blocks. Sonny spoke first.

"He wasn't a bad guy. He sure was loyal. There's something to say for that, you know? What's going to happen now? This really sends a powerful message to the next guy who takes on these cases."

"I'd say that's the main purpose of this. Things just might turn cold now." Jake stayed quiet for a moment, then he spoke again. "This surely has been one sour couple of days, what with Wade and now this—"

"I'm going home," Sonny said. "I'm tired. I've got school most of tomorrow. With Wade in the slammer, I'll have to find out how he was in contact with Doctor Vincent. I'm surprised the Feds didn't show up with a search warrant for Wade's computer and such. Guess that might have been tough, with all his client info in there—then too, all the local judges seem to like Wade. Getting a warrant might be problematic. A Federal judge in Albuquerque though…"

"I've got to see Flint at the station at midnight. I'll write up the story, then knock off," Jake said. "Might see you around somewhere tomorrow night."

"Yeah," Sonny said, "maybe tomorrow night."

★★★

Danny ran to the truck when Alice pulled in the next day at lunch time.

"Alice, Alice, Alice!—" he said as he gave her a hug. "How's that baby colt?"

"Getting big. We had another one last night."

"Ahh. I gotta see that. Whatcha gonna call it?"

"Don't know. Haven't even named the last one yet. Usually something happens that gives them their name. Once we sell them, the new owners usually pick their own name anyway. You're lookin' good. That Maria's a good cook, now isn't she?"

"Great. Me'n Anton play games a bunch. Got friends I play ball with too."

"I'll have your daddy back before you know it. Don't you worry none about him."

"Yeah. I'd kinda like to go with him…"

"You'll be going home soon now. I just believe it." "Yeah. Ain't sure that'd be good."

Alice tussled his hair, and then waved to Maria. Al came over to the truck clutching a small bag with the disks.

"Be good, Son. I'll see you soon."

"Me'n Anton will be just fine, Maria too," Danny said as he looked at Maria, who'd walked over with Al.

"Be careful," she said to Al, a look of concern in her eyes. "I want you back, safe and sound. I'll take care of Danny. Don't you worry about anything. Just come back."

"As soon as I can."

"Gotta run, Maria. I'll talk to you when we come back," Alice said as she started the truck, turned it around, and then started up the road.

"Sit back and relax, Al. This is all going to work out. You and Danny will be able to start your own real new life before you know it."

"I feel as if I'm going into the mouth of the lion, but I've got to do this. If something goes wrong…"

"A little faith, Al. Just have a little faith."

★★★

Red Conners looked at Evelina Vincent as she sat across his desk. Six weeks ago he'd wanted to get as close to this woman as he could. Now there was a part of him that wanted to tell her to get out and leave him alone. Still, she intrigued him. She had such a cold way about her, and something about that iciness attracted him in some strange way.

"Send off a copy of this picture to every university and community college library in Arizona, New Mexico, and Texas, maybe Oklahoma too. He's out there somewhere using those public internet outlets. Take a fistful of these and start up and down the interstates, showing them at all those travel and truck stops. Someone has to have seen him by now. He's such a nerd. He can't be out there alone. I want him before the FBI gets their fingers on him."

Why? Red wanted to ask. The internet was everywhere now. He could never find what Evelina wanted him to find. However, when she wrote out another four-figure, bonus check…. He was in this too deep to give up now anyway. Even thinking of quitting sent a shiver down Red's spine. What would this woman do to him if he bailed out?

"I'll head out in the morning," he said.

"Find them. Then we'll talk about a place for you in the Saints of Seven. I think you're our type."

Red slowly nodded his head—but his heart was having serious second thoughts.

★★★

Alice drove up the ranch road to the little meadow where Bacho had dropped Al and Danny off that night that now seemed like many months ago to Al.

"I'll wait. I think we're about an hour early."

Al sat tapping his fingers on the window edge. He closed his eyes and leaned his head back.

"I see my attorney is in jail because of me. That makes me feel awful. What I'm doing now could backfire also. Somebody else could get in trouble. I surely wish there had been a different way."

"But there wasn't. You've done what you had to. That boy of yours, he's going to be something special someday. He'll make you really proud. I just feel it."

"Just remember, I don't have custody of him. If this all comes to an end, I might never see him again. I could be charged with kidnapping and

186

who knows what all and he could go back to his mother. I try not to think of that, but it's a real possibility."

"Hadn't thought of that," Alice said. "Mercy, you surely do have a lot on your mind."

"First of all, we've got to hold this country together for the next generation and so on," Al said. "We've got to defeat all these terrorists who want to tear us apart. I don't want to live as they do. But I see that coming if we don't stand together and defeat them. I want to do it somewhere other than here, too. I know that means a lot of our young people have to go to wherever, but that's better than them having to line our streets to save us, I guess."

"Lost my husband in Vietnam," Alice said quietly. "My only son in the first Gulf War. My dad was shot to pieces back in WWII. It burns me to no end that some here want to just roll over and let some god awful way of life take over. If it ain't those radical Muslims it's those crazy environmentalists who want to turn us back into cave people. I for one am getting mighty fired up at some of our sissy politicians. I'd like to go down there myself and show them what a backbone is."

They sat in silence for several minutes. Then Al heard a distant drone of an engine.

"Something's coming."

"Yeah, I hear it too," Alice said. "It's probably Bacho. He's usually early. He likes to leave time to skirt a storm or whatever."

In a few minutes, Bacho set the chopper down and gave a big thumbs up to Alice.

"Thanks again, Alice. I owe you a bunch," Al said as he opened the truck door.

"Save the country. That'll be good enough for me."

Al grabbed his bag, lowered his head into the whirling wind of the flailing rotor, then ran for the chopper.

"Howdy, Amigo," Bacho greeted him. "How's the little guy?"

"Doing a lot better than I am. Are we going to pull this off?"

"Relax. You know how it is. Let old Bacho do his thing, and nothing will go wrong," Bacho said as he grabbed a roll of camo-print duct tape and tossed it to Al. "Jump out and put strips of tape over the numbers." When both sides were covered, Al jumped back into the passenger's seat, tossed the tape into the back, strapped on his belt, then grabbed the bar on the dash as Bacho opened the throttle. Both men waved to Alice as they lifted off.

"We got our orders, Boss. We need to get in, and then get back out. The rest is a dream," Bacho said, then gave one of his big grins.

Al nodded. The sun was behind them. They were going almost due east. That wasn't the way to Los Alamos. Al knew better than to ask where they were going. He'd learn where they were at when they got there.

The sun was behind the mountains to their west, turning that sky a bright orange, when they put down on a pad at a small airstrip unfamiliar to Al. He'd seen a large lake as they'd crossed the mountains moments ago. He figured that was Elephant Butte. This had to be the Sierra County Airport.

"Why here?" he asked.

"As I was told, the feds have one of your co-workers covered like bark on a tree, but the other one seems to be pretty free. That was who you wanted anyway. This guy made it known he was coming down to the lake to fish and clear his head tomorrow. He's to be here any minute. Hopefully, he wasn't followed."

Al nodded. That would be Kurt. He hoped the exchange was quick, so he wouldn't have to listen to any of Kurt's criticism.

"Should be him now," Bacho said as a car came down the road and turned into the airport drive.

"Yeah, that's Kurt's Corvette."

Kurt pulled up to them, then quickly got out.

"You got it all solved? Tell me you got it all solved."

"Hello to you too, Kurt," Al said. "All but one section. That part's really weird. I'll keep at it though."

"Hey!" Bacho yelled, pointing to two dark sedans with no lights on coming down the road. "They must have hidden a locator in your car. Guess they'll give you an escort back to the lab. This stuff will be good and safe now for sure. Time for us to vamoose, Amigo."

Al jumped back in and slammed the door. As the chopper lifted off the two cars flipped on both their flashing headlights and their portable, dashboard red strobes as they raced towards them. As Al looked back, the last thing he could see was a man jumping out of his car and pointing a gun at Kurt.

"That best be the feds. I surely wouldn't want those disks to get into the wrong hands."

"Those were feds. I could smell them coming. I'm going up. I don't think we can hide. It's getting dark and I don't want to try and stay below radar. Some local sheriff or the like might get above me, trying to be a hero by attempting to force me down. Someone on the ground could pop off a round through us too. I'd rather get up in the clean air and have lots of room below. Keep an eye out for company."

"What do you mean?" Al asked.

"We're about a hundred miles to the border. If there's anything already up waiting for us, they'll pick us up any minute. If they have to scramble a couple of birds from Holloman or Biggs, I figure it'll take them about half way there to catch up. Hot diggity, this gets my blood going."

"They won't shoot us down, will they?"

"You're the golden egg, Amigo. They want you alive. You're safe, man. You're in my hands—the best. They're just gonna try and force me down. That's why I want lots of air below. Hang on to your stomach."

Al closed his eyes and leaned his head back. After a while, he started looking around. He looked at his watch. They'd been in the air about twenty minutes. Maybe nothing was coming. Maybe Bacho was just playing some silly game. Another ten minutes went by.

"Maybe we're OK. Shouldn't we head back to Arizona?" Al asked.

"They're coming. Five more minutes, I'd say. They'll have to back off about five miles from the border, so we've got about fifteen minutes of fun."

"Maybe—" Al was cut off. It swooped in from their left. Big, black, and spewing fire right across in front of them. Then another one banked up on its side and cut across from the other side. The little chopper shuttered as it cut the wake left by the banking jet.

"Yooooeee!" Bacho cried, and then let out a big laugh. "Down we go, Amigo."

Chapter 21

Danny and Anton sat out on the patio, eating chocolate ice cream.

"How 'bout a game of checkers?" Anton asked.

"Naah."

"Your ice cream is melting. Come on now. Your daddy is just fine. He'll be back before you know it. No sense frettin' about it. Eat up, now."

Danny slowly ate his ice cream, and then slid the empty dish across the table.

"I've got a good story about the Indians I haven't told you yet. Want to hear it?"

"Naah. Tomorrow, maybe."

"Hey, like I said, my little friend, this'll all be over soon. Then you can go home."

"But that's just it, Anton. I don't ever wanta go back home."

Pulling up out of his short dive as the pursuing planes made another sweep, Bacho banked left, then again dropped what seemed to Al to be hundreds of feet. Al closed his eyes and grabbed his throat. Suddenly, they were climbing again.

"Come on boys. I beat off every demon Mig that ever came my way. I'll beat you too. Hang on, Amigo."

The two jets made another crisscross sweep in front of them, this time closer. Bacho swooped right as he again dropped below the rippling airfoil.

"One more then they'll have to go home. Bet they're having as much fun as we are. This is the real thing for them. Here they come."

This time the jets both came from the left side, one above the other. Bacho powered his craft right through between their paths. Al hit his head on the door as the rough air whipped them side to side.

"Down we go. That's the border, those lights over there," he nodded down to their left. "Goin' low now so we'll get out of Las Cruces and El Paso radar."

"Where to then?" Al asked, hanging on as they dove toward the lights on the ground.

"Gator's. He's an old army buddy of mine. He's got a little ranch of sorts on down here. We'll hole up there."

"How long?"

"As long as it takes. Man, you're too tight. I'll get you to where someone can find you, and then I'll call Lollypop. Think I'll swap choppers with Gator for a while. He's got one about like this, only a faded orange color. Anyone looking for me will be looking for this drab, olive one. I'll wait on the wind or a storm to bring down the aerostats, then go home."

"The aerostats?"

"Those radar balloons strung out along the border to detect low flying aircraft."

"You mean like us?"

"We're in Mexico, Amigo. I can taste the tequila already. We made it. Your stuff got delivered safely. Your friend will have a good escort back to Los Alamos. Everything's cool."

"You said this would be a dream."

"It is, it is. A little bit like a nightmare, but this is fun. I haven't had that much fun since, well, I don't even know."

"How am I going to get back out of Mexico?" Al asked. "With all this trouble, I really don't want to be here. Can't we just head for Arizona now?"

"They'll be watching the entire border tonight. Relax. You'll get back out of here. Piece of cake. You're too uptight, Al. The sun will come up tomorrow, and we'll live another day. If not... gotta go someday."

They skirted the flatland for what seemed to be an hour or longer. Al looked at his watch: It had only been forty minutes. On they flew. Al looked at his watch often. Looking again, it had been nearly two hours now since they'd crossed the border. Then, apparently seeing some landmark Al didn't see, Bacho made a quarter turn to the right.

"Not far now. I've never put down here at night. Maybe Gator'll turn a light on for us."

Coming upon a faint light in what soon was revealed to be a house, Bacho made several circling passes. Soon an outdoor light came on, and he set the chopper down near what appeared to be a barn.

As the blades wound down to a stop, an almost gaunt looking man in torn jeans and Harley Davidson t-shirt came hobbling out to meet them. The turbulence from the still turning rotors blew his long ponytail over his shoulder. He reached up with his tattoo-covered arms to help Bacho.

"I shoulda known you'd be a showin' up. Got a call on the short wave from old Froghead up in the tower in Cruces and he was tellin' me about some fool duelin' with two fighters on the border. I should have known it had to be you. What are you up to anyway? What's the hot load?"

"This is my friend Al. We, uh, we need to hide for a spell."

"What's the gig?"

"Kinda secret."

Gator pointed at Al. "You gotta be that code fella from Los Alamos. Hot dog."

Al stared at Gator, not knowing what to think.

"It's cool. It's cool with me. My lips are sealed. I'm still on their wanted list too. Stay as long as you need to."

"I'll need to swap birds for a while," Bacho said.

"She's all fueled up and ready to go. Anytime, Bacho, anytime."

"Got anything to eat?" Bacho asked.

"More than plenty. Let's get inside. This light'll run down my batteries in no time. Man it's good to have some real company. Fella gets to itch'n for someone to talk to sometimes. Oh, I hop over to the village now and again to get supplies and the like, but that's not like real folks, not really."

Gator went about fixing Bacho and Al up a plate of eggs with a healthy slab of steak on the side. As they ate, Bacho and Gator talked on, Al sat and listened.

"How's the leg?" Bacho asked.

"'Bout the same. Dug out a dime sized piece of shrapnel 'bout a month ago that had worked its way out to the edge. Got to hurtin' like a hot iron every time I put weight on it. Arthritis, or whatever, is a gettin' worse. Get to thinkin' sometimes I shoulda just let them take it off when they wanted to. One of them plastic ones might not be so bad after all."

"Got my Ka-Bar out in my bird," Bacho said. "I know you got a bottle of tequila on a shelf somewhere. You get gassed up good on that, then bite down good on that broom handle, and I'll go to it."

"How 'bout we just do a practice run? We just get gassed on the tequila and forget about cuttin' off my leg."

"Last time I was here you'd about sworn off that stuff and were keeping steady company with old Mary Jane."

"Oh, I ain't cut back on the weed at all. I've just got ta washin' it down with a little liquid smoke. I saw a bottle of that on the store shelf and thought somebody had the right name, just the wrong ingredients. How 'bout you, Al?"

"Ah—well, I don't care what you do. Myself…"

"Let me guess. You're a wine guy. Yeah, I'm sorry I didn't have the right vintage to go with them eggs. What would that be anyway?"

"No, I mean, I'll have a little tequila, sure."

"Sociable guy, I like that," Gator said. "Got some Corona too. Kinda mild, but maybe more to your liking."

"Well, yeah. That would be better."

Gator rose and hobbled over to a small gas powered refrigerator. He opened it and took out a longneck bottle and tossed to Al.

"Thanks," Al said. "I really appreciate your taking me in."

"Don't know how you and Bacho got hitched up, but any friend of his is cool with me. I just ain't much on the social ladder. That doesn't mean I don't know the other side. Grew up in New Jersey. Whole family is high society. All but me and my older brother. He fled to Canada to avoid the war. Me, I went in guns blazing and came back a bonafide hero. Ribbon and star decorated, so I was. Yet, here I hide in Hell. Thanks to the good old US of A," Gator said, spitting on the floor. "My brother can't go there because he refused to go to a stupid war. I went, came back all shot to pieces, then protested what was going on, and now I can't go home either. Go figure. Of course, I've got to tell you, my protesting involved more dynamite than words."

Gator took a jug of tequila off the shelf, handed it to Bacho, then got two glasses. He grabbed a quart sized metal can and half a dozen cigarette papers off the table, and then slumped back into his old chair.

Al looked around, and seeing nothing any better, stretched out on the floor. He rolled up a blanket lying there and made a pillow. He thought about his son. He was in good hands. Maria would take good care of him. Maria... just what all was she up to? What all was she carrying across the border? When would he see her again? How would he make it to the border, then across it safely?

After several hours of drinking and smoking, the other two men seemed to forget Al was there. Gator talked most of the time, while Bacho listened. Part of the time, Al did too.

"We're gonna have to pay some day. Yes sir, you know some day we're gonna face some God or whatever, and they're gonna know what all we did over there."

Bacho said nothing as he rolled up another joint.

"I mean it was the right thing to do," Gator said. "You know we did good. I mean..."

There was silence for a minute. Then Gator started talking again.

"You still believe all that God stuff like we did over there? Was that all just somethin' to lean on when bullets were a flyin' and blood was a squirtin' all over all night long?" Gator paused for a minute, and when Bacho didn't respond, he then rambled on. "All night long. Bullets a flyin'. Blood all over. Remember that kid? The one we dubbed Cowboy?"

Bacho still said nothing.

"Came at me with a grenade. He came at me with... why'd he come a killin' at me? Why'd I have to shoot the little toad? I still see his eyes as he came a runnin' at me screamin' like a Comanche."

Gator took another drink, then slowly rolled and lit a new joint.

"Blood went everywhere. I still see li'l Cowboy's blood goin' all over the place. God's gonna get me for that."

"My god takes care of his people," Bacho said. "You're a white man. Maybe all that God stuff we lived over there fits you, but I got my old ways. Navajo ways. Navajo god. He's got my back. Got me covered."

"Got us a ribbon for getting that info outta them gooks at that old snaky swamp, remember? You remember?" Gator asked. "We saved lives, the Major said. We were heroes, the Major said. God was on our side, the Chaplain said. I still see the look of fear in the eyes of those boys when we took'em way up in your chopper and started pushin' em out, one at a time."

There was silence for several minutes. Gator then started talking again.

"Three. I pushed out three of them boys until one of the others started singin' like a robin after a rain. We got our ribbons. We saved lives. You and me buried them busted up bodies so's no one would see how we got it all done. I remember shovelin' in the dirt on top of them. Blood everywhere. Bullets flyin'. God's gonna get us someday, Bacho. Me'n you are gonna pay. I'm already in Hell. I don't know what could be worse, but I fear it's comin'."

"You think too much," Bacho said. "We did what was right. Forget it. Move on. Find some excitement and get your mind off the past."

"Bullets. Blood everywhere. I didn't want ta shoot ya, li'l Cowboy. God's gonna get me someday."

★★★

When the sun rose the next morning, so did Al. He quietly went outside and sat in the shade of Bacho's chopper. He hadn't slept much on the hard, dirty floor. The conversation of last night didn't help. Now he pondered what Gator had said about his Vietnam days. How would he have handled being faced with what these men had been faced with? Could he kill a child? Could he get critical information at any cost?

Then he got to thinking about God. Was God out there to punish everyone in the end as Gator perceived? Was that what God was all about? Al always tried to shut out the things Carla tossed out about God, but now found he remembered many of them anyway. Love, forgiveness, new life, peace, wisdom, compassion, strength… she'd used all these words when talking about God and his place in her life. Who was right, Gator and his fear of judgment, or Carla and what Al saw as utopian optimism? Or was he right for rejecting the whole thing as imagination.

★★★

Sally Browning sat at her kitchen table. She'd pushed back the dirty dishes—not just today's dishes, or even yesterdays'. From when they were, she didn't remember. After making room for the newspaper, she then spread it out in front of her. Until a few minutes ago, she'd not gotten the papers off the porch for several days, so she hadn't seen the pictures of

Max or read of his arrest. She picked up a kitchen knife and started stabbing Max's picture.

"You killed my Kreg," she cried out. "It was you. I know it was you." On and on she went while she stabbed the front-page picture until it was unrecognizable. Then she threw it across the table where it landed on a large pile of mail. People had sent her checks. The newspaper had set up a fund, but all of this lay in a pile, un-cashed and unused. Sally then reached over and grabbed the paper and threw it on the floor. She then stomped on it with all the force she had.

Finally, she slumped back onto her chair. She put her head in her hands and let the tears flow again, as they had every day since Kreg disappeared. Soon she drifted off into a shallow, dream- controlled sleep with her head resting on the hard kitchen table. Then the dream came again, the one she'd had time after time. There she was, reaching out for Kreg, but never quite getting a hold of his outstretched hands. Then he slowly drifted away into darkness, disappearing with one last scream.

Sally then jolted awake, as with every time before. She looked at the mutilated paper at her feet. The time had come to do something. Moments later, she moved slowly across her driveway, her tattered bathrobe clinging to her bony shoulders while the bottom flapped in the breeze. She moved slowly, deliberately, more like a carnival mime than the youthful woman she really was. She entered her garage and, with all the strength she could muster, dug out an old wooden stepladder, and half carried, half dragged it into her house.

She spread the ladder's legs under the entryway hole in the laundry room that led to the crawlspace above. She stepped up on the first step, then the next. She pushed up the square of sheet rock that covered the opening. Pushing that aside, she next pushed back a piece of pink, fiberglass insulation. She pushed herself up another step, then another. Soon she was using all her strength to push herself up through the hole, into the dark, cramped attic space. She sat on the piece of loose plywood used for a floor to store several trunks of things. After her eyes adjusted somewhat to the darkness, she pushed herself through the dust over to one of the trunks. She knew this was the right one. She lifted the lid, and then reached inside. She first took out the flag she'd been given from her late husband's casket. His dress uniform was next. She held the jacket to her chest and touched each of the medals and ribbons. The tears she shed were absorbed by the heavy, woolen cloth.

"Buck," she whispered. "I miss you so. Guess you know about Kreg. Maybe he's with you—he's not with me anymore. I might be with you soon too. I don't know."

She reached back into the trunk. There were many other things there, but they held no interest to her today. She felt around the bottom, and then she felt it, smooth and hard. She drew it out and held it against her pounding heart. She reached back in the trunk and found a small but heavy cardboard box. She withdrew that also, then put the uniform and flag back in. She slid over to the opening and dropped her feet down to the top step of the ladder. Slowly, she made her way back down. Once down she didn't bother to put the insulation or cover back over the hole.

She went back to the kitchen table, picked up the paper then re-read the story on Max. She looked at a calendar, then her watch. She flopped open the cylinder of the old duty revolver. Then out of the cardboard box, she took one bullet for each of the six chambers. She dropped each into the empty chambers, one at a time. Then she rotated the cylinder back into the gun frame. She slipped the loaded gun into her purse. She headed for the bathroom. She had time for a much needed shower. When was the last time? She turned on the water, and then took a towel out of the closet.

She knew what she'd wear: that black dress, the one she'd worn to Buck's funeral. Half an hour later she sat putting on make-up and fixing her hair. She then stared at her face in the mirror. She hadn't seen that face, not really, for over a month now. Then, feeling hungry for the first time in days, she went to her refrigerator and found a half-full bowl of soup. She stuck it in the microwave. Finishing that, she felt a burst of energy. She got up and started for the door.

Al sat out in the shade for several hours. He remembered that back at the lodge he thought he might get hungry somewhere along the trip, so he'd put a granola bar in the paper sack he'd carried the CD's in. He wasn't going to get any hungrier than he was now. He was pretty sure neither Bacho nor Gator would be up to any breakfast, or even lunch. He opened the chopper door and retrieved his oatmeal-laden, energy bar. He was nearly finished with it when Bacho emerged from the little, plastered-adobe home.

"Whooee," he said as the sun hit his eyes. "We gotta get that bird under roof. Satellite photos, you know. Should have done that last night. We best get you out of here real soon. We'll swap with Gator, then head for Cananea. I'm sure Lollypop can have someone meet you there."

"Where's that?" Al asked.

"Not too far from Nogales. On this side of the border. I'll come back here for a few days. Let's get the gear swapped out." Bacho started toward a barn with an open center. Al followed, and once near the barn, he saw the other chopper in the open runway. Bacho hooked a chain on the skids. After several tries, Gator's old pickup truck started, and Bacho backed it towards the chain. Al looped the chain around the ball hitch, then hooked the grab hook over the chain. Bacho then slowly pulled the helicopter out into the open. He was pulling his into the barn when Gator joined him.

"You ain't leavin' so soon, are ya?"

"I'll be back. I want to take Al over to Cananea. I'll get him all fixed up to get back into the states, then be back. Figure I owe you a jug of tequila anyway."

"Yeah, but it stays corked tonight. Man I can't do that like I used to. Bring me some eggs and bacon too. Maybe in a day or two I'll feel like eatin' again.

A short time later, Al and Bacho put down at a little airstrip. Bacho went to a phone and called Lollypop. It took about half an hour to work out the details, but he finally was told to leave Al there. Someone would pick him up in a couple of hours.

"I'm gonna hitch a ride over to the town. Do some shopping and what not. If you're still here when I get back, I'll wait 'til your ride comes. If you're gone, then I'll know you're on your way to wherever. Hey, ahh… last night—just forget about Gator, OK? He gets all uptight when he gets juiced up. He's alright, really he is."

Al nodded. "Thanks, Bacho. I really needed you to help me. Be safe. Don't get into any trouble over me."

"Trouble? Man, that's the most fun I've had in years. Let's do it again sometime." At that Bacho gave a big laugh and slapped Al on the shoulder. "Later, Amigo."

Al went over to a bench against the shady side of the building and sat down. He sensed that everyone there was keeping tabs on him, wondering what he was up to.

Any of these guys connected to any of that drug trouble? What's my chances of ever getting out of here? My son—I've got to get back to my son.

Thirty minutes went by, then forty, then an hour. As Al tried to take a nap, a produce truck pulled up and parked along the road. The driver got out and came over to Al.

"Señor, you be Meester Al, friend of Maria?"

"Yeah. Sure, I'm Al. Yeah, I'm Maria's friend."

"She ask me to geeve you ride to Nogales. Come, Señor Al. We go in me trucka to Nogales."

Chapter 22

Al followed the driver to the truck and climbed in the passenger's side. He noticed that on the driver's door the name "Nacho" was painted in hand-lettered, gold colored script. Once inside the truck, Al attempted to have a conversation with the driver.

"On the door it says Nacho. Is that you?"

"Sí. Nacho Garza. Thees be me trucka. Haul fruit to you country. What you do here? How you get here?"

"Long story. I was down here with some other fellows, and something's come up that I need to go back home."

"You friend of Maria. You lucky man. She one fine Señora. Ehhh, one fine wooman as you say."

"That she is," Al said. He leaned his head back and closed his eyes. In a couple of hours, barring any trouble, he'd be back at Maria's. Nacho reached over and turned on the radio to a Spanish music station. That suited Al. Now he didn't need to try and make conversation, or answer anymore questions. Now he could sit here and worry.

★★★

Wade Hawkins sat in the little visitation room across from his mother.

"You OK, Son?"

"Yeah, I'm doing alright. Don't worry, Mother. This can't be for long. Yesterday I heard I was to be transferred to the Federal holding in Albuquerque, but today the guard said that's been canceled. Maybe they'll let me go. Maybe they've learned that I can't tell them any more than I have because I don't know anything."

"Things aren't the same at home without you. I could be happy if you'd gotten married and moved out but—"

"Please, Mother. Just remember to feed Kicks. I'll be home soon."

"You can't believe the calls at the office. Some want to dig up dirt, but most are outraged. I've had TV reporters from all those big networks. The FBI was in and wanted to search everything. They didn't have a warrant. Guess no judge would give that. They've no real cause to be rooting through all your case files and such. Of course I told them to scat. Sonny's been a big help. I think he looks to you somewhat as the father he lost as a youngster. Everyone at church sends their best. Oh Son, I— you know I'm very proud of you. However, I sure do wish you'd have found some other way to do this."

★★★

The produce truck pulled up to a small building up the street from a truck stop and weigh station. Al saw Maria's Cadillac parked in a carport off the side of the building.

"Theese ees it, Meester Al. Maria, she be inside."

Just then, the door swung open and Maria stepped through it. She put her hand to her forehead to shield her eyes from the sun. She smiled when Al opened the truck door. As he turned to back down out of it, he reached over and shook hands with Nacho.

"Thank you. This was very important to me. What do I owe you?"

"Owe, Señor? You friend of Maria. You owe nothing. You go back home you country now. Is good day you go home."

Al nodded. "I will be glad to be back home. Thank you again, Nacho."

Al stepped down from the truck and turned toward Maria.

"Hurry. Come inside where it's cool," she said, stepping back into the office. Al followed her through the door and closed it behind him.

Without even thinking, he threw his arms around Maria, and they embraced tightly for several minutes, then he let loose.

"I'm sorry. I—I, well that just happened. Forgive me," Al said.

"Forgive you? Never—but I do thank you. You don't know how much I missed you and worried about you. I didn't sleep a wink last night. Even your son slept more than I did."

"How is he?"

"Playing ball when I left. He's been quiet, but he's OK."

"I was quite concerned for a while," Al said. "I didn't know how things would turn out."

"There was a news report about a helicopter and two fighter jets, and I just knew it was you. That must have been some trip."

"I just want to go home, back to my room that is. I really shouldn't talk about it."

An hour later, they were across the border and back at the inn. Danny came running and threw his arms around his dad.

"I was all scared, Dad. I knew you was in trouble. I went out and played ball with the guys 'cause I didn't wanna tell 'em no and have to say you was gone and—"

"Slow down. That was good thinking. I'm home. Let me go get a shower and well, I really could use a nap."

"That's OK, Dad. Now that you're home and everything's cool, I'll go play. See ya later."

By the next morning Al was rested. He was ready to go back to Maria's office and get back to work on the one troublesome section of code.

"Hey Dad, it's church tonight. Can I go?" Danny asked his dad at breakfast.

"Oh, yeah, sure. How are you getting along with those new friends of yours?"

"We get along real good, Dad. Me and Anton do too," Danny said, looking over at the old man who smiled back.

"If you keep beating me at checkers that might change," Anton said. "I'm about out of jobs for you to do. You work too quickly sometimes."

"I like helping you, beings you can't—well it's easier for me to get down on the ground I figure," Danny said.

Anton sat there in his wheelchair and laughed. Maria got up to do the dishes. Al quickly moved to help her.

"I need to stay over on this side today," Maria said to Al. "I hate to ask, but could you run an errand for me over in Mexico? Over to the office where we met yesterday."

"Mexico? You want me to go into Mexico by myself? I… ahh, yeah. I wasn't paying any attention. I don't know if I could find it."

"I'll draw you a map and, well, you'll be just fine, I'm sure. I know all the trouble you had down there with Alice, but I've never had any trouble here in Nogalas."

"Well… if you go over there by yourself, surely I can. I mean—."

"You mean that if a girl can do it, you being a man can surely do it? A bit chauvinistic Al?"

"No—I mean—maybe I am. Old school I guess. I'm not the bravest guy around. You and Alice put me to shame sometimes."

"I'd say you've just never needed to do some of these things. What you're doing for Danny is braver than anything I or Alice has done for you. It's proof you can be very brave when circumstances dictate."

"Maybe so. How long should this trip take me?"

"That depends on the crossings. It might only take you half an hour, but might take two hours. I could hire a courier."

"No, don't do that. I'll do it," Al said.

"With Danny going to church tonight, let's go have dinner," Maria said. "A real dinner, not pizza."

"Sure, although I enjoyed that pizza, that whole thing really, you know what I mean." Al felt his face flush.

It only took ten minutes to get into Mexico. Al drove slowly, following the map Maria had drawn for him. He had a large box of various sized envelopes, all stuffed with multiple sheets of paper. He got to the office easily, then he made an exchange of boxes. He then started back the way he'd come. Less than an hour from the time he'd left, he walked back into the office and Maria.

"You made it! That didn't take long. No trouble, right?"

"No trouble," Al said. He really hadn't wanted to go back to Mexico after his experience with Alice, and also with Bacho and Gator. Then too, he also had to admit that something about Maria and all her businesses still made him suspicious. It wasn't Maria. It was—well, it was just some of the things she did. He was very relieved to now be back in Arizona.

Later that evening, Al and Maria drove to Tucson where Maria took a package to the airfreight terminal. Al waited in the car until she returned. They went to a quiet restaurant and ordered dinner.

"You have any brothers or sisters?" Maria asked.

"No, only me. Guess that's why I sometimes have trouble relating to people. I've been accused of being selfish, but I think that's just because I've been alone most of my life. I guess I never learned to share."

"That makes sense," Maria said. "I'm an only child too. I came along late, and mother died when I was in high school. I guess that's why dad and I are so close. He's been everything to me. I often think I'm the son he never had. Then when he got shot—"

"You're afraid of what you're going to do when he passes on, aren't you?" Al asked.

"You can tell? That's going to be a tough time. He's failing. He keeps up a good front, but he's in a lot more pain than he lets on. Someday…"

"You'll get along," Al said after a minute of silence. "You're the type to survive. You've got that spunky attitude."

"I hope you're right."

They talked on through their meal and when finished Maria looked at her watch. "Hey, we better get home. Danny will be getting there about the time we do."

"Yeah," Al said. "I've ah, this has been nice." "Yeah, I agree," Maria said.

But, what did you take to the airport? What did I take and bring back from Mexico this morning? Was it just paperwork? Just who are you anyway?

These questions and more ran through Al's mind while they drove back to Nogales, then on out to the Inn at Patagonia. No sooner had Al gotten to his room than he heard the bus bringing Danny home.

"Hi Dad," Danny said when he burst through the door. "I had a good time tonight."

"Did you go back to Wal-Mart?"

"Yeah, but not the TV section. I stayed far away from that." Danny kicked off his shoes, then went and brushed his teeth. He then lay down on his bed. He looked over at his dad who sat at the little desk, reading something on his computer screen.

"Hey Dad, you know Anton paid me $20.00 for the work I helped him with."

"Yeah, you told me that the other day."

After a moment of silence, Danny asked his dad, "Is it OK to give money away?"

Al turned away from his computer and looked at his son. "What brings on this question?"

"Oh, I was just thinking."

"Just thinking?"

"Well, tonight Pastor Hec talked about buying some shoes and other things for some really poor kids down in Mexico, and I thought about Pedro and those other kids at that orphan place and I got to thinking that I have everything I need and," Danny finally took a breath. "I gave $5.00 to those poor kids, Dad. Then we went over to the store and at the snack bar, well the guys didn't have much money, so I took the money you gave me plus what was left from Anton and bought us a big pizza and I, well, it felt good to be able to help them, Dad."

"And now you want to know if it was right?"

"I guess so. I've never heard you talk about giving anything to anyone, so I didn't know what you'd say."

"Well, I've never done much giving. That's why I've not talked about it, I guess. It seems I'm thinking about things like that a lot more myself now. People sure have been giving to us. All these people give us a place to live, food to eat, protection from those who'd send us back into trouble. It seems their giving is surely helping us. I don't know what we'd be doing without the things all these people have given us. I think that's one area I need to change greatly, once I get out of this mess we're in."

"Yeah, maybe I can earn some more money from Anton so's I can help some more. Me and you are learning a bunch together, aren't we Dad?"

"Yeah, a bunch—together."

★★★

Wade Hawkins sat in his cell reading a book. The guard came down the hall and stuck the key in his door lock.

"Got a visitor, Mr. Hawkins. It's sort of unusual, but the warden says it's OK."

Wade walked out through the cell door and down the hall toward the interrogation rooms. The guard opened the door. Wade stepped into the room. There sat Max Pace.

"Hello, Hawkins. This sure seems odd, me and you being in here like this. I never thought—well, I guess there were times when I did fear something like this. Sit down, please, talk to me. I've been thinking about things for days now. Now I need to talk to someone—you really."

Wade walked over to the table and sat across from Max, but found himself unable to look Max in the eye. He slid his chair around some and looked off to the side.

"In a round-a-bout way you're the reason I'm in here, Hawkins. Well, not really, but—well, it was about five years back when I heard you speak to some men's thing I'd been invited to. You talked about how your faith in God got you through the loss of your wife and son. It really moved me. I could tell you were talking the truth—it was for you anyway. I wanted something like that, but I didn't want to become some pansy, church-geek, you know? So I started looking for something else to get connected to, besides the normal old church God. Know what I mean? I got to reading lots of stuff, and I tried out most anything I read about.

"At the library one day I met Evelina Vincent. Yeah, she seemed to have what I wanted. I not only wanted what she had, I wanted her. Guess I got both, somewhat, but I sure didn't get what you've got. I've got nothing but hell-on-earth from all of this." Max took a deep breath, then leaned forward and started talking again.

"I'm scared of what Hell, the real thing, will be like. I think I've seen some of what the devil can do here. If he's gonna be in Hell...."

"Talk to me, Hawkins, what can I do to make things right?" Wade cleared his throat.

Why me, Lord? I don't want to do this.

Wade looked over at Max in silence for a minute, unable— unwilling really—to speak to him about what Max wanted to hear. He looked away again.

Wade's mind started popping up Scriptures buried deep in its memory.

...He's not wanting for any to perish, but for everyone to come to repentance... anyone who believes in Him will have eternal life... God sent his Son to save the world, not condemn it... for all have sinned and come short...

Finally, he spoke to Max.

"You want me to talk to you about God? I'm sitting here wanting to choke the last ounce of breath out of you, and you want me to tell you God will make everything alright? Yeah, Max, God is willing to forgive you— He'll do that a whole lot easier than I can. How could you do what you did to those kids? How—"

"Please, Hawkins. Not now. I can't think of that now. I just need to know if I'm beyond help, or if that God of yours will give me another chance."

"You—that's all you still think about, isn't it? When it comes to anyone else, you don't give a...." Wade was silent for a moment, and then answered Max as he knew he should. "As I said, God will forgive you, Max, but that doesn't mean you don't have to pay for all you've done. You know you're probably going to face a life in prison sentenced by some jury. God's forgiveness doesn't mean he's obligated to stop that, or any other kind of just and legal punishment or consequence."

The pictures he'd seen, and stored in his mind, of happy, innocent little Kreg Browning and Melissa Vincent, as well as those Sonny had taken of their ashes and minute fragments up at the satanic alter up in the wilderness, now stared back at Wade from the gray, block wall he faced.

"I can't do any more than tell you what the Bible says, Max. Maybe you should talk to a preacher. Someone not attached to all of this."

"That's so hard, Hawkins," Max said, ignoring Wade's advice. "I mean the Bible was written by a bunch of men, right?"

"They penned it. Look, you had a secretary, right? If you dictated a letter to her, and she wrote it for you, is it her letter or yours? If a secretary takes notes of a meeting, is it her meeting, or her notes of her observation about someone else's meeting?"

Max slowly nodded his head. "That makes some sense—go on."

Wade paused for a moment, and then went on.

"Because the first man rejected God, and broke his bond with Him, none of us are born right with God. We all need to be restored back to him. He gave us a way, one way." Wade went on for over an hour answering Max's questions and explaining God's redemption plan.

"Cut to the chase, Hawkins," Max finally said. "I thought I could say some creed thing or something, you know, do something as a penitence, or give some money or—"

"No, Max. Nothing you do will make up for the evil you've done. The ability to get forgiveness for what we've done isn't yours—it's held by God himself—to be freely given if we truly repent and accept His way, as I've explained to you."

"God and I haven't been on speaking terms for a long time now, Hawkins."

"It's the only way, Max. The only way."

The door then opened and the guard stepped inside. "Time's up, fellows. Court time for you, Max. You've got a hearing over at the courthouse to settle that attorney thing. Wait here, Hawkins. I'll be back in a minute."

★★★

Several hours later, Max was being led out the back door of the courthouse to the prison van. A car in the parking lot moved up close behind the van. The deputies leading Max stopped near the van's back door and stared at the car. The door opened and out stepped Sally Browning.

"Mrs. Browning," Max said. "What are you doing here?"

"You're going to have to move back, lady," one of the deputies said. "We're taking the prisoner back to jail and—"

"I just came to see Max for a moment," Sally said as she quickly raised the hand she'd kept hidden behind the car door and shoved the old revolver straight at Max. She squeezed back the trigger. The gun cracked. She squeezed the trigger and it cracked again, then again. Max's knees buckled and he slumped to the pavement.

Chapter 23

Sonny Horn was driving up I-25, coming from the University of New Mexico in Albuquerque, when his phone rang. "Sonny, Jake here. Just got the report back from the lab. You were right on. Some of those bone pieces are human—child really. Some of the blood is human too. Now all we need is some sample of DNA from those two kids, old hair or something."

"Wow. Guess we both knew it though. I hope now we can wrap this up for sure. What about Sally Browning?" Sonny asked. "Does the jail have a counselor or someone who can break this news to her? I know this still isn't proof it's her son, but really. Anyway, someone is soon going to have to tell her. Someone will have to get something of his for a DNA match."

"Yeah, maybe this might bring some sense of confirming what her mind has been telling her for weeks. I don't know who should do it. I don't think the Santa Fe police are the right ones. I'll check that out though," Jake said.

"What's the latest on Max? Is he going to pull through?" Sonny asked.

"Doesn't look good. I hear he'll never walk if he does. I came out here from California to get away from all that messy blood and guts. This case is as bad as any I've ever worked on. Hey, why don't you stop by my office? I should have this story wrapped up by the time you get here."

"OK, see you later then," Sonny said, and then he closed his phone and slid it into his pocket. Some of the major happenings of this case ran through his mind while he drove up the interstate. Dr. Vincent and his son were still on the run somewhere. Rhea Thatcher was dead. Luke Lane was dead. Max lay crippled in the hospital. Sally Browning was in jail. Wade sat in jail. Evelina Vincent would surely soon be in jail. Homeland Security was in a panic. The President planned to address the nation in a couple of days with what was rumored to be devastating news. It was something to do with what Dr. Vincent was working on. What would things be like if Dr. Vincent hadn't gone on the run? Would they be any better? Or would Tucker by now be a statistic, also?

Sonny looked at his watch. He'd stop by and see Nita for a minute before going to the newspaper office. She'd know how Wade was doing. He'd take Wade a paper in the morning with the Lab findings' story. Maybe there'd be something on Evelina Vincent by then, too.

The next morning, Sonny and Wade sat in the small visiting area of the jail. Wade read the story about the findings of the samples taken from the Pecos, and then he folded the newspaper back together.

"I stopped by to see Nita yesterday," Sonny said. "She's doing a lot better. I think she realizes this will be over soon."

"The whole thing's screwy," Wade said. "Here I am in a city jail, arrested by the FBI. If they had any plan to do anything but harass me, I'd be in the Federal Pen in Albuquerque. I sometimes wonder if the FBI office in Washington even knows what those guys here did. Do they know I'm in a local jail?"

"You ever see those two agents, that Miles and Simpson?" Sonny asked.

"Not for days. I think they'd like to turn me loose now, but don't want to have to explain why they put me here in the first place. I don't think either one will be up for a promotion over this."

"Kicks misses you," Sonny said. "I exercised him some the other day. He'll be as glad to see you as anyone."

"Sure could use a good ride about now," Wade said. "A good long ride."

Footsteps came down the hall. A guard brought in a woman wearing a nurse uniform.

"Hawkins, this lady has a message for you. It's from Max Pace," the guard said.

"Mr. Hawkins, I—Max died a couple of hours ago. I worked the night shift. He knew he was dying and asked me to give you a message. He said to tell you that he had that conversation you two talked about, and that everything was alright. He said you'd understand."

Wade slowly nodded his head, and then spoke. "Thanks. Yeah, I understand. Thanks for telling me."

The nurse and guard then left. Sonny and Wade sat in silence for a minute and then Sonny rose.

"Best get going, Wade. Surely, someone will pick up Evelina Vincent soon. I'll check back later."

Wade nodded. "Yeah, OK, Sonny. Strange how life goes, isn't it?"

★★★

Later that morning, the guard came back to Wade's cell.

"You're a popular guy, Hawkins. You've got another visitor, a woman. I'll have to stay in the room with you."

"Sure, who is it?" Wade asked.

"Another inmate, that Browning woman," the guard said while opening the visitation room door. Wade went in and slowly approached the woman waiting for him. He sat at the table across from her.

"Mr. Hawkins?" Sally Browning asked. "I've met your friend, Sonny Horn. Such a nice man. I'm Sally Browning. I guess you've heard about me."

Wade looked at the woman who'd risen to greet him. She looked like a cross between an anemic little girl and a frail old lady. She was neither, but Wade knew she was a woman in great emotional pain.

"I've heard much about you, Mrs. Browning. I'm pleased to meet you."

"Guess you heard Max Pace is dead. I killed him. I need you to be my attorney. I'll plead guilty, but I know I need someone like you to help me."

"Why?" Wade asked. "Why did you do that?"

"It was the best way. Don't you see? He took all I had. I'd lost my husband. I don't have any other family. All I had was Kreg. I know I'll go to prison for a long time. I can live with that. Maybe someday I'll get out, and then it might be over. Maybe then I'll not be tormented by all of this. Maybe the dreams will be gone. The hate will be gone because Max is gone. If he was still walking around... I can live with the prison—I've been in one a long time now—but without doing something drastic to Max, I'd never get over this. Now, there's a chance."

Wade shook his head.

"I already have a client in all of this. This somehow might be a conflict."

"I want you, Mr. Hawkins. You can do it. Please don't turn against me too," Sally begged.

Wade closed his eyes, and then slowly nodded his head.

"Well—I can't think of anything that would be a problem. If something comes up, we'll make a change then. Alright, I'll see if I can help you. Once I get out of here, that is."

"Thank you," Sally said. "See, things are going better for me already."

Evelina Vincent took a long, lavender scented bath, and then put on a flowing, black gown. She put on her favorite old Navajo pawn jewelry. She stared at herself in a full length mirror, nodded her head and smiled. She then went into her closet and took down a small wooden chest.

"It's time to go now. I can't do anymore here, so I'm coming to you," she said. "I wanted to bring your brother along too, but I guess that's not to be." She put the chest under her arm, and then casually walked through the house and out into the garage. She pushed the door opener button then she started her Hummer. Once on the street, she headed for the interstate.

She got off at the Pecos Wilderness area exit, and started back through the roads she'd driven so often these last few years.

"It's such a beautiful day, isn't it? You haven't been out here for a while. We'll have lots of time together now. No more cares of this world. You know all of that already, don't you?"

She pulled into the area where Sonny had parked his Jeep days before. She got out and carried the chest with her to the altar area. She set it on a flat rock in the outer ring of rocks. She opened the hand-carved box, then took out a deeply tinted, glass bottle, then drank its thick, dark syrup. She placed the empty bottle back into the box, then took out a spherical object that was wrapped in a folded, silk napkin. Then she reached back into the chest and retrieved a long, slender dagger.

She walked over to the altar, spread her gown across it, then lay down and emptied the napkin of its contents. The tiny skull of her daughter rolled out on her chest. She picked it up, placed it over the handle of the dagger. Then she placed the tip of the pointed blade on her rib cage over her heart. Then she started chanting.

After several moments of ever escalating, but less and less coherent, chants, she let out a cry then shoved the knife deep into her heart. She again started up the chants while she pulled out the blade and stuck her fingers into the warm, spouting gushes of crimson blood. The chants became weaker. They reduced to a whisper. Then there was silence.

Two days later, down in Nogales, Al checked his e-mail while eating lunch at a truck stop. Again there was nothing. He'd not received anything since he'd given Kurt those discs and gotten word that Wade Hawkins was in jail. He was standing in line to pay his bill, when he saw a man approaching the front door. *Red Conners!* Al quickly turned off to the side, then reached up and pulled his western straw hat lower on his forehead. With his hat and a nearly two-month old length of beard, he knew he looked very different than his picture, but still.

Red walked up to the cashier and cut in line. "Looking for this fellow," Red said while he stuffed a picture under the cashier's nose. "Might have this kid with him," he went on as he showed another picture.

"I've never seen either of them," the young girl said.

"What about any of you?" Red said when he turned the pictures around for those in line to see. "This kid's in danger. If you've seen them—well, a waitress at a truck stop out east of here swears he was in there last month. Said he was a computer paper salesman."

"No, Señor," Al said, shaking his head while he looked at the picture with his head tipped low enough that his hat brim hid his eyes from Red's.

Red Conners then walked quickly back toward the truckers' lounge area. Al paid his bill without looking the cashier in the eye, then slowly walked out. He got into Maria's car and started back to her office. Would anyone at the truck stop recognize him? Would they associate him with Maria? Had he gotten careless?

When he pulled into the office parking lot, he asked himself another question: did it matter anyway? If they couldn't stop this terrorist attack, what would be left of the country? How would things change if Islamic terrorists took control? He was still thinking about these things when he sat down at his computer back at Maria's freight office.

"You OK?" Maria asked. "You look a little pale."

"Things aren't good. I just had a close call with an investigator who's looking for me. Maybe I've been here too long. Maybe I need to contact that Lollypop lady and move on. Then, maybe none of that matters."

"Why would you say that?" Maria asked.

"Oh, this project I've been working on—well, it looks as if we've failed and the country is going to be subject to a major attack. I shouldn't be telling you anything about this, but—I hear the president is about to tell everyone all about it tonight anyway."

"Do you want to move on?" Maria asked.

"No! I don't want to leave you. I mean, we're just getting settled here, and—I'm just so tired of running. If I've failed, I've failed. I don't think I could have done any more being at the lab. This was just one of those impossible projects. I'll get blamed for the failure, though. They'll have to have someone to blame—that'll be me. If there's still an America, I'll probably go to jail. Then what about my son? I've failed all the way around."

"Don't feel that way, Al. I've found that when I'm at my lowest, that's when God steps in."

"Don't start on me with any of that God stuff. Everyone believes in God, that He's with them and all that. I don't get it. He's not with me—so I don't believe any of it."

"Oh, He's with you all right. You just don't know it. I believe you will—soon, too. You say I'm brave for doing some of what I do, well, I know God's with me all the time. I ask Him for his protection, and thank Him often for it," Maria said.

Al had no response. He felt somewhat embarrassed. A few months back his atheistic belief was strong. He believed God was a myth for the weak. Now, he wasn't as sure of his belief. Actually, lately he'd had more doubts than belief. That bothered him. The fact that he was having glimmering thoughts that God might be real, was a weakness to him.

"Hey, maybe a drive would do you some good. I planned to take this bundle over to the other office. You want to do it?" Maria asked.

"You mean Mexico?"

"Yeah," Maria said.

"Why not. Sure, I'll take it."

"That Presidential speech is at six," Maria said. "I'd like to watch it with you."

"Sure. Maybe he'll put out a price on my head. You can collect the reward."

★★★

Sonny Horn stopped by Jake Bonner's office after lunch. FBI agents Huck Miles and Sig Simpson were in J. Quinton Sedwick's office.

"What's with the Feds?" Sonny asked Jake.

"Looking for Evelina. Nobody's seen her. Her garage is empty and it's like she's faded off the earth. It's hard to hide a black Hummer."

"Hey, you two, in here a minute," J. Quinton motioned to Jake and Sonny.

"You both know these Feds, right?" J. Quinton motioned to the two FBI agents. "They got warrants for you two. They figure one or both of you was responsible for finding those samples up in the Pecos."

"So," Sonny said. "What's with the warrants?"

"Disturbing a crime scene. Withholding evidence. There's more," Agent Huck Miles said. "Look, we need to find that thing in the Pecos and process it as a crime scene."

"What do you think?" J. Quinton asked, looking at Jake, then Sonny. "They're also looking for Evelina—she's vanished, so it seems. It's a possibility she's up there. With Max gone and— well...."

"I think Wade would like to go for a little ride. What do you say we take him with us?" Sonny asked.

"Don't get smart—" Sig Simpson snapped.

"Sig!" Huck cut in. "Look, let's not talk about Hawkins right now. This is about those two kids and the dame, not the run-a-ways, alright? This could all be over after the President talks tonight anyway. Sounds as if the whole world might be about to come apart or something."

"Alright," Sonny said, "Tear up those warrants, give me your word new ones won't be served, and let's get going."

They drove with little conversation the entire way until they turned off the interstate. Once Sonny started directing them through the maze of roads, Huck seemed to get nervous.

"Something's not right," he said at one point. "I can just feel it."

Sonny directed Sig to drive the car off the road, and onto the path leading to the altar. When he rounded the last bend, there sat the black Hummer.

"I knew it," Huck said. "Where is she?"

Once Sig parked the car, Sonny got out and started up the path around behind the boulder outcropping. Jake had his camera out and was snapping pictures. Then Jake saw the altar and stopped instantly. "I'll be—look at that." His camera started clicking again. Huck walked right up to the altar. Sig dropped to his knees, bent over, and then grabbed his stomach.

★★★

Al sat in line, waiting to cross back through the border check from Mexico. It was hot; that added to his nervousness. What if Red Conners found out he was here? Should he hole up at the inn and not go into town at all?

Just as the line started again, the car in front of him stalled. He could tell the driver was trying to restart it to no avail. Out of nowhere, several young men came and offered to push the car out of line and over under a tree where they could work on it. The driver got out.

Miles Groman!

It was his old colleague and friend from the lab. While under investigation for passing secrets on to enemy countries, Miles up and totally disappeared. No one knew where he went. He just vanished.

"Miles—hey Miles!" Al yelled while getting out of Maria's car. The other man froze. He didn't turn around. He seemed unsure of what to do.

Chapter 24

"Hey Miles, it's Alex Vincent." At that Miles turned around and looked back at Alex.

What have I done? I've blown it all. How could I? Al's mind raced. Now what?

"What are you doing here?" Miles asked while he slowly walked back toward his old friend.

Maybe it won't make any difference. It's all too late now anyway. I've failed,

"It's a long story," Al said. "You've got car trouble. Need a lift across the way?"

Make the best of this. Maybe you can still cover things. If Miles has been in Mexico, maybe he doesn't know what's been going on in the States.

"Yeah, that would be great. I just bought this old clunker for the trip up here from the coast. Almost made it. Hot, though, no air conditioning. Let me tell these guys what to do with this thing, and then I'll take you up on that lift. It's boiling out here."

Al watched Miles give one of the young men some money, then grab two suitcases from the old car's trunk.

What do I tell him? Why am I here? What's he doing here? Think. Think of something quickly.

Al popped the trunk release and, after putting his suitcases in there, Miles walked to the passenger side and got in, then he looked at Al.

Stall… you need time to waylay Miles, then grab Tucker and get out of here.

"What's up with you? You're not here on lab business, and this sure isn't a vacation."

"I'm, ah, I'm buying a mine down here. You know, a childhood dream—Roy Rogers, cowboys and Indians thing, I guess. The mine's old. It's been closed for years. It was really active back before the Civil War. The neat thing is, I've developed a new extraction system that I'm sure will make it profitable again."

"Gold, huh? I never figured you for the type," Miles said. "Going to be an alchemist, turn sand into gold, huh?"

"Not quite that easy," Al said. "It's silver and lead out here anyway. What about you? You just vanished off the planet."

Miles was quiet for a minute. Then he motioned to the customs people when the last car in front of Al pulled through.

"I'll tell you once we're across."

Al hesitated pulling up to the checkpoint.

"You're not going to get me into trouble, are you?"

"No, no, nothing like that," Miles laughed, but Al knew Miles was nervous. He drove up to the guard, then stopped and lowered his window.

"American citizens, both?" The agent asked

"Yes," Al said, Miles affirmed.

"What are you bringing back that you didn't take over?"

"Just this box of paperwork. It's for—"

"I know who it's for," the agent said. "You were in two cars back there."

"My car died," Miles said. "As luck would have it, my old friend Alex came by."

Don't say Alex! My driver's license is for Albert Tucker.

"Old friends?" the guard asked.

"We worked together for many years up by Santa Fe," Al said.

"What's in the trunk," the agent asked.

Al sensed nervousness when Miles answered, "Just my suitcases. The usual travel stuff, you know."

"Open it," the agent ordered. Al looked at Miles, who was now pale and had perspiration running down his forehead. Miles nodded. Al pushed the trunk release button.

Another agent walked a dog around the car. With pounding heart, Al watched in the mirror. He was sure Miles had something hidden in his suitcases. The agent reached up and closed the trunk once the dog moved away.

"Have a good day, Señors," the first agent said, and then he looked back at the next car.

When the gate popped up, Al moved ahead quickly. He drove away from the border for several miles, and then pulled into a convenience store.

"Thirsty?" he asked.

"Sure am. I'll buy. What do you want?" Miles asked.

"Water, big bottle."

Through the store window, Al watched Miles get the water and pay for it. This was going to be some game of wits. Al knew what he was hiding, but what was Miles' game? Just what was this guy up to anyway? Miles got back into the car and handed Al one of the water bottles. Miles opened his and took a long drink as Al pulled back out onto the street.

"Guess you're still wondering what I'm doing down here. I've got some time. Why don't we go out to that mine of yours, and we'll have us a talk? I think I've got something for you, something you can't turn down."

"It's a ways out there, might as well start talking now," Al said.

"You always were all business," Miles said. "That's one of the things I always liked about you. You stood up for me too. When the charges started to be thrown at me, you stood up for me. Now I'm about to repay you that favor. Of course I've first got to tell you that you were wrong. I was guilty of all they said, and more."

Al's head jerked as he took a quick look at Miles.

Guilty? Miles was admitting he was guilty?

"Surprises you, huh? Oh, I wasn't at first. I was as loyal as an old dog for the first ten years I worked at LANL. Ten years where three foreigners and two unqualified minorities got promoted ahead of me. They'd come over here, get off the boat, get a job and in two years be my boss. Or claim racial preference and threaten a discrimination suit. I flat got tired of it." Miles said nothing more for a few minutes while he seemed to be deep in thought.

"Remember that trade show we went to in Paris that summer? I got pretty drunk in a motel bar one night and must have voiced some of my gripes to someone. Anyway, the next night I was whisked away in a limo and met with none other than Aswad Hamal himself."

Aswad Hamal? That's what Miles is up to. Yes, he's behind this whole code thing.

"For my last two years in Los Alamos, I fed him everything he wanted. When the suspicion around me got too hot, he got me out of there and set me up in my own lab. You're sitting here now thinking that I'm the one who designed this highly sophisticated code you and your team has tried to decode so frantically. I've got everyone in a panic, right up to the President. I can see things are clicking in your mind."

Miles took a drink of water, and then went on.

"I know about you. You're not buying some old mine. You're hiding out there. I still read American newspapers, you know. You're a hot property. Of course what I've got isn't really what your intel thinks it is. That computer that Abba Saad had—it was a plant. He was getting too greedy. We let him think he was sneaking into Washington to sell some of our secrets to some new Iranian group. Yeah, we took him out. It worked slick as wet ice. We got rid of him and you all fell for the whole thing.

"All that code," Miles continued. "I'm surprised how long it took you to break all that easy stuff. I thought I made that easy enough you'd have that in weeks. That section you still can't get, forget it. It's just mumbo jumbo. Just something to keep you all sweating." Miles took another drink of water.

Al picked up the cell phone Maria kept plugged into the accessory socket in her car. "I've got to call a lady friend of mine and tell her to add you to our party tonight."

"Party? Whoa now, what kind of party?" Miles asked.

"People you'll like—militia types, real anti-government, you know what I mean."

"How'd you get into that group?" Miles asked.

"If you know about me, then you know I needed someone to hide me. They jumped at the chance to pick my brain. You're not the only one who's sitting on a big surprise. What would you do if someone else beat you to the punch with a hit bigger than you've got planned? Ever think about that?" Miles was silent. Al turned off the paved highway. He looked at the phone. He'd be out of cell range in moments. He punched through the speed dial addresses on the phone and found one marked "office." He punched it. On the second ring Maria answered.

"Maria, it's Al."

"You alright?"

"No, not really, but that's OK. Hey, I'll get you these papers when you come out to the mine later. I ran into an old friend of mine. Fellow I worked with for many years. We're already on our way out there now. Don't worry, he's alright, someone we might be able to work with."

"Whatever are you talking about? Al, what's going on?"

"About our party tonight. You did invite Corky and those friends of his, right?"

"Corky? You mean my cousin? His friends? What—wait a minute. The mine—are you saying you want me to send Customs out to the mine?"

"Sure do. Those others too."

"Border Patrol too? Any law I can?"

"That sounds like a lot of fun. Can't wait to hear what the President has to say. What's he going to say when something totally different happens? Won't that whole bunch look like fools? We'll be awhile. Yeah, we're just crossing the Santa Cruz now."

"I'm losing your signal, Al. I don't know what's going on, be careful."

"Lost the signal," Al said when he snapped the phone closed. He picked up his water bottle, twisted off the cap, then took a drink. "Where were we?"

Miles didn't say anything for a minute. Then he turned and looked at Al.

"You're putting me on, aren't you? You don't really have…." He didn't finish his thought. Al could tell that Miles was deeply troubled. "Alex, come in with me. You and I will be an unbeatable team. I'll make you my top assistant—whatever title you want. You're smart, you're loyal and you must want to live. Bring your group in with us."

"Come on, Miles. You're the one on the outside needing a place to get in. I'm already here. So are all my people and all our toys. You don't really think you and Aswad Hamal can tear down the United States with a couple of little bombs, do you? Look at the Twin Towers. That just made things stronger. We've got something totally different planned."

"But what we've got planned is different also. I've got some really good minds and…." Miles seemed to be very flustered.

"Look, Alex, you remember the Trojan Horse story?" he went on. "Sure you do. That's what I'm using Aswad Hamal and this Islam thing for. Don't you see it? No other military in the world is going to overcome the military might of the U.S. But with its policy of religious tolerance, even with something as radical as hard line Islam, that's what's going to let us in and take right over. You think I care about any of that Allah crap? It's just a cover. Think about this. You're a U.S. military commander, and I come at you in fatigues and with arms—you shoot me. But I come at you wearing a head-rag and robe crying Allah, and you roll out the red carpet, then I pop the bomb I've brought in with me."

"So you're now some kind of Muslim?" Al asked. "Is that your game?"

"It's a game alright. Can't you see? The religion thing is a cover to take over America first, then the world. Once all the governments have fallen, I tumble Islam. Those guys have been out in the sand for so long they don't see that part of it coming, but that's my end game. Come on over with me. I'm the way of the future—I am the future of the whole world. They'll rewrite every history book. Forget about the Greeks and Romans and the British Empire, forget them all. It's me, Miles Groman, who's going to rule the entire world. Soon, Alex, soon. Once we have the U.S., then everyone else will fall to their knees and beg."

"You serious?" Al asked.

"Couldn't be more so."

"Just what is your plan?" Al asked

"It's all scare. Mostly smoke and mirrors. I've got everything in one bag right in your trunk now," Miles said.

"That dog would have sniffed it."

"Not this type of ricin stuff in a sealed glass container. Besides, dogs are trained for explosives, not bio agents," Miles said. "Look, it doesn't take much to burst open a glass vial and spread those germs. Just a magnetic solenoid set off by the dash clock of a car. I'm going to be at the Saint Louis airport in two days. Right in the heart of the country, with people leaving there in all directions. I've got a car already wired and ready for this vial. I park the car in the long term lot, that's up wind from the terminal, and at exactly noon the next day, poof. A little pop as the plunger smashes the vial, then a small fan kicks on and away the little germies go.

"In twenty-four hours the entire country will be in a panic. I'll put out the word that ten more of these devices will go off all over the country in seventy-two hours, unless our demands are met. That's it, Alex. You can't top that, so come in with me."

Al's mind raced as he tried to come up with something that would throw Miles off.

"Got you beat, Miles. I'm using a simple bi-metal switch inside one of those reusable, plastic ice blocks that campers and others use in their coolers. That'll stay frozen for hours, then when it melts, surprise," Al forced a laugh. "As I said, the little bi-metal switch, and the infrared sender attached to it, is inside one of those empty ice packs, taped to a real, frozen one. The bio- agent, a tiny pinch of plastic explosive, along with the infrared receiver, are all hidden inside an empty juice bottle. The whole thing fits inside a lunch bag." Al laughed again. "So innocent looking—yet so deadly."

"You'll kill all the germs in the blast," Miles said.

"You know better," Al said. "It won't take many bugs to survive to create the panic I need. It's not the damage or even body counts that I need, just panic."

"You're not serious about this whole thing. You're dreaming," Miles said. "You're like a kid with a new comic book. You've heard about what's going on, and you've dreamed up all this like a boy with tin soldiers. We get your friends together at that party tonight; I'll show you some things then. When you see what I've got in my computer, you'll believe. You'll be a full believer."

Al could tell Miles was shaken. He now sat silently, slowly shaking his head.

"Hey, where's this mine at anyway?" he finally asked.

"Just a mile or so more," Al said when he made the last turn. "Wait until you see what all's there."

"Good. Living like a hermit out here or what?" Miles asked.

"Underground house. An old mine shaft, really."

Miles didn't say anything when Al pulled the Cadillac up the drive, then hid it behind an old stone building.

Is anyone here yet? Will they rush in with their trucks or swoop in with choppers? What about the noise?

"How far do we have to walk?" Miles asked.

"Quite a ways. We can leave your bags here until some of the guys get here to carry them for you."

"NO! I mean, I'll take them now. Boy, this sure is out of the loop. How'd you ever find this place?"

Al took the opportunity to lean against the car and start talking. "You know how Evelina got into that Indian religion stuff? She bought a lot of books about this area back when the Apaches ruled. I read about some of the old mines once. Then when I started looking for some militia group to hide me, I saw this one here and, well here I am."

"Let's go, huh?" Miles said. "I've got things to show you too, open up."

Al pushed the trunk release button, and then looked around while Miles removed the two bags.

Where are you guys?

"I'll take one of them," Al said as he closed the trunk.

"I'd rather carry them myself, thanks anyway," Miles said. "Lead the way."

Al started walking up the upper trail, the one that was the most open, so they could be more easily seen, and so Miles would tire more quickly in the intense heat.

"This is quite a layout," Al said while he moved forward very slowly. "There's grates over all the air shafts and all the horizontal shafts have iron plates welded across."

In only minutes in the one-hundred-plus degree heat, Miles was gasping hard for air while they climbed the steep, rocky trail.

"You got power up here? Air conditioning?"

"Generator," Al said. "It's not bad really, if you can put up with the snakes and the like."

"Snakes! Right in where you live?"

"It's not bad really," Al said while Miles started intensely searching the ground around them. Al looked off down the road. He was sure he heard an engine coming near them, and then it went quiet. Off the other way, down toward the border, he saw dust rise from where the road cut through the cedars. He counted three different spots, each some distance apart. Help was coming, but how would they get in close without tipping off their presence?

"There's a spot of shade over there," Miles nodded with his head. "I need a break." He walked to the shade, then set his bags down and took out his handkerchief and wiped the perspiration from his face. Al looked out across the area again. The dust was closer. Then, way off behind it, he saw a black spot in the sky. A chopper! But that would give itself away minutes before it arrived. Surely, they—

Suddenly, out of nowhere an F-16 fighter swooped down in front of them, and did a vertical spiral up into the deep blue sky, then a second one followed suit.

"What the—" Miles said, staring into the sky.

"They're from the reserve unit over in Douglas. They come out here to train. There's no one here—not supposed to be anyway. Watch, here they come again." The planes swooped down to merely a few hundred yards from the cedars, then inverted and cut upward again.

"One of the first things I'm going to do, once I'm in control that is. I'm going for a ride in one of those," Miles said. "Wouldn't you like to be in that right now, Alex? Don't tell me you wouldn't."

"I don't know," Al said, purposely walking across the path over to the edge where it dropped off radically to an old air shaft below. Miles followed, leaving his bags now out of his reach.

"I get sick in a commuter jet," Al went on. "When they go upside down, like right now, oh, my stomach turns over even standing here."

"Just once, I'm going to do it just once," Miles said.

Al looked over to where he'd seen the chopper. It was now out of sight, probably circling behind them. He had to keep Miles's attention on the jets for another few minutes.

"You were in the Air Force, weren't you?" he asked.

"Yeah, but they wouldn't let me fly. I had asthma. With that they won't take a chance on you having an attack at the stick of a multi-million-dollar machine. Once they're mine, I'll take the stick anytime I want to. Whew, would you look at that," he said when the two planes dove towards them again. Just when they split apart, another sound could be heard above the roar of the jet engines—the pulsing flail of a chopper popping over the ridge less than one hundred yards behind them.

Chapter 25

Miles spun around and pointed at the chopper dropping into a wide spot up the trail. He shot a look at Al, and then yelled at him.

"You set me up! Why'd you do that?" He rushed for his bags. Al grabbed him around the neck and tried to pull him down. Miles elbowed him in the ribs, and then grabbed his bags when Al fell to his knees.

By this time, the chopper was on the ground, and four men burst from it, their weapons pointed toward Miles and Al.

"Don't shoot!" Al yelled. "There's a vial of ricin in one of those bags!"

Miles started down the trail, but down by the Cadillac there now was a white SUV emptying out other armed men. He turned toward the edge of the drop off to the air shaft. Al grabbed one of the bags and tried to strip it away. Miles hit him with the other one and knocked him back. By this time, the chopper rotor had stopped and so had the men. Miles stood at the edge of the nearly hundred-foot-drop off and looked back and forth at the two groups of men.

"Tell them again, Alex. Tell them what I've got and what it will do to them. Tell them I want a ride out of here in that chopper, or I go over the edge and break open the vial of bugs at the bottom. You'll all be infected and there's no antidote for what's here."

"It won't spread. Without an explosion, it won't get anyone but you," Al said.

"Wrong. It's packed under pressure. It'll spread for several miles in a matter of hours."

Al now stood in front of Miles, who had his back to the drop off. Below them Al saw several men rushing toward the embankment. He had to stall until they could make the hard climb up behind Miles.

"Let's talk this over, Miles. What is it you really want?" Al asked.

"I want that pilot to take me and my bags back into Mexico. I want one of those rifles left in the chopper, because I'm going to kill you when we lift off. I was so close. I trusted you, Alex. How could you do this to an old friend?"

"This isn't about you and me, Miles. We're talking about the lives of millions of people, a way of life, America. How were you going to take care of the complexity of running a government system?"

"The weak will die. Only the smart and dedicated are useful. That could have been you."

"Wrong. The weak have just as much right to a life as anyone. I've learned—"

"Ah, cut it Alex. You're beginning to sound like some soppy preacher. Tell them, go on, tell them they're all dead, unless they do what I say."

Al couldn't see the men climbing the wall of loose soil and rock behind Miles. *How far up were they by now?*

"Listen up," Al yelled to the men by the chopper. "This man is Miles Groman. He wants a ride out of here on your chopper, back into Mexico. He wants the rest of you to move out of the way, but stay where he can see you."

"The gun, tell them to leave me a gun," Miles said.

"Oh, yeah, he wants one gun left in the chopper. He says he wants to kill me before he leaves."

"This is Corky, Al," came a yell from the group of men over by the car. "Tell your friend to set those bags down nice and easy and step away. We're not going anywhere. If this is what you say it is, we've got specific orders from Homeland Security on what to do. We'll give you sixty seconds, and then we'll do what we have to."

Al looked at Miles. He saw fear and knew Miles was about to panic.

Without warning, there came a noise from one of the men climbing up the slope as he slipped and started tumbling and sliding down the steep slope toward the covered air shaft. Miles swung around and when he did, Al grabbed one of his bags and gave a yank. Miles jerked against him but lost hold of the bag and dropped backwards to his knees, and then he slid, clawing and screaming, over the edge.

Instantly, one of the other agents who'd been climbing the cliff, trying to get behind Miles, dove across him when he started down the slope. A small scrub oak bush caught them. Miles let go of the suitcase he still held, and it started sliding down the slope too. Another of the men reached out and with one hand grabbed it. He pulled it against his stomach, then he slid and bounced on his back all the way down to the bottom. Another of the agents quickly took the suitcase and helped the man who'd slid down the cliff to his feet. Everyone was silent for a minute. Nothing happened inside the suitcase. Once the first agent moved, in seconds all of the other Customs and Border Patrol agents swarmed across the area where Miles still clung to the scrub tree.

Al slumped down in the middle of the trail and buried his head in his hands. He wasn't able to stop his body from trembling.

"Al! Al, are you alright? Oh Al," Maria cried when she sat beside him and put her arm around him. Was this for real? Did he really have that stuff?"

"Maria? How'd you get here?"

"I came with Corky."

"What time is it?" Al asked.

"Twenty to six, why?" she asked, looking at her watch.

"Your satellite phone. That's all that will work out here. Do you have your sat-phone?"

"Yes, but—"

"I've got to make a call," Al said, then he quickly pushed himself up.

"You OK?" Corky asked when he reached out a hand to help steady Al."

"I've got to get on her phone and make some calls right now," Al said. "Where's your phone?"

"Corky's car," Maria said.

Al ran down to the path toward the SUV.

"Wait for me, Al," Maria called out when she fell behind, having gotten a rock in her left sandal.

"I can't," he yelled back to her.

Dumping out Maria's purse on the car hood, he grabbed the satellite phone, then he leaned against the car and started punching the keys. The phone rang, and on the second ring it was answered.

"Los Alamos National Laboratory, how may I direct your call?"

"Area 622 lab, quickly, please."

Again the phone rang. Just when Al was about to hang up, a voice said, "Hello."

"Carla, this is Alex."

"Alex! What on earth?"

"Can't talk now. I need that private number of Secretary Kingston's. I've got to get a hold of him right now."

"He's going to be on the platform with the President for the speech. We're going to watch it here. I don't think you could get through to him now."

"I've got to. I've got the whole thing—the whole attack plan. I've got to stop that speech."

Carla quickly read off the number. "Thanks, I'll talk to you soon," Al said, then cut off the call and started dialing the direct line to the Secretary of Homeland Security. On the first ring the phone transferred, then on the next ring someone answered.

"Homeland Security."

"I need to talk to the Secretary immediately. This is an emergency."

"Who is this? How'd you get this number? The Secretary is on his way to the Presidential speech. We're walking that way now."

"Tell him Alex Vincent has stopped the whole plan—do it now!"

In the background Al heard the message being relayed. Then Clayton Kingston's voice thundered across the phone.

"This better not be some kind of joke. Just who is this?"

"It's me, Alex Vincent, sir. You've got to stop the President. I've got the whole thing stopped right here. I have the mastermind's computer. I've got it all, or rather the Custom's officers here do."

"Where are you?" Kingston asked.

"Nogales, Arizona. Actually, a ways out into the country from there. I'll let you talk to the agent in command, wait a minute until I can get him to the phone, please, don't hang up." Maria was already running back up the trail to get Corky. He saw her waving for him and quickly started her way.

"In just a minute he'll be here, sir," Alex said.

"Where have you been? Maybe—"

"No—look, sir, the whole code thing we found was a red herring," Al cut in. "We'd fallen for a ruse. I can't tell the whole story now, but you can't let the President throw this country into a panic when we've stopped all of this now."

"How do you know your information is real and not a plant or something?" Kingston asked.

"The mastermind was Miles Groman, a former employee at the lab. You remember him, I'm sure. He was under suspicion, and then he disappeared several years back?"

"Sure, I remember his story. Miles Groman, huh," Secretary Kingston said. "Where's he now?"

"Being loaded into a chopper, cuffed and all. Here's agent Corky Cortez. He'll confirm what I've told you."

When Corky took the phone, Al walked over to the old rock wall where he and Maria had shared their pizza that night. Maria came and sat beside him. She said nothing. In a few minutes Corky joined them.

"I'm to keep you and everything else in custody. Guess you understand that. Gotta get your computer too."

Al nodded.

What now? Am I going to have to go to jail for running and taking that hard drive? Will I be vilified or exonerated?

The chopper carrying Miles and his suitcases started rotating its huge blades and in minutes lifted off into the hot, southern Arizona evening sky.

"Am I under arrest?" Al asked once the noisy craft was racing away from them.

"No, but you're in my custody," Corky said.

"One thing," Al said. "You've got to tell me. How'd you get those F-16's into this? They sure were a diversion."

"It pays to have friends," Corky said. "If this had turned out to be nothing, I'd have some tough explaining to do. I called in a favor owed me by the reserve commander down here. He just happened to be in the air at the right time. I guess now I owe him."

"We might as well get out of here," Corky said. "Follow me to my office," he said to Maria. "Hey, it's almost six. The President will be on the radio in a few minutes."

Maria got into the driver's seat of her car and started following Corky. Al sat on the passenger's side but neither said a word. Maria turned on the radio and within a few minutes President Daugherty started speaking.

"Good evening my fellow Americans. I come to you tonight with great news. I was prepared to deliver to you the most dire speech ever given by any President. We were under imminent threat of attack and did not have a good defense against this highly sophisticated threat.

"However, in just the last few minutes I've been informed by Homeland Security Secretary Clayton Kingston that his department has broken this case wide open. I don't know many of the details at this time. Much more information will be given to you as we work through what has just happened. This case has been the top priority for every department under Secretary Kingston. I'm not exaggerating when I tell you we were in grave danger—in fact, our very existence as a nation was at risk. This is truly a glorious victory, and I extend my personal gratitude to all who had any part in this happy turn of events.

"You know by now that it is customary for me to end my addresses to you with the plea that God bless America, but tonight I'd like to deviate. Tonight I declare that God has blessed America. Good night and thank you."

Neither Al nor Maria said anything for several minutes. Maria turned off the radio when the after-speech speculation by the news people started. Finally, she spoke softly to Al.

"Well, I guess this means you'll be leaving. I'm going to miss you."

"Maybe I'll be in jail," Al said. "I did some things that could put me away for a long time. If the government wants to make an example out of me, I'm in big trouble."

"I think the public sentiment will make you a hero," Maria said. "I don't think the government will want to buck that."

"I don't want to be a hero—not to the public. Guess I don't really know what I want. I'm not the same person I was three months ago. The problem is, I don't know who I really am now. Things were on such a smooth track before, now—"

"I wish I could help you," Maria said.

"Maybe you can," Al said. "Look, I'm no romantic. I'm just a guy who deals in facts and figures. The fact is I've become attracted to you—you know that. I've gotta tell you though, you scare me about as much as the thought of jail does sometimes. There's so much about you I can't figure out. There are some things—" Al cut off his thought and looked out the window.

"I know what you mean. There are some things I can't explain to you right now. I just can't until I'm sure about—about, well, I can't tell you tonight."

"I've been wondering, is finding me staying at your inn going to blow your cover with this Lollypop Railroad thing?"

"No. I'll cover that. You were just a guest who showed up here. You were researching some environmental project as far as I knew."

"Good," Al said. "I don't want to be the one to ruin all the good that organization does. Maybe you best call that Lollypop lady from a pay phone—guess you know how to handle that."

"Yeah, I'll take care of it."

Neither one said anything while they approached the lights of the town. Then Al turned and looked at Maria. "Guess this is goodbye for now."

"Please, Al, don't forget me."

"It's Alex—Alex Vincent. Danny is Tucker." "Oh. Alright Alex, that's easy, but Tucker?"

"You'll adjust." Alex was silent for a few minutes, and then spoke to Maria again. "I've got to call Tucker and tell him some of what's gone on."

"I'll talk to Dad," Maria said. "Tucker can sleep back in his room again tonight—for as long as needed, really. I still have a cot set up in there. Guess you'll have to spend the night in the lockup at the Custom's office. I imagine Corky will come out and get your computer and such. I'll come see you in the morning."

"I'd like that," Al said.

They pulled into the Custom's office parking lot and parked beside Corky. Maria picked up her cell phone and called Anton. Alex got out and looked around.

Well, the running and hiding and all the lying is over—but now what?

Later that evening, after Maria was back at the inn, she walked over to the courtyard where Anton sat in his wheelchair playing checkers with Tucker. "Hey, Danny or Tucker or whatever your name is, how about some chocolate ice cream?" Anton asked. "I'm due for some, you know, and I don't like to eat alone."

"Yeah, OK," Tucker said. "Might as well."

Anton and Tucker stayed in the courtyard while Maria went inside to get the ice cream. Just when she opened the freezer door, her satellite phone started ringing in her purse. She grabbed it and stepped to the side door. Pulling out her handkerchief from her jeans pocket, she covered the microphone with a double layer of the thin cloth before speaking.

"This is Lollypop," she then answered quietly, closing the door behind her.

★★★

A week later, Alex and Tucker sat in Wade Hawkins' office.

"I'm so sorry about your ending up in jail on my behalf," Alex said to Wade. "I surely never expected that. I don't know what I can do to make that right."

"You haven't gotten my bill yet," Wade said. "If I took my hourly rate times the hours in jail, let's see—no, of course I can't do that. Here, I have something for you." Wade handed Alex an envelope with a Homeland Security return on it. Alex opened it and stared at it.

"It was ruled that you met all the qualifications. You certainly stopped the attack. You'd been terminated by the lab, so there was no employee conflict. It's yours—you deserve it. There's no doubt now, since Miles Groman has told all that he had planned, you saved our country."

"One million dollars. Wow. I don't know what to say."

"Any plans?" Wade asked.

"Oh, I've got a few things I want to do. I've met some people who could use a piece of this. There's this little orphanage down in Mexico, you should see how they live, and—wow, I just don't know."

"We're gonna go back and see Maria," Tucker said. "Anton too."

"Maria?" Wade asked.

"Yeah, well, I don't know. We hit it off pretty well and, maybe—who knows?"

"That would be great, good for both of you guys," Wade said.

"I've read a lot of the papers. Guess things were really wild around here," Alex said, and then he looked at his watch. "Well, I've got to go up to the lab. I'll check with you before I leave town or anything like that. Think I'll put my house up for sale. Hey, thanks again, Mr. Hawkins, I really mean it."

★★★

Once in Los Alamos, Tucker found some old friends, and he went off to play ball with them. He was enjoying his new position as a celebrity. Alex drove his BMW up the familiar road to his old office at Area 622. He parked the car, then got out and walked to the building entrance. Lester greeted him.

"Good to see you, Doc Vincent. Mercy, you surely had you a time of it now, didn't you. You came through in the end, though. I knew you would. I just knew you would."

"Lester, I'm sorry for all the trouble I got you into."

"No trouble. I knew you had good intentions. I got me a couple of weeks suspension, but I needed the time off anyway. Now that you're a hero, I even got my back pay for the time off."

"I'm glad. Good to see you, really it is," Alex said. "I know I don't have clearance anymore...."

"Clearance? You're a hero here," Lester said. "You go on back and see Mrs. Hunter now. She's mighty concerned about you."

Alex walked back the hall to the lab. He stood in the doorway. Carla looked up and saw him.

"Alex! Oh, Alex! Come on in here. Kurt's in Washington this week. He'll be sorry he missed you. When are you coming back?"

"Come back here? No, this isn't for me anymore. I—well," Alex said while he looked at Carla. "Guess I've changed—really changed."

"Give it some time. Don't make any hasty decisions, Alex. How's Tucker? How's he getting along?"

"Surprisingly well. You won't know him. He's so grown- up now. I don't know if this was too hard on him or not. In many ways, it was good for both of us. As far as his mother... he doesn't say anything. I think things between them had been awfully strained for some time. There weren't many feelings towards her from Tucker, nothing much but fear. Maybe he just hasn't had time to think much about any of that yet. Hey, what about you? How are things here?"

"Both are somewhat back to normal. It seems as if I'm loafing when I come in at eight and go home at five. Hey, why don't you and Tucker come over for dinner tonight? I'm sure Bill and the boys would love to see you and hear some of the stories you have to tell."

"Yeah, sure. I'd like that." Neither spoke for a minute, then Alex continued. "I'm sorry for all the trouble this caused you. I really put you on the spot. It wasn't fair, my involving you, and then running out. I wasn't thinking about anyone but myself, and Tucker."

"You did the right thing," Carla said. "No matter how you look at it, you did the right thing. You don't know what might have happened to Tucker—then look how you solved the whole thing. That never would have happened if you were here. You were right where you needed to be at the right time."

There was silence again. Then Alex walked over to the window as he'd so often done over the last many years.

"I've seen Him," he said while staring out into the canyon.

"Who?" Carla asked.

"You're right—I know it now. I've seen Him. He was behind this whole thing."

"Whoever are you talking about?"

"God."

"Oh."

"Well, I don't mean with my eyes," he said, turning to look at Carla. "But I saw a little bit of something beyond explanation in most of those people who took us in and protected us and fed us and risked all they have for us. I've carried my whole load myself for too long. I've got to find what you and these others have. I've got to fill this aching hole inside."

"That's great, Alex. We'll talk about this when you come over tonight."

"Yeah, OK, please, let's do that," Alex said. "I think I'm even beginning to understand that faith thing. Maybe I can't prove everything in a lab." Alex was silent for another moment. "Hey, I've got to run now. I've got to go watch Tucker play ball. I'll see you tonight."

"It's so good to see you, Alex."

Alex looked around the lab. He stared at his desk for a moment, and then walked out the door. He waved to Carla, "See you later."

Alex drove back across town to the ball field where Tucker was playing baseball. Alex parked his car and sat there watching his son. How quickly kids adjust. That's one thing he needed to learn from his son. He closed his eyes and thought about Maria. He picked up his phone and called her.

"Hello," she answered.

"Hi, it's Alex."

"Alex! How are you? You OK?"

"Yeah. Things are good, really they are."

"How's Tucker?"

"He's doing very well. I'm sitting here watching him play ball with some of his old friends. I've read a bunch of the papers about all that went on around Santa Fe. Guess things were a real mess. All the charges have been dropped. I'm a free man. President Daugherty invited us to the White House to meet with him over the weekend. They're sending out a plane just for us. That'll sure be something. I—I wish you could go with me, but…." Alex didn't finish his thought.

"Next week, after I get back," he said. "I'm going out to see a fellow in west Texas to give him some money for an orphanage he helps down in Mexico. I'm thinking that maybe after that, maybe by then I'll come over and see you. Guess we've got lots of things to talk about. Maybe—"

"I'd like that," Maria said. "I do have much to tell you. I guess it's time I put my trust in someone again."

"Yeah, I know what—oh my! Tucker just smacked the ball over the outfielder's head. He's really running hard. I think he's going to make it all the way to home. Keep running, Son! Keep going! Go on… go on! Yes! Go… keep going! He's safe! Wow! Hey, Maria, I've got to go and congratulate him. I'll call you back later."

Alex got out of his car and started down the sideline toward Tucker. When his son saw him, he came running toward him, arms outstretched. "Did you see that? Did you see that, Dad?"

Alex dropped to one knee, then Tucker threw his arms around him. Alex hugged his son. "I saw that. That was great. You've gotten really good."

"Life's gotten really good, Dad," Tucker said. "Especially you and me, right Dad?"

"Yeah, Son. Especially you and me."

"Me'n you've gone from hiding like bad guys to being treated like we won the World Series or somethin'. No more runnin' for us, Dad."

"Yeah. No more running. No more hiding. No more telling stories. No more carrying everything on my own shoulders. Just about everything seems new, Son. Yeah. I'm ready for a whole new life."